# SUMMER
# SHADOWS

To
SARAH,
ALL The
BEST!

Killarney Traynor

This is a work of fiction.
Names, characters, businesses, organizations, places, events, and incidents are either products of the author's imagination, or are used fictiously. Any resemblance to actual events, locales, organizations, or persons (living or dead) is entirely coincidental.

ISBN: 1500751987
ISBN 13: 9781500751982
Library of Congress Control Number: 2014914062
CreateSpace Independent Publishing Platform
North Charleston, South Carolina
Author photograph provided by Monica Bushor of Bushor Photography

For Janie and Jenna:
You believed.
Thank you.

Life is real! Life is earnest!
And the grave is not its goal;
Dust thou art, to dust returnest,
Was not spoken of the soul.
- Henry Wadsworth Longfellow

# 1

Just after one o'clock on a Tuesday afternoon in June, Julia Lamontaigne turned into the short driveway of her sister's house. The house was dark. If her eleven-year-old-nephew, Ron, was his usual diligent self, it would be locked tighter than a drum.

*Welcome home, Julia,* she thought. She put on the parking brake, pulled out the key, and sank back into her seat.

*Oh, Lord.*

In the yard next door, blades hacked through twigs and leaves without pause while their operator glared at Julia, sitting in her little silver Audi. Mrs. Gouldman, the retired neighbor, had pruned her hedges the same way for over twenty years and could probably do it in her sleep.

Julia could feel her disapproval.

*Let her stare.*

In the four or five months since Julia moved in, she had never been home on a weekday earlier than five in the afternoon, when her elderly neighbor was returning from her daily trip to the mail-box. In the morning, Julia always left promptly at seven a.m., when Mrs. Gouldman was either sweeping snow from her porch or water-ing her roses. The two of them were like clockwork.

Now, Julia was screwing up the whole routine, causing a rip-
ple in the peaceful universe that was Mill Street in Springfield,
Massachusetts.

Mrs. Gouldman glared. Julia could imagine her thinking:
*Should I go to the mailbox now? Or did I go already? These young women!
Always messing things up! Bad enough they come moving in here like they
own the place...*

How would Mrs. Gouldman feel if she knew that Julia, in addi-
tion to being the single guardian of three children, was also newly
unemployed?

"No, not fired. Laid off," Julia said out loud. "'Manly Stanley'
made that very clear, didn't he?"

He had called her into his office at noon, then launched into
his script like he was hyped on caffeine. He was very sorry, but the
company's revenue was not what it was, cuts had to be made, and
she had to go. According to company policy, she had to clear out
her desk under the supervision of the Human Relations Manager
and be off the property within the hour.

Julia was stunned. She had gone over her personal budget just
last Saturday and figured out how to survive the rest of the year.
Now she would have no income.

"Sir," she'd stammered. "I really can't afford this right now – not
with..."

But Manly Stanley, so nicknamed by the office managers after a
particularly disastrous company outing, was firm.

"I'm sorry, Ms. Lamontaigne," he said. "But times are tough on
all of us. If there's an opening, we'll call."

And eight years of service ended.

Julia leaned back against the cushioned seat and closed her
eyes, partly to ignore her neighbor, but also to calm the tornado of
thought in her head. She tried to create a sense of order out of the
chaos.

The air in the car became heavy as the heat crept in to replace the air conditioning, but Julia welcomed the humidity like

a soothing blanket. If only she could wrap herself in it and sleep the day away, she thought. Perhaps today had only been a nightmare. Perhaps she'd find that everything that had happened since Valentine's Day had been a dream. She would wake up and find herself clutching the pale blue comforter of her bed back in her old Taunton condo.

Encouraged by this fantasy, she opened her eyes.

No such luck. She was still here, it remained June, and she was in Springfield, sitting in front of her late sister's house.

How could she face Ron with the news? How could she tell Dana or Jack, Ron's siblings and her other wards?

Her heart sank at the thought.

A sharp rap on her window startled her from her gloomy thoughts. Julia jumped and saw Mrs. Gouldman, still holding the shears and glaring down at her. She made an impatient rolling movement with her fingers. Julia waved the older woman to the side and carefully opened the door.

"Yes?" she said, with some trepidation. The elderly matriarch was a formidable woman and, judging from the actions of the people on the street, Julia wasn't the only one who was a little afraid of her.

"You sick or something?" the other woman asked sharply. The shears opened and closed unconsciously in her hands.

"No, I'm fine, thanks, Mrs. Gouldman."

But she was not to be put off.

"Kind of strange for you to be home in the middle of the day and then just to sit in your car," she pointed out.

Julia had to acknowledge that this was not her normal behavior. She nodded and swung her legs out of the car, smoothing her black pencil skirt as she stood up.

"It's such a lovely day today," she said, hoping to give the impression that she was playing hooky.

The game was over when she opened the rear door, however. Standing where she was, Mrs. Gouldman couldn't possibly miss the

3

cardboard box loaded with personal office equipment on the back seat.

Julia sent up a quick prayer that this would be misinterpreted; apparently, the suggestion was taken under consideration and rejected.

"Got the ax today, huh?" Mrs. Gouldman asked with her customary tact.

Julia bit back a snarky remark. *Awesome,* she thought. *Now the whole town will know.*

Not that she cared about the whole town. She couldn't care less about the town, but she didn't want the news to reach Ron, Dana, or Jack before she had a chance to talk to them about it, aunt to nephews and niece. She'd even gone so far as to consider putting it off a few days, to buy herself some time and get some interviews set up to take the edge off of the situation. Mrs. Gouldman, who never spoke to children unless she had something frightening or depressing to say, would be sure to catch each one of them when they returned home this afternoon.

Julia knew just how Mrs. Gouldman would do it, too. She'd sit out on her big front porch, which she only used for situations like this, and find something home-spun to do, like shelling peas or clipping coupons. She'd nod to all the people who passed by, commenting on the weather and how terrible it is that some people seemed to get nothing but the shaft in life.

Then, when neighbor asked for clarification, Mrs. Gouldman would tell them about Julia being fired, and those poor orphaned kids of hers. "I don't know what they'll do with no money. Move in with their grandparents or go on welfare, maybe. It's sad, you know. Once somebody's on welfare, they never get off."

*Over my dead body!* Julia thought. *I've never taken charity and I won't take it now. I'll work twenty-four seven, minimum wage before I do that.*

And then Mrs. Gouldman would wait until the three Budd children were going up the drive before saying something disguised as sympathy, like, "You just tell your aunt that if she needs any home cooked meals or anything to let me know. It's going to be tough on you kids, now that she doesn't have a job and all."

They would be shocked. Then Dana would start crying, because that's all that she ever did lately. Jack would join in because he didn't understand, but wanted to sympathize with his sister. And Ron would grow more stone-faced and distant as he ushered the younger ones inside.

*Thanks, Mrs. Gouldman. Remind me to TP your house someday.*

Then Julia, becoming angry by her own prediction, did something that was quite out of her nature. She lied.

"Just redoing the cubicle, Mrs. G," said she, using the nickname that the woman hated. "Got tired of the same-old, same-old and wanted a fresh look, a change. You know what I'm saying?"

There was a moment of silence. The shears breathed quietly as their owner glared at Julia, clearly disbelieving and waiting for a crack in the façade. But Julia maintained her bright expression, refusing to turn away.

Finally, Mrs. Gouldman ended the standoff by saying, "Seems to me you've had enough changes for one year."

And with a snap of the shears, she stomped around the fence and disappeared into her tool shed.

Julia waited until her neighbor was out of sight before she hauled the heavy box out of the car and up the front steps. She wedged it between the door jam and her hip as she fumbled about for the keys and opened the door.

The house alarm, which she'd forgotten about, immediately began its countdown just as Julia's cell phone started to ring. She dropped the box, wincing at the tinkle of broken glass that accompanied it, and dashed for the key pad. By the time she put in the code, her cell phone was quiet and the corner of the box was beginning to get wet – she'd forgotten about her snow globe.

With an aggravated sigh, she practically threw the box into the foyer and slammed the door shut behind her. The house was quiet and dark, and humming from all the automatic appliances that her deceased brother-in-law, Timothy, had been so fond of. It was cooler than outside, but Julia knew that the AC was off – it was set to turn on at 3pm, which would give it enough time to cool the place before the children got home from their after-school activities.

Her cell phone rang again, but she left it in her purse. She wasn't in the mood to talk. It might be her mother or, worse - Miriam Budd, the children's other grandmother. Both had a habit of calling, both liked to interfere in the daily running of the house; but while Julia's mom did it out of concern, Mrs. Budd was quite another story. Julia felt nervous about telling her parents about her unemployment, but that was nothing compared to the chill she had when she thought about telling Miriam Budd.

*Not until I at least have an interview,* she thought, as she hefted up the box again. *Although, I'll be in almost as much trouble for keeping it from her. I'll have to caution the kids against texting her.*

Not that she thought Ron would. He was pretty introverted.

She brought the box over to the table and began to empty it. Some of her paper memorabilia was wet beyond saving, so she tossed them away without a second thought. She scooped the glass into some old newspaper, and then laid the rest of the things out on the counter to dry.

Only then did it occur to her that the phone call might have been from one of the kids. She was still new at parenting, so her instincts were slow; but once the idea struck that one of the children may be in trouble, she nearly panicked. She pawed through her bag, found the cell phone, and saw the ID: Sherri Lawton.

She relaxed. It wasn't an emergency. Sherri Lawton was the realtor who was trying to sell the condo.

Julia put the phone on the table and took a deep breath. Then she pulled out a chair and sat down at the table. She ran her fingers along the velvety edge. It was an elegant monster of a table, dark and rich in tints of red and brown. It suited the kitchen perfectly. The room was all stainless steel and dark paneled cabinets, perfectly modern, so perfectly like her sister, Amanda.

None of it felt like home. Her own kitchen table had been made of pine wood with a colorful inlay, surrounded by slender-legged chairs equipped with thin cushions that were forever slipping off of the seat. All of her furniture had been like that: simple, bright, and welcoming. It was all gone now, sold in an open house along with a lot of other things in preparation for the sale of her condo. The bright, cheery little condo with the blue walls and the familiar creaks and groans was now empty and quiet. A *For Sale* sign stood on the lawn. Who knew how many strangers had tramped their dirty shoes over Julia's hardwood floors.

She hadn't minded the sacrifice. Not really. She was needed here and wanted to be here, but she did miss the homey feeling. After all these long months, Julia still felt like she had to knock on the front door before entering, or ask permission before she used the coffee machine. It was her sister's kitchen. This was her sister's house, her sister's furniture, her sister's decorations, and her sister's kids. Not Julia's. The name on the property might be Julia's, but it really belonged to Amanda and Timothy Budd.

Julia's hand had left prints on the shiny finish. She rubbed them out automatically, thinking, *Amanda hates when I leave fingerprints.*

Hot tears stung at the back of her eyes. She still couldn't think of her sister's death without crying. It seemed that she and her niece Dana had more in common than she had thought.

Julia's older sister, Amanda, had been a fun-loving spendthrift who adored travel, fashion, adventure, the finer things in life, and fun. Although several years separated the sisters, they had been very close until Amanda went off to college and discovered her dual-calling: corporate accounting and Timothy Budd. They were an ideal match: he was studying banking, and loved all the things that a young Yuppie is supposed to value. When they married, the wedding took place in a church, but the reception was at the exclusive country club that Timothy's family had belonged to for decades. It was the first and last time that Julia had been inside of it.

After the wedding, the two moved from place to place until they found the house in Springfield and, between travels, managed to have three children: Ron, now eleven; Dana, eight; and three-year-old Jack. Having children didn't slow them down: they either took the children with them or, more often, left them with one of the two sets of grandparents.

Although Julia saw them at the family get-togethers and was invited to the house now and then for dinner, their lives were too busy to keep much personal contact. Julia had her career and her condo, and Amanda was always just getting in from one foreign country or another. Julia could still hear her chipper voice on the phone when she called from the airport.

"Back on USA terra firma," she would say. "I'm so glad to be home!"

"How long are you going to stay this time?"

"Don't be fresh, young'un. How's life?"

"The same."

"You should come with me sometime, Julia. We'll see the world together! Paris is sooo nice this time of year. Well, any time of year, actually."

Julia would laugh. "I wouldn't want to cramp your style."

"Nonsense. I would – oops, sorry, Ron's tugging at my sleeve. Got to go. Come for supper some night?"

"Wouldn't miss it. I'm glad you're home, Mandy."

"Dana, now please stop sniffling. Hang on a second, Ron, Jack's crying again – good grief. Love you, Julie. Bye."

The phone rang.

Julia jumped and her heart squeezed so much that it hurt. But it was only Sherri again and, as she needed a distraction, Julia answered this time.

"Hello?"

Sherri's voice was both frantic and happy. "Juuulia! I've got *great* news for you!"

"Oh yes?"

"The Petersons absolutely fell in love with your condo, and they just made me an offer. The number is lower than what we had stated, but it really is a good offer, especially in this selling climate. I'm just so excited! We've only had it on the market for, what, three months? Want to hear the offer?"

Julia did, and Sherri told her.

"It is lower," she agreed. "But I can live with it."

"I thought so. Shall I get the ball rolling?"

Julia hesitated. Letting it go was the right thing to do, but it felt as though she was losing much more than just a home. It felt like she was letting go of a past in favor of a present, one that no longer included her sister or brother-in-law.

That little condo had been her first piece of real estate. It was on a private drive, with quiet, respectful neighbors, and only ten minutes from her place of work. Her *former* place of work. It belonged to another era, an era that had ended, and there was no point in crying about it.

"Go for it," she said. "Keep me informed."

"Awesome. I'll get the bank on the line. Want me to call you back when I've got their okay?"

"Sure. Please."

"No problem, bye, now."

Julia ended the call and looked at the clock. 1:24 p.m. - the kids would be home around 5. She had time to get cleaned up and do some chores around the house.

She looked around the spotlessly clean kitchen and grimaced. Of course, Ron wouldn't have left without making sure everything was done. Julia may have been named guardian of the three Budd children, but it was Ron who really ran things. He was the silent watchman, the one who never seemed to say anything but everything got done, thanks to his influence. He was, without a doubt, the most mature, adult, responsible person Julia knew, and he was only eleven.

She remembered a conversation she had with Amanda a week or two before the accident. Amanda called asking to borrow a set of DVDs from Julia's collection, explaining that she and Tim were going north and were hoping to get caught up on the series. Of course, it was no big deal and Julia, to be polite, asked for details about the trip.

"We're going to Stratton Mountain for a little marriage rejuvenation," said Amanda. "Just Tim and me and no kids. They have a special Valentine's Day package. It'll be *so* romantic."

"Where will the kids be staying?" Julia asked.

"Oh, Ginny's coming over to stay with them."

"Ginny Rossetti? The party queen?"

"She was available. It's only for a few days."

"Yeah, but…"

"All she has to do is be present. Ron takes care of everything while we're away. In some ways, he's a better parent than Tim or me."

Julia didn't join in on the laughter. "That's a lot of responsibility for an eleven year old," she said.

"Trust me," her sister answered, "he can handle it. And if anything happens, we're only a phone call away."

That conversation was the first thing that Julia thought of when she received the call on the night of February 14th. She could vividly remember her mother's incoherent sobs on the other end of the line and her father's toneless explanation of the accident. The children were still at home, he said, but Ginny had gone to pieces. He and her mother were at the hospital. Would Julia go to the house to be with the kids?

Of course she went. She bundled herself up against the cold, snowy winter night and made her way through the slippery streets.

The drive took longer than the usual fifty minutes, with Julia fretting the whole way about the kids.

Ron was frightfully calm when he answered the door. When she asked how he was doing, he replied only that he was fine, and the kettle was on if she wanted something hot to drink.

"Thanks for coming," he said, as an afterthought.

The house was noisy and sad. Miriam and Walter Budd were already there, comforting the sobbing Dana and the frightened Jack. Ginny had gone home. Ron had mugs with instant coffee in them, and the kettle was whistling, ready to be poured. In a stoic tone, he explained that his mother didn't like him to handle the kettle and would Julia pour?

What she remembered most about that night were the tears of Mr. and Mrs. Budd as they stroked Dana's hair and held Jack. She'd never seen them so emotional, or so protective: they wouldn't let her near the children.

She and Ron sat off on the sidelines, watching. Julia felt useless and uncomfortable, as well as sad, but there was no room for her grief here. Ron seemed to feel the same. The expression on his face never changed.

When the hysterics seemed to be growing worse rather than calming, she got up and went to stand in front of Mr. and Mrs. Budd. They looked up at her, resentful.

"It's getting late. The children need baths and to go to bed," Julia said kindly but firmly. "Let me take them."

The grandparents were reluctant to let go. As Julia moved in scoop up Jack, Ron slipped between her and them. He took the two children and led them upstairs like it was the most natural thing to do. The three adults were left to themselves.

After a moment of strained silence, Mrs. Budd turned to Julia. "Why are you here?"

Julia drummed her fingers on the kitchen counter.

Of the three children, Ron worried her the most. He never cried, never lost his temper, never laughed, and never seemed to relax. In fact, the only emotional expression that she could remember was when the lawyer, Steven Hall, had the three children in his office, explaining that Julia was their mother's choice of guardian.

Julia was surprised and flattered when she'd learned about the guardianship. For Amanda to have put only Julia's name on the will spoke volumes of what she felt about her younger sister. The responsibility was not one she took lightly, and it never occurred to her that she could pass it on to anyone else. She was insulted when the Budds suggested it.

At the lawyer's office where the will was read, the Budds had been outraged that the children had not been left to them. They didn't like the idea of their grandchildren being entrusted to an unmarried aunt on the Lamontaigne side.

Mrs. Budd made a snide remark about Julia's salary and her condo. Tim's sister followed this with a snarky question about how Ryan, Julia's boyfriend at the time, would react to this news. But the look of surprise, doubt, and worry from her own parents was the worst to bear.

When the children were informed about her guardianship, Julia watched anxiously for their reactions. She nearly came undone when Ron's face fell, and his veneer of smooth control disappeared. He looked at Julia with anxiety and doubt.

Whom he had expected for their guardian, he never said. Dana said later that they had thought one of the grandparents would get them, but she was glad it was Julia, because their grandparents sometimes smelled funny.

Ron's disappointment nearly ruined Julia's confidence. She would have signed the papers transferring guardianship right there and then, if Jack hadn't jumped out of his seat and run over to throw his arms around her legs. For the rest of the meeting, he didn't leave her. He kept his little blond head on her shoulder, his arms and legs wrapped around her tight, as though he were afraid that she'd go driving off into the night and disappear, too.

Then Dana, who looked the most like Amanda, came over and gave her a hug.

"Are we going to move into your house?" she asked, after looking anxiously at her brother.

"It's too small, Dana," Ron put in. "We'll stay in our house."

Dana frowned. "Then where will Aunt Julia sleep?"

"We'll figure that out later," Julia said soothingly. "Right now, we've got a few other things to take care of, okay?"

Dana nodded and sat down again. She hadn't smiled, but she hadn't flinched either. She looked back at Julia with a quizzical expression in her wide blue eyes. Julia smiled at her, and the little girl breathed deeply and her shoulders relaxed.

But when Julia looked at Ron, his face was smooth and calm again, and he even gave her a little nod. She knew what that meant: he didn't know if she could measure up. The weight of the responsibility, his gaze seemed to say, remained on his slender shoulders.

"Poor kid," Julia muttered.

The sound of her own voice, echoing in the empty kitchen, startled her out of her reverie. She remembered, with a renewed sense of failure, that she had been fired. Julia Frances Lamontaigne was thirty years old, jobless, and single. There was no unemployment money coming, because she'd worked for a non-profit. She had three kids that needed food, shoes, clothes, education, and medical care. There was a house with a mortgage, a weakening roof, taxes due, a huge credit card bill, and a car in need of a tune-up. She had her savings, some money still coming to her from the insurance, and whatever was left after Sherri took her cut from the sale of the condo.

Perhaps Miriam Budd had been right. Maybe it was too much for her to bear.

If she couldn't handle the relatively simple things like bills and finances, how on earth could she ever have thought that she could handle the bigger things? She had three young children in her care. They were still grieving and, in spite of all her tender, respectful care, she wasn't reaching any of them. Ron was as distant as he was the day his mother died, silently going through the motions of living, and never even once talking to Julia about anything more pressing than tomorrow's lunch plans. Dana was an emotional wreck who never made it through a day without a breakdown, and Jack still wouldn't sleep by himself.

Maybe everyone had been right. Maybe she couldn't do the job. Maybe she should give up, hand the kids over, and…

She stopped herself. Just the thought of giving up the kids felt like she was ripping her heart in two. But keeping them for her own sake was selfish, no matter how much she wanted to honor her sister's memory and wishes. She had to do what was right for them, regardless of what it did to her.

Amanda wanted the kids with her. She left a letter to Julia, explaining what she wanted.

*I can't imagine anyone better to care for them, including Mom and Dad,* she had written. *When I suggested it to Timothy, he agreed: you and no one else. I hope you never have to read this, Julia, but if you do, know that I leave them to your care with gratitude and confidence. I love you, little sister.*

Julia began to sob, breathless and ragged, like she had when Amanda died.

# 2

When her sobs subsided and the tidal wave of pain ebbed, Julia whispered a spontaneous prayer: *Please, please help me.*

She didn't really expect an answer, but when she looked up, she caught sight of a framed picture in the hall in front of her. There it was: the answer, just as she had requested.

Actually, she thought it was more of a first step. Julia rubbed her eyes and stared at the picture, taking a step forward to look at it more closely. It was Amanda and Timothy, in the first year of their marriage. He had taken their picture by holding the camera at arm's length from their faces, and it was a nice shot, displaying their youth, vitality, and happiness.

But it was the building behind them that caught Julia's eye. An older building, two stories, possibly built in the 1920s or 1930s. There wasn't much of it visible behind the couple; however, it was enough to start a chain reaction of thought.

It brought to mind something that Julia had forgotten, something that Steven Hall, the lawyer, told her when they were settling the estate.

"The Springfield house is mortgaged," he told her. "Your sister took out a twenty-five year mortgage on it about five years ago and..."

He talked on, but Julia was caught by the phrase "the Springfield house". At the first break in his monologue, she asked, "Is there another house? I thought they only had one."

He looked surprised. "Oh, no. There's also the Franklin property."

"Franklin? Where's that?"

He shuffled some papers while he answered. "In Franklin, that is, in New Hampshire, a little north of Concord."

"The capitol?"

"Right. I have the paperwork right here…"

"When did they buy that?"

"About ten years ago. The place was a bank foreclosure, I think. In any case, they bought it for a song and I believe it's completely paid off… Aha! Here we go." Steven opened the file and scanned it quickly before nodding with satisfaction. "Yes, they paid it off two years ago."

Julia was puzzled. "But, what did they use it for?"

"They rented it out," he said, still examining the pictures. "I think they wanted to make a summer cottage out of it eventually, but they never got around to it. It's not very big, just three bedrooms and the basics, fully furnished. It needs minor repair and the caretaker tells me that it could do with a makeover."

Julia grimaced at the idea of this added expense. "Is it still rented?"

Steven Hall conferred with his papers again. "No. It's been locked up since September. Franklin is not exactly a thriving community, and renters were only interested during the summer. It's near Webster Pond, you see."

"Ah."

"It might be worth your while to make the repairs and do over the place. As it is close to the capitol, you may be able to sell it to someone who works there."

"Does anything have to be done immediately with it?"

"Oh, no. The caretaker there is paid monthly out of this office, and she looks after things pretty well. I'll send her your information in case anything comes up."

"Thank you."

The subject was dropped. Then, while dealing with the challenges of moving out of her condo and into her sister's house, adjusting to sudden family life, and making the myriad of decisions that came with the new responsibilities, Julia forgot all about it.

She took up her purse and keys again, and went upstairs in a pensive mood. In her room, she changed into a robe, turned on the bath, and sat on the edge of the tub while it filled. She selected a soft, fragrant soap and poured in a generous amount, but she had difficulty shaking the Franklin house from her mind.

All at once, she made a decision. She stopped the water and went back into the bedroom.

Amanda, in an uncharacteristically old-fashioned whim, had installed a land-line telephone on the nightstand, right next to where Julia's cell phone was charging. Julia sat on the bed, located Sherri's number, and dialed it into the landline. She pulled her hair free of its bun and swung her feet as she waited through the rings.

Sherri sounded puzzled when she answered.

"Hi, Sherri. It's me, Julia, again," said Julia.

"Hi, Julia!" She sounded as though she was talking through a mouthful. She coughed and then said, "Sorry, I was confused for a moment. My ID said you were calling from home."

"That's where I am."

"Oh, nice! Day off?"

"Not exactly." Suddenly, Julia felt the urge to share the news with someone. She spoke quickly, "Actually, I was let go today."

"What?"

"Yeah. It was a surprise."

"Oh goodness! Oh, I am *so* sorry."

"Thank you..."

"Well, I guess this condo thing came through just in time then."

"You said it."

"I'm working with the bank now. I haven't got exact figures for you yet, but everything is going really smooth. We'll be able to close quickly."

Julia twisted the phone cord around her finger. "Awesome."

"But how about you? What are you going to do now?"

"I'm not sure yet, but something will come up. Actually, I'm calling you for another matter. Have I ever mentioned my sister's place in Franklin?"

"New Hampshire?"

Julia could hear Sherri's fingers already pounding away at her keyboard and grinned. Sherri was the consummate realtor who lived for the next commission.

"Yes. It's a rental place, not very big. I think it was on…"

"134 Whipple Lane?"

Julia was impressed. "Yes. So I did mention it."

Sherri's tone was less than enthusiastic. "You did several months ago and told me that you might be interested in selling. I did some research on the place. I know a realtor in the area and got him to do the leg work for me."

"Oh, okay."

"Yeah, he's a good friend of mine. His name is Charlie Jean, if you know anyone who needs a realtor in that area. Anyway, he went up there to have a look at the place about a month ago. The caretaker wasn't around to let him in, so he just peeked in the windows and looked around the outside. He says that, structurally, it's pretty sound, except for a few shingles missing from the roof. He couldn't tell about the heat, or the pipes, naturally, but it looked like everything was pretty well packed up. It needs a lot of cosmetic work, though."

Julia was impressed. "You are amazing, Sherri."

"Well, don't congratulate me yet. The market up there is dead. Nothing's moving. Charlie says he hasn't sold a house in

Franklin in a year and a half, and he has all the better properties to sell. Your house isn't on a bad street, but it's small, run down, and old looking. Families want newer houses and bigger neighborhoods. They can't afford fix-me-ups. I'm sorry, Julia."

Julia sighed. So much for her big revelation and the sudden source of income. Now all she had was a crumbling, crummy old house, eating up her savings in tax dollars.

*Wonderful.* She ran her hand through her hair again and willed herself not to cry.

Sherri must have felt sorry for her, because she said, "Look, maybe if you did the place over, fixed the roof, and made the place look gorgeous, we'd have a shot at it. People who work in Concord don't want to live there, and I'm sure between Charlie and me, we could swing something. But getting a handyman and decorator in there will be expensive, and I can't guarantee that you'll earn it back in the sale."

Julia heard Sherri typing as she spoke, but the wheels in Julia's head were turning.

*Cosmetic work...*

"But, look..." said Sherri, in the tone she always used when proposing something that Julia might find objectionable. "If you are looking to rid yourself of one of your properties, I have a proposition for you."

"Oh?" Julia couldn't hide the wariness in her tone. She knew what was coming and braced herself. "What is it?"

"I've gotten a lot of calls lately for people looking for homes where you are now. I know this is a stretch, but I could get you a real nice deal for your Springfield house if you'd be willing to put it up for sale. Springfield's become a hot spot in the market – I could sell this house, get you into a smaller one a few towns over, and leave you with a considerable sum in the bank."

Julia sighed. "Sherri..."

"I know there's an emotional attachment and that it's always difficult to downsize, but you need money and you have that huge mortgage attached to that house. Add all the upkeep and the taxes and the yard, not to mention all the bills that kids run up these days, and economically speaking, moving into a smaller, more manageable place would be the wisest thing to do."

"Thank you, but this is their home, Sherri. I can't just uproot them. There are too many memories here and they're still so fragile."

"Sometimes the best thing for grief is a change of scenery. When my mother died, I was a mess. I was crying every day and eating chocolate like it was going out of style. I wouldn't go out or anything." She sighed, then continued, "Finally, my husband had it. He booked a vacation in Bermuda, without asking me, and we went away for two weeks. By the time I came back, I was a new woman, ready to face the world again. I'm telling you, it worked wonders."

"I've just been *fired*, Sherri. I have four mouths to feed and three young, growing bodies to clothe. I can't afford a Bermuda vacation."

"Not in that house. It's a money pit for you, Julia, and the only way to fix it is to get out of there and into something more practical. I actually have several properties in the neighboring areas that you could have for a song. Let me pull some up here – some are bank foreclosures, but most are ready to be moved into on a moment's notice. Let's see… Three bedroom, small ranch…"

She rambled on and Julia let her talk without hearing what she was saying.

She looked around the master bedroom. Amanda's room. Her sister was in every nook and cranny, in the color scheme, the decorations, and the arrangements. Julia hadn't been any more thrilled at the idea of moving into that room than the children had been, but it was the only bedroom available.

She recalled the day she moved in, the three children standing in the doorway, watching her with big eyes as she invaded their mother's sanctuary. Ron eventually ushered them away, despite Julia's invitation for them to keep her company. The subject was never again brought up, but their silence was telling enough.

Sherri was still talking, and her voice was starting to annoy Julia. She rubbed her forehead and sighed heavily, but the other woman was in full sales pitch and showed no signs of slowing down.

"...is completely tight and the basement shows no signs of flooding," she was saying, "The school district has a good reputation, and the tax bracket is one of the lowest in the area. I can arrange a viewing if you are interested...?"

It took a few moments for Julia to realize that she was waiting for an answer.

"I'm sorry, Sherri," she said, "but it's just a little too soon for me to be considering a move. I just got let go today, and I don't want to go through all the expense and the upheaval of a move, just to have to move again if I find a job in, say, Boston."

"I totally understand. There's no pressure, I just wanted to let you know that you do have options. Springfield is considered a great place to move to, so you can always get rid of the house whenever you want."

"Thank you," Julia mumbled. She heard a phone ring in the background.

"Oops, that's my other line. It's probably the bank. You'll have to sign some paperwork and stuff, but that will be easier now, I guess, since you don't have to take time off from work."

"Yes..."

"I'd really better answer that. Bye!"

Julia put the phone down and stayed where she was on the edge of the bed, staring at the chocolate brown and raspberry trim walls.

"Raspberry, Amanda?" she'd said, when first given the tour several years ago.

Amanda had laughed. "Taryn told me how she'd re-done her and Brian's room in lavender and pink and all I could think was, 'that poor man! Talk about emasculation!' So I asked Tim what his favorite manly color was, and he said brown. I thought, 'Perfect!' Brown and pink go so well together, so now we have a room that's a perfect compromise – manly and womanly and stronger because of it. What do you think?"

The memory faded, leaving Julia alone in the cold room with the echoes of the question.

"I think it's like living in a mausoleum, Amanda," she said. The sound of her own echoing voice startled her, but her growing frustration made her continue. "I can't breathe here and the kids can't grow. What am I going to do with them, Amanda? You left them in my care, which is fine, great and all, but *now* what?"

Her words were swallowed up in the empty room. Amanda was not there with her usual bright answer. Julia found her hand on her phone, with a half-formed idea to call her parents, but she stopped herself.

They were in Florida full-time now, looking after her maternal grandmother, Jean. The move had been in the works ever since last June, when Jean was diagnosed with Alzheimer's. Her mother didn't want to leave Jean to face the disease by herself, so they put their Massachusetts house up for sale and prepared to move into their winter place for good. Half of their furniture was already in Florida when the accident happened, and by then, the house in Massachusetts had an offer. In the wake of the tragedy, they considered giving up their plans, but Julia wouldn't hear of it. Besides the fact that Jean needed support and was too fragile to be moved back north, Julia knew intuitively that she and the kids needed some space. They had to do this on their own. Her parents never quite understood that and felt a little left out. But they honored her decision, and carried on with the move.

She couldn't call them, not yet. This was her problem, not theirs.

She took her hand off the phone and went into the bathroom.

A few minutes later she was in the tub, listening to the classical music station playing a Bach concerto, blissfully losing herself in a swirl of warm water and fragrant suds. One thing she was grateful for was Amanda's expensive tastes. Although paying for it all was a headache, she enjoyed the luxuries of driving the Audi, the exquisite furnishings, and relaxing in the hot jet streams of a Jacuzzi.

Julia let the music and the water take away her cares and thought of nothing but violins and soft grassy meadows.

Then a commercial came on for a summer camp for the offspring of the rich and bored. She was reminded of an incident a few weeks earlier, when she was going over the bills and budgeting the summer.

Jack had been drawing pictures in the high chair next to her. Dana and Ron were doing their homework. It had been a quiet night, and if it hadn't been for the bills and the depressing state of her finances, Julia would have been feeling very much at peace. But she had come to a conclusion from her research, and she could no longer put off telling the kids.

She cleared her throat, and Dana and Ron looked up expectantly. Jack was oblivious, and busily decorating his tray with the washable marker.

"I'm sorry, guys," said Julia hesitantly. "I have some... disappointing news."

Dana shot Ron a look of dismay, but Ron never took his eyes off of his aunt.

"I've been going over the books and, well, I'm afraid..." She shook her head and gestured toward her ledger sheets. "There's just not enough for summer camps this year. I'm so sorry."

She expected tears and outrage. It was a Budd tradition that the children each got to go to a special camp each summer, with the younger ones going to day camp. This would have been Dana's third year at a summer art camp in a place that Julia had never heard of for an astronomical sum that she could not justify. It was what their parents had done, and so Julia wanted to do the same, only she couldn't. Going over the past several years of her sister's bookkeeping, she couldn't figure out how they managed it, even on two salaries.

"We can't go?" Dana asked.

"I'm sorry, honey," she said, with another wave at the check-book. "We just don't have the money this year." She added, "Except, Ron - your mom paid for yours back in January, so you can still go, if you'd like. Um… Well, the rest of us will just have to have a great time here on our own, that's all."

She was flushing now. It felt terribly awkward.

Dana looked at Ron as though for instructions. Ron said, in his implacable way, "We're in trouble?"

"No, no," Julia said, hastily. "No, we're doing fine, as long as we stay within our means, and, for this year, camps are out of our means. But I'm going to start putting away money now, so that next year you can all go. I am sorry, guys."

Ron appeared thoughtful and Dana looked hesitant. Jack took his red marker and drew a line on Julia's sleeve.

"Can you get a refund?" asked Ron.

"Sorry?"

"My camp deposit. Can you get a refund?"

"Well, um, yes, but…"

He nodded and returned to his homework as though the matter was settled. "Cool. Then we can put it towards next year's camps." He looked up at her again and said firmly, "For *all* of us."

Julia felt chastised. She thought she ought to say something, in-sist that Ron go in honor of Amanda's wishes, but she couldn't. The matter was closed. Ron had diplomatically turned a tragedy into a triumph of self-sacrifice. His gesture had cleared his sister's face of all disappointment and jealousy.

He went back to his homework, and indicated that Dana should do the same.

Dana said, in a happier tone, "We can start collecting money for them. I could sell lemonade like last year. I'll bet we make pots of money!"

Jack added a purple stripe to Julia's red one, as she wondered how she was going to manage to keep happy and busy three active young children for two and a half months.

As Julia sat in the tub, listening to the snap of the suds, she thought that at least now she didn't have to worry about working a full-time job at the same time. Until the money ran out, she had all the time in the world.

She sighed and drew her head underneath the bath water with a quick jerk. Under, she couldn't see and all she could hear were the jets. She let the water caress her face, felt her hair flow freely about her ears, and her shoulders relaxed. At last, the air in her lungs gave out and she had to surface.

The first thing she saw when she opened her eyes was a bunch of dusty pink silk roses in a brown vase on the shelf over the tub, a display she never would have picked herself, and a blunt reminder that this wasn't her tub. Someone else had picked out the colors, bought the equipment, installed it, tested it, and enjoyed it. It was something that Julia wouldn't have bought, partly because she couldn't afford it, and partly because, until recently, she hadn't been a bath person. That had been Amanda's favorite way to relax...

Suddenly, Julia couldn't get out of the tub fast enough. She nearly slipped on the cool tiles as she scrambled for her robe, gritting her teeth as she shut down the jets and let the water drain. She hurriedly left the bathroom, and found herself standing in front of the full length mirror.

She had never been fond of full length mirrors. She had found them to be much more honest than flattering, and she avoided them whenever possible, but increasingly, in the past few months, she found herself standing in front of the mirror. It had become her one confidante and she needed one now.

She scowled at the image of the soft, curvy figure in front of her.

She said, "I can't stand this house. It's closing in on me – we can't breathe here, we can't grow here, and we can't forget here. Every time I turn around, I expect to run into Amanda or Tim. The kids can't move on. I can't move on. I can't even run the household without thinking first if what I'm doing is what Amanda would do. And if I find that it isn't exactly what she would want, I change it until I'm so tied up in confusion that I can't do anything. I can't break free and I can't go on like this!"

She stopped and took a deep breath. She took in her reflection, her tousled hair and weary, sad eyes. Then she realized how very much her eyes looked like Ron's. The shape, the color, the unwavering gaze, the spacing, and even the lashes were alike. It was the first time she'd ever thought of there being a physical resemblance between her and the children.

This realization pleased her. It did more than that: it steeled her.

"These are my children now," she said, very calmly. "They are my responsibility and no one else has a claim to them. There's me. Just me. Only me."

It was terrifying, but freeing. Although this wasn't the first time she'd said these words to herself, it was the first time that she actually believed them.

"So, if I decide that something is in their best interests, I have the right to carry it out, even if others disagree. Even if *the kids* disagree."

She nodded and smiled weakly at her reflection.

With a shuddering sigh, Julia turned and looked around the room again. The ghosts of Tim and Amanda hung heavily in here. She could feel them pressing in on her again, clouding her judgment. She grew unsure – her resolve was slipping.

She turned back to the mirror.

"We've *got* to get out of here," she announced. "Or... or just tear everything out of this house and start all over."

She stopped and thought for a second. Yes, she could do that. She had done extensive work in her condo when she first bought it, and she grew up helping her father with his part-time handy man work. She knew how to paint, remodel, and fix. The cost would be much more manageable if she did the work herself, and she could get the kids to help her, too. It would be a great summer project, a good way to keep her busy in between interviews. The family would grow closer together, the kids wouldn't be bored, and she could redo the entire house, room by room, until it wasn't...

Then she thought of Ron's face, Dana's fragility, and Jack's bewilderment. It was bad enough that she couldn't send them to camp like their mom would have done and that she stole their mother's room. Now she has to tear down every last trace of her world.

No, not this house. Not yet.

"Then we can't stay here," Julia declared. "Amanda, I can't stay here all summer with nothing for us to do but mourn. Look at your son – he hasn't laughed or smiled since you died. He can't even act like a kid any more. We need something to do, something to build together, or a new place for the four of us to explore."

*Franklin.*

She'd never been there. In fact, she'd only been to New Hampshire twice, both during the skiing season. And, according to what the lawyer told her, the kids had never been there either. It was new territory – completely new for all of them.

Just like that, she had a plan. It was perfect. A little New England town to explore. A month, maybe two, where it would just be them, working on the renovations to make the place sellable. She could work off all her anxieties through the demolition and rebuilding. Ron could help, or he could ride his bike and just be a little boy for a few weeks. Dana and she could get closer by cooking the meals and such. Jack would be able to play outside in the yard, because of course there'd be a yard – it was New Hampshire, after all.

She still had some savings, and if she didn't get work right away, they could make it for a few months without resorting to peanut butter sandwiches. They were due another payment on the insurance, and there was that guy across the street who had offered her a nice sum for the Audi. With all that, the savings, and some ingenuity, they would have enough for the repair supplies, too.

*Brilliant.*

There was a lake, so they could all go swimming. They could attend the fireworks in Concord or even just in town, if they had them. They could get ice cream cones and drive up to Maine for a day on the coast. They could walk the country lanes or go to the state capitol and hang out in the museums. They could, for once, just act like a real family, not like a broken one.

The kids wouldn't like it. Not one bit, not at first. But the more Julia thought of it, the more she became convinced that it was not only what she ought to do, but the only thing she *could* do.

She dressed quickly. There was much to do in a short space of time. She wanted to have all the information at her fingertips when the kids got home, before Ron could come up with an argument.

The first person she called was Sherri.

"Hey, Sherri? Listen, do you have a phone number for the caretaker at my place in Franklin?"

If she hadn't been so excited, she might have noticed that it was the first time that she had referred to any of these properties as her own.

# 3

The old rattle trap of a bus pulled away from the curb, leaving the taste of exhaust in Ron Budd's mouth. He stood on the sidewalk with his backpack in one hand and a trumpet case at his feet, glad the day was over. It had been a long day of studying, social pressure, and extra band practice in preparation for the graduation ceremony that was one week away.

Ron was always the first one home, and the one responsible for unlocking the house and turning off the alarm. The kids, as he referred to them, would arrive at 5:15, and Aunt Julia at six. It was 5:00 now, so he was surprised to see his aunt talking with their neighbor, John Kehoe.

She stood with her arms folded, watching Kehoe run his big hands all over the engine of the Audi. Kehoe shot rapid-fire questions, typical of a used car dealer, and Aunt Julia answered in what Ron thought was an eager sort of way.

Julia caught sight of him and waved, so he gave her a brief wave back.

Ron shook his head, wondering why she wasn't at work. He hated when the schedule was disrupted and he wasn't informed ahead of time; besides, he didn't like John Kehoe very much. He was a greasy, dirty-minded man who made Ron feel uncomfortable.

Still, it did him no good to stay there and watch. He gathered up his things and looked up to see Julia coming over to greet him

Her wet hair was pulled back into a pony tail, and she was wearing her weekend jeans and T-shirt, all of which told him that she had been home for some time. This confused him even more. Did she take the afternoon off? That would be way out of character.

When she spoke, her voice was heavy with concern. "Hey, Ron. Are you okay?"

He straightened his shoulders. "I'm fine," he said. "You're home early."

Julia looked around furtively, and Ron followed her eyes. Knitting on her front porch, Mrs. Gouldman looked completely at peace with the world, and that was a sure sign of trouble. She never looked that way unless something was wrong.

Ron's heart sank as he wondered what else had happened. He thought, *there can't be anything else. I can't handle anything else.*

Instantly, he was ashamed of himself. Was that any way for the man of the house to feel? He couldn't waste time feeling sorry for himself. What would Dad think?

Just before Dad left for the trip in February, he had told him, "You're the man around the house while I'm away. Take care of things for me, will you?"

Ron replied, like he always did, "You can count on me, Dad."

"I know I can, Ron. I know I can."

Dad always said the same thing when Mom and he went off on trips alone and, every time, Ron felt like he'd grown two inches in height. His dad, who knew how to do everything - except how to screw in a light bulb, if Mom was to be believed - had needed Ron to look after the little kids and keep everyone safe.

Those were the last words Dad said to him. The second to last, actually: the very last had been, "Goodbye, guys!"

Ron could not let his father down. Not for a moment. No matter how tired he got.

Ron was faithful to his promise. He looked after the kids, helped poor Aunt Julia, and always double-checked the locks on the doors of the house after everyone else had gone to bed. He knew that Dad would be proud of him, but not if he started whining now.

It wasn't as if Dad had been the only one to point out his new responsibilities. Dad's lawyer, Steven Hall - on the day they were told who was to be their guardian - took advantage of Aunt Julia having to use the ladies' room to give the orphans some advice.

"This is a new situation for all of you," he had said. "Your aunt is a capable woman, but she is young and doesn't have any children of her own. This will be a very difficult experience for her, at least at first, while she is still getting used to everything. We don't want to make it any harder for her, do we? I hope that you will all do your best to give her as little trouble as possible, and to help her any way you can. Do I have your word?"

They gave it as solemnly as he had asked for it. He seemed relieved as he sat back in his chair.

"I'm sure you'll be no trouble at all," he said.

Dana had raised her hand and asked the question that Ron was too reserved to ask: "What would happen? If she doesn't like us, I mean."

"Well, I'm sure she likes you. But if she or the courts felt that she was unable to handle the responsibilities, you would be taken somewhere else to live."

"With Gran and Gramp?" Dana asked a little doubtfully.

"Perhaps. Or maybe with another family."

"And we'd stay together?" asked Ron, a little more fiercely than he had intended.

Mr. Hall's answer was slow in coming. "We would certainly try for that."

It sounded to Ron like a death knell of sorts. The lawyer must have realized this, for he repeated, with a wan smile, that he was sure the children would be no trouble at all. It was at this point that Jack managed to work the cover off of his little jug of milk and fling the contents all about the office. Aunt Julia returned just in time to see them scrambling for the paper towels.

She wasn't angry with them, though. She only seemed sorry for Mr. Hall, whose attitude changed when she came back in. Dana mentioned this to Ron in private later that day.

"I think he likes Aunt Julia," she said.

"Oh?" Ron was not very interested in what Dana thought.

"I hope she doesn't like him."

"Why not?"

"He smells funny."

"You're such a child," Ron sighed.

"Am not!"

They all agreed that they would give Aunt Julia no reason to complain, and formed a sort of team: Ron was in charge of chores and discipline, Dana was to keep Aunt Julia happy and Jack occupied, and Jack was to avoid being a nuisance.

Their grandparents thought it was too much for Aunt Julia. Every time they came over for dinner, Gran and Gramp Budd would ask about money, health, and business. They tried to insinuate that it was overwhelming Aunt Julia and that they would be better placed somewhere else. Ron always defended her as much as he could, but what frightened him was how quietly Aunt Julia took the abuse. Didn't she know that the grandparents were trying to take them away?

Once, when he was listening at the top of the stairs, he heard Gran Budd say, "It's a heavy responsibility, Julia. I hope you know what you're doing. You know that you have options and you don't have to be ashamed to consider them."

Aunt Julia surprised Ron with her sharp, quick answer. "There's only one option that I've ever considered, Miriam, and that is carrying out Amanda's wishes. She wanted them with me, so they are. We are doing just fine. I don't regret a single moment and that's the end of the discussion, all right?"

Gran was angry. Ron could tell from her tone. "You're being foolish. I'm only trying to look out for my grandchildren, to do what's best for them."

"Aren't we all?" asked Gramp.

Aunt Julia had reluctantly apologized, Gran stiffly accepted it, and the matter was closed for the moment. Ron went to bed a little more secure, but he knew that, if absolute peace wasn't kept and the household didn't look like it was being run in pristine condition, the naysayers would return and he might not be able to stop them.

It was a heavy burden sometimes, but Ron couldn't put it down. The stakes were too high.

Julia was still standing in front of him, looking back at Kehoe.

Ron asked, "Is everything all right? What's going on?"

She gestured to the Audi. "I've decided to let the Audi go. We don't need three cars and I can get the best price for this one. I'm letting Kehoe make an offer first."

She put a hand on Ron's shoulder. He could feel her inquisitive gaze, as though she was silently asking him, "Is this okay with you?"

He wanted to throw the hand off of his shoulder. He wanted to shout at her, "No, it's not okay! That's my Dad's car! My *Dad's* car! And you're just giving it away!"

But he restrained himself. It wasn't Aunt Julia's fault that his parents were gone. It wasn't her fault that bills had to be paid and things had to change. It wasn't her fault that the only room in the house that she could move into was Mom and Dad's room. When people died, things changed. People changed. He fought against the changes as hard as he could, for Dana and Jack as much for himself, but they couldn't fight everything. As the man of the house, he had to appreciate that, grit his teeth, and move on, so that he could handle the other kids when they came home.

He swallowed hard. It wouldn't be easy. Aunt Julia hadn't seen the look on Dad's face when he unwrapped the Audi's keys on Christmas morning. He had been so excited that he swept Mom up in his arms and gave her one of those movie kisses that always managed to both gross Ron out and make him happy at the same time.

Aunt Julia didn't know things like that.

She was a bit of a mystery to Ron still. She was hardworking and obviously caring, but she didn't take charge like his mother did. She was very hesitant and so apologetic that it made Ron wanted to shout sometimes. But she did seem to love Dana and Jack and, for that, he was willing to overlook her shortcomings. After all, he couldn't expect her to be Mom. He wouldn't have wanted that anyway.

He said, "Kehoe sells cars, so he probably knows what they're worth."

She gave his shoulder a grateful squeeze, which he appreciated. He was relieved, though, when she took her hand off of his shoulder. Physical contact was something that he preferred to limit.

She picked up his trumpet case, and they walked the few steps up the driveway.

"How was school?" she asked.

"Long," he said.

"Worried about the results of the finals?"

"No. Not really." He thought for a moment and added, truthfully, "But I'll be glad when it's over."

She smiled sympathetically. "I always hated the end of the year. Loved summer, but hated the finals. I don't know why, though. I was a pretty good student and I wasn't likely to fail. But I always thought I would. Actually, I was always positive I would and I was always so shocked to find I had done okay. I'm glad I don't have to go through that anymore."

For a moment, they were so comfortable that Ron was struck by the idea that, in other circumstances, they might have become very close friends. He was about to confess that he was too anxious to eat breakfast on test mornings, when Kehoe called out to his aunt and took the opportunity away.

"Mind if I take it out for a test drive?" he asked.

Julia stopped mid-step and laughed. "No, but you know perfectly well that it purrs like a kitten, Kehoe. You saw me drive out with it this morning."

"Ever hear of sawdust, Julia?"

"Okay, okay! Just don't get into an accident while you're out."

Kehoe asked, with a lecherous smile that was intended to be charming, "Why don't you come with me and make sure that I control myself."

Ron was annoyed, but to his surprise, Julia hesitated. He could see her calculating the risks in her head and turned to Ron with a pensive look.

"I probably should," she said. "It'll only be a few minutes. Do you mind?"

Ron was disappointed. Was Aunt Julia really going to go with Kehoe? A few weeks ago, Mrs. Gouldman had made a casual, but calculated remark to Ron, commenting on how friendly Kehoe and his aunt were getting. She hinted that it wouldn't surprise her if they started dating or something. The idea was so abhorrent to Ron that it kept him awake long into that night.

"No," he muttered. "I don't mind."

She squeezed his shoulder again, grateful. "I'll just be a few minutes," she said. She gave Kehoe a nod. As he turned to go into the house, Ron thought the grease-streaked man almost did a little happy dance.

Aunt Julia called to him, "We have to have a family meeting tonight, okay?" she said. "Just you and me before we talk to the younger two."

He froze. "Something's happened."

"Yes, but…"

A blast from the car horn. Kehoe was impatient.

She waved a hand to silence him and quickly said to Ron, "Everything will be all right. Something has happened, but I need more time to explain. And I've got a plan for the summer that I want to tell you about. It'll be fine. Actually, it'll be great. We'll talk about it when I get back. Stay away from Mrs. Gouldman in the meantime, okay?"

She ran over to the Audi passenger door to join the increasingly excited Kehoe. Ron watched him back out of the driveway and take off down the street. With his heart sinking into his stomach, the man of the house turned and went inside.

"We're moving *away*?"

Dana Budd's mouth fell open, and her dinner of chicken fingers, mac and cheese, and string beans was completely forgotten. She looked from Julia to Ron as her wide blue eyes started welling up with tears. "But… But why? Where are we going?"

Julia reached across Jack's plate and took her hand. Jack, finding this an intrusion, made his displeasure known by dumping a spoonful of ketchup on her arm.

Julia snatched her arm back and wiped the sauce with her napkin, somehow winding up with a blob on her clean white shorts. "Oh, Jack!" she wailed.

"Sorry," Jack said. He went happily back to smearing mac and cheese and ketchup around his plate in colorful designs.

Ron explain, "We aren't moving, Dana. We're just going there for the summer to fix the place up."

He felt like adding, *Shut up, Dana, and eat. We'll discuss it later, when Aunt Julia isn't around.*

But his sister was not adept at telepathy. In the crush of the last few days of school, and with growing accustomed to the new way of life, Ron thought she'd been slacking in her duties. No doubt it was time to remind her of what might happen should Aunt Julia be unable to provide them a home.

While he was thinking this, however, the conversation moved on.

"Why?" Dana asked, sniffing. "Why can't we just stay here? I *like* it here."

"Well, I like it too, honey," Julia answered, still swiping at the ketchup on her shorts. "I just thought it would be nice for all of us to have a change of scenery and to get out of the city for a little while. I know that you were all disappointed when I told you we couldn't do camps this year – well, this will be like going to camp, only longer and with all of us. I think it'll be fun." She turned and gasped. "Jack! We do *not* put cheese *or* ketchup in our hair."

"Sor-ry!" he sang in reply.

"But what are we going to do up there?" asked Dana.

"Mom and Dad had an old house in New Hampshire," Ron explained patiently. "We're going to go up there to fix it up so we can sell it. Like on one of those reality shows that you like. You know – we'll be giving it a makeover."

"But we won't be just working," Julia added quickly. "There's a lake up there for swimming, and a park, and a big yard for you to play in. We'll have picnics and we can bring all of your bikes and swimsuits and lots of sparklers for the Fourth of July. But no video games or anything like that. I want you guys to run around in the sun and just live it up. It'll just be a fun, old fashioned sort of summer, you'll see."

"But Colleen and I were going to do a lemonade stand together," Dana protested. "We were going to raise money so that we could buy some cute little puppies."

Ron saw Aunt Julia's face fall. Dana had wanted a pet ever since she was six and her desire had only grown with time. Ron knew that

Aunt Julia considered pets a luxury that they couldn't afford, but still he couldn't help wishing that they could give Dana her way. She was desperate for something to care for, and Jack was getting too big. Surely a pet mouse or a rat wouldn't be too much to ask.

Julia said, "We'll be back a few weeks before school starts. You can do your lemonade stand then."

"But summer will be almost *over*! Colleen will already have enough money and she won't want to *do* it anymore."

"Well, I'm sorry, Dana, but I think that this is the best idea for all of us right now. I think we need a little time to get away, see someplace new, and get to know each other a little better. I know it doesn't sound like it'll be much fun, but I think you'll be surprised at how fast the time goes by."

Dana opened her mouth to protest again, but Ron gave her a gentle kick under the table. She stopped, gave him a look of hurt surprise, and closed her mouth again as she folded her arms and sat back in her chair. She was trying not to pout, as Ron had warned against earlier, but the effort was costing her.

Julia didn't notice. She said, in her usual gentle tone, "We also need some time as a family, to sift through what we need to do next. The past few months have been difficult for all of us, but I think we've done very well. Now we have to take the next step. Since I don't have to go to work, we can go away for a month or so, on the cheap. We're going to have to spend very carefully now until I find another job."

Dana looked at Ron, alarmed. "We don't have any money?"

Julia was quick to respond. "No, we have money and we are going to be all right. You don't have to worry about that. But we just may find that we don't need *everything* that we have. Like, for instance, the Audi. We decided that we don't need three cars and so we're selling that one. That's not too bad, is it?"

Dana was getting confused, but under Ron's steady gaze, she was too polite to offer any kind of protest. "No. It isn't."

"This is sort of the same thing. If we can fix up the house and sell it, the money will buy me some more time before I absolutely have to get a job. Hopefully, there'll be enough to put aside some for those summer camps next year. That would be good, wouldn't it?"

"Yes!" Jack laughed, slapping both palms onto his tray. "Good! Very good!"

Julia smiled. "Good boy, Jack. *That's* the spirit. Are you ready for a summer adventure?"

"Yes!" He brought both palms down into the mushy remains of ketchup and cheese.

"Eww, Jack! That's gross!" Julia cried.

"No, it's good," he insisted. He grabbed a handful and shoved it at her. "See?"

"No, thanks, Jack, I'm full. Eat another chicken finger, okay?"

"Okay!" He took the chicken nugget that she offered him and dipped it in his unique mixture.

Then Julia looked at the two older ones. Dana was still leaning back against her chair with her arms folded, while Ron tried to stare her into submission.

"How about you guys?" she asked. "What do you think?"

Dana shifted and Ron nudged her with his foot. She frowned at him, and then turned to Julia.

"I think it'll be fun," she said, her tone flat.

"Thank you, Dana. You can bring out the box of cookies from the cupboard now, if you like." Julia looked at Ron. "And you, Ron? Anything you want to ask me before we go? Anything I should know about?"

Ron looked down at his plate for a second, and then met her eyes. "I think it's a good idea," he said, sounding more confident than he was.

Julia blinked in surprise.

"Thank you," she murmured.

Dana came back in with the cookies, and Jack clapped with delight. After a few had been distributed, Ron asked, "When will we leave?"

"I'm thinking we could go as early as the Saturday after school is out. You're out on Tuesday, Jack's out on Wednesday, so that will give us a few days to finish packing and to shut down the house." She crunched on a cookie thoughtfully. "We'll have to remember to bring a lot of DVDs. We won't have any cable up there."

"How about computers?" Ron asked, alarmed.

She shook her head. "We can bring the laptop, but we'll have to use the Wi-Fi wherever we can get it."

Calmer, Ron said, "That's fine. Whatever."

"Who will stay here to watch the house?" asked Dana.

"My friend, Sherri, from the real estate office," Julia said.

"She won't go in my room, will she?"

"No, she won't really be staying here – she'll just stop by every once in a while to check up on things." She looked around and sighed again. "Jack, we don't put cookies in our hair either. I think it's time you had a bath."

"No!" Jack replied firmly.

Ron gestured to Dana and she jumped up. "I'll do it, Aunt Julia," she said, and hurried to gather Jack in her arms. "Come on, messy!"

Julia rose halfway from her seat to protest, then sat down again. She seemed disappointed, almost hurt.

"All right," she called after them. "But remember – only a few inches of water in the tub."

"I remember!"

Ron was clearing the table when Julia turned back around.

"Just you and me on clean up tonight?" she asked, smiling.

"I can do it, Aunt Julia. I know you've got a lot to do," he said.

Her eyes clouded over again. "Not that much. I've got plenty of time now."

"No, really," he insisted. "It's cool. I need to clear my head anyway before homework. I can handle this."

Eventually, she gave in and left for the study. Ron made short work of the dishes, and then raced upstairs to where Dana was struggling to get Jack dressed.

"He won't hold still!" Dana said, frustrated.

Ron plucked Jack from Dana's grip and held him out in front of him. Jack protested by shouting, squirming, and kicking his legs, but his older brother had gotten very good at this sort of thing and was not about to let go.

"Now, listen here, you," he said sternly. "Remember what we said? No trouble, right?"

Jack kicked in reply.

"Jack, do you want to sleep alone in your room tonight?"

That got his attention. Jack hadn't slept alone since their mother had died. He always slipped out of his crib to curl up with Dana or Ron or, when the two older siblings didn't catch him in time, with Julia. He would cling to them, sometimes dreaming dreams that would have him wake up sobbing. Sleeping alone was not an option for Jack. Even his ever-present Yellow Teddy was not enough to soothe his troubled sleep.

Eventually, he calmed down and let Dana put his night clothes on.

"Why do we have to go, Ron?" Dana whined. "I don't want to leave this house. I don't want to go away."

"We have to go and get that other house ready to sell, Dana," Ron said curtly.

"But why?"

"Because we don't have any money to hire someone else, that's why. Aunt Julia's been *fired*, Dana. She doesn't have any money coming in any more. If she can't sell this house, she'll be in real trouble, even if she does get a new job. Do you know how much it costs to keep two houses?"

"Do you?"

"No, but I know that it's a lot and we can't afford a lot."

There was silence for a moment. Jack had caught on to the seriousness of the matter, and was listening carefully.

Dana asked, "What will happen to us if she can't sell it?"

Ron looked solemnly at them both. "Well, the lawyer said that we couldn't stay with her if she couldn't take care of us, right? So, I guess they'll take us away and give us to someone else. Maybe Gran and Gramp Budd, if we're lucky."

"But they *can't*," said Dana, panicking. "We belong with Aunt Julia – that's what Mom *wanted*!"

Ron looked at her. "Then I guess we're going to Franklin," he said softly. "And make sure that we do everything that we can to get that house to sell, right?"

Dana sighed. "Right."

"Shake," Ron said.

They shook on it.

"And," he warned, "I don't want any more trouble out of you two, you hear? We are going to be the most helpful kids anyone's ever seen, right?"

They shook on that, too.

# 4

The days passed quickly. Julia was busy job searching, preparing her resume, and arranging everything for their summer trip. She called the caretaker of the Franklin house, a woman by the name of Sheila O'Reilly. She was initially taken aback by the terse way the woman answered the phone, but Sheila's tone softened when she realized who she was talking to. She had heard about Amanda and offered Julia her sympathy.

Julia thanked her, then asked her to open up the place for them.

Mrs. O'Reilly was happy to oblige. "The house is in need of a clean, I'm afraid. There was a leak during the winter, but my old man got it all patched up nice and tight for you, no problem. All the furniture's still there, including some mattresses and stuff. Most of it was in good shape. Shall I call the electric company?"

"Please."

"Sure, no problem. What number can I reach you at?"

Julia gave it to her, and Mrs. O'Reilly wrote it down, saying, "I'm glad to hear you say that you're coming to fix the place up. It's really a nice little house, and we've got a great neighborhood and a good school. It'll be nice to have some new faces here."

"I'm afraid we're only going to be up there for the summer, Mrs. O'Reilly. I'm just coming to fix the place up to sell."

"Oh? Well, you might change your mind. Franklin may be past one heyday, but we're on our way to another. Anyway, I'll open the place up for you and give you a call to let you know what I find."

"Thank you," Julia said.

A week before school got out, Julia went down the realtor's to sign the final papers and hand over her keys to her condo. Sherri was in a very good mood that day, having sold three properties in a week.

"This is a great idea of yours," she said, as Julia was trying to decipher the fine print on the contract. "Getting out of town for a few weeks is just what you and the kids need."

Julia shuffled the papers noisily. "Thanks," she said, hoping she'd take the hint.

Sherri didn't. "I'm glad you took my advice. In fact, I'm so glad that I'm going to offer you another piece, free of charge." She leaned forward, forcing Julia to look up from her paperwork. "Let me show the house for you while you're gone."

Julia was puzzled. "I already told you that you could, once we've gotten finished renovating it."

"No, not Franklin. I'm talking about the Springfield place."

"No. Absolutely not, Sherri. I told you, that is the kids' home, and I'm not about to uproot them. They've been through enough."

"But Julia, you have no idea of the market that's opening up here. I'm telling you, with the right buyer, we could make a killing. You wouldn't have to go back to work."

"No."

"All right, but think about this for a minute: Springfield's building a new school next year. When that place gets built, they're going to need more teachers, more computers, more supplies, more programs, and more buses. In the next few years, taxes on a place your size, which is too big for just for the four of you anyway, are going to go through the roof. Unless you really strike gold with the new job, you may not be able to afford it."

"Sherri, stop," Julia snapped.

Sherri clasped her hands together as if she was begging. "Please, Julia, let me at least show it. I'll just put out some feelers, and see if there's any interest. I won't make any deals until you're sure, but let me get some bids here at least, even if only just to satisfy my own curiosity."

Julia relented, but with conditions. "I won't agree to anything other than showings right now. And the kids are not to know, so wait until we're gone before you post it."

Sherri was more than happy to agree to the conditions. Julia left the office minus one condo, and with the suspicion that she had bitten off more than she could chew.

She cleaned the house from top to bottom, working until her arms felt like they were going to fall off. The children chalked her flurry of activity up to the summer vacation, and cheerfully volunteered to help.

Julia also began packing. She boxed up enough toys, games, DVDs, and books to see them through the month and stacked them by the doorway. She called the post office and the newspaper, and composed an email to all their friends, explaining their absence. It wouldn't be sent until the day that they actually left Springfield, a detail that Julia thought important for the preservation of her family's peace.

The Monday before they left, Julia sorted through their tools and bought two small tents, a smoke detector, a carbon monoxide detector, and a first aid kit.

Tuesday was the graduation, and Ron's band played to great acclaim. On Wednesday, they sorted through clothing and discovered that new wardrobes were needed for everyone. Thursday was spent in various department stores, trying on clothes and trying not to lose tempers.

That night, Yellow Teddy disappeared. They made a frantic search for the little bear while Jack cried hysterically. Dana wore herself out trying to comfort him. Just when Julia was about to give up, Yellow Teddy was discovered wedged between Jack's car seat and the wall of the minivan. Disaster was averted.

On Friday, they went to the grocery store and bought supplies and packed everything into the minivan. They discovered that there was room for everything but Jack and Dana. They took everything out, then resorted, repacked, and tried again, this time with slightly better results: they would have to leave only Dana behind.

Tired, sweating, and hungry, Julia decided that they would need only one tent. They put the other into the basement, along with one of the coolers and a 24-pack of soda, which she decided could be bought in New Hampshire.

Dana looked doubtful. "Will they have soda in New Hampshire?" she asked.

"Of course, honey. It's not the wild, wild, west."

"I thought it was a camp ground place. You know, like Uncle Tyler's."

"Uncle Tyler lives in a trailer park," Ron sighed. "Not a camp ground."

"We're not going to a trailer park, Dana," Julia said. "It's a normal neighborhood, like here. I showed you the picture, didn't I?"

"Yes..."

"Well, then, you know it's a normal house, don't you?"

The little girl shrugged. "I don't know. It was hard to see. Mom and Dad were in the way."

"Well, it will all be fine, I promise. We just going to another state, you know, not to Timbuktu."

After dinner that night, they treated themselves to the rest of the ice cream from the freezer. Jack fell asleep in the middle of his sundae, and was so dead to the world that Julia was able to slip him into his crib without waking him.

When she tucked Dana in, the little girl said, "When will we be back, Aunt Julia?"

"By mid-August at the very latest, but maybe before then."

Dana sighed and stroked her comforter. "I'm going to miss this house," she said. "It'll be lonely without us."

Julia smiled softly and ran her hand along the child's face. "It'll be fine," she said gently. "It'll still be here when we get back, all rested and ready for some noise. Besides, my friend Sherri will be checking in on it, too, to make sure everything's okay. It'll be fine."

Dana nodded, but she still looked troubled.

"Is there something else, Dana? Something you want to tell me?"

The little girl opened her mouth, and then an expression that Julia couldn't identify crossed her face. Dana mouth snapped shut and she shook her head.

"No, I'm fine."

"Are you sure? We can talk about it. Sometimes that helps, you know."

But she only shook her head again and buried herself deeper under the covers. "No, I'm okay. I'm just tired now."

Julia hid her disappointment and kissed the little girl good-night, taking a moment to stroke the child's brunette curls.

"I love you, Dana," she said softly.

Ron was waiting outside Dana's door.

"I've checked the house," he said. "All the doors are locked and everything's all set for the night. You just need to set the alarm."

"Thank you," Julia said. Then, knowing that he wouldn't be comfortable unless he watched her set the alarm, she went over to the panel and turned it on. Maybe it was because she was tired, or maybe it was because his steady gaze was distracting her, but whatever the reason, Julia punched in the wrong code and nearly set off the alarm in full mode. After a few seconds of frantic punching, she finally got it under control.

"Is there anything else that needs to be done before tomorrow?" Ron asked.

Julia sighed in relief. "I've got some last minute packing to do, but other than that, we're good. Why don't you get to bed early and rest up? Tomorrow will be a long day. Thanks for everything. You've been a real rock, you know."

He nodded solemnly and padded off to bed.

Julia left her bedroom door open while she packed and put on one of her favorite old movies to keep her company. She was just about done when she heard Jack sobbing.

Jack was in the middle of his crib, rubbing his eyes and crying. Julia gathered him up with his blanket and Yellow Teddy and brought him into her room. She noticed Ron's door silently shutting as she passed and was pleased that he would have an undisturbed night.

She deposited the sleepy little boy in her own bed and let him watch the movie while she finished the packing, laid out the next morning's clothes, and got ready for bed.

Curled up together, both were asleep before the credits started to roll.

Julia figured the trip should take about three hours and ten minutes. Leaving at eight o'clock would allow them to get to Franklin in time for lunch, thus leaving the whole afternoon free for moving in and getting settled. Accordingly, she had the kids ready to go a half-hour before their start time.

Sherri was late getting to the house, of course. Julia thought she should have known better than to expect her to be on time for a job that did not include a sale. At 9:00 a.m. Sherri called to say that she was on her way. At 9:15, she was pulling in the driveway.

Sherri hopped out of her car, beaming. "Sorry I'm late! I had a breakfast meeting with one of my clients and she would not stop talking. Do you mind if we skip the walkthrough, and just hand over the keys? I've got another appointment in fifteen minutes."

"Not at all," Julia said. She pulled out the spare set and handed them to Sherri, along with a folded up sheet of paper with the passcode on it. "Thanks for looking after everything."

"Well, it's the least I can do. You're doing me a favor, too, you know." Sherri tucked the paper, unread, into her purse. "Have a great time in New Hampshire. I hear it's really nice up there during the summer."

"I hope so," Julia said. "Thanks again."

Sherri left. Julia and Ron walked through the house once more, checking everything before setting the alarm and locking the front door.

She glanced at her watch as they walked down the front steps to the waiting van.

"Nine-thirty," she said. "An hour and a half late. Not a great start to our big adventure, but still, not as bad as it could have been."

Ron waved to Mrs. Gouldman, who was watching them suspiciously. "Nope. Not as bad as it could be."

They got in and strapped on their seat belts. Julia pulled out the list that she had left the night before on the dash board. "Okay, last minute check list. Do we have the map?"

"Check," Ron said, waving it.

"GPS?"

"Check."

"My purse?"

Ron sighed. "Check."

"Yellow Teddy?"

"Yellow Teddy!" Jack shouted, waving him happily.

"Four bottles of water?"

"Check," Dana said.

"Piles and piles of luggage?"

Ron rolled his eyes. "Definitely check."

Julia folded the list. "And we have one driver who is in desperate need of some caffeine. Good. Let's roll, guys."

As they pulled out into the road, Julia spotted three faces turning towards the now deserted house. With wide-eyed sadness, they watched until the van turned a corner and the house disappeared from sight. She heard a collective sigh as they all settled back into their seats and composed themselves for the long journey. Even Julia felt something at the thought of the weeks it would be before they saw home again.

Even so, she couldn't help but feel a rush of excitement as they pulled out on to the main road. This was it. They were on their way.

Summer had begun.

# 5

The trip took longer than expected. Traffic was heavy, and bogged down in several places. They passed a dreadful-looking accident involving a truck and two small cars, which horrified Dana and fascinated Jack.

"Aunt Julia," he said, sounding awed. "They hit each other."

"Yes, Jack."

"Why did they hit each other?"

"I don't know."

"They hit each other," he said again, "and then they blew up."

"I don't think they blew up."

"Yes, they did. That's why police are there."

"Oh, *Jack*," said Ron. He was white-faced from fighting carsickness.

"What?"

Julia sighed. "Let's listen to the music, guys, okay?"

They had to make a bathroom break and then stop for lunch at a crowded restaurant that had very slow service. Jack became cranky and ended up with most of his meal on his shirt. Dana was homesick, and the still-queasy Ron didn't feel like eating much.

They managed to make it through lunch and got back on the road. With a meal and some ice cream soothing the kids, they became sleepy and the van was quiet.

It was well past two o'clock when Julia finally passed through Concord, New Hampshire. She sighed with relief and turned down the air conditioner. The day had gone from warm to hot very quickly, and the noise of the fans was starting to irritate her. She turned down the radio, too, and glanced in the rear view mirror.

The two youngsters in the back looked like withered flowers. Jack slept in the warm sunlight that fell on his seat, the stains of lunch still prominent on his shirt. His golden curls shone like a halo on his head. Dana was curled up in a little ball, her head on a stack of suitcases, one arm around her rag doll, and her mind far into a dream world.

To Julia's right, Ron was very quiet, as he had been for the entire trip; however, he was feeling better, thanks to some Pepto Bismal from a local gas station. His blue eyes watched the passing scenery with a dreamy concentration. His hand had grown loose on its grip of his iPod, and Julia could just make out the faint sounds of the song that was playing.

The scenery grew more and more luxurious. Tangles of trees, brush, and thick grass made it seem as though they were driving through a sort of northeastern jungle. Julia even spotted some rare Lady Slipper orchards, and the horticulturalist in her grew excited. She remembered Mrs. O'Reilly telling her about the remains of the garden out back. It would be fun to work on it, weeding and planting. Maybe Dana would like to help with that. She was looking for something to nurture, after all.

Once again, Julia went over her to-do list. First thing was to see if the house was clean enough to stay the night. If not, she'd brought a tent, a portable grill, and the sleeping bags. They could camp in the backyard until the house was ready. Although Mrs. O'Reilly didn't think there was any problem with the place, Julia wanted to leave nothing to chance.

The second thing was to visit the local hardware store to pick up cleaning supplies. Space constraints forced Julia to leave all but the bare minimum behind. She could also look for paint and other supplies while there. She was looking forward to the work: there was nothing she liked better than a simple home improvement project. It would help take her mind off of the job hunt.

She had already sent her resume to several companies with open positions. Hopefully, something would come up soon. Any sort of home improvement would cost money, and that was in dwindling supply.

Ron, who was studying the directions, pulled an earplug from his ear. "Take the next right," he said. "Almost there."

"Yep," Julia smiled. "I'll be glad to get out of the car."

Ron didn't answer. He had plugged himself in again, and they were separated by a wall of music.

They followed the directions to Sheila O'Reilly's house, passing through downtown Franklin as they did so.

Ron kept careful watch at the window, not terribly impressed by what he saw. Franklin had once been a busy and prosperous city; but for every open business, there were two that were closed. Although the websites he had visited spoke of the city's renaissance, Franklin was still suffering. There weren't many people on the broad, straight streets. A police car idled by a stop sign.

The directions took them through the city center and into the outskirts of Webster Lake. Here, old streets with small houses were interspaced with wider, more modern streets and newer houses. Their carefully trimmed lawns, backyard pools, and patios made Ron feel a little better. He sat up straight and pulled the ear plug out.

Sheila O'Reilly lived on High Top Ridge, a street built into the side of a hill near Whipple Lane. She wasn't home. She'd left an envelope taped to her door containing a note and a key, which Aunt Julia brought back to the minivan.

"Sheila forgot that they were going out this afternoon," she said. She showed Ron a bunch of shiny keys. "But we're in."

"Doesn't seem like a very safe way to leave someone a key," Ron remarked.

"It isn't, but I guess it doesn't matter now. We've got the keys and that's the main thing." She started the van and turned back on to the street, shaking her head ruefully. "The note says that the lawn is covered in ticks. There goes my backup plan – I don't want to tent in a tick-infested lawn."

Ron read the directions to 134 Whipple Lane. As they drove closer to the lake, the houses grew smaller and sat close together in a cozy fashion. The enormous pines and maples testified to the fact that it was an older section of town. Some of the back-yards had toys, while others simply had hammocks. An old woman sitting on her front porch frowned at the van as they passed by. A trio of pre-teen girls walked down the street, talking and texting each other.

"Take the next left," Ron read, and Julia turned onto Whipple Lane.

It was a wider, more open street than the one the O'Reilly's lived on, and the properties were better kept up, with mowed lawns and drivable cars in the driveways. Julia slowed down as they came upon a green and weather-worn mailbox with the let-tering *134* on it in chipped white paint.

The grass from the tiny unkempt front yard at number 134 came nearly halfway up the leaning post. In front of the house, day lilies and tulips fought against the encroaching lawn.

A maple and an oak stood at the front corners of the prop-erty, the oak with the petrified remains of a wooden swing hang-ing from one of its limbs. A rotting, waist-height fence, in serious need of paint, leaned against its trunk. Someone long ago had planted little clusters of white, blue, and red flowers at each of the fence posts, but they were overrun with weeds.

Ron barely noticed these details, however. His attention was taken up by the house itself.

He was prepared for a small place. Aunt Julia had told them that it was only a cottage for people visiting the lake, but he was still disappointed. Wide, cracked cement stairs led up to an old one-and-a-half story bungalow with a roofed front porch, where a large front door stood between two double windows. Above the porch roof was a gable and a tiny set of windows in what was probably the attic. There were chimneys on either side of the house, and Ron wondered if there were fireplaces. He regretted the idea that they would not have an opportunity to use them, if there were.

Although it was large as old summer-by-the-lake cottages go, compared to his two-and-a-half story place in Springfield, this house looked positively cramped.

Julia pulled into the driveway. On closer inspection, the house looked even less inviting. The cream colored paint was cracked and chipped and the windows were dusty and full of cobwebs. Ron found himself wondering if the house had cockroaches.

He had just managed to clear the expression from his face when his aunt turned to him.

"It's bigger than I expected," she said.

Ron nodded.

She studied it for a moment. "You know what it reminds me of?"

Ron wanted to say, "The House on Haunted Hill?" but he contented himself with, "No, what?" in a mildly curious tone of voice.

Julia tapped her window and, in a tone like that of an archeologist with a significant find, said, "It reminds me of those pre-fab homes that they used to sell in the 1920s and 30s. Sears used to have catalogs full of them. You'd just order the kit and dig the foundation and presto, you had a home."

This was the first he'd heard of it. "Really?"

"Yes. I used to have an old catalog from Sears, back when I was studying architecture. This house looks so familiar, I wonder if it was in that catalogue." She gave a winsome smile. "These sorts of houses were a big deal then. They were cheap, easy to build, and ordinary families could afford to have their own place outside of the city. It must have been a dream come true for some of them."

This did not look to Ron like anyone's dream come true. "You studied architecture?"

"Mmm hmm. Just for a little while. I used to like to walk around neighborhoods and try to guess what year the houses were built. I got to be pretty good at it." She smiled at him apologetically. "I'm sorry, Ron. I'm jabbering on and on, and you probably want to get out and stretch your legs."

"I'm fine," he said quickly.

"I know, but it's almost three and we've got a lot to do. Now you wait here, and I'll take a quick walk through the house before we wake the others."

Ron, who really did want more than anything to stretch his legs, said hopefully, "Would you like me to come with you?"

"No, you stay here with the others. I just want to be sure we don't have a tenant living in there that Mrs. O'Reilly forgot to tell us about. Sometimes, when these houses are left alone for a period of time, people move in without permission." She opened the door and looked at the house with some trepidation. Then, with a glance over her shoulder, she said, "I'll be right back. Keep the door locked."

She shut the door behind her and waited until he put the lock down. After trying several keys, she managed to get the side door open, and was swallowed up by the darkness inside.

Ron unlocked the doors again, just in case, and unbuckled his seat belt. Twisting around, he shook Dana until she protested and slapped his hand away.

"Dana, we're here," he said.

She sat up, her hair mussed, her eyes heavy with sleep. She looked around.

"Where are we, Ron?"

"We're at the cottage," he said. "Aunt Julia's gone inside to take a look."

Studying the house, Dana looked shocked. "It's all *broken*," she cried. "And *dirty*! We're going to live in there?"

Ron sighed as he faced front again. "I guess so. Just for a few weeks, anyway."

He could see Dana pouting in the rearview mirror.

"It's all dirty and gross," she said. "I don't want to sleep in there. It'll be all buggy and stuff. We should just go home."

"We can clean it up," he replied sternly. He privately agreed with Dana, but didn't want to spark a mutiny. Not on the first day, anyway. "Oh, buck up, Dana. It'll be fine."

"It looks creepy. Like it's haunted or something."

"Aunt Julia won't let us stay in any place that's dangerous. And besides, ghosts don't exist and you know it."

"Well, maybe not, but I..."

As she said this, Jack woke up with a start, saying, "Oh! Oh, I need to *go*, Ron! I need to *go!*"

"You have to wait, Jack. Aunt Julia will be back any minute."

Just then, the side door opened and Julia came out. She looked preoccupied as she approached the van.

Ron said hastily, "You just keep quiet, Dana. We don't want to bother Aunt Julia, right?"

"Whatever," Dana mumbled, but Ron knew that she'd obey.

Julia opened the sliding door, and her face brightened when she saw Dana. "Oh, good, you're awake! You can get out now, but stay out of the grass."

"I have to *go!*" Jack moaned.

"Oh, good heavens! Hold on one second, buddy."

Ron got out of the car while Julia took Jack out of his car seat and swung him up onto her hip. Jack was still half asleep and he rested his head on her shoulder as she turned to the house.

"Well, guys," she said hopefully. "This is it. What do you think?"

"It looks dirty," Dana said, before Ron could stop her.

Julia nodded. "I'm afraid it is. We have a lot of cleaning to do before we can start to relax, guys. Want to see inside?"

"I need to *go!*" Jack reminded her.

"Ron, run and get the wipes from the van. Don't go near the grass. Dana, come on."

Dana followed her reluctantly. Ron darted back to the van as quickly as he could, grabbed the wipes, and made it to the house before Dana got through the door.

Just inside the doorway was a staircase leading upstairs to a shadowed second floor. On their right was a closed, battered, and ominous-looking door. On the left were two steps that led up into the kitchen. They followed Julia as she turned a sharp right down a short hall and stopped just short of the door at the end. She turned to Ron.

"Got the wipes?"

He tossed them to her and she caught them neatly with her free hand. "I'll take Jack to the bathroom. You two can look around, but don't get into anything."

She and Jack disappeared into the bathroom.

For a moment, Ron and Dana stood staring at each other. The house was cool, dark, and dry, with a hint of a musty smell to it. Shafts of mid-afternoon sunlight came in through the kitchen windows and made an effort to light the hallway. There were doors all around them, all of them shut.

"Come on, Dana," Ron said, suddenly filled with the urge to explore.

He started with the door across from the kitchen. It opened up into a small room with a banged up desk, a sagging computer chair, an empty bookcase, and a window. There were marks in the dusty rug from where other furniture once rested, and dead flies decorated the window sill.

"Boring," Dana said. "Come on!"

She opened the door to the front room. It was a larger room with a set of double windows, a wooden floor, cheery but peeling yellow wallpaper, and a stone fireplace. There was an old TV and console, and a tattered sofa, all covered with dust sheets. To their left, a pair of open double doors led into a dining room with a tiny chandelier, a scarred dining set with six chairs, and a hutch with glass doors. Another door led back into the kitchen.

They returned to the hall. To the left was a little bedroom with a closet, a shabby dresser, and a cloth-draped bed with no mattress. To the right of the bathroom was a dark, creepy storage room of sorts, loaded with boxes and draped things. It smelled mustier than the rest of the house did.

"Phew." Ron made a face as he closed the door. "I'm not looking forward to cleaning *that* room."

"Let's go upstairs," Dana said.

They darted down the short hall, back through the kitchen, and up the narrow staircase onto a railed landing. There were two rooms up here, one on either side. Both were long and rather narrow, with tapering walls. The larger of the two rooms held a cot and a night stand. A set of tiny windows overlooked the front porch.

The other room had just a cot and a larger window that looked out the back. Both had closets that were dry, but in need of a coat of paint.

It was much warmer here in these rooms than it was downstairs, but they seemed cleaner somehow, despite the layers of dust and dead insects.

Dana stared out the window into the backyard; and after inspecting the closet, Ron came to join her. There wasn't much to see. There was a good-sized, over-grown yard with fencing along the back, a weed-choked garden, and tall shrubs that protected it from the view of the neighbors.

Dana asked, "Do you think we'll be sleeping up here?"

Ron looked around and shrugged. "I don't know. It's not too bad and it doesn't have that funny smell."

"It's hot."

"I don't think Aunt Julia has the air conditioning on yet."

"I thought I heard you two up here." Julia came in, holding Jack on her hip. She looked around the room with a critical eye. "Have you seen everything?"

"We didn't get to the basement," Ron said.

"Well, there isn't too much to see down there. Just the furnace. Have you picked out which rooms you want yet?"

The two exchanged glances.

"We get to pick?" asked Dana, surprised.

"Sure, if you have a preference. Dana, you'll have your own room, but," she turned to Ron, "I'd like to pair you and Jack up, if you guys don't mind. We only have three rooms available for bedrooms right away and Jack said he'd prefer to stick with you. Is that alright?"

Ron nodded.

Dana said, "It's really dirty in here, Aunt Julia."

"I know. The whole house needs to be cleaned and painted, but we'll deal with that in the next couple of weeks. Right now, let's just figure out where everything's going. So, which room do you want?"

Dana looked at Ron and shrugged. "I don't know," she lied. "It doesn't really matter."

Julia looked at her steadily for a moment, and then nodded slowly. "All right, then. So you don't mind if I pick?"

She shook her head.

"And you, Ron?"

"I don't really care," he said politely.

Julia hoisted Jack and looked around the room. "Then, why don't we make this your room, Dana, and the boys will take the larger one down the hall. How does that sound?"

Dana brightened – Aunt Julia had chosen well. Ron genuinely didn't care and was glad to see his sister smile.

"Okay, let's get a move on," Julia said. "We've got to unpack the van, and I want to take a run into town as soon as we have room in it for some supplies."

"We're going shopping?" moaned Dana, as they trooped down the stairs.

"Just a quick hit, Dana. We have to get some spray for the ticks and some cleaning supplies for the house." She opened the screen door, looking around. "And, if we manage to find a hardware store that's open, we can pick up some paint chips. Start thinking about what colors you'd like– we can do whatever you want."

Julia was excited, but both Ron and Dana, who were trailing behind on the stairs, stopped in mid-step and looked at one another. Julia went out the door, but came back in when she noticed that they weren't following.

"Did I say something wrong?" she asked.

Ron noticed the circles under her eyes and hesitated, not wanting to irritate her. But he was unnerved by this decorating idea. Was it a scheme to get them to want to move up to Franklin permanently? This house was too small for them; and anyway, there weren't too many jobs up here. Everyone said so. Besides, he didn't want to leave his home – the very idea hurt. But how could he say any of that?

Dana had fewer inhibitions than he did. She blurted it right out: "But we aren't staying here."

Julia's frown deepened. "Well, we are, actually."

Dana's face fell. "We are?"

"For the summer, Dana," she said patiently. "We're going to fix the place up to sell, remember?"

Dana shot her brother a puzzled look. "So, we aren't *living* here, right?"

"No, of course not. What would make you think that our plans would change?" Then, to everyone's relief, Julia caught on and shook her head. "Oh, for goodness *sake*. When I said you could pick the colors, it wasn't because you would live in them for the rest of your lives. I just thought it would be fun for you to have a hand in it. We're only staying here until the fifteenth of August, then we go back to Springfield to get ready for school. You have my word on it, okay?"

"I'm sorry, Aunt Julia," Ron began, but she dismissed his concern with a wave of her hand.

"Not a problem. But if we don't get that van emptied soon, we won't be able to get to the store before it closes, and that means we won't have enough supplies to clean with. So let's get a move on. Ron, you and Dana start unloading and put everything in the dining room for now. That seems to be the cleanest. Jack, you can stay in the kitchen and play with Yellow Teddy until you wake up all the way."

"I want to watch cartoons," he said.

Julia laughed, shifting her grasp on him. "So do I, pal, but let's wait until we have the van unpacked."

# 6

Julia had spotted a hardware store when they went through town earlier, so she knew exactly where they were going when she piled the kids back into the van. Looking at their drawn, tired faces, she felt guilty about dragging them back out on the road again, but she simply couldn't let them sleep in the house as it was. Thanks to the profusion of tick-infested grass, sleeping outside in the tent was no longer a possibility.

She jotted down a quick list of things to pick up at the store just to get started. As she buckled Jack in his seat, she thought of more items, but decided against adding to the list. She didn't want to try the children's patience any more than she had already had done.

She buckled herself in and started the minivan. With more cheer in her voice than she felt, she said, "Well, we're on our way."

Ron, silent again, nodded. Dana wore a wounded expression and kept her eyes focused out the window. Jack was busy eating animal crackers, and didn't notice that she had said anything.

Julia backed the car carefully out into the street, noting with some envy the tidy lawns of the pretty houses on either side. She reflected that soon enough, she'd have her house in equally good shape. She wished for a few more hands to help, but decided it was no use moaning about what could not be changed. They would have to do what they could with what they had.

As they pulled away, Ron craned his neck to look back at the driveway, then turned to her with concern.

"Shouldn't we have locked up the bikes?" he asked.

They had left the bicycles leaning against the side of the house with no chains or locks. Julia wanted to face-palm herself for over-looking them, but she also wanted to spare the boy worry.

"Oh, no, they'll be fine," she said. "They'll be safe for an hour or so. This is a nice, established neighborhood – the people here won't be going around stealing unsecured bicycles."

"But I thought you said it was a rental community, and that everyone here was outsiders."

Julia decided that she'd have to reconsider her policy of full disclosure to the kids on all major subjects. A little mystery, she thought, was a good thing.

"True, but not this street. Besides, this is a very safe town. I was talking with Mrs. O'Reilly about it. She said the police are overpaid for the amount of work that they have to do."

Ron thought about it, and silence settled over the van. Dana stopped listening in and looked out the window again. Julia relaxed, and was not prepared for Ron's next statement:

"I guess they need a larger police force here because of the prison."

Her foot slipped off of the pedal. "The – *what?*"

"The prison. There's one on the outskirts of town, near the state nursing home. I looked it up online before we left."

Julia did not like the sound of this at all. "There's a state prison here in town?"

"Yep."

She shook her head, mentally smacking herself again. "Yes, that would be a good reason to have a large police force in town. Is it a big prison?"

He shrugged as Dana said, "Aunt Julia, are there criminals in town?"

"Yes, but they're locked up safe and secure, sweetheart." Privately, she was thinking about door alarms, shotguns, and German shepherds. She had the first, but was now feeling a keen need for the latter two.

She knew that any tension or nervousness on her part was sure to be picked up on by the kids, and that she had to hide her fear and stay alert without frightening them.

Julia changed the subject. "Ron, when we get to the hardware store, why don't you and Dana go over to the paint section and see what they have for decorating ideas and paint chips. We can bring some pamphlets home and discuss it over dinner."

"I want purple walls with orange around the edges," Dana said brightly.

Julia imagined the horrified expressions of potential home buyers as they saw the room. "Uh, that's pretty strong coloring for a bedroom."

"Besides, the people who come to look at the house may not like it," Ron added. He had a strange habit of picking up on her inner thoughts and verbalizing them. He twisted around in his seat to look at Dana. "We have to think about what they would want when they come looking."

Dana scowled. "But *I* like purple and orange."

"We can't just do what we'd like, Dana," said Ron. "We have to think about what people will want to buy."

"But..."

"We can talk about this all tomorrow, guys," Julia said firmly, hoping to cap what seemed like a rapidly-degenerating conversation. "We're all tired from our trip, and we still have a lot to do. So we're just going to pick up a few things, and then we'll head back to the house. We'll do a little cleaning, Ron will set up the TV, and we'll have a relaxing night. Sound good?"

"Sure," Ron said. "Right, Dana?"

Dana muttered something that sounded like she agreed, and then fell silent.

Ron faced front, and the car became quiet again. Julia wondered whether that was a victory or a loss. She suspected that it was something in the middle.

The downtown was also quiet. There was nothing to indicate that there were any vacationing families in the area, enjoying a warm Saturday afternoon, and Julia noted the abandoned appearance of the buildings and the sad old houses that seemed to slouch as they passed.

The one exception was an ice cream shop, which was doing some good business. The lines stretched to nearly the end of its parking lot.

Dana perked up. "Can we get some ice cream?"

"We already had some," Ron said wearily.

"Please, Aunt Julia?"

Julia eyed the line. "Not today, Dana. The line's so long, I'm afraid we'll miss the hardware store."

Irwin's Hardware was a large place with a big front porch overrun with summer goods. Its sign was edged in green, lettered in orange, and under it, another sign proclaimed *Summer Sale!* in big red letters. The parking lot was nearly empty.

Julia pulled up to the porch and stopped, peering through the gloom of the front porch, seeing a light from inside. It was 4:15, and the place was still open. She breathed a sigh of relief and thought, *I don't have to go looking for a motel tonight.*

"All right, everyone out," she said.

Ron beat her to getting Jack out of his seat. The little boy was rosy-cheeked and covered with animal cracker crumbs. Julia brushed him off and felt his forehead; he was very warm, almost too warm. She thought she might have to stop to get some ice cream after all.

"Okay, little buddy," she said. She swung him up onto her hip. Although small for his age, and being almost unfairly cute, he was getting heavy. She wondered if she was inhibiting his growth by carrying him so often; but he wrapped himself around her and fastened his arms around her neck with a panicked grip. She could almost hear his thoughts: "Don't let go – don't lose me!" and her own grip tightened instinctively.

*I won't lose you, buddy. I've got you.*

Perhaps she was inhibiting him. But he was a little boy who'd lost his mother, and he was still healing. She couldn't - and wouldn't - rush him.

"Let's go get some supplies."

She hadn't realized how hot she was until she opened the door and received a blast of cold air. The van's AC was weak and probably in need of some repair, and there was none at the house yet. Jack squealed and buried his hot face in her neck. Julia was surprised by her rush of maternal affection.

She grabbed one of the carriages by the door, plopped Jack into the seat, and looked around to get her bearings.

It was a low-ceilinged, orderly place with an open layout and clearly marked aisles. At the far right was the paint aisle. At the far left was the checkout line where a teenaged girl sat reading a magazine. There were only two other people: a sales associate and the man he was talking to. Both were engrossed in their conversation and barely glanced at the newcomers.

Julia turned to Ron and Dana, gesturing towards the paint counter.

"You can go look at the paint samples and see if there's anything you like," she said quietly.

Dana folded her arms. "But no purple and orange, right?"

Julia gave her a stern look. "I said that we would decide on that tomorrow. Right now, you go and bring back chips of whatever colors you like, okay?"

Dana nodded glumly, and Ron took her hand.

"I think," he said, "that maybe it would be quicker if we helped you instead, Aunt Julia."

"That's very nice of you, Ron, but you will be helping me by getting me those samples."

Reluctantly, the two of them turned toward the paint and wallpaper. Julia shook her head in exasperation, and then reached into her purse. "All right, Jack. Ready for some speed shopping?"

He nodded eagerly. "I like shopping."

"I know you do. You're a boy after my own heart. You want to hold the list and the pen?"

He did, and proceeded to doodle over the entire thing while she gathered the items on it. After filling the page, he started on his arms and then his legs. Julia noticed just in time to save his shorts from a similar fate.

"Good heavens, *Jack*," she said, snatching the pen from his hands. "You need a bath."

He looked hurt and his lips trembled with emotion. A meltdown was prevented only by the fortunate discovery of a lollipop in Julia's purse. As he sucked on his pop, Julia examined what she could read of her list again and saw that only tick killer remained.

She hesitantly fingered the plastic bottles of insecticide. Each listed ingredients, promises, and warnings. Some were organic, some boasted that they were as strong as the professional grade stuff, and suddenly Julia felt overwhelmed by the choices.

Help arrived then, in the form of a sales associate whose nametag read *John I.*

John was shorter than Julia by two inches, and most of the hair on his head had migrated to his exposed legs, but his smile was friendly and he knew just the right thing to say.

"Can I help you, ma'am?"

"Oh, I hope so," she said, gratefully. She explained the situation to him, and he knew exactly what she needed. He pulled out a jug of insecticide, gave her instructions on how to use it and how long to wait before she let the kids play in it, and then related his own experiences with a tick-infested lawn.

"You should cut it first," he said, as he walked with her to the checkout line. "Otherwise, you'll be wasting a lot of insecticide."

"Oh, shoot," Julia said, stopping short.

*Do we even have a working lawnmower?*

John was watching her with concern, so she said, "I don't even know if I have a lawnmower at this point. We just moved in today and it didn't occur to me to check."

"You just moved in today?"

"Yes, we just came here for the summer, but you know, I always forget how much work is involved in getting from one place to the next."

"It's a bigger hassle when you have so many kids," John said. "If you're really strapped for a lawnmower, though, I got a few older models that I could let you use. Or better, I know some people who do lawn care. I could give you their card, if you want."

Julia did some quick mental calculations, trying to remember what she had available in the check book, then surrendered to necessity and nodded. "I'd appreciate it."

John went behind the counter, where the teenaged girl ignored him. Rustling about a drawer for a few minutes, he pulled out a business card that was a little crumpled around the edges and handed it to her. "It's my son's business, actually, but he's a good hard worker and a few ticks won't bother him. Whereabouts is your house?"

"We're on Whipple Lane," Julia said. She read, *John Irwin III, Handyman, Lawn and Garden Care.*

She looked up, surprised, "So, you're John Irwin?"

He smiled. "Yep, that's me. John Irwin, Junior."

"This is your store, then?"

He smiled again, seeming proud as he started up the cash register. "My dad started it back in the sixties, and my brother, Michael, and I took it over. Then Mike left for Vancouver and now there's just me. So, whereabouts are you on Whipple Lane?"

"I'm at the Budd's house. It's the one with the jungle for a front lawn."

Jack tried in vain to reach the candy display as Julia began to unload her cart. From somewhere, a bell rang, announcing a new customer in the shop.

"The Budd house?" John shook his head. "I'm afraid I don't know the Budds."

"I don't think they ever stayed in the house. They just used it as a rental property. I didn't know it even existed until a short time ago."

"We've got a few of those in town. A lot of people like to come up to Webster Lake in the summer."

"So I've heard. I was wondering, can you tell me anything about the neighborhood? Is it quiet?"

"Oh, real quiet. A lot of longtime residents live there. Which end are you at?"

"We're at 134."

"134?" He paused. "Oh, wait, the old Purcell place? You're moving into the old Purcell place?"

"If its 134, I am."

"Permanently?"

"No, just for the summer. I'm cleaning the place up to hopefully sell in the fall."

"You are? Well, you're in luck. That place is sound and sturdy. I'll bet all it needs is a lick of paint and some cleaning."

"I sure hope so, but I am a little nervous with the children. So, it is a good neighborhood?" she asked again.

"A good neighborhood?" He chuckled. "One second, ma'am." He craned his neck, looking around the store, then raised his hands to his mouth and hollered, "Robert! Got someone here I want you to meet!"

He smiled reassuringly at the startled Julia. "You know, I've always liked the old Purcell place – I might be placing a bid myself when you put it on the market. Franklin is a real nice place to spend the summer. There's the lake, and the Fourth of July celebration, and Concord's right down the street. We're a real old fashioned community, and…"

Julia handed him her credit card. Still talking, he slid it through with the ease of a practiced hand. She was astonished. She'd heard that New Hampshire natives were cold and standoff-ish and John Irwin Junior seemed to be going all-out to welcome them.

He handed her the receipt and a chewed-up pen to sign it with, then nodded over her shoulder.

"Ah, Robert," he said. "Meet the new neighbor. This young lady and her little family just moved into the house right next door to you."

Julia looked up from the receipt and did a double-take. Robert was a tall, lanky man with dark, almost black hair and a boy-next-door face. He was carrying some supplies, including a box of nails and a new tape measure, and his stance reflected the easy familiarity of a frequent visitor. He gave her a friendly nod.

But none of these particulars were what took Julia by surprise, or what filled her with a sense of relief. It was the fact that he was wearing a policeman's uniform, complete with a heavy belt and a strapped-down automatic. She felt a gush of relief, almost affection. Her next-door neighbor was a cop? That was better than a shot-gun or a German shepherd any day.

She caught herself with start. *Easy. Don't want to give him or John Irwin Junior the wrong idea.*

Robert said, in a tone of polite and friendly interest, "Oh really? That's great."

John Irwin Junior explained, "She's just moved in today and she was asking about what kind of neighborhood she was living in. Bet you're glad to know that you live right next door to a cop, aren't you, ma'am?"

"Um, yes," said Julia.

Robert smiled sympathetically.

"Oh, stupid me," said John Irwin Junior. "Forgot to introduce you. This is Mrs…" He stopped, realizing that he had no idea who Julia was. He looked the credit card in his hand.

Julia extended her hand with a quick smile. "Julia Lamontaigne and this is my nephew, Jack Budd."

The officer's smile warmed as he shook her hand. "Robert Wilde," he said. "Pleased to meet you, Ms. Lamontaigne. Are you just here for the summer or is this a permanent move?"

"Just for the summer," she replied. "We're doing a little work on the house and taking time out to just relax. I've heard that Webster Lake is one of the area's greatest unsung natural wonders."

"Oh, it is," John assured her. "It's got great beaches and boating. Fish and game has been stocking it with rainbow and brown trout for the season, if you're interested in little fishing."

"I'm not really an outdoors person," Julia admitted. "I don't think I've ever been fishing."

"Well, you've got two of the best fishermen in the county standing right in front of you, if you're ever looking to start," he said proudly.

Wilde grinned and shifted his stance.

Julia said, "Thank you very much for the offer, but I think we're going to be a bit too busy with all the housework to have much time…"

Jack had been staring at Officer Wilde with a mixture of awe and hero-worship, and it took him until now to collect himself enough to ask the question that was clearly uppermost on his mind. Pointing to Wilde's badge, he asked, "Are you a policeman?"

Officer Wilde looked to his badge as if for confirmation, and then grinned. "Yes, I am."

"One of Franklin's finest," John assured him.

Officer Wilde didn't respond to the praise. "And who are you?" he asked.

Jack was awed by this confirmation of his suspicions. "I'm Jack," he said.

"Are you enjoying your summer, Jack?"

This was too much. Jack turned and buried his head in Julia's shirt, forcing her to make some hasty adjustments to her apparel.

"It's been a long day," she said, putting a hand on his back. "I've been an absolute slave driver, haven't I, Jack?"

He nodded, shook his head, and finally gave up trying to answer and just made a sound that was something between a cry and a yelp. Julia decided that it was time to retreat before he succumbed to exhaustion. She thanked John for his son's card, and took her cart and the still-huddled Jack to the entrance, calling for Ron and Dana as she went.

They met her outside at the van. Dana had her hands full of paint cards and color-scheme pamphlets. While Julia struggled to get Jack into his car seat, she happily chattered about a princess theme that she particularly liked.

Jack's face grew more and more flushed. It was obvious that he had reached the end of his tether, and all Julia wanted was to get him in the car and back to the house before he exploded. Ron put his brochures on his seat and tried to help, but his efforts only made Jack complain all the louder.

Amid all the commotion, Office Wilde came out of the store. Jack immediately went still, Dana fell silent, and even Ron paused.

Wilde seemed unaware of his effect on them. He nodded at Julia as he got into his car.

Julia returned the gesture, and took advantage of Jack's fascination to buckle him down.

Ron return the cart to the store as Julia got into the van to start the air conditioning.

Dana buckled herself in. "Who was that, Aunt Julia?"

"That was Officer Wilde," Julia said, lowering the windows as she spoke. She was amazed at the van's ability to absorb heat in such a short span of time. Wearily, she thought about the cleaning ahead of them, and then wondered if the microwave was working. "He lives next door to us."

"A cop? Really? Do you know him?"

"We said hi."

"Oh."

Julia turned on the car.

Dana said, "I've changed my mind about the orange walls."

"Really?"

"Yep. I want green and purple instead with princess stickers on them. I've got the picture right here. It's *so* pretty that I'm sure all the house buyers will want it. Here you go."

She handed over a pamphlet for a very girly bedroom, complete with purple walls, green wainscoting, pink trim, matching furniture, and a lace canopy over the bed. It was easy to see why Dana had changed her mind.

Julia caught a glimpse of Dana's anxious face watching her in the rear view mirror. She smiled at her and handed the pamphlet back.

"I think they would love it," she said.

The little girl settled back to stare at the photo with delighted anticipation. Ron got back into the car, and they started out for home.

# 7

When they got back to the house, Julia sent the children to open all of the downstairs windows, while she set up the three fans she had found in the storage room. She decided that until the bedrooms got a thorough cleaning, everyone would camp out in the living room. The kids did the cleaning there while she started on the kitchen.

When the living room was in decent shape, and the kids thoroughly worn out, she had Ron set up the TV with the DVD player while she and Dana set up the sleeping bags in the living room. Dana was charmed by the idea of sleeping in sleeping bags *inside* the house. Jack was thrilled and wanted a fire, too.

Julia was relieved by their enthusiasm.

They unrolled sleeping bags, found their sleepwear, microwaved TV dinners, and put a favorite movie in the DVD player. After sponge baths in the kitchen sink, the three Budds ate their dinner by TV light.

Julia, plagued by thoughts of lice and cockroaches, continued to clean. She washed out the old refrigerator, then started on the kitchen cabinets. Several of the cabinets were barely hanging onto the walls by two or three rusting screws. A few others had water damage, their bottoms soft to the touch.

Julia found the tool box and took down the cabinets that seemed ready to fall. She put them outside by the shed, intending to break them down and dispose of them later. On her last trip to the shed, she stopped for a moment and breathed in the night air.

It was much quieter than Springfield, with a silence as deep as though sound were fighting against a vacuum. The stars were sharp points of light in the dark navy dome of the sky. Lights shone from the windows of the surrounding houses, and she could just make out the droning, distant sounds of a variety of TV programs. She heard a door open and close, and someone pacing on their front porch.

Julia sat on the side-door steps. A few mosquitoes hovered around her legs and arms, but she was too tired to pay attention to them. The warmth of the night air, the good ache in her tired arms, the hunger in the pit of her stomach, and the ceaseless roaming of her mind over the events of the past day made her recline against the door, exhausted. She tried to process everything: the early morning wakeup, the final lock-up of the Springfield house, the long drive, the house, the hardware store, the neighborhood – all came back to be examined, judged, and sorted.

When they had gotten back to the house, Dana looked to see if the patrol car was in any of the neighbors' driveways, but it wasn't. The kids were hoping to view some police action, figuring that if a cop lived next door, adventure and danger couldn't be far away. Julia had the opposite impression: if one of her neighbors was a policeman, there had to be a decreased chance that any of her other neighbors were mass murderers or drug dealers.

Julia laughed at herself. She used to snicker at young parents who panicked at every minor detail, and who imagined all sorts of horrid and far-fetched scenarios - and here she was, doing the same thing.

She decided that she would call John Irwin III, the lawn care guy, tomorrow. With everything they had to do for the house, and her conscience bothering her about putting the kids to work on their school vacation, she really didn't relish the idea of pushing a rusty old machine through swarms of ticks. Much better to let the professionals handle it.

Her mind went back to the list of things that needed doing. It was already lengthy and she hadn't even looked at the bathroom or the basement. It was likely to get even longer: the kitchen cabinets had been a surprise.

She thought about the kids and began to worry again, wondering how she could do everything that needed doing in the house and still have time to make it a nice summer for them. They needed to relax and have fun, not be working all day, breathing in fumes and dodging falling cabinets. Maybe she should have listened to the hesitation in her parents' voices when she had outlined her plan a week ago. She could have just swallowed the cost, taken out a loan, and hired professionals. Maybe this was nothing but a huge mistake. The children would be miserable, or worse - something might happen to one of them. Then they would be taken away and put in foster care, or sent to live with the Budds, and she'd be relegated to seeing them only on the holidays that she was invited to.

Tears sprang to her eyes at the thought. She was about to give way to them when the door opened from behind her and she fell through the doorway.

She found herself looking up at Dana, who jumped and gave a little scream before recovering.

"Jack fell asleep in his plate," she explained. "He's got mashed potatoes all over his face. Ron's trying to wake him up."

"*No*, don't wake him up," Julia said, struggling to get to her feet. "Hang on a second, I'm coming."

Dana watched her with concern. When Julia finally was upright, she asked, "Are we going to Mass tomorrow?"

"Mass?"

"Tomorrow's Sunday."

She could hear the weariness in Dana's voice and put a reassuring hand on her head. "We'll see. I don't want to tire Jack out too much."

Dana looked relieved and turned to go back into the living room. "Good, cause I don't know where my dresses are."

Julia learned early that Dana could not and would not go to church without wearing one of her fancy, lacy dresses. Julia didn't know why, but it was a fact, and an insurmountable one.

"We'll go next week," Julia said. "That'll give me time to find a church and you time to find your dresses."

Dana was impressed by this logic.

Julia found Jack so soundly asleep that she was able to retrieve him from his plate, clean his face, change his pajamas, and put him into his sleeping bag without waking him. The older two finished the movie while Julia tossed out the paper plates and washed their cups.

By the time the credits finally rolled, Dana was asleep. Ron's face was white with exhaustion as he stumbled about brushing his teeth. Julia tucked them both into their sleeping bags, then placed a fan on one side of the room and opened the window at the other, hoping to create a breeze.

With the house quiet, Julia took a flashlight and checked the rooms upstairs and the basement. She set the door alarms and the alarm clock, made her own dinner, and sat down to eat it in front of the TV. She managed to finish her meal before nodding off herself, mid-program.

She woke up several hours later to find the TV still on, and Jack and Yellow Teddy curled up in a tight little ball next to her.

# 8

Ron awoke with a start, having no idea where he was. He
fought a sudden panic as he wiped his eyes. He wasn't in
bed – the covers were plastic-coated, and there was a crunch-
ing sound when he moved. Sweat plastered his pajama shirt to his
back and his hair was damp and sticky. His blanket was up over his
head and he could hear a sort of dull roar coming from nearby.

Someone stirred next to him and Dana muttered. Ron forced
himself into a sitting position and shook his head. Reality solidified,
and the roaring became the sound of a fan at one end of the room.
At the other end, light poured through a window, open so that he
could hear a passing car honking its horn. Beyond the sound of the
fan, he heard the clinking of dishes and someone humming. The
scent of cinnamon and coffee mingled with the crisp smell of the
grass, and the maudlin smell of slept-in covers.

He wasn't home, and Dad hadn't taken them on a trip. He was
in a dingy living room with Dana after moving to a little cottage for
the summer. The humming woman wasn't his mother, it was Aunt
Julia. Mom and Dad weren't there.

He heard a squeal, and Aunt Julia said, "*Shhh*, Jack. You don't
want to wake Ron and Dana, do you?"

"Are we going to play today?" asked Jack.

"Sure, but first we have to do some work. Eat your bun and don't rub your fingers in your hair, okay?"

Ron looked at his watch. To his dismay, it was nine o'clock. He had slept well past his alarm time of six-thirty, and it was Sunday, when they always went to Mass. They were going to be late. Aunt Julia was already up, and probably made breakfast. Ron prided himself on breakfast – it was one of the many responsibilities that he had taken off of Aunt Julia's shoulders, and he hadn't missed a one since his parents died.

*Until today, that is,* he thought. It sounded like Aunt Julia and Jack were already eating. Perhaps he could still make it for himself and Dana.

He began to scramble out of the tangle of sleeping bags, giving Dana a shove.

"Wake up, Dana," he said.

She grimaced and turned away. He wriggled his way out of the sleeping bag and stood up in the middle of the living room.

There was a nice breeze blowing in through the open windows. In the morning light, the peeling wallpaper was more stained than he remembered. Aunt Julia's sleeping bag was rolled up and neatly tied in front of the couch, with Jack's Yellow Teddy sitting jauntily on top. In a nearby basket, their clothes from yesterday sat in a folded stack with their shoes lined up in front. Ron collected his clothes and shoes and a dry towel, and gave his sister a shake.

"*Dana,*" he said sharply. "Time to get up."

She moaned softly. He was about to give her another shake when he noticed Aunt Julia in the doorway. She was dressed in jeans and an old t-shirt with her hair pulled up tightly into a bun. In one hand she held an unfamiliar mug of hot tea. She'd been awake for hours.

A wave of guilt hit Ron.

*You're the man of the house while I'm gone, Ron. Take care of everything, will you? I'm depending on you.*

"Oh, you're up."

Julia's face showed no sign of disappointment. In fact, she seemed happy to see him.

"Did you sleep well?" she asked.

He nodded. "I'll be dressed in a minute. Dana's waking up now. I'll shake her again."

To his surprise, Julia shook her head. "No, don't wake her. I wanted you all to sleep in this morning, and it's only nine. Come on – I just pulled some cinnamon buns out of the oven. You'd better eat them while they're hot." She saw the clothes in his hands and smiled. "You can get dressed after breakfast this morning."

"Cinnamon buns?" His mouth watered at the thought. He hadn't had cinnamon buns in ages. Mom was always big on whole grains, and all-natural sugar substitutes in the morning.

"Yep. Fresh from the can." Julia's eyes danced as she watched his delighted reaction.

He looked around. "I don't know where my robe is."

"Oh, don't worry about the robe. It's just us here. Come on. I'm just about to put the frosting on – they taste best when they're hot."

She turned and went back into the kitchen. Ron watched her go with some astonishment. Eat breakfast… in his *pajamas?* At nine in the morning? Dad would have pitched a fit and Mom would have been just as bad. The rule in the Budd house was no meals without first having brushed your teeth, washed your face or taken a shower, and dressed.

The buttery cinnamon smell intensified, and his mouth watered as his stomach grumbled. Aunt Julia was right about one thing: cinnamon buns *were* best when they were fresh.

The kitchen was small, with wrap-around counters, peeling linoleum, and a recessed area for the oven. There were gaps showing raw, yellowing paint on the wall where Julia had removed some of the sagging old cabinets. On the shelves were some grocery supplies, and paper and plastic dishes. The electric kettle steamed on the counter beside a stack of unfamiliar china and silverware. The kitchen smelled of butter, cinnamon, and pine-sol. Ron thought that Aunt Julia must have been up and at work early.

At a tiny metal folding table in the middle of the room, Jack sat in a freshly scrubbed chair on a stack of books, half-way through his cinnamon bun, hard boiled eggs, and orange juice. He looked up and smiled a sticky grin as Ron lowered himself into one of the matching chairs, which he recognized from the dining room. The table was old, and so small that Jack's breakfast things took up half of it. Cramped though it was, it was already set for two more people.

Julia frosted three fresh cinnamon buns at the oven. On the counter, her iPod played softly. The kitchen window and the side door were open, letting in a rush of warm, summer-scented air.

Ron sat at the table, feeling undressed and a little revolted by Jack's careless dissection of his cinnamon bun. He was distracted enough that he was startled when he heard Julia speak.

"You can pour yourself some orange juice, Ron. I'll have these done in a second."

Dana stumbled through the doorway, rubbing her eyes. Her brunette hair was an enormous, tousled mess, and her face was creased from a deep sleep. She blinked and stared at the unusual sight of both of her brothers at the table, dressed in their pajamas. Then she sniffed, and her eyes grew wide when she saw the cinnamon buns.

"Well, good morning, sleepy head. Did you sleep well?" Julia said. She placed a dish filled with two eggs and a cinnamon bun in front of Ron. The warm scent wafted up, and he almost drooled.

"Cinnamon buns?" Dana asked, awed.

"Yep. I've got one here for you."

That was enough to snap her out of her sleepy state. "I'll get dressed right away!" she shouted, and was about to run back into the living room when Aunt Julia stopped her.

"They're warm now – you can get dressed afterwards."

Dana hesitated, but when Julia put a third plate on the table, she slid into a chair.

"You can say grace to yourselves," Julia said, turning back to the stove.

They did, rushing through the prayer with only one thought on their minds.

Ron picked up his bun and bit deep into it. He closed his eyes and savored. It was every bit as good as it smelled.

He opened his eyes and saw Dana with cinnamon and frosting all over her mouth. She grinned at him.

"You have frosting on your nose!" she giggled.

He tried to wipe it off, but his hand was sticky, and he only made it worse. Julia came to the rescue with a wet paper towel, which he used while she deposited the last cinnamon bun, neatly and fairly divided into thirds, on each of their plates.

Julia pulled a bottle of ketchup out of the refrigerator and put it in front of Dana, saying, "Make sure you eat some of your eggs, too."

"Yes'm," she mumbled.

They were far too busy eating to make conversation. Julia sat down with her mug and a notepad, squeezed between the oven and the edge of the table. She took a sip of her tea, and began to jot down notes on a sketch of the floor plan that Ron hadn't seen before.

She looked up with the pencil in her mouth and smiled. "I guess you guys were hungry."

"Yeah," said Dana. "Hungry for *cinnamon buns*." She took another bite.

Ron said, in a big-brother-knows-best tone, "Thank you, Aunt Julia, for the nice surprise."

Dana swallowed her rather large mouthful and dutifully said, "Yes, thank you, Aunt Julia."

Ron noticed that Julia got that solemn look in her eyes again as she so often did when they tried to be helpful. She looked both sad and analytical, as though she were monitoring them and wasn't too sure of the results. Ron didn't really understand her expressions, and it annoyed him at times. Perhaps it was just a girl thing, he thought.

Before he had too much time to wonder about it, Julia said, "My pleasure. We've got a lot of work ahead of us before we can really start enjoying the summer, so I thought it would be good for everyone to have a little treat."

Jack was done eating. "Can I go play?"

"Not yet, old man, just wait a second. And don't move around too much - you'll knock yourself right off that chair."

"What do we have to do today?" Ron asked, eager to show that he, too, was work-minded.

Julia showed them her sketch: it was a rough floor plan for the house, including windows and doorways. In each room, she had written a list of what needed to be done and what supplies would be needed. As promised, the two rooms on the top floor were listed as *Dana's Room* and *Ron and Jack's Room*. Ron leaned in to see what needed to be done in his room. On top of the supply list were the words *AC Unit*.

"All right, guys, here's the house," Julia said cheerfully. "I've gone through and made a list of what I think needs doing in all of them. We're actually in good shape – there's a lot less to do than I thought. What I'd like to do is go through one room at a time, starting with the most important ones, and get them all fixed up."

"The kitchen and bathroom first, right?" asked Ron.

She nodded. "The kitchen and the bathroom both need a good scrubbing, but other than the cabinets for this room, they're in good condition. We can put off whatever repairs they need for the present and focus on the more crucial renovations."

"What's that?" asked Dana. "The living room?"

"Oh, no. I was thinking your bedrooms."

They were both surprised, and Dana couldn't hide her delight. "Cool!" she said.

"But…" Ron was confused. "Wouldn't it be more important to fix up the kitchen and the bathroom first? I mean, we all need those."

Julia nodded. "You're right, but, like I said, the only thing really wrong with them is that they need a scrubbing and a face lift. The face lift can wait and the scrubbing is pretty much done. What I'm more concerned about is you guys smothering to death in those sleeping bags or catching fleas from lying on these musty old rugs. The rooms upstairs don't need too much." She consulted her list. "Floors need scrubbing, the walls need painting, the baseboard in your room, Ron, needs to be replaced and I'd like to get an AC unit up there. Oh, and I think the closets need new shelving."

Dana tried to contain herself, although why she was getting so excited was beyond Ron. After all, they weren't going to be in those rooms for very long. Before the end of the summer, they'd be back in Springfield, using their own beds and their own computers.

Ron sighed at the thought of his computer. It would be a long summer without his PC. Why had Aunt Julia insisted on no computers and no videos games? They were his one escape from an otherwise responsibility-fraught world.

"We might need to look at the flooring." Julia interrupted his thoughts again. She was tapping on the pad. "Now that I think of it, I didn't really take a good look at it last night and I haven't gone back up there this morning."

"So…?" asked Dana.

"So, let's go have a look at it together," Julia said, jumping to her feet. "Come on, guys."

She led the way out the kitchen door and up the stairs, Dana close on her heels. Ron helped Jack off of his perch and would have carried the little boy, only he was so excited that he slipped out of Ron's grasp and went for the stairs by himself. He half climbed, half crawled up the steep stairs and Ron followed close behind, anxious that his little brother might fall.

"Jack all right with those stairs?" Julia asked.

"I've got him," Ron said.

"I'm *fine!*" Jack insisted. "I'm a big boy now, Aunt Julia."

"Yes, you are," she assured him. "But I want you to grow even bigger, you know."

Jack made it to the top step, and pulled himself upright with a look of pride on his little face.

Julia examined the narrow stairway with some concern. Dana was already in her room, pulling up the patched old window shade; but Jack went around to the narrow landing, and tried to put his face between the bars of the railing.

Ron pulled him away. "Come on, Jack," he said. "Let's go look at the room."

Jack pulled his hand out of Ron's grasp and scampered into Dana's room. Ron didn't bother to chase him. He took hold of the railing and shook it. It stood firm.

"That's good to know," Julia said, watching him. "I'll get one of those gate things to put at the head of the stairs. I don't want Jack to go down by himself. Maybe it would be better for him to stay downstairs with me."

"No," Ron protested. "He'll be better upstairs with me."

Julia nodded thoughtfully, and then they went into Dana's room where they found Dana holding Jack up to the back window.

Ron looked around. Aside from some nail holes in the wall and scuff marks on the wooden floor, it seemed a sound enough place. It badly needed a cleaning: it was dusty and cobwebs were everywhere, and the blue and red walls were spattered with stains. He went to where Julia was poking her head into the closet.

She stepped out and pointed inside it. "See those shelves?"

He looked. They were thin, flimsy looking, and lined with flowered, peeling paper.

"Those were probably put in there in the 1970s," she said. "They weren't meant to last longer than a decade. I'm surprised they weren't pulled out when the place was renovated in the eighties."

"We should take them out, then?"

"It would be more useful to have a bar in here to hang clothes. But I guess that's not all that important. That belongs on the second tier of repairs." She looked around. "This room would look a lot bigger if the walls were white. It would also look a lot more attractive and peaceful."

"Why?"

"White reflects light and tricks the eye into thinking that there's more space." She explained. "It would make this room much easier to sell to potential buyers, too."

Ron nodded.

Julia jotted down some notes and said, "Let's have a look at your room."

It was much the same, perhaps slightly larger, and it had the added benefit of two skylights. The walls were painted a dark gray, which made the room look like a cave.

Despite that, Ron liked the room. He stood under the skylight, looking up into the bright blue sky, and wondered what it would be like to lie under it at night and wake up to the morning light. It would be almost like camping. He loved camping with the Boy Scouts: the quiet and the danger of living outdoors, the smell of the campfires, and the constant learning curve of trying to make do with less. It was something that he had always longed to do with his father, but Dad hadn't been much of an outdoorsman - his idea of a day in the wild was a bike ride in the local park.

Julia was saying, "Okay, it looks like we know what we need to do."

Dana asked, "Are we going to pick up the paint now?"

"Not yet. We have to prep the walls first."

"How do we do that?" Ron asked.

"First we need to clean the rooms. Why don't you and Dana go get dressed and start on that while Jack and I tidy the kitchen? You'll want to sweep and dust it thoroughly. We'll wash the floors after we've painted everything. Sound good?"

"Great," Ron said, relieved to have something to do. He felt a surge of energy. "Come on, Dana. Let's find the stuff." He charged out of the room and down the stairs, taking them two at a time. Dana followed, hollering, "Wait for me!"

They went into the dining room, where Ron found the broom and the dustpan. It took them both a few minutes to find the dusters and the spray.

They had to cross through the kitchen to get back to the stairs. Julia and Jack were nearly done cleaning up breakfast. Julia's cell phone rang as they slipped by, and she answered it, her voice echoing in the small room. Being naturally nosy, the two siblings stopped to listen.

"Hello. Oh, hello, Mr. Irwin? Thank you for returning my call… Well, it's not very big, but it is infested… Yes, I have the insecticide. In fact, your father sold it to me… Yep… Yep… Well, as soon as possible. Tomorrow? Oh, that would be fantastic. Yes, thank you very much."

Ron and Dana exchanged glances.

Julia spotted them. "While you're doing the rooms," she said, "don't forget to clean out the closets and the landing. We're going to want to paint them, too."

"All right," Ron answered.

"Who's coming over tomorrow?" Dana asked.

"I've hired some people to come and take care of the lawn for us. They're going to be here pretty early, so we'll have to make sure that we are up on time."

"Sure, no problem," said Ron, gesturing to Dana with his head. "Let's go, Dana."

Ron and Dana quickly finished the boys' room, closet, and the landing. While they were in Dana's room, Dana began to talk about the colors she wanted for the wall. She pulled the pamphlet from her pocket to show Ron, chattering excitedly.

Ron studied the picture. It was carefully folded, and she had drawn little notes and heart symbols around the edges.

It was, Ron noted, a stark difference to Dana's room at home. Mom's best friend had decorated all of their bedrooms only about a year and a half ago, and she had paid the most attention to Dana's. Her room was enormous compared to this tiny little thing in the attic. It was pink and white, all delicate and lacy and coordinated right down to the bedclothes, which were heaped up so high on the four-poster bed that it was sometimes difficult to find Dana in it. Mom called it "the perfect little girl room".

"And we could paint the closet door purple, too," Dana was saying, as Ron continued to scan the brochure, looking for prices. "It'll be *such* a cool room."

"Dana," Ron sighed. "There's no way we can get your canopy bed to fit in here."

Plus it was a far cry from the peaceful, sellable white paint that Aunt Julia had wanted. Dana's colors were definitely full of personality, and they would probably make the room shrink again, if it was really possible for paint to do that. Ron knew he was going to have to change her mind. After all, they couldn't expect Aunt Julia to shell out money for different paint for every room in the house. That would be far too expensive. Ron flipped to the back of the brochure, where some prices were listed.

"It doesn't really matter about the bed, I guess," Dana answered. "I was thinking that we could paint the dresser green with pink drawers and..."

Ron sighed again, stopping his sister mid-sentence.

"We don't have that much time, Dana," he said patiently. "Aunt Julia has to make over the whole house and she can't spend all of her time on our rooms. Besides, we're not going to be here long enough to make it worth it. We're better off picking colors that older people would like."

"Older people?"

"Sure. I heard that lady, Sherri, say that the only people who would really be interested in a house this size are old people."

"So?"

"So, if we want to sell it, we should decorate it with them in mind." He paused. "And your paint costs twice as much as what old people paint costs. See?"

He showed her and her enthusiasm withered away. Ron got no joy out of deflating her like that, but he had a job to do. Keeping things easy for Aunt Julia was at the top of his list.

Julia called them from the bottom of the stairs, ending their conversation, and they went out to see what she wanted.

She was downstairs, talking with a plump, middle aged woman. Dana stopped at the top of the staircase and didn't move until Julia beckoned them down.

"Come and meet Mrs. O'Reilly," she said.

"Oh, please," the woman said, with a wave of her hand. Her makeup-encrusted face was creased in a smile. "No need for all that. Just call me Sheila. Everyone else does."

"Go on," Ron whispered to her and Dana descended reluctantly. He followed her and Julia introduced them.

"Hi, kids," Sheila said cheerfully. She smelled very strongly of cigarette smoke and her teeth were yellowed, but her eyes were bright and her smile was friendly. She had a Tupperware container in one hand and waved it with every sentence she spoke. "How are you enjoying the summer?"

Timidly, Dana said, "Very nice, thank you."

"Quiet bunch, aren't they?" Sheila asked, not unkindly. "Not at all like my grandkids, let me tell you. They were born screaming and they haven't stopped yet. My husband says that they're strong minded like me, but I know better than to mistake that for a compliment! Oh, that reminds me." She gave Julia the Tupperware container. "My Katy baked these for you. Hope you like them."

Julia mumbled, "Uh, thank you."

"She likes baking, that one. She's a wild card, but she sure knows her way around a kitchen. I don't know where she gets it from. I wasn't like that at her age. I was out wasting my youth on boys and love-ins. I was at Woodstock, you know."

"No," Julia said with a faint smile. "I didn't know. Would you like to come in and have a cup of coffee?"

"I would, but I have to run and pick my grandson up from camp. He's staying with me for the summer, or maybe longer. My daughter is taking some time out to pull herself together. I'll take a rain check on that coffee, though, if I may."

"Of course."

"I just wanted to welcome you to the neighborhood and make sure that you found everything all right."

"I think we're doing well, but to be honest, I haven't had enough time to look around much."

"Well, if you need anything let me know. You're probably strapped for furniture right about now, right?"

"Well, actually..."

"A lot of that stuff in the storage room is in really good shape – it had belonged to the previous owners, I think, and the renters just shoved it all in there to make room for their own stuff. Before you buy anything, I would have a good look around in there. Odd that they didn't use it," Sheila mused.

"Well, perhaps they felt more at home with their own things."

Sheila shrugged. "Maybe. Probably they just didn't like the idea of using what the previous owners had used. I can't blame them. This house had some weird people in it before the bank took it over, I can tell you."

Ron felt a shiver go down his spine, and he looked at Dana. Her blue eyes were wide and she looked frightened.

"What do you mean, 'weird'?" he asked.

But Sheila didn't hear him. A blast from a horn filled the air, making them all jump.

Sheila scowled, her whole face turning dark, and she stuck her head out of the side door.

"Won't kill you to wait a second!" she screamed into the morning air. "Lord Almighty!"

Julia's eyes went as wide as Dana's, and they all recoiled a little when Sheila swung back around to give them a wide smile.

"My old man's getting impatient," she said. "I have to go, but I'll stop by later this week to see how you're getting on. Ah, man, I could just eat that little one up!" She reached for Jack.

Jack froze with terror. Thankfully, another blast from the truck stopped Sheila short.

"All right, all right, I'm coming!"

She stepped outside, then poked her head back in.

"Forgot to mention I'm having a Tupperware party this Wednesday, and you're invited."

"Why, thank you," Julia smiled.

Then Sheila was gone again.

They all breathed a sigh of relief when the truck pulled out of the driveway. Julia turned to Ron and Dana.

"What a character!" she laughed. "Living with her must be exhausting."

Dana, however, was not in the laughing mood. "Aunt Julia, what kind of weird people lived here?"

She shrugged. "I don't really know, but I wouldn't worry about it. People like Mrs. O'Reilly sometimes exaggerate their stories. How are you getting along upstairs?"

"We're all done," Ron said proudly.

She looked shocked. "Already? Good grief, you must have been moving fast! Well, that's awesome – now I can get to work on sanding and priming right away."

"I can help," Ron offered.

"I'd better do the sanding myself, but you can help with the priming if you want. In the meantime, you guys can watch Jack and start cleaning up the living room again. Later, we can go pick up the primer and the rest of the paint. Oh, have you decided what colors you want your rooms to be?"

Ron looked at Dana, who was examining her toes, so he stepped forward and pulled the brochure from his back pocket. He opened it to a white-walled room with the brown trim.

"Yes, Aunt Julia," he said. "We both want this one."

"You both agreed?"

She seemed impressed until she saw the picture. She looked puzzled as she raised her head.

"This is what you want?" she asked.

Ron nodded vigorously, forcing a smile. It was one of the most boring ideas for a room he had ever seen, but they were going home in a few weeks anyway. "Yes, it's great, right, Dana?"

"It's really pretty," she said weakly.

Julia still looked hesitant.

Ron steeled himself for questions, but Julia only said, "All right, then, if that's what you like best. Let's get to work."

The two siblings charged up the stairs. While they were collecting their tools, Dana asked, "Can I have my brochure back?"

Ron looked at her sternly. "You aren't going to change your mind, are you?"

She shook her head, miserable, and he reached into his back pocket, but the brochure was no longer there.

# 9

Ron and Dana worked up a sweat as they moved every-thing into the crammed dining room. They dusted again, cleaned the windows, then swept and washed the floor, taking much longer than they did upstairs. By the time they were done, the floor was damp but sparkling clean and the entire house smelled of Pine-Sol.

When Aunt Julia came down, they made lunch and ate it outside on the front porch.

"I want to play," Jack said when he'd finished.

Ron shook his head. "We have to get back to work."

"Actually," Julia countered, "why don't you guys take a break and play for a bit. I have to finish sanding the walls upstairs and prime them, and it would be good to let the living room dry out."

"Yes!" Dana said, quickly. "Let's go, Jack!"

"Yay!" Jack shouted, while Ron sighed.

Julia called after them, "Watch out for Jack, don't play in the front lawn at all, and don't get hurt."

"We won't," Dana answered.

"I'm gonna ride my bike!" Jack exclaimed, scampering after her through the front door.

Julia cocked her head at Ron. "Aren't you going with them?"

Ron knew that Aunt Julia was trying to do the parental thing by letting them play, but she didn't understand that he was no longer a child. He had to find some way of letting her know. After all, raising the two kids was their job together, and it was more his burden than hers. But it wouldn't do to insult her by stating it openly. It was better done subtly.

He selected his words carefully. "I was really hoping to do the priming with you," he said. "I've never painted a room before and I want to learn how. I mean, I used to watch all those make-over shows with... Mom... but they don't always show you step by step and anyway, it's not as good as doing it yourself."

He gave his best blue-eyed gaze.

Julia looked surprised and impressed. "*Absolutely*! It's always more fun to do it with someone else. But first, go and run the two younger kids ragged, so they'll be too tired to do anything other than watch TV while we're working, okay?"

Ron beamed. "They'll be ready to sleep in a half-hour, you can count on me."

"I know I can," she said.

Now that he'd squared things up with Aunt Julia, Ron was eager to get moving. He hurried over to the bicycles, strapped on his helmet, and hoisted himself onto the pedals, swinging his leg over the seat as he rolled off. It was a method he'd copied from movie cowboys, and a habit he'd never gotten out of. As soon as he was rolling down the sidewalk, feeling the breeze in his face, he felt the urge to race. He bent over the handlebars and began to pedal furiously.

He passed Jack, who was playing with his cars in the driveway, and Dana, who was still searching for her helmet among their toys in the plastic tub.

"Wait up, Ron!" Dana shouted. "I'm not ready yet!"

Ron pretended that he couldn't hear her over the wind blowing in his ears. He kept up a furious pace, passing house after house without noticing them, until he came to the end of Whipple Lane. He slammed on the breaks and dragged the back wheels around in a semi-circle. To his immense satisfaction, they left a thin layer of rubber on the white sidewalk.

He grinned and looked up. That's when he first noticed the house.

Sitting at the base of Whipple Lane, where Old Kobold Street crossed it, was an eerie Victorian house - large enough, in Ron's estimation, to be called a mansion. A short, weedy gravel path led to sagging steps up to a darkened front door.

The house was three stories tall, with peeling, dark gray paint and white trim. Two windows jutted up from the roof on the third story, the panes so dirty that they appeared brown in the summer sunlight. Trees, bushes, and shrubs had grown wild, making it almost impossible to see the lower-story windows. The whole thing had a look of neglect and darkness – even the "No Trespassing" sign was stained from months of exposure, and the mailbox listed to one side.

Through one window Ron could make out tired-looking white drapery. A crow cawed from somewhere close by and an invisible branch scratched against glass pane.

An icy sensation crawled up and down his back. Ron stared at the house, unable to take his eyes away from it. It seemed to loom up over him, an evil specter on an otherwise harmless street.

In the distance, Ron heard Dana's plaintive shout, and he was glad to turn his bike around. As he pedaled back up the slight incline to their house, he sensed the cold stare of the Victorian on his back.

Dana sat astride her pink and white bike, waiting for him with her arms folded, pouting.

"You went too far!" she scolded, in a high pitched tone. "Aunt Julia said to stay at the front of the house."

"No she didn't," he sighed. Arguing with Dana was like arguing with a terrier – she just didn't know when to give up.

"Did too."

"No, she said to stay on the sidewalk. And I did."

She tried a different approach. "Well, it's dangerous to just be riding off on the road like that and I think…"

"Dana, *look*. There's the cop car."

Dana's mouth snapped shut. They studied the black and white cruiser in the driveway next door. It was parked in front of a garage next to a one-story, tan house with a porch. Although it was probably the same size as the Budds' cottage, it seemed more spacious, and it was certainly kept up much better. It was a nice, friendly house, and a far cry from the Victorian at the bottom of the street.

"Think there's anyone there?" Dana asked, quietly.

Ron shook his head.

"Maybe they're at church," she said.

"Maybe," Ron said. "Come on. We don't want to stand here all day."

Ron and Dana raced up and down the street, sticking to the sidewalks and without leaving Jack too far behind, although he seemed so happy with his cars that he wouldn't have noticed. Only one or two cars passed during that time and, except for the occasional dog barking at them through a window or from behind a fence, they saw and heard no one.

They raced until they were breathless and sweat poured off of them, then they called a truce, and walked their bikes back up to their house.

Ron had a stitch in his side, and the start of a headache from their time in the hot sun, but the exercise had done him good. He was feeling better than he had in months.

Beside him, Dana was pink and wheezy, but glowing.

"Pretty good riding there," Ron said, with a grin.

"I beat you that time," she said, her voice triumphant.

Ron had let her, but she didn't need to know that. "I know. You're fast."

"I like biking. We can go a lot further here."

"Yeah, you're right."

"And we haven't heard one siren the whole day."

Ron had to admit that it was remarkable. They often heard sirens back in Springfield. Ron's school was shut down a couple of times because of bomb threats, but no bombs were ever found. He thought that the real pain in the neck about the bomb scares was the reaction the teachers always had: they got nervous and cracked down hard on the students, which put everyone in a bad mood. Ron wondered if the schools in Franklin ever had bomb threats.

They were approaching the cop's house when Dana said, "I wonder if they ever have bank robberies or anything here. It seems so quiet."

"They probably don't," Ron answered. "That's why people come on vacation here."

"Probably..."

"Hi!"

It came from their right. They turned to see a girl about Dana's age, standing on the bottom rail of the fencing in front of the cop's house. She was small, with enormous hazel eyes and extremely curly brown hair. She wore flip-flops, shorts, and a sparkly top, and she seemed at the same time both friendly and shy. She kept lowering her face to hide it behind the top rail on the fence, then looking up, like she was playing peek-a-boo.

Dana and Ron exchanged puzzled looks.

"Hello," Dana said. "Who are you?"

"I'm Amelia," the girl said.

"I'm Dana Budd and this is my brother, Ron. We're staying next door."

"I know," Amelia said, still hiding her face.

"Do you live here?" Ron asked.

She nodded. "I live here with my dad and my cat." She looked up then. "Do you want to see her?"

Dana pounced on the invitation. "Sure!"

"Wait right here."

Amelia turned and ran to her house, banging the front door closed after she raced through it.

Ron wiped the sweat from his forehead, squinting through the bright sunlight to where Jack was playing cars. Jack's face was flushed, but he was very absorbed in his playing and hadn't noticed the stranger. Ron didn't dare look down the other end of the street. Even from where he was, he could feel the Victorian, and it made him uncomfortable.

Then Jack came running over to them. He grinned brightly and hopped up onto to the bottom slat of the fence.

"What are you doing?" he asked.

"We're going to see a cat," Dana said.

"If she ever comes back," Ron mumbled. "Let's go."

"But..." Dana protested.

"Come on," he insisted.

No sooner had they turned their backs than the front door banged open again, and Amelia came running across the lawn. She clutched a squirming, meowing, fluffy white cat against her chest. She was breathless, and her arms were freshly scratched, but she was triumphant.

"This is Dorita," she said. "My dad gave her to me."

"Dorito?" Jack giggled. "That's a funny name for a cat!"

"It's not 'Dorito'," she said, struggling to hold the increasingly annoyed cat. "It's 'Dorita'. It means 'gift'. Ouch!"

With a swipe of her claws, Dorita won her freedom.

Dana was aghast. "Are you all right?"

Amelia lowered her head with a barely visible nod. The scratch wasn't very deep, but it was starting to bleed. The little girl held her arm, fighting back tears, obviously embarrassed.

Ron wanted to ease the moment.

"Dorita's a nice name," he said. "It's Spanish, isn't it?"

Amelia nodded, sniffling.

"I really like your cat, Amelia," Dana said. "I've always wanted a cat or a dog, but my Dad is – was allergic to them. So we couldn't."

Dana had touched on the subject nearest and dearest to Amelia's heart. Her face brightened, and she began to talk rapidly.

"Oh wow, then you are going to *love* Mrs. Jurta!"

Dana blinked. "Mrs. Jurta?"

Amelia nodded and hopped back onto the fence. "Uh huh, she lives across the street right there," she pointed, "in the green house and she has *so* many dogs that you wouldn't believe it. She gets them from the pound and helps them to learn to live with people and other dogs and stuff so that the new owners won't have any trouble. This week, she's actually gotten *two* puppies – a Great Dane and a mutt."

She stopped and took a breath, grasping the fence.

"Do you get to play with the dogs a lot?" Dana asked eagerly.

Amelia nodded. "Oh, yes, all the time. When my dad isn't home, I stay with Mrs. Jurta and she lets me take the little ones for a walk. It's a *lot* of fun. Would you like to do it sometime, too?"

"Sure!" Dana was delighted. "That would be cool!"

The girl's face lit up with excitement and she kept her eyes locked on Dana, seeming to forget that the boys were there. In fact, when Ron spoke, she jumped at the sound.

"Do you know everyone on this street?" he asked.

Amelia nodded, then reconsidered. "Well, not *everyone*. But most everyone. The Willis family lives next door, in the white house. They're old, and they've lived here forever. Mr. Willis is a nice man, but Mrs. Willis has a dog that likes to bite, and she's pretty grouchy. And then there are the Durkins…"

Ron interrupted. "Do you know who lives in the house at the end of the street?"

"Which end?"

"The spooky, old one at the end of the road down there," Dana said, thrusting her arm in the general direction and missing Ron's face by a half an inch. "The one that looks haunted."

Ron hadn't realized that she'd noticed it, but the description was accurate.

Amelia leaned over the rail and squinted. "Oh, that place? No one lives there. It's empty."

"Who used to live there?" Ron asked.

She shrugged. "I don't know. It's been empty as long as I can remember. I heard Mr. Willis tell Daddy that someone wanted to buy the house and tear it down to build new homes, but they couldn't get enough money or something. I'm glad it didn't work. I kind of like it. It must have been pretty when it was new. If I had enough money, I would buy it and fix it up and put a pool in the back."

"But it's so spooky looking!" Dana objected. "It's like those houses in haunted movies. You couldn't pay me a million dollars to live in there."

Ron saw how Jack and Amelia were looking at his imaginative sister. "Let's talk about something else."

"I wish we had a pool," Dana said. "I love swimming."

"We've got one," Amelia said. "It's kind of small, but maybe you could come swim in it some time?"

"That would be *awesome,* wouldn't it, Ron?"

He rolled his eyes. "Dana…"

"What?"

"Nothing."

"Of course, we'd have to get Aunt Julia's permission," Dana said, assuming this was the cause of Ron's reluctance.

"You came with your aunt?" Amelia asked.

Dana nodded. "Yep. We're spending the summer here and fixing up the house so we can sell it."

"My dad says that paint is the cheapest way to redo a house," Amelia said authoritatively. "When we moved here, he let me paint my room whatever color I wanted."

"Aww, man," Dana said, enviously.

"Speaking of which," Ron said, not liking where the conversation was going, "I think it's time that we went home. Aunt Julia might need our help now."

Dana gave her customary pout. "But she said she wouldn't need us until tomorrow."

"I think we ought to check anyway."

"Oh, whatever! I'll see you later, Amelia." She took off with Jack on her bicycle, leaving Ron alone with their new neighbor.

She looked admiringly at his bike. It was a camouflage off-road bike with sixteen gears and a matching water bottle - the coolest bike that Ron had ever owned. He had gotten it the Christmas before, so it was still new and didn't have any scratches on it yet. That was something he hoped to change.

He put a foot on the pedal and smiled. "It was nice meeting you," he said.

"You, too," she said. "I have a bike, too."

"Oh? Why don't you ride it?"

"Dad doesn't like me riding on the sidewalk." She brightened. "But maybe he wouldn't mind if I did it with you guys."

Ron shifted in his seat. "Well, maybe, but…"

"I'll go ask him!"

She turned and ran off.

Ron pedaled away as fast as he could and coasted into the driveway. So much time had passed: Aunt Julia must be nearly through with the priming by now.

He found Julia standing at the kitchen table, which was now covered with a drop cloth. She stirred a bucket of white paint with a wooden stick, and her face was almost the same shade. Dana and Jack were at the refrigerator, getting drinks.

"Did you have a good time?" Aunt Julia asked Ron.

He nodded and dropped into the kitchen chair. "I'm ready to work now."

# 10

Julia woke early the next morning. Her arms and back were sore from the painting she and Ron had done; but when she went upstairs with her cup of morning brew, she was so pleased with the results that it made the aches and pains seem worthwhile.

The strong, clean scent of fresh paint was refreshing. She ran her fingers lightly over the wall in Dana's room and rubbed them together.

*Already dry – nice. Moving the fans upstairs must have done the trick.*

She went into Ron and Jack's room and found that it, too, was dry. She stood amid the drop clothes, buckets, and closed cans of paint, sipping her coffee and thinking.

She reached into her bathrobe pocket and pulled out the decorating pamphlet that Ron had dropped. When Julia picked it up, she noticed that one of the pages was covered in Dana's scrawling handwriting, and she recognized it as the picture Dana had shown her in the van. Little hearts decorated the borders and arrows pointed out objects of interest. The color scheme was a far cry from the delicate pinks and white of Dana's room in Springfield, and further still from the tan and white picture that Ron had pointed out.

No doubt Ron was trying to be responsible again and talked Dana into picking a boring, but more saleable palette. Julia decided that she'd have none of it. Despite what she told Ron about white being preferred, she couldn't imagine doing an entire house exclusively in white. The place would look like an institution. As long as they were stuck with having to repaint and redo an entire house for the summer, they were going to have some fun doing it, even if it did cost a little more.

Besides, she didn't like the idea of Ron pushing Dana around, even he did so for what he thought were good reasons. She was going to have to let him know, again, that she was in charge. But knowing him as she did, she thought it would be best if she could find a subtle way to tell him.

Julia slipped the pamphlet back into her pocket and went downstairs.

Shafts of early morning sun lit up the drab interiors and filled Julia with a sense of wellbeing, despite the almost overwhelming amount of work that needed to done. She felt empowered today, something she hadn't felt in a long time.

Jack woke up first. He stumbled into the kitchen where she was preparing breakfast, rubbing his eyes. He looked so cuddly in his superhero pajamas that Julia was tempted to stop and scoop him up.

She told Jack to wake the others for breakfast, and by the time she had finished, they were fully dressed and ready for the day.

"What are we doing today?" Dana asked, around a mouthful of cereal.

Ron poured the last of the gallon of milk into his bowl and Julia made a mental note to buy more.

"We have to run some errands," she said, checking her watch. "We have to go to the grocery store, then the hardware store to pick up the paint we need. The lawn care guys will be here around ten-thirty."

At the word, "paint", Dana and Ron exchanged glances that Julia pretended not to see.

When breakfast was over, they piled the dishes in the sink and left. It was 8:30 a.m. and the street was still quiet. Dana noted that the police car was still in the driveway.

"I guess he doesn't work on Mondays," she said.

Julia noticed its neat and tidy appearance. "That's where Office Wilde lives?"

"Yes, with Amelia."

"Amelia?"

"Wilde's daughter," Ron said.

"Oh, I didn't know he had a daughter."

Dana leaned out the window. "Hi Amelia!" she called out.

"Hi, Amelia! Hi!" echoed Jack.

On the sidewalk with Amelia, a tall, elderly woman walked briskly down the street, holding the leashes of five energetic dogs. They were of all breeds and mixes, all sizes and ages, from older dogs to just out of puppyhood.

The woman's face was a mask of concentration, her short white hair pulled back from her face with a kerchief. She pulled so hard on the leashes that her back was at almost a ninety-degree angle with the sidewalk.

Behind her, Amelia concentrated on her two little charges: a dark gray dog and a smaller tiger-striped puppy with perky ears. Both together were nearly as much of a handful as the five bigger dogs.

"Amelia!" Dana yelled again.

Amelia heard this time. She turned and her face broke into a smile. Julia slowed down as they came up beside her.

Dana was almost beside herself.

"Ohmigosh, those puppies are so *cute!*" she gushed.

*Uh oh,* Julia thought.

"Which one is the one you want?" Dana asked.

Amelia indicated with her head. "The striped one," she said proudly. "His name is Tiger and Mrs. Jurta lets me help with his training. We're, like, best friends."

"He's so cute!"

"Oh, hi, Ron!" Amelia chirped. "Where are you guys going? Are you going to the lake?"

"Nope, to the grocery store," Dana said. "See you later today!"

"Cool!"

Julia pulled away from the dog walkers as Dana rolled up the windows, then settled back in her seat with a sigh.

"So that's Amelia," Julia commented. "She seems nice. Whose dogs are those?"

"Mrs. Jurta's —she lives across the street and Amelia goes over there when her dad's at work," Dana supplied. "She says that Mrs. Jurta gets them from the pound and that's there's two cute little puppies and she wants to adopt one, but when she asked her dad, but he was like, 'Well, maybe, we'll see.'"

"Good grief, Dana!" Julia laughed. "Did you get her date of birth and baptismal records, too? How long were you talking with her?"

"Only a few minutes," Dana said. "She said that she'd ask Mrs. Jurta if I could come and help with the puppies sometime. Can I go if she says yes?"

"I'll think about it."

She gave a disappointed sigh. The answer was not to her liking.

Julia wanted to pacify her without backing down. "I'd like to get to know Mrs. Jurta a little before I let you work with her, just to be on the safe side. You know the rules about speaking to strangers, right?"

"We know," Ron interrupted. "We'll be careful."

Julia nodded, but added, "Even in a small town like this, creepy things can happen, you know."

"Like at the haunted house," Jack whispered.

"The haunted house?"

"There's a haunted house at the end of our street," Dana explained. "Didn't you see it?"

"At the end of the street?"

"The one that's empty and creepy."

"Oh, the old Victorian: It does look creepy, but who told you it was haunted?"

"No one," Dana sighed. "But it's obvious. All you have to do is look at it."

Julia raised an eyebrow at Ron. He rolled his eyes and shrugged.

She switched on the radio, and they listened in silence until they reached the grocery store on the outskirts of the city.

They stocked up on groceries and went on to the hardware store. There, after much discussion, Julia succeeded in having her own way with the paint selection. Dana got her purples and greens and Ron selected green and blue for the boys' room.

John Irwin, who was mixing the paints, got into the spirit of things and asked, "Are you redoing the whole house?"

"Yep!" Dana said cheerfully. She stood on the end of the carriage, running her finger around the edge of the purple paint can. "We're fixing it up so we can sell it."

"That is a big job," he confirmed. "I hope you have lots of help."

Julia smiled confidently, but she couldn't help thinking: *Julia Lamontaigne, what have you let yourself in for? You're going to be painting from now until September.*

Dana handed her two neon chips of paint, one orange and one yellow.

"How about this for the living room?" she asked.

As much as Julia hated stomping on their artistic flourishes, she felt obliged to point out, as gently as she could, that the living room should not resemble a police crime scene.

# 11

They were having such a good time in the paint department that Julia completely forgot about her lawn care experts. It was only when Ron happened to mention the time that she remembered. She instantly panicked, imagining hordes of teenagers all over the lawn, breaking things by accident, and suing her for damages to their equipment.

She hurried the methodical John along, raced through the checkout, and drove quickly back to Whipple Lane.

While the street was quiet, Julia's house was not. An old pickup truck with a new paint job and a long, empty trailer was parked in front of their house, and the lawn was a hive of well-organized activity. Two lawnmowers were plowing through the tall grass in the front of the house, navigated by two goggled individuals wearing tall boots. Another figure followed them with a rake and a trash bag. A tall, extraordinarily thin man wielded a weed-whacker with practiced precision, while a heavy woman in a tank top sat in the bed of the pickup, working industriously at something that Julia couldn't see. On the side of the pickup a sign declared *John Irwin III's Lawn and Garden and Handyman Work.*

Already the difference was dramatic: in the space of a few short hours, the house at 134 Whipple Lane had gone from looking like a haunted reject to a slightly neglected family-friendly home. It was actually welcoming.

"Oh, wow!" Julia exclaimed, slowing the van down for a better look.

"They're here already," Ron commented. "They work fast."

As the equipment was blocking the driveway, Julia parked on the side of the road just in front of the pickup truck.

She stepped out into the hot, humid morning, and went over to the side of the pickup truck. The woman there was a teenager with a face that looked nearly as young as Dana's did. Julia was surprised to note that they were all teenagers - the operation was so smoothly run that she had expected to find an adult overseeing everything.

Ron hopped up onto the pickup's tire to look into the bed. The girl was opening a bag of lawn seeding treatment.

"Hey," she said. She was pretty, about thirty pounds overweight, with gorgeous blue eyes. Her brown hair was short and carefully styled, and her earrings glinted in the morning light. Her jeans and boots spoke of the business at hand.

"Hello," Julia said. "I'm Julia Lamontaigne. Is John Irwin here?"

"Oh, yeah." The girl indicated behind her. "He's coming."

The tall, skinny man, still holding the weed-whacker with one wiry, muscular arm, came loping around the corner. He pulled off his goggles to reveal a friendly face framed by dark hair and a thin reddish beard, no older that the girl who sat in the back of his pickup truck.

John Irwin III pulled off his glove and wiped his streaming forehead with his sleeve.

"Mrs. Lamontaigne?" he asked.

"Ah, no," said Julia. "No, just Julia Lamontaigne. Are you John Irwin?"

"The third," he said, extending his hand for a quick shake. "But call me J. C."

"J. C.," she smiled. "You've gotten so much done already."

"Oh, well," he shrugged. He had an easy kind of effect, laid-back and completely non-confrontational. "We like to move it when we're working, you know? Actually, I'm glad you came when you did, because we weren't sure how much you wanted us to do. I have your work order here..."

The girl in the pickup truck rummaged in a bin for a second, and then pulled out a slightly crumpled piece of printed paper which she handed over.

"Oh, this is my girlfriend and associate, Derval. Derval Raye."

"Nice to meet you," said Derval Raye.

"Very nice to meet you," Julia answered. Jack pulled insistently on the corner of her blouse, so she bent and picked him up. "This is Jack, Ron, and Dana."

"Hi!" Jack chirped.

"Hey, buddy," J. C. said, then showed the paper to Julia. "I noted that you wanted the front lawn trimmed and treated for ticks and that you had the insecticide and stuff, but I didn't know if you had wanted us to seed it, and do the flowers and the back lawn, too."

Julia looked over the bed of the truck to the work that was already done. The three teenage boys stood in a group, talking to each other and chugging sports drinks. The lawn was immaculately shorn, and now she could see thin patches where the grass was burnt or gnawed at by grubs. The edges of the lawn had been carefully trimmed so as to avoid the flowers, which now looked even sadder since they lost their covering. She could see that it needed a lot of work.

J. C. said, "We could do it all today, if you wanted. We brought everything just in case. It's up to you."

Julia couldn't help asking, "You run this business all by yourself?"

He didn't seem offended; in fact, he flushed with pleasure, and his chest swelled a little when he answered.

"Yes, ma'am!" he said proudly. "All mine. I started it last fall, doing leaf cleanup and snow removal and stuff. It's going pretty well.

The boys and I handle the heavy work, and Derval helps both here and with the paperwork and stuff."

"I'm impressed. Starting a successful business is a daunting task. But you seem so young - have you graduated high school?"

"I will this year."

"Oh. And do you plan do this through college?"

"Nope." He grinned. "Why should I? You go to college to be able to make enough money to support yourself, right?" He gestured at his crew. "Well, with a bit of elbow grease, this will be doing that by the end of the school year, and if it isn't, I've still got my part-timer with a handyman on the other end of town."

"Sounds like you have it all figured out," Julia commented.

"I think so. I'm having trouble convincing the old man, though," he said. "I think he's afraid that I'm going to be a lay-about hick."

Then, apparently thinking he had said too much, he abruptly got back to business. "Now, back to your lawn. I don't want to push you into anything, but you do have grubs both here and in the back yard. If you don't hit them pretty hard now, you probably won't have much of a lawn in a few weeks, and they'll get into the back garden as well. And, like, the whole thing would look a lot better with some seeding and treatments, too, but that's up to you."

"What about the ticks?" Julia asked.

"Just mowing the lawn will take care of most of them, but we'll spray it with that stuff you got from my dad the other day, just to be sure. You won't want to let the kids walk on it for a day or two after we do it."

"That sounds good," she said. "And I'd like the backyard trimmed and treated as well."

"Okay." He felt around in his pocket and then held out his hand. "Derval, pen, please."

John made some marks on the page as his three employees found their way over to the pickup truck. He noticed them when he looked up.

"Oh, this is Billy, Mitch, and Connor. Guys, Mrs...."

"Miss."

"Oh, right, sorry. Miss Lamontaigne."

"Please, call me Julia," she said, feeling quite old all of the sudden. "Nice to meet you all."

They nodded and said hello. All of them were sweating profusely and Mitch, as he took another sip, commented to Connor about the heat. He used an epithet which both surprised and annoyed Julia, especially as he said it in front of the kids. After receiving an elbow and a dirty look from Billy, Mitch promptly apologized.

"Sorry, ma'am." He added, "Sorry, J. C.," to his boss, who nodded.

Julia turned and handed Jack to Ron.

"Why don't you three start bringing the groceries into the house," she said, giving Dana the key. "Just put it all in the kitchen."

The threesome trudged off.

J. C. said, "Mitch, take the guys and go start on the back yard. Don't do the garden or the borders yet, and watch out for the little kids."

The threesome turned and went back to their machines, elbowing and kidding each other while Derval and John exchanged nervous glances.

"Sorry about that," he said. "They're a bit rough around the edges, but they're all right."

Julia detected the sincerity in his voice. She decided that she was going to like John Irwin III.

"I'm sure they are," she said. "What does J. C. stand for?"

"John Christopher," he said. "It's so people don't confuse me with my dad. Now, would you like to schedule your next treatment while we're doing paperwork?"

After arranging all of the details with J. C., Julia locked up the van and went into the house. The air was heavy with the scent of freshly cut grass and throbbed with the sound of machinery.

The kids had left the side door open. Julia stepped through to find Ron hauling two paint cans up the steep stairs, with Amelia right behind him.

Surprised to see her, Julia said, "Well, hello."

Amelia turned to give her a huge, infectious smile.

"Hi, Mrs. Lamontaigne!" she said.

"Miss," Julia corrected her with a wince.

"My dad said I could come over and help today if you wanted me," Amelia continued. "He's working in the garage today and said that I couldn't stay for lunch, but I could come back in the afternoon if you needed me."

"He said that, did he?" asked Julia. Her opinion of Robert Wilde plummeted: what sort of person just let their kid go hang out with a brand new neighbor whom they had barely met? Why hadn't he come over to check this out with her first?

It went against the strong first impression that he had given her. Perhaps it was wishful thinking, but she'd taken Wilde as a man who could be even more protective than she was.

Before she had time to decide what to do, Ron was speaking.

"We're bringing the paint upstairs now," he said. "That way we can start on it right away."

Julia had to speak loudly over the sound of the lawnmowers. "Be careful on those stairs. Those cans are heavy and I think the stairs are uneven."

"I'm alright," Amelia declared. "Mrs. Jurta says I'm as strong as an ox, and Mrs. LaVallee says that I can climb like a mountain goat."

"Mrs. LaVallee?"

"She's my Girl Scout leader. She said that mountains are a symbol of life and all its struggles and that it's only by going through the struggles and stuff that you can make it to the top and see the view. She says…"

"She says an awful lot," Ron interrupted. "Come on, Amelia, my arms are killing me."

He started up the stairs again. Amelia followed with a chipper, "Not me! I'm not tired!"

Ron looked back at Julia and shook his head, amused.

Smiling, Julia went into the kitchen. It was surprisingly in order. The sacks of groceries were unpacked on the kitchen table, sorted by box, bag, or can size. The bags had been thrown on the floor in one corner and the stuff from the hardware store was piled up in the doorway. Dana knelt in front of one of the cabinets, neatly stacking the cans that Jack handed to her.

Julia complemented the children on their organization while she opened the kitchen window. Ron and Amelia clamored back downstairs, Amelia still talking a blue streak. Ron's face had grown impassive, as though he had shut down his hearing.

"Hey, Amelia!" Dana called out, breaking into the conversation. "Want to give me a hand with the groceries?"

There was a plaintive, lilting tone in her voice – she was jealous of the attention that Ron was receiving from their new friend. Julia wasn't surprised to hear it, but she suddenly realized that Dana didn't really have any girlfriends, now that Colleen was no longer next door. That meant, aside from Ron, Jack, and herself, Dana had no one. No wonder she was desperate for a friend.

Amelia hesitated, and looked from Dana to Ron.

Ron said. "Why don't you help Dana? You guys need some girl-talk."

Julia watched the emotions play out on Amelia's face. She thought that they ran the gamut, which was surprising for a decision of such little import. Why such a big deal when she'd come over here to hang out with Dana in the first place?

When Amelia gave Ron a sidelong look, Julia understood. Amelia had a crush on Ron. It was cute, and definitely innocent, but Julia wanted to stifle it as quickly as possible. The last thing they needed was to incite an adolescent summertime romance.

She straightened up and checked her watched, clearing her throat as she did so. The four children looked at her.

"Actually, here's what I need done. Girls, I want you to open all the windows downstairs and start the fans. Ron, you can do the same for the upstairs, and then start sanding the walls. Make sure to wear the mask."

Ron seemed relieved. "Sure!" he said, bolting for the stairs.

"Can I help with the sanding?" Amelia asked.

"Me, too?" Dana added.

"No, I've only got two masks and I'm going to need one. Besides, I need you two to look after Jack and start things going for lunch. Dana, we'll be using the hot dogs and vegetables for lunch today. You can make your dip, if you like."

Dana's face lit up and she grabbed Amelia's arm.

"Want to help me make dip?" she asked.

Amelia nodded quickly. "Okay! That sounds like fun!"

"First the windows," Julia warned. "And take Jack with you."

She caught a bit of the girls' conversation as they pulled up the windows in the dining room. They had to speak loudly to be heard over the sound of the lawn mowers. Dana told Amelia about how she'd found the dip recipe while watching a cooking show on TV.

"It's really good," she said, proudly. "You'll like it – are you staying for lunch?"

"Oh, sure!" Amelia replied enthusiastically. "My dad said I could stay all day, as long as you guys needed help."

The two girls chattered on, tugging Jack into the hallway, while Julia stood rooted in place. Robert Wilde wouldn't have told Amelia both that she could and couldn't stay for lunch. And if Amelia was lying about that, then there was a good chance that he didn't even know she was there. Amelia could have told him that she was going to hang out with the dog lady who, Julia had gathered, was a frequent babysitter as well as dog sitter.

Julia checked her watch: 11:30 a.m. Time for a little tattling before lunch.

She went to the foot of the stairs and called for Ron. He didn't respond, but she could hear the soft scraping sounds of the sandpaper at work. He probably had his ear buds on.

She took the stairs two at a time and found him in the boys' room, his iPod in his pocket, working the sandpaper like a pro. He spotted her and pulled a bud out of his ear.

"I have to go next door for a minute," she said. "Could you keep an ear out for the kids downstairs?"

He nodded and pulled the other bud out. "No problem. What do we do after I sand?"

"Wipe the walls with a damp rag," she said. "Not too wet, but just enough to remove most of the dust. I'll be back in a second, though, so don't worry too much about it."

Julia left the house with the side door propped open and hurried down the driveway. One of the lawn mowers had gone quiet, and the members of J. C.'s crew were wrestling with large bags of seed and mulch. She had a momentary doubt about leaving the kids alone with them, but shoved it aside – she wouldn't be gone long and there was a cop next door, for heaven's sake. They would be safe.

The Wildes' driveway led right up to the attached garage. The doors were open, and she could hear the soft sounds of classic rock playing on an old radio while tools clinked methodically. An avocado-green two-door car from the 1970s sat on blocks in the center of the garage. There were patches of white on the body and doors, spare parts on the bench and scattered around on the cement floor, and the hood was raised. The owner was nowhere to be seen.

Julia stepped in and rapped on the side of the door. "Hello? Mr. Wilde?"

He popped up like a jack in the box from behind the car. His clothes were worn and grease-streaked. His face and hands were dirty and he rubbed a tool in a filthy rag as his face creased in a friendly smile.

"Oh, hi!" he said.

Julia said, "I don't know if you remember me, but I'm the woman who just moved in next door. We met on Saturday."

He came from around the back of the car. "I remember. Julia Lamontaigne, right?"

"Yes. You have a good memory."

He shrugged with a self-deprecating grin. "Sometimes." He bobbed his head in the direction of her house. In the clear midday air, they could hear J. C. issuing orders to Mitch and the others. "I hear that you hired Irwin's son to do the lawns."

Some of Julia's self-righteousness slipped away. He seemed so nice and unconcerned that she hated to spoil his day by telling him that his daughter had probably lied to him.

"Yes," she smiled. "There were ticks in the lawn and, well, I'm kind of squeamish about bugs."

"I don't blame you there. We've had a few cases of Lyme disease in the area and it's not an easy thing to get rid of. But J. C.'s a good kid – you won't have any complaints."

"He seems very efficient. I am impressed."

"The Irwins are a good family. They've been around here a long time."

"Have they?"

"At least for three generations. Franklin's a pretty old city, and quite a few of the founding families are still here."

"You sound like an expert. Are you a founding family?"

He grinned and leaned against the car. "Nope. I'm a recent immigrant."

Julia nodded. "Well, that makes me feel better. I was starting to feel strange around all the natives here. Are you from Massachusetts?"

"No, Manchester, but I went to school in Mass. Boston University."

"Good school."

"That's what they tell me."

"Don't remember much?"

"I remember being overwhelmed a lot. I'm not much of a scholar."

She waved a hand at the car. "You have to know quite a bit to restore one of these things."

He turned and smiled at the car. "Yeah, it can be tricky, but finding parts is the most difficult thing."

"Ah."

There was a moment of silence. Julia was still trying to figure out how to bring up Amelia when he said, "So, do you like the new place? Are things working out for you?"

She saw an opening. "It's going very well," she said. "It's tight for the four of us, but we're managing. There's been so much cleaning and arranging that I haven't had time to decide whether or not I really like it."

"It's been empty a long time. You must be finding a lot of things to repair."

"Actually, no. So far we've been lucky. The cabinets in the kitchen are shot, but that's it. What it really needs is a face-lift and, to be honest with you, I'm not sure how Ron and I are going to get it all done before school starts again. There's a lot to do."

"Well, if ever you need an extra hand, be sure to let me know. I like doing handyman work – I worked as a painter and handyman during summer breaks when I was a kid."

"Oh, really?" she said, and saw an opening. "Well, I'll be sure to call on you sometime, when we need an expert opinion. Right now, we're doing well. And thank you so much for sending Amelia over – she's been a real help, and I think Dana's been a little lost for female company right now."

Wilde straightened up and looked at her, confused.

"Amelia?" he said. "Amelia's at your place? My Amelia?"

"Yes. She's helping Dana with lunch. Actually, that's why I came over here – she told me you'd given her permission to stay for lunch, and I wanted to check with you. We don't really know each other very well, and I just wanted to make sure that you were comfortable with that."

Robert was looking toward her house, tapping the wrench into the palm of his hand. His frown deepened.

"Is everything all right?" she asked.

He looked at her. "It's just that she was supposed to be with Mrs. Jurta and her dogs today. I had no idea that she was over at your house."

"Oh, I'm sorry."

"It's not your fault. I'm glad that your daughter and her get along, but..."

"I understand," Julia said quickly. "She's more than welcome to stay, but I'll understand if you need to, you know, lay down the law and all that." She blushed when she remembered that she was talking to a cop.

He regarded her sympathetically. "I'm sorry," he said. "I've... well, Amelia's been getting a little difficult to handle lately. She'll agree to do one thing, then go out and do another without telling me. I don't get it – she never told a lie her entire life."

Julia hastened to reassure him. "I think all kids go through that. You know, testing and trying to see how much they can get away with. I did it when I was young. I drove my poor mother crazy."

"You're probably right," he said. She could tell that he didn't believe it. Or if he did, he thought it little help.

He continued, "But I can't always be here, obviously. Today, when I thought she was with Mrs. Jurta, I really had no idea where she was. I'm relieved that she's with you and safe, but she could have been anywhere and I would have no idea."

Julia shifted uncomfortably. She was new to this whole parenting thing and had no experience to offer him.

"Should I send her home?" she asked.

At that moment, a bloodcurdling scream ripped through the air. It was like being doused with icy water.

Julia froze.

"Dana!" she gasped.

Another scream followed, and the two of them went racing down the driveway, their hearts in their throats.

# 12

They found the children huddled in a group around the side door with J. C.'s boys moving around them in a protective, if confused, circle. Julia's relief at seeing them whole and apparently unharmed quickly reverted to panic when she realized that the two little girls were crying, and Jack's face was smeared with blood.

She raced over and scooped Jack up. He clutched at her, burying his face into her shirt. It was only with difficulty that she managed to pull his face up and see that he had a split lip. The two girls ran over to her as she examined Jack's head for further damage.

"What happened?" she demanded. "Jack, tell me what happened."

"I fall down!" he cried.

"The girls found an animal inside," Ron said. He looked scared. "It's still in there."

"We heard the shouts and came over to see what was happening," J. C. added.

"Did it bite anyone?" Julia asked, and relief rolled over her when everyone shook their heads. "What is it?"

"A wolf!" Amelia shouted.

"A wolf?" J. C. sounded skeptical.

"Amelia," Wilde said. There was a warning note in his tone that caused the girl to fall silent.

"Dana, what happened?" Julia adjusted her grip on Jack.

"We..." Dana gulped back tears. She was barely able to talk. "We were playing by the fireplace and then a *fox* came down it! He tried to bite us!"

She burst into tears and buried her face into Julia's jeans. Amelia was quick to follow suit, and Jack was already soaking her collar. It was a comical and embarrassing scene.

"They must have loosened the damper," J. C. said.

"What's a damper?" Ron asked. He had his back plastered to the screen door, as though he expected claws and teeth to shred the metal mesh at any moment.

"It's a sort of door in the chimney that keeps stuff from coming down it when you're not using it," Wilde said.

"But a *fox*? In the fireplace?" Julia said.

"More likely a squirrel," Wilde said.

"Yeah," J. C. agreed. "They nest in unused chimneys, like bats and birds. You haven't had this chimney cleaned out yet, have you?"

"Er, no," Julia answered. "I wasn't expecting to use it. Should we call animal control?"

Wilde shook his head. "Why bother them? The boys and I can chase it out, can't we, boys?"

"Count me in," Connor said. "Beats weed whacking!"

"What if it has rabies?" Derval asked anxiously.

"Bring it," Mitch said, snapping his shears with mock ferocity.

Arming themselves with gloves and rakes, Wilde, J. C., Mitch, Connor, and Ron went into the house in search of the squirrel. Outside, all Julia could hear were the faint sounds of battle. After a few moments, the squeaking rodent fled out the front door and they returned triumphant, singing Ron's praises.

"He was able to slip right past the squirrel and open the door," J. C. said, clapping him on the shoulder. "Slick work."

Wilde nodded, the grin reaching his eyes. "I think he was smarter than the rest of us combined."

"Ron's the smartest guy I know," Dana said proudly.

Ron shrugged. "Oh, it wasn't anything."

But he looked very pleased, and even swaggered a little under the praise.

Wilde and the boys searched the house and declared it rodent free. The crisis was over, but the living room was a mess. Sticks, soot, and indistinguishable garbage spilled out from the fireplace, and there was a fine layer of darkened dust over everything, disturbed by human and squirrel feet. Small, dark brown pellets were scattered all around, even in the hall.

To Julia's surprise, J. C. , Billy, and Connor were already cleaning up the nest and the pellets while Mitch made huge gestures with his arms, giving a detailed and exaggerated blow-by-blow of the great squirrel hunt to the two gaping little girls. Ron and Wilde joined the cleanup crew and started to help.

"Dude, so disgusting," Connor said, making a face as he accidentally smeared something he was cleaning.

"That's what they do when they're panicked," J. C. said.

"Do you have any bleach or disinfectant?" Wilde asked Julia. "This will smell if we don't clean it up right now."

"I'll get it!" Ron hopped up and raced out of the room.

Feeling unnecessary, Julia took Jack into the kitchen, washed him up, and soothed his wounds. When she came back into the living room, everything was cleaned: the damper was put back in place, the soiled bedclothes were in the laundry basket, and the boys were standing around chatting.

J. C. was leaning on his broom, surveying the room. "When I came here this morning, I wasn't figuring on this much excitement," he said.

"Neither was I," Wilde laughed. He turned to Julia, and the talk died down as everyone looked at her expectantly.

Jack turned and buried his face in her neck, and Julia had to adjust her grip on him before she spoke.

"I just want to thank you all so much," she said. "For pitching in like that, helping us get rid of the squirrel, cleaning up the mess – I just don't know how to thank you."

"You could buy us lunch!" Mitch offered, raising his hand.

Billy clipped him playfully with his hat, but Julia smiled. "I'd really be pleased to offer you all lunch. It'll just be hot dogs and salad, but you are welcome to it."

To Ron's evident delight, they accepted. Amelia offered the cookies she'd baked the day before, and J. C. volunteered the soda he had packed in coolers in his truck. Wilde offered to help cook the hotdogs. When they discovered that the old grill in the shed had no charcoal, he and Amelia cheerfully wheeled their own over from their back porch.

Julia was almost overwhelmed with offers of help. She fussed with the salad while Amelia and Dana swept the porch and spread a picnic cloth on it. Before long, dogs and buns were grilling on the flames.

It turned out to be an unexpected party. J. C. and his friends tried to outdo each other in stuffing their mouths. Amelia and Dana huddled together giggling, while Derval and Julia chatted. Ron discussed the renovations with Wilde. Julia, sitting nearby, overheard some of it.

"You're both doing nice work. You did those rooms in just two days?"

"Aunt Julia did most of it. I've been helping."

"It's a big job. What colors are you using?"

Ron told him and Wilde approved. They talked for a few minutes about application and drying times, and matte finish compared to gloss. Wilde told Ron about redoing his old house and all the trouble he'd had removing the wallpaper.

"That's a mess," he said. He spoke comfortably, man-to-man, as though they were almost the same age. "Trying to get that guck off the wall made me never want to use wallpaper again. Give me paint any day."

"A whole bunch of the rooms downstairs are wallpapered," Ron sounded worried. "I guess we'll have the same trouble."

"Yeah, it's a lot of work. If you two decide you need a hand, let me know. It's been pretty slow around here lately and I'll be glad to have a project to help with."

Julia saw Ron look up at Robert with new interest. The officer, busy helping Amelia with her food, didn't seem to notice the boy's burgeoning hero-worship.

By the time the food was gone, an hour had passed and J. C.'s crew had to go to their next appointment. Before leaving, Derval made a deal with Julia to watch Jack a few times a week while they worked on the house. Wilde and Amelia left too, having made plans to go see a movie.

After cleaning up the picnic, Julia set Dana and Jack up to watch a movie in the living room while she and Ron went upstairs to finish the sanding.

When they were upstairs, donning their masks, Julia said, "Well! That was exciting."

"Yeah."

"It's nice when you make friends at a new place, isn't it?"

"Yeah, it sure is."

They worked with the sandpaper for a few minutes, then Ron said, "Aunt Julia? Do you think I'll be as tall as Robert?"

Julia was glad that the mask hid her grin. "You'll probably be taller. Your dad was."

She regretted the comment instantly. Ron's expression, so open and innocent, closed again into his usual stoicism, and he didn't mention Wilde again that afternoon.

# 13

Ron woke up feeling refreshed. Aunt Julia had let them all sleep on sheets and blankets on the bare living room floor. While his back was a little sore, it was far less stuffy than it had been in the sleeping bags. For the first time since they had arrived, he didn't wake up damp with sweat.

Dana and Jack were still sleeping as he lifted himself up off the floor. As he padded past the kitchen, he spotted Julia, already dressed in her paint-stained jeans, working on her computer at the kitchen table. By the time he was dressed, she'd set the table with his favorite cereal.

He was hungry and ate two bowls. Julia sipped her coffee and nibbled on her breakfast bar as she alternated between scrolling and typing quickly.

Ron watched her work. Her lips were tight – what she was working on wasn't making her very happy. He thought it wasn't fair that she got to bring her computer when she wouldn't let him bring his, but he knew that she was trying to find a new job and keep in touch with the woman that was minding the house.

She finally broke the silence.

"I heard from your grandmother this morning," she said.

She meant Gran Budd, his dad's mother. She and Gramps were on a trip around the world with a whole bunch of their friends and didn't expect to be back for a few months. Gran had promised to call all of them every day that she was gone. So far, Ron hadn't received a call.

"They're in Puntarenas, Costa Rica, and having a marvelous time," Julia said cheerfully. "She said to tell you that she loves you and misses you. They wanted to talk to you, but Gramps didn't want to wake you."

Ron nodded. He knew that the Budds didn't like Aunt Julia, even before his parents' accident, and things had only gotten worse after she'd refused to give up custody. He remembered standing by when Aunt Julia told them, over the phone, about their summer plans. Although Julia hadn't said anything to him, he knew his grandparents well enough to know that his aunt would have been raked over the coals. Gran Budd claimed to love the children dearly, but they all knew better than to cross her.

"I've never even heard of Puntarenas," Julia continued. "She said it's lovely, and that the sun has been out every day. It sounds great. Anyway, I promised that you guys would call later, so please don't let me forget."

"I won't," he promised.

"Cool. I had a look at the walls this morning and I think we can go right ahead and put the next coat on. It's drying beautifully. You've got a good eye for colors, you know, just like your mother."

Ron said, "Everyone says that I'm just like Dad."

"Yes," she said. "You're a lot like him, too."

To change the topic, Ron asked, "You have internet here?"

She looked at her computer. "No, I'm afraid not. I think we're going to have to schedule a trip to someplace that has free Wi-Fi. I haven't been able to access my email in nearly a week. Maybe we'll go out this afternoon."

"After we do the walls again?"

"After we do the walls," Julia agreed. "I'd like to see if I got any feedback from those job applications."

She poked at her keyboard for a few minutes while Ron played with his cereal. Then he asked the question that had been bothering him for two weeks.

"If you don't get a job, what will happen?"

Julia looked up at him thoughtfully. She folded her arms and leaned on the table in front of her laptop and said, in a careful, even tone, "I *will* find a job. That isn't the problem. The only real problem that I can see is that when I do get the job, we may have to move to accommodate it and it will probably not pay as much as my old job, which will mean that we'll have to cut more corners. But we'll be okay. It'll all work out."

Ron met her gaze steadily. "How long will the savings hold out?"

"Long enough. We're good until December at least - providing, of course, that the repairs here don't cost more than I expect them to."

"Do you think they will?"

"Nah. Between the two of us, I think we can pull off the renovations and save a bundle on contracting costs. Your help is making it take half the time I thought it would."

Ron flushed with pleasure.

She shut down the laptop and got up. "Why don't we get back to work? If we can get to the walls early enough, we may be able to put the final coat on this afternoon."

He felt much better. He put his dishes in the sink, washed his hands, and went upstairs to work.

They put the second coat on the boys' room, then carefully painted the two-toned walls of Dana's room.

By the time the walls were finally finished, Ron's arms were sore and he was sweating again. Julia was tired, too. When they came downstairs, they found Jack on his back, screaming and kicking his heels on the hallway floor, while Dana leaned against the wall with her arms folded, pouting.

When Julia snapped, "*Jack!*" they weren't too surprised. He had it coming. They waited for her next move, watching warily.

Jack stopped kicking and screaming, but he was still crying. He rubbed his eyes and reached to wrap himself around Julia's leg, sniffling pitifully.

Julia sighed and looked at her watch.

"It's 11:30," she said. "I want you guys to go out and play *nicely* on the sidewalk until I have lunch ready, all right?"

"Do we have to?" Dana grumbled.

"Yes, you do."

"I don't want to go outside!" Jack whined.

"Well, I need you to go outside anyway. I want you out of the fumes."

"Do you need help with lunch?" Ron asked.

"No thanks," Julia said. "You guys go out and I'll call you in a few minutes."

Sitting outside on the sidewalk a few minutes later, Dana said, "It's boring out here."

"It's boring," Jack repeated, but then his attention was captured by a parade of ants.

Ron knew better than to agree.

"I'm bushed," he said, leaning back into the sun. He welcomed the rest. The day had grown hot, and a few lazy butterflies circled them. The roar of a plane could be heard competing with the birds and the tree frogs; across the street, a sprinkler system started up and made a grating noises. Fluffy clouds floated by the sun, occasionally casting shadows.

Dana was right. It was boring.

"I wish I had my game system," Ron said.

"It's not fair," Dana pouted. "Amelia says that there's a great big lake and a beach to swim at and we can't go because of the stupid house."

"We have to fix it, Dana, to sell it."

"I know! But I don't like it. Paint smells."

"It smells good," Ron insisted. He was proud of his efforts that morning. He rubbed at the paint stains on his pants and smiled. "It's looking nice up there. Jack, don't go into the bushes!"

"You'll be eaten by a tick," Dana warned.

"No, I won't!"

Ron and Dana got up from the pavement and retrieved him, wriggling and squealing, from the depths of the jungle-like growth. Jack wasn't happy, but Ron tickled him and that took his mind off the indignity of it. They sat on the pavement again, and amused themselves by throwing tiny stones to the sidewalk on the other side of the road.

They were enjoying themselves; then Dana, who had gotten to her feet to see where the last stone had landed, froze in place. Her face, expressive even in the calmest moments, had gone white. She was staring towards the old Victorian.

Ron got up and touched her shoulder. She jumped.

"What's the matter?" he asked.

She looked wide-eyed at him, then thrust her finger towards the mansion.

"Did you see it?"

Ron looked towards the house, always in shadow thanks to the trees, and saw nothing.

"See what?"

"Something *moved*," Dana insisted. "One of the branches by the porch. Like someone's *there*."

Ron's heart was pounding, but he couldn't let the younger ones see that. They'd panic. Besides, he wasn't sure he *wanted* anything to be there.

"No one's there, Dana. Amelia said it's empty. It was probably just the wind."

She threw up her arms. "What wind?"

She was right. There wasn't even a breeze.

"Maybe it was a cat."

She gave him an exasperated look.

"Sure," she said, her voice dripping with sarcasm. "An awfully big cat."

Ron shuddered.

At that moment, however, they heard something that put all thoughts of ghosts and prowlers right out of their heads. Behind them, at the other end of the road, came a parade of yapping dogs, managed by the sturdy figure of Mrs. Jurta and trailed by Amelia. The dogs jumped around so much that Ron couldn't count how many there were.

Jack, frightened by the noisy animals, drew near to Ron and took hold of his jeans with one hand. Ron could feel his trembling through the cloth.

Dana shrieked, "Amelia!" and ran to meet her.

Mrs. Jurta struggled to keep the dogs under control, but Ron had serious doubts about her ability, so he moved to pick Jack up just in case. But before he could, the little boy bolted for the house, screaming Julia's name.

Mrs. Jurta yelled, "Quiet! Down! Hello, there, young man," she said to Ron, speaking loudly over her charges. "It's all right, they're all friendly."

Some of the dogs tried to escape their leashes, but with a few more commands from Mrs. Jurta, the dogs sat - except for one small black and white dog. He strained at the leash, his tail going a mile a minute.

"I think Packer likes you," she said.

Ron took a step closer and put out his hand. Packer sniffed and joyfully licked it. He patted Packer's back, and the dog leaped all over his arm, trying to lick his face. Ron noticed that one of Packer's ears had been torn and healed over.

He observed Dana sitting on the pavement with a large, coal-gray puppy in her lap, licking her face. Amelia was next to her, cuddling a tiger-striped puppy, and the two were chattering away.

"No doubt about it," said Mrs. Jurta, taking advantage of the quiet to wipe her forehead. "He likes you."

A bang at the side door had all the dogs on their feet and barking again.

Julia, with a cringing Jack wrapped around her neck, hurried over and stopped short when she saw what the fuss was about.

"Oh!" she said. "Hello!"

"Sorry about the ruckus," Mrs. Jurta greeted her. "They get a little excited when they meet new people."

Jack shuddered and buried his face in Julia's neck.

"Not at all," Julia said. "We just aren't used to having dogs around, are we, Jack?"

He shook his head, and Mrs. Jurta clucked her tongue sympathetically. She lifted a hand full of leashes.

"If you ever decide that you need a dog," she said, "let me know."

Julia laughed. "I think we're all set, but thank you. I don't think we've met before. I'm Julia Lamontaigne. This is Jack, Ron, and Dana."

"Helen Jurta. I'm awfully glad to see a young family moving in. It's nice to have a young, stable presence in this neighborhood, not to mention that Amelia's been looking for someone to play with. Do you want to play with Packer?"

She offered the leash to Ron and he took it, feeling a little awkward. Packer, after leaping around him for a few minutes, sat down for a long, hard scratch.

"I'm afraid we're not staying," Julia said. "We're just here for the summer."

Ron thought that Aunt Julia must be getting tired of explaining that to everyone.

"Oh?" The older woman glanced at Amelia. A mixture of pity and concern crossed her weathered face, but it faded quickly.

She brightened and turned back to Julia. "Well, you never know. You might change your mind. When I first arrived here, I had no intention of staying. Now, nearly fifty years later, people are starting to wonder when I'll leave!"

The two little girls squealed suddenly as the gray puppy licked Dana's face. She giggled and wrapped her arms around the dog who seemed content to stay right there.

"Now *that*," said Mrs. Jurta, "is a nice thing to see. You know, that poor little puppy was abused before I got him. Wouldn't even come out of his crate, and he took two weeks to adjust to Amelia. And now he's thick as thieves with Rona there..."

"Dana," Aunt Julia corrected.

She carried on like she hadn't heard, "...just as if they'd been pals for years. That's love at first sight if I've ever seen it."

"Yes..."

Ron heard the caution in his aunt's voice. Dana was prone to getting attached to things quickly, and she'd wanted a dog for years. Dana's potential obsession had to be stopped before it started. Ron stood with leash in hand, wondering how to do that while Packer, having scratched every reachable inch of himself, went to the end of the leash to sniff around in the bushes.

Julia asked, "Where do you get all of these dogs?"

Mrs. Jurta looked at them with pride. "I'm their foster mother," she said. "Whenever the ASPCA gets overloaded with rescues, they send some of them to me. I care for them, train them, and report any anomalies to the office. In return, they pick up the vet's bills for me."

"That must be a lot of work."

"It can be, but I'm retired so I've got the time. Amelia is a big help when she can make it. I've always loved animals, so this is sort of a dream come true for me."

"How nice," Julia commented politely.

"It is. I've taught here in Franklin for twenty five years and I've lived here twice that. I think I know just about everyone who lives here, and I'm friends with most of them. You'll find this to be a friendly, safe neighborhood, Mrs. Lamontaigne. Even though some of the tenants in your house were a bit... well, strange. We haven't had any violence here in, oh, twenty years now. Yes, just twenty years ago this year, as a matter of fact."

Packer came dancing away from the bushes and began to sniff around Julia's feet, causing Jack to cling even tighter. Ron, intrigued by the last remark, tried with no avail to convince the dog to go back to the bushes.

Julia struggled to loosen Jack's death grip. "That's certainly good to hear."

"Just tell Packer to sit," Mrs. Jurta advised Ron. "He's a good dog, but he needs a firm hand."

Ron did as he was told and Packer dropped to his haunches, cocking his head at Ron and looking wounded. Then he was up again, running in happy circles around him.

"He's energetic," Julia observed.

Ron couldn't stand it anymore. "Mrs. Jurta, what happened twenty years ago?" he blurted out.

He hadn't realized that the girls were listening in until Dana said, "Did it have something to do with the haunted house?"

"Haunted house!" Mrs. Jurta chuckled. "What haunted house? Don't tell me you kids believe in *ghosts*."

"She means the old house at the end of the street," Ron said patiently.

"The one that's empty," Amelia added. She nodded at Ron, as though they were in this together.

"Ohhh..." Mrs. Jurta nodded sagely. "The Lang house. It does look spooky, doesn't it?"

"But it isn't haunted, right Mrs. Jurta?" Julia asked pointedly. Jack seemed to be shrinking in her grasp. "It's just an old, sad, empty house."

"Yes." Mrs. Jurta caught on. "Yes, it's a very sad house, with a very sad history."

She turned to Ron. "The crime you were asking about happened there – twenty years ago, a man beat his wife to death in that house."

Dana gasped and exchanged horrified glances with Amelia. Ron felt a cold shiver run down his back. Mrs. Jurta was pleased with their reaction and seemed to be waiting for a cue.

Ron was happy to supply it: "Why did he kill her?"

"Oh, jealousy, of course. Stephanie Lang was an artist - young, beautiful, and talented. She was from a good Boston family, and she was already becoming famous when she and her husband moved up here, must be twenty-two years ago now. Such a tragic loss."

"What happened?" Ron persisted, ignoring the warning look that Julia shot him.

Mrs. Jurta ignored her, too, and settled in to tell her story.

"Well now, I didn't really know the Langs much at all when they first moved here," she said. "I still had my kids at home and I was busy teaching, but Stephanie was everywhere. Her husband spent most of his time out of town working, or so he said, but she stayed here. She set up a studio in the house, and there were always people going in and out of it. She had this way about her - she knew how to make you feel comfortable.

"I first got to know her when she asked if she could paint my daughter, Elizabeth. Liz was a cute kid in those days, so of course I said yes." She paused, smiling nostalgically. "They got to be good friends, the two of them. Stephanie gave Liz one of the sketches she had done, but the portrait - she submitted that to a gallery in Maine. It's still there."

Despite the roundabout way she was telling the story, Ron found himself fascinated by it. It sounded like something he'd see on TV or in a movie. Julia and the girls seemed interested as well.

He asked, "And what about her husband?"

Her eyes narrowed. "Oh, he was a very different story. He was a very ambitious man, very handsome." She paused again, thinking. "His name was Brad, well-educated, from a political family somewhere. He worked in the art world, too, but he was a dealer, not an artist - he owned a gallery in Concord. Real snob, liked to drive around town in his fancy car and make a big show."

"Why did he kill her?" Dana asked, almost whispering.

"Well, Stephanie was gorgeous and talented, and her husband didn't like it one bit. He wasn't an artist, and he didn't really have any talent as a business man. He was possessive, jealous of her abilities. They kept up a good front, but it was easy to see that there was trouble. I tried to talk to Stephanie about it, but she just brushed me off and told me everything was fine. I didn't push it, mores the pity. Maybe if I had, she'd still be alive today."

She paused for dramatic effect, and then continued.

"One cold night in October, Brad came home in a bad mood. He was losing money and, just a week before, his gallery had been robbed and the thieves took almost everything. His insurance would cover what had been taken, but he had been in debt long before that. Lang had burned all his bridges with the banks and friends, and he had no one to turn to. So he came home early that night and accused Stephanie of seeing other men. They started to fight and he began hitting her. By the time he was done, she was dead."

Dana and Amelia both looked sick and Julia seemed horrified. Ron wanted to urge Mrs. Jurta to finish, but she was busy trying to calm the dogs down again. When she was able to speak, she said, "Where was I?"

"Brad had just killed his wife," said Ron.

"Oh, right. He was a cold one, that man. To put the police off the scent, he called 911 and reported finding her dead and the house robbed. He put on a good show. The police believed him, and even took him to the hospital for a sedative."

"What's that?" Amelia asked.

"It's a knock-out pill," Ron answered, wanting to get back to the story.

Mrs. Jurta nodded. "As I said, they took him to the hospital and everyone was all worried about him and sending meals to his house and everything. And then it came out that his wife had a million dollar insurance policy on her life. Presto – just like that, everyone knew."

"Knew?" Julia asked.

"That he'd killed his wife for two reasons – jealousy and money. He needed the money to pay off his bills, you see, and the quickest way to get is was by bumping off the woman he'd grown to hate."

Mrs. Jurta stated her conclusion like it was the summation in an Agatha Christie novel. She seemed to enjoy it far more than what Ron thought was right; but still, it was an exciting tale.

He looked down the street at the old empty house and shuddered when he tried to imagine the scene.

Dana asked, "Then what happened? Did he get away?"

"Oh, no, he didn't get away. He was arrested, tried, and sentenced to life. That house has been empty ever since. They say that his family refuses to sell it, that they still think he's innocent, but *I* think that they *can't* sell it. No one wants to live in a murder house, whether or not it's haunted."

As though on cue, a breeze whipped down the street and tugged on their clothing, cooling their skin. The trees and bushes swallowing up the old house waved and bowed toward it, then grew still again.

*As silent as a tomb,* Ron thought.

An alarm went off. Mrs. Jurta looked at her watch and said, "Time to feed these hungry critters. Hand Packer over to me, young man. If you feed him, you'll have to keep him. It was nice meeting you, Mrs. Lamontaigne."

"'Julia'."

"All right, then you must call me Helen. Come along, Amelia."

"Oh, good bye, Horatio!" Dana bent and hugged the dog close. "Isn't he the cutest dog you've ever seen, Aunt Julia? He's only a month old and he already knows how to sit."

"Horatio?" Julia said. "That's an unusual name for a dog, isn't it?"

"One of the volunteers at the ASPCA is a big Shakespeare fan, and he thought it'd be funny to name him after one of the characters in Hamlet." Mrs. Jurta sighed. "He's a very smart little pup. He'll make a great pet."

"Isn't he a little big for a puppy that's only a month old?" Julia asked.

"Actually, he's a little *small*. He was the runt of the litter and someone saw him being thrown from a car on Route 101."

"That's *horrible*," Dana gasped.

"Feel free to stop by whenever you want," Mrs. Jurta said cheerfully. "And if you ever want to take Horatio for a walk, you be sure to let me know, okay?"

"Oh, gosh, sure!"

"Come along, Amelia," Mrs. Jurta said, lifting the leashes. The dogs jumped up and jerked forward, pulling their foster owner along. "It was nice meeting and talking with you all. We should get together some time."

Dana waved and ran alongside of Amelia for a few steps before stopping at Amelia's driveway. Horatio kept looking back at Dana, confused that she was not going with him. Amelia urged him to keep going, and soon they disappeared into Mrs. Jurta's yard.

"Come on, everyone," Julia said. "It's lunch time. They're gone, Jack." She kissed his head. "You can let go now."

The two of them went into the house, and the screen door snapped shut behind them. Dana trudged slowly to where Ron was standing, her shoulders slumped.

"What a cute puppy," she said. "I miss him already."

She wanted sympathy, but Ron wasn't feeling it. He was still thinking about the house. It loomed at the base of the road, an eyesore to some and a mystery to him. The murder had been solved, justice was served, and the matter was done. But something about the house seemed disturbed and unsettled, restless even.

It spoke of unfinished business.

Dana followed his eyes to the house, squinting in the sunlight. "Do you think it's haunted by her?" she whispered.

*What if it is?* he wondered. *What if Stephanie Lang still wanders the halls, asking why he killed her?*

It was a good plot for a movie, but this was real life, and Ron Budd didn't believe in ghosts or fairy tales.

Dana persisted. "What do you think, Ron?"

His stomach growled loudly.

"I think I'm hungry," he said.

They went inside and left the ghosts to themselves.

# 14

The sun had long since set when Julia slipped outside on the porch with her rosary and her journal. It was quiet, the street dimly lit by flickering blue television lights through the windows of her neighbors' houses. She settled on the steps, brushed away a mosquito, and took a deep breath of the sweet scented summer air – exhausted, but not ready to go to sleep yet. She fingered her rosary and started her prayers, but her mind jumped through to-do lists and events of the past day, making it difficult to concentrate.

The kids were asleep inside, curled up side by side on layers of blankets and pillows. She hoped that it would be the last night they would have to sleep on the floor.

Crickets sounded in the night air. A car passed by the house, its headlights shining briefly in Julia's face. She shook her head to clear her thoughts and hastily finished the rosary. After she was done, she opened her journal, adjusted her position on the porch so that the porch light shone on the page, then nibbled the end of her pen as she tried to figure out what to write.

She hadn't written anything in a couple of days. So much had happened.

She thought about the kids. They hadn't been in Franklin all that long, and yet already she was seeing them relaxing. Dana, of course, was excited about her room, her budding friendship with Amelia, and the puppies. They couldn't adopt the puppy, and she'd be leaving Amelia behind when they went back to Springfield. What kind of toll would that take - not just on Dana, but on Amelia as well? She was a sweet kid, but a liar. And where was her mother? Julia couldn't recall anyone having mentioned her.

She pushed that aside and thought of Jack. He was still clingy, yet he was eagerly helping wherever he could, and even leaving beloved Yellow Teddy inside whenever he went out to play. That was an improvement, for sure.

Ron was a different story, of course. He was subtly fighting her authority on most things. The other kids still instinctively obeyed him first. In all the time that Julia had been guardian, she had yet to see a smile crack his solemn expression.

Yet there was hope there, too, she thought as she recalled the incident with the squirrel. It had been nice to see how her new, temporary neighbors had stepped in to help, without her even having to ask. It made this whole summer adventure seem a little less lonely. She thought of the girls clinging to her, terrified by the little rodent - and Ron, thrusting himself into the fray and earning the admiration of the older boys. The expression on his face had been interesting: embarrassed, pleased, and almost pathetically eager to receive it. Perhaps it was a good thing that she had decided to hire J. C. and his crew to fix up the lawn. At first she'd done so only get rid of the grubs and make the house more marketable. Now she thought that Ron might enjoy the chance to interact with other boys a little closer to his own age.

Ron seemed to take a shine to Officer Wilde, too, listening to him and watching him with keen attention. Julia wondered how much Ron was missing his father. He'd be too proud to admit such a thing, of course; but at his age, he probably felt his father's absence more than the others.

Julia yawned. She looked at her watch, surprised to see that is was 11 o'clock. It explained why she felt exhausted.

She wrote quickly, *Good day today. Painted kids' rooms and met a neighbor, Mrs. Jurta. Learned about the spooky house at the end of the street. Will have to make sure the kids aren't unnerved by the story.*

She closed her journal and stood up, stretching. In the distance, the old Victorian house loomed ominous and dark. She could just make out some details, and despite herself, felt a cold shiver wiggle down her back. It looked like a haunted house out of a movie. No wonder the kids had been frightened by it. Thank goodness the murder had been solved and the murderer caught.

Yet as she turned away from it, Julia couldn't help feeling that she was being watched.

*Honestly, Julia, there's nothing there. You're as bad as the kids.*

She didn't notice the non-descript black car that was parked several houses down from hers and, of course, she didn't see that the car was occupied. Even if she had, she wouldn't have been able to see that the driver was watching her house, gripping the steering wheel tightly, thinking, *the matter is closed. There's no reason for anyone to suspect. I'm safe.*

Nevertheless, the driver remained, watching as Julia went inside.

The driver knew that as long as the kids and their aunt were in the neighborhood, there was that slight, slight chance that they would uncover what had been hidden. Surely there was no reason for them to go poking around, but what if they did?

*Stephanie...*

Some problems never went away. Even after death, Stephanie still seemed so present, and just as dangerous as she had been in life.

*No one will find out. I won't let them.*

If necessary, something would have to be done about the little family. Too much had been risked, too much endured to allow things to fall apart now.

The idea that summer would soon be over and that the family would return to Massachusetts was reassuring. *Surely,* the driver thought, *there won't be enough time for them to cause any damage. Yes, they'll leave, and I'll be safe.*

Only when the lights went out in the little house did the nondescript black car leave.

# 15

Despite her exhaustion, Julia tossed and turned on her makeshift bed, going in and out of dreams, most featuring loathsome men with blood-stained knives or bats. She woke up soaked in sweat, with Jack's arm draped around her neck.

She groaned and turned to look at the clock. 5:30 a. m. The dawn was still lavender-gray, and it was no use trying to go back to sleep.

She dragged herself out of bed and paddled into the kitchen. She needed coffee.

A list of needed supplies was taped to the refrigerator door. Julia snatched up a pencil and wrote in bold, heavy lines, *Air conditioner for the living room.* She underlined it three times. It was an expense that she'd hoped to avoid, but now she didn't care about the money.

"No wonder the wallpaper's peeling," she said aloud. "It's so awful in this house."

She prepared herself a strong cup of instant coffee and dropped an ice cube in it, then sat on the porch steps where it was somewhat cooler.

She sipped her coffee slowly, relishing the bitter taste and the feeling of the caffeine coursing through her deadened senses. She felt like a zombie coming back to life.

Her nerves were still shaky from the dreams, and she was too restless to sit quietly. After finishing her coffee, Julia went inside and changed quickly into her jogging clothes and sneakers. She grabbed her iPod as she went back outside, but she was too nervous to put her earphones on and risk blocking out any sounds of distress from the kids, so she left them on her shoulders and was content to listen to her music from a distance.

As she jogged, her lungs worked hard against the oppressive humidity, but she could feel her spirits brightening. She ran faster and faster, almost giddy from the adrenaline rush. Worries and cares fell to the wayside. A favorite song came on and she found herself singing along in between gasps for air. As the music swelled to a crescendo, she closed her eyes, just for a minute, and belted out the last few words.

That's when she ran into the police car.

She bounced off the door and back into the present, hearing Wilde's laughter through the open window.

"Assault on a police vehicle," he said. "Very unusual. Are you all right?"

She pulled the earphones off and returned to the window. "I'm sorry, I wasn't paying attention," she said.

"I could see that. You all right?"

"Oh, fine, just embarrassed. I was caught up in a song."

She was dripping sweat and dressed in mismatched, stretched out workout gear. He was dressed in his dark blue uniform, his black hair brushed, remarkably alert for so early in the morning.

"Hey, it happens," he said. "I like to embarrass Amelia sometimes by singing along with her pop tunes. Can't stand them, but I know the lyrics."

She laughed. "There's a healthy relationship. How is Amelia?"

*And now that I think of it, how's her mother? Where is her mother? How come no one ever mentions her?*

"She's good. I just walked her over to Mrs. Jurta's." He looked up at the sky. "Looks like it's going to be a nice day."

Julia made a face. "I guess it would seem that way if you're sitting in an air conditioned car. It's a sauna out here."

"We're going to have thunderstorms later tonight."

"That's good to hear." She wiped her face, trying not to think what her hair looked like. If it were true to form, it would be frizzing in the humidity, not exactly the model of sophistication. She wished that she'd thought it over more before going outside.

"It should break up the humidity, anyway," Wilde said. He nodded towards the house. "How are things going?"

"Good. We found some beds in the storage room yesterday, so I can get the kids off the floor and into real beds."

Actually, the storage room was crammed with enough furniture to stock at least three yards sales. Apparently no one who'd lived in the little house ever thought to throw anything away. Julia had no idea what they were going to do with it all.

Robert was saying, "Nice. My offer still stands, by the way - if you ever need help with something, just let me know. Things are slow around here this time of year, so I can make the time."

Julia hesitated. It was a nice offer, with no strings attached, and he seemed very sincere. She could use an extra hand, especially since the bureaus they found were too heavy for her and Ron to lug upstairs.

But what about Mrs. Wilde? Was there even a Mrs. Wilde? Robert didn't strike her as the type of man who wouldn't marry the mother of his child, but there was no ring on his finger. Amelia spoke constantly of her babysitters and never of her mother, but that could mean anything.

"Is there something wrong?" he asked.

Julia hadn't realized how long her contemplative pause had lasted. Scrambling to cover, she found herself saying, "Actually, I have some furniture that's too much for Ron and me to move alone. I hate to ask, but would you mind...?"

He held up a hand. "Say no more. Just let me know when."

"Thank you so much. That would take such a load off my mind, not to mention my back."

Wilde smiled back at her. His smile touched his eyes and crinkled them at the corners.

"Any time," he said.

A door creaked, and one of the neighbors waddled out to get the newspaper. Julia took a step back from the car, keeping a friendly smile on her face.

"Well, thanks again," she said. "I'd better let you get back to work and catch some bad guys or jaywalkers or something."

"Jaywalkers, if we're lucky," he said. "It's a never-ending crime scene here in Franklin. See you around, neighbor."

And with that, he was off.

Julia waved to the neighbor across the street and then started for the porch, shaking her head.

"Oh, I need a big strong man to move furniture," she muttered to herself. "Way to be a modern feminist, Julia. Your suffragette fore-mothers would be so proud." Still, it was nice to have a friendly neighbor. Especially one as cute as Robert Wilde.

A noise caught her ear and she turned to see Mrs. Jurta walking briskly up the street, preceded by a dark Labrador. Julia's first instinct was to run for the shelter of the house, but then Mrs. Jurta spotted her and waved.

Julia was caught. She stopped and waved back.

"Good morning!" Mrs. Jurta chirped. She stopped to let the dog sniff appreciatively around the mailbox.

"Good morning, Mrs. Jurta."

"Please, call me Helen. I was just taking Dexter here for a walk."

"Another pound puppy?" Julia asked.

"No, actually, this is my dog. We met when I was going to the pet store for some food and he was just a little guy. We took one look at each other and that, as they say, was that."

She patted Dexter's back, and Julia was just about to make an excuse and jog away when Helen nodded sharply down the road.

"Was that Officer Wilde I saw you talking to?"

"Yes, it was." Julia cursed her innate politeness, which rendered it impossible to simply excuse herself. She didn't want to listen to another long story about some other old city scandal. She began to jog in place lightly, hoping that Helen would get the message.

She didn't seem to notice. "What a nice man," she said. "He hasn't been here long, but he and his daughter are both peaches. They came up from Manchester, you know."

"I didn't."

"Oh, yes – right after his wife left him, I think, but I don't know too much about it. He doesn't say anything about it, but Amelia does and sometimes she gets the story mixed up."

"Poor Amelia," Julia said. "Does she see her mother?"

"On occasion. She's got visiting rights, but can't squeeze her daughter into her busy schedule. Her mother's a doctor, you know. I think she shouldn't allow her work to interfere with her daughter, but Amelia doesn't see it that way. According to her, her mother practically walks on water and can't make the time because she's saving the world from disease. I don't have the heart to tell her any differently."

Julia couldn't help but think that honesty was the best policy, even if it would be painful. In perpetuating the lies about her mother, Amelia was falling into the habit of avoiding every discomfort by the same method. What kind of a strain was it putting on her father?

But this was a family issue, and Julia couldn't get involved. It wasn't as though she didn't have enough family issues of her own.

"I've got to get going," Mrs. Jurta said, returning to her cheerful self. "Dexter needs his exercise and so do I. If you need anything, Julia, you be sure to let me know. I've lived in this town a long time, and I know everything and everyone in it. You need something, or if one of the kids does, you just say so."

"I will," she promised.

Julia jogged for about ten more minutes, and then went inside for a shower. She managed to eat something and was busily washing floors when the kids got up. Ron was, as usual, the first one up and the first one to volunteer to help with the work.

They went upstairs together to inspect the bedrooms. It was stifling there, despite the open windows and the fans.

Julia wiped her moist forehead and turned to Ron. "If we stay in this house with this heat, I'm going to have a meltdown. We'll do some errands and find a restaurant with air conditioning."

They went to find Dana. She seemed nearly comatose in the living room, watching cartoons.

"Everyone up," Julia said. "We're going out."

"Where?" Dana asked, brightening.

"Somewhere with air conditioning. Ron, grab my list from the fridge, will you? Jack, go find your shoes. Dana, put on some shorts that don't have holes."

They took off as Julia packed up her laptop and grabbed her phone. There were several messages, including - to her surprise - one from the kids' paternal grandmother, Miriam Budd.

Miriam had been Julia's main opponent in the "amicable" custody battle. Although it was a civilized dispute, handled largely through lawyers and emails, Julia lost ten pounds from anxiety during that memorable month. After all the thinly veiled accusations of neglect, pride, greed, and inability, it was a wonder that they were still on speaking terms. The only good thing about the whole mess was that they'd managed to keep the kids out of it. Although there had been moments when Julia found herself wishing that Mrs. Budd would just disappear, she didn't want the children to have to pick between their grandmother and their aunt.

At the sound of Mrs. Budds' voice, it struck Julia that she had completely forgotten to have the kids call. She felt a twinge of guilt and apprehension.

*Oh, am I going to be in trouble.*

Miriam Budd's voice was measured and carefully controlled. Having lost the legal battle, she had reverted to icy friendliness. It was difficult to miss the pointed sarcasm.

"Hi, Julia, it's Miriam. I'm just calling to say good morning to the children. I'm sorry I missed their call yesterday. I know you have a lot to do fixing up that old place, so please just have them call me whenever it's convenient. Goodbye."

Julia deleted it, feeling her stress levels elevate. Lingering behind every encounter with Miriam was the threat of a renewed attack. When the victory had been declared, Miriam made no bones about the issue merely being postponed. Every time she came over to the house, she made a big deal about noticing what little changes there were, or questioning the children about their meals and bedtimes. Julia felt like a bug under a microscope, alive but in danger of being pinned at any moment.

And then, of course, there had been that crack about her then-boyfriend, Ryan, way back in the beginning. It wasn't bad enough that Miriam and her daughter insinuated that he'd leave Julia rather than help with the new responsibilities: they had to be *right* on top of that.

*Ryan.*

Julia hadn't thought about him in a long time, and the image brought a lump to her throat.

She pushed the memories aside and looked at her phone again. The last message was from her parents, just saying hello. She saved that one.

Julia put her phone in her purse and then checked her reflection in the TV. Her hair was a little disheveled, so she spent a few moments fixing it. Her emotions were all over the place, and her fingers shook as they tried to tame her unruly dark hair. She shouldn't let Miriam get to her so much. It was only right that she be worried about the children. They were her grandchildren, and her one remaining link with Timothy. Julia, having won, could afford to be more generous with both Miriam and her husband.

Ron came in. "Do we need the grocery bags?"

"No, I don't think so," Julia said. She thought she was too con-templative – her family had always teased her about overthinking things. She was going to have to learn to stop that. There was too much danger in mulling the past.

She flashed the serious boy a smile. "Let's go."

# 16

R on was glad that they were leaving the house for the day. Although Aunt Julia took way too much time picking up the simplest of supplies, it was still better than hanging around the overheated house, listening to Dana talk about that dog. Of course, if he'd been able to convince his sister to check out the old Victorian with him, that would have been a different matter. But Dana was convinced that the house was haunted, and she refused point-blank.

Julia was solemn after checking her phone messages. Although she put on a good show, neither Dana nor Ron were fooled. Both knew that there were lean times coming, and they'd been plotting and planning ways to both make and save money to help out.

"Maybe we can ask the lawyer to give us our money early," Dana suggested while they waited for Julia to come out of the post office. The kids were sitting outside on the shaded steps of the building, but it was still awfully hot.

Ron knew that Dana was referring to the trust fund that their parents had set up for them. He remembered Hall talking to Aunt Julia about it right in front of them, as though they couldn't understand.

"That's for college," Ron replied.

Dana shrugged. "I don't care. I don't want to go to college."

"Yes, you do."

"No, I don't - and anyway, it'll help Aunt Julia, so I think we should give it to her now. What do you think, Jack?"

Jack nodded.

Ron considered it. Perhaps it was a good idea. It would buy them some more time and take some of the worry from Aunt Julia's face. But hadn't Hall said that they couldn't touch the money until they were a certain age? Maybe if they all asked for it together and insisted, he would give it up. It was their money after all.

He was still working this through when Dana, exasperated, said, "When are we going to leave? I'm dying out here!"

Jack's face was pink and Ron tried to fan them both with his hands. "She said it'd only be a minute. Come on, guys, keep thinking of other things we can do."

"Yard sale?" Dana shrugged.

Julia came out at that point, and they abruptly ended their discussion.

The next stop was the hardware store. Ron and Julia needed chair rail, and John Irwin Junior had a good stock on hand. Ron and Dana loaded it into the cart while Julia talked about the renovations with the curious store owner.

When she learned that the chair rail was for her room, Dana became very excited. She pestered Ron with questions, like why it was called "chair rail".

"I don't know," Ron answered. "I guess maybe it keeps the chairs from bumping against the wall." He held out a rail. "Put this one back."

"Why?" Dana scowled. "What's wrong with it?"

"It's got a crack in it, see?" He pointed.

She put it back and got another, giving it a cursory once-over before handing it to him. "When do you think the room will be finished?"

"Probably two or three days," Ron said, proud to be able to show off a little of his knowledge. "We have to let the paint dry and with this humidity, it takes a little longer."

151

Dana clapped her hands. "I can't wait! It's going to be such a pretty room."

"Yeah, it'll look all right."

"Do you like yours? Is it what you wanted?"

Ron considered it. It was going to be a bright, but thoroughly male room. With the vaulted ceilings, he could mount a hoop for some basketball and even mark the hardwood floors to make the place really look like a court. There was room for his desk and computer, all his equipment, and Jack's toys from home - provided, of course, that the two of them got rid of some stuff.

Yes, he thought it would be pretty close to what he'd want, if he was staying. But there was no use in getting attached to the place, when they'd just leave it at the end of summer.

"It's all right," he said. "Jack likes it, don't you?"

Jack looked up from his seat in the front of the cart. He was quiet today, earnestly studying a design brochure that Julia had given him earlier. His blonde hair looked limp and tired from the heat, and his heavy eyelids spoke of a bad night's sleep.

"What?" he asked. "What did you say?"

"Do you like your new room?" Dana asked. "The one you're sharing with Ron?"

He nodded. "And the ducky bathroom."

"Oh, yeah, that's *way* cool," Ron assured him.

Jack went back to his brochure, looking pleased. Then he looked up again, his face crestfallen. "Where's Yellow Teddy?" he asked.

"You left him at home," Dana said.

Jack pouted.

"Oh, stop," Ron said, tickling his neck. "You always lose him in the stores, remember? Then we have to go and find him before they throw him away."

"Stop! Stop!" Jack giggled, and when his brother did, the little boy threw his arms around Ron's neck and clutched him tight. After a second, Ron pulled away and ruffled the boy's hair.

"Good boy, Jack," he said.

They waited for Julia and John Irwin to finish talking. Dana sat down on the extended bottom rack of the cart, resting her head in her hands.

"I've been in town ever since I was a kid," Irwin was saying. "I always like hearing what people are doing with their new places. My dad was a contractor and he helped out redoing nearly every old house in town, so Mike and I grew up in and out of all sorts of buildings. We knew every cubby hole, every secret entrance, every covered up window in town. My dad even worked at that old convent outside of town and we used to play in the underground tunnel over there."

"Underground tunnel?"

"Yep. They had an orphanage and a school, and it used to be so bitterly cold in the winter that they built a tunnel under the road separating the buildings so the orphans wouldn't get frostbite going to school. Your kids would love it. It's too bad the place was sold – otherwise, I'd have been able to show you around."

"It's all right," she smiled. "I think we've got enough to do with the house as it is."

"It doesn't sound like your renovations will take too long."

"No, not unless I need to replace that wall in the back room."

John looked puzzled. "The wall?"

"Oh, just the paneling, I think. It looks really, really tacky and it's starting to buckle. I'm probably going to have to tear it out, might rip out some of the wall with it."

Julia turned, relieved when she saw the cart filled. "Are we all set to go?" she asked hopefully.

Ron thought, *she's trying to get away from John Irwin.*

He didn't blame her: John Irwin Junior could talk almost as much as Mrs. Jurta, only he was less interesting. Maybe it was a New Hampshire thing.

"All set," Ron said.

"Excellent," Julia said. "Let's be on our way."

"I can check you out at that register there." John pointed to an unattended one.

The same bored-looking teenager was there, reading a different magazine. She seemed no more inclined to help than she had been the other day. She looked annoyed when they pulled the cart up next to her station.

Julia was swiping her credit card when the front doors opened, letting in a swirling mass of hot air and cigarette smoke. Ron didn't need to look up to know who had come in.

Sheila O'Reilly declared loudly, "Well, *hello* Budds! How are you this fine day?"

She stood with her fist planted on her hips, her faded shirt loosely covering her generous girth, and her short, dark hair plastered to her head from the heat.

Two teenagers flanked her. The girl looked a little like Sheila, with long, dark hair and bold make up. She was dressed very casually, her tight jeans making the most of her long legs.

"Oh, hello, Sheila," Julia said with a genuine smile. "How are you surviving the heat?"

"I'm loving it. This is my kind of weather. I keep trying to convince the old man to move to Florida, but he likes the snow, he likes his couch and TV, and there's no point in uprooting him. It'll just make him wither even more, right, Katy?"

Katy shrugged and muttered, "Yeah." She wore a set of oversized sunglasses and hadn't looked up from her cell phone since she first walked in.

Sheila gestured to her companion. "Have you guys met the grandkids? This is Katy and Dylan. Katy's fifteen and Dylan's nearly fourteen. Guys, Julia Lamontaigne and her entourage: Ron, Dana, and Jack. Say hello."

"Hello," Katy muttered. Her voice was musical, despite her disinterest.

"Hey, sup," was Dylan's response. Dylan was shorter than Katy, with curly reddish-brown hair, bright eyes, and an open, friendly expression. He put his phone away and gave Ron an approving nod. His legs and arms were scratched and bruised. Ron thought he must be a skateboarder.

"'Sup," Ron replied.

Dana seemed put off by them. Jack's only response was to take hold of Julia's shirt again.

"Whatcha getting today? More paint?" asked Sheila.

Ron wondered how she knew that they had gotten any paint.

"Just some chair rail to finish off the rooms," said Aunt Julia. "We're nearly done with the upstairs. By the way, thank you for telling me about the furniture in the storage room. It looks like we have everything we need now."

"Well, I'm glad someone's using it. My husband had to put up with my rants for days about people being so wasteful. By the way, the last time I was in the house, I noticed a few things that…"

Julia signed the receipt while nodding her head to Sheila's stream of talk.

Unsure of what to do, Ron shoved his hands in his pocket and listened. Dylan began nudging Ron's elbow. Ron ignored him until the nudging became a painful pinch. He turned, rubbing his elbow.

"What?" he asked, annoyed.

Dylan put both palms up. "Easy. I just wanted to know - you guys are in that house on Whipple Avenue, right?"

Ron was puzzled by the question. "Yeah. So?"

"So, nothing. I just wondered if you've noticed the old Lang place yet, that's all."

"The old *what* place?"

"The old Lang place. You know, the cobwebby one that looks like it's from every horror movie ever made."

"The haunted house?" Dana asked.

"Yeah, that one."

"We've seen it," Ron said. "What about it?"

Dylan stepped in closer to speak quietly. "Have you, you know, checked it out yet?"

"No," Ron answered.

"It's closed up," Dana said. "No trespassing."

"I don't mean break in," Dylan said. "I just meant, have you been up close? They say, at certain times, you can still hear the screams."

A cold chill raced down Ron's spine.

"What screams?" Dana whispered, turning white.

"Of the murdered woman, of course. Some of the locals around here say that she's still there, wandering. She doesn't know her husband killed her."

"They didn't bury her?"

"He means," Katy broke in, "the *ghost* of the woman who was killed. Come on, Dyl, you're scaring the kids."

"I just want to see if they've heard anything." He studied them, curious. "Have you?"

"I don't believe in ghosts," Ron said firmly.

"Everyone believes in ghosts, no matter what they say. How about you, Dana? You've heard something, I bet. Am I right?"

Dana bit her lip and looked at Ron for direction.

Dylan grinned. "You have! What did you hear?"

"Nothing," Ron said quickly. "We haven't gone near the place."

"Too scared?" Dylan sneered.

"No time," he shot back. "We've been helping Aunt Julia."

"Well, that's as good an excuse as any."

"Knock it off, Dylan!" Katy said.

"Only little kids believe in ghosts," Ron snapped. "And I'm not scared of anything that's dead."

"But you're afraid of the house," Dylan taunted.

"This is stupid. It's just an old building." Ron tried to calm down. He had to set a good example for Dana and Jack. "There's nothing there."

"How would you know if you've never been near it? You can't be sure that there *isn't* something there."

"Neither can you, Dylan," Katy said. "It's not like you go and hang out there either, you know."

Dylan rolled his eyes and returned to Ron. "Okay, look, here's the thing - everyone knows that place is haunted. It's a fact and I want to prove it by getting something on camera. Have you seen anything even slightly mysterious?"

He seemed so sincere that Ron felt sorry for being so defensive. He shook his head. "No, sorry, I haven't."

"But I have," Dana piped up.

Dylan whipped around. "You *have?*" he squeaked.

"It was just the wind, Dana," Ron said nervously. He didn't want to get Dylan's hopes up and anyway, there was too much going on to start a ghost hunt.

Dana's chin lifted. She was going to be stubborn.

"It wasn't the wind. Something moved those bushes. I just couldn't see who..." she paused for effect, "or what it was that moved them."

"When was this?" Dylan demanded.

"Yesterday."

"What time?"

"Lunchtime."

"Ghosts don't come out in the daylight," Katy drawled. She pulled off her over-sized sunglasses to reveal large blue eyes. "They only appear at night when everyone's too tired to be very observant or smart."

"No, she could have seen one," Dylan said thoughtfully. "I mean, there are all sorts of apparitions and they all have their own rules."

As Dylan started grilling Dana on what she'd seen, Ron and Katy exchanged glances. She rolled her eyes and he grinned at her. Ron thought the whole topic was silly, but decided to let Dana and Dylan have their chills and thrills and be done with it.

Katy seemed to think the same thing. She shook her head again and returned to her cellphone.

Ron was momentarily disappointed in that she didn't want to talk with him, but he understood that she was a lot older. It was a compliment that they'd even shared that brief moment of sympathetic annoyance.

Dylan was saying, "We've got to stake this place out and watch it. If we can capture something on film, that'd be awesome."

"I don't have a camera," Dana said, "but Ron has a camera phone."

"No, I'm talking video," he responded. "My grandfather has a digital movie camera at home. I'll talk him into letting me borrow it. If we all work together on this, we can take shifts and get it all on film. What do you say?"

"Come on, Dylan," Katy groaned.

"It's not like they have anything better to do," Dylan shot back. He turned to Ron and Dana. "Come on, guys! How often is it that you have a real live ghost in your backyard? This is, like, *epic!*"

Dana looked pleadingly at Ron. He didn't get her at all. When he'd suggested investigating the house, she told him that he was nuts. Then Dylan suggests it and now she's for it. To say that she was changeable and confusing would be putting it mildly.

He hesitated. He did want to investigate the house, and hanging out with another guy would be cool. Ron had been wishing for someone to hang out with, who knew how to shoot hoops and do guy things.

But there was Dana to consider. She was so easily swayed by other people, and Dylan seemed like he might be trouble. Cops usually didn't like it when people hung around boarded up houses and, if they got in real trouble, it might interfere with Aunt Julia's guardianship.

Of course, except for Officer Wilde, he hadn't seen a patrol car near the street and Ron thought it was more than likely that they'd never be caught. If he agreed, he risked getting into trouble with Aunt Julia and the law. If he didn't, he'd look like a coward. It didn't take a genius to see that Dylan would never let him live it down, even if Dana did.

Ron was spared making a decision. Just then, Julia glanced at her watch and exclaimed loudly about the time.

"We have to get going, too," Sheila O'Reilly said. "Lots to do today. We should get together sometime. Are you coming to the Fourth of July picnic?"

Julia shook her head. "This is the first I've heard of it."

"You should definitely come. It's the highlight of the Franklin social calendar, and we'll all be there. There are games, food, and a fireworks display, provided it doesn't rain."

"Like it did last year," Katy said flatly.

"That was disappointing. You should come. It's a good way to meet the neighbors."

"I'll think about it, thank you," Julia said quietly.

"And don't forget about my Tupperware party tonight," Sheila added

"Oh, I don't think I can make it. I'm sorry."

"No worries. It was nice to have the young ones meet today. We should get them together again sometime, right, guys?"

Dylan jumped right in. "*Totally*," he said. "Actually, we were already planning to hangout so we can trade skating techniques, right, Ron?"

He shot Ron an anxious look, and Ron nodded. "That, and shoot some baskets," he agreed.

"Absolutely." Relieved, Dylan feigned a toss and then gave him a victory sign. "Got to get ready for the Celtics. They'll be calling any day now. Okay with you, Grandma?"

"I don't have a problem with it," she said. "How about you, Julia?"

"No, that's fine."

"Takes a load off of my mind. Do you have any idea how hard it is to occupy two teenagers for an entire summer? It's more than this old lady can handle. Come on, you two. We need shingles. Later, guys."

She walked away. Dylan gave Ron a thumbs-up signs as he and Katy followed.

Julia didn't say anything until they were in the minivan and driving towards Concord.

"Sheila's grandkids seemed nice," she said.

"They are," Dana answered. "Dylan knows all about…"

Ron shot her a cautionary look, but she pretended not to notice and continued, "…skateboarding. I can't wait to try it!"

"I don't want anyone getting hurt on the skateboards," Julia said. "They make me nervous. You can do them for now, but if I say 'no more' that's it."

Ron felt irritated. He wasn't stupid – if they started getting hurt on the skateboards, they would stop right away, on his say-so. They didn't need hospital bills on top of everything else. And, anyway, when had he ever disobeyed a direct order?

"Yes, Aunt Julia," was all he said.

"Yes, ma'am," Dana said quietly. But her eyes, as they met Ron's, glittered with excitement.

# 17

"**G**rande peppermint tea?"

It was late in the afternoon, and the youthful barista glanced around the little café with the steaming cup in his hand. He looked new and a little out of place that afternoon. Despite the fact that he'd been the one to take Julia's order, he didn't seem to recognize her when she stepped up to claim it.

"This yours, ma'am?"

"Yes, thank you."

"Cream's over to the left," he said, and turned to go back to work.

Julia held the cup under her nose and took a deep breath. The steamy sweetness was like an embrace from the inside out, and she could already feel herself relaxing in response. Still taking in the fragrance, she made her way back to the little table where her laptop was waiting for her.

It was a slow afternoon at the bookstore. Even the presence of a local author, with a stack of books and a hopeful expression, failed to disturb the aura of calm. The cool, quiet atmosphere was just the tonic Julia thought they all needed. It had been a long day of shopping.

After the hardware store, they'd gone to a department store to pick up necessaries like light bulbs, lamps, and seeds for Dana's garden. Dana was very excited about her garden and kept up a steady flow of questions about planting, harvesting, and whether or not Julia thought Amelia would be interested in gardening with her. While there, they ran into Mrs. Jurta and Amelia.

"What a coincidence!" Mrs. Jurta beamed. "Twice in one day."

"Astonishing," Julia agreed wryly.

"We're helping Mrs. Ojacor," Amelia said, smiling at Ron. "We're shopping for the food pantry. You know Mrs. Ojacor, don't you?"

They had to admit that they didn't and went with them to meet her. Caroline Ojacor was a beautiful Kenyan woman with dancing eyes and a wide smile who spent most of her time helping refugees get acclimated to New England.

"She's a living, breathing saint," Mrs. Jurta said.

Mrs. Ojacor simply smiled and asked Julia if she was bringing the children to the Fourth of July picnic.

"We haven't made any plans yet," Julia answered.

"Oh, you *have* to go to it," Mrs. Jurta said. "It's the social highlight of the annual calendar. Lots of fireworks and food and fun – your kids will love it."

"I'm going, too," Amelia announced.

"You really ought to go," Mrs. Ojacor agreed, and the matter was settled.

It was after lunch at a local diner, where Jack dumped his soda on Dana, that Julia decided that they needed some quiet time. They mopped Dana up and drove to the bookstore, where Julia could check her emails and the kids could wander around.

"Stay together," she'd said when they first arrived. "You can look at the books, but if you damage anything, you'll have to pay for it out of your allowance."

"Naturally," Ron said.

"I'm still wet," Dana pouted.

"I'm sorry, but we can't do anything about it until we get home. Why don't you see if they have the second book in that series you're reading?"

They scampered off with Ron taking charge as usual, and Julia settled down to business. It had been a week since she'd had an opportunity to check her email, and she was anxious to see if she'd gotten any replies to the job applications she'd sent out just before leaving Springfield.

Julia drummed her fingers on the table as her computer connected with the Wi-Fi. It had been foolish of her to wait so long to check. She was either going to have to make this a regular thing or find a way to cheaply set up internet at the house. Perhaps there was a computer at the local library. She would have to look into that.

Her mail box was full of messages. Julia scanned them quickly, weeding out the junk mail and sale notices. There were several emails from Sherri the real estate agent, three from Julia's mother, Rachael, a few from friends, and then some from the job application sites. Heart pounding, she clicked on those first.

To her intense disappointment, all of these emails were form replies: *Thank you for your interest in this position. Your application has been received and will be reviewed by a member of our staff. You will be contacted should further information be necessary.*

Julia tried to be philosophical. In this economy, she told herself, it would be a miracle to get a position on the first round of tries, and she could reasonably expect a wait of a few months before something came her way. She had to be patient, which was tough —only two weeks since her dismissal and she was already biting her nails with anxiety.

She archived the job emails and tackled Sherri's next.

*Hi Julia –*

*Hope you're enjoying Franklin and this lovely weather! How's the house? Be sure to send me photos as you finish the rooms. I'll put together a portfolio and see if we can't drum up some interest in the place.*

*With regards to your Springfield house, I've got a couple who are very interested in moving into that neighborhood. They're a young family with a two-year-old and another on the way and, really, this house would be perfect for them. I don't think I'd be talking out of turn if I told you that money is no object for these people. I'd like to give them a tour – they already said that they were interested in it – but I wanted to get your approval first. Let me know ASAP: they're in the area and leaving shortly. Thanks, toots!*

Julia sighed and took a sip of her tea. Letting Sherri show the house had been a bad idea. She'd done it only to get the persistent woman off her back, but as usual, her inability to stand up to Sherri put her in the more embarrassing spot of having to tell her that she wasn't selling yet.

On the other hand, if a lucrative offer did come in, didn't she also owe financial security to the children? They did have an emotional attachment to the place, but with the job market looking so poor, would she really have the right to refuse a legitimate offer?

She replied:

*Hi Sherri,*

*I'm still not comfortable with selling the place yet. If you think it's a good idea, go ahead and show it, but please make it clear that we're not sure about letting it go. Thanks for everything you're doing for us!*

She sent it and got a reply almost immediately.

*Great, will do. I'll keep you informed of developments re: Springfield. Hope the kids are enjoying the lake!*

*Sherri G.*

Julia made a note to take some pictures of the Franklin house, then she opened the email from her mother. It was a long and chatty message, filled with stories about their Florida adventures. Dad was starting to fish and was hoping to catch an alligator "by accident", so he could have some photos for the park newsletter. Mom was jogging with some of her friends and had already started losing weight. Both sent their best wishes to the kids. Mom worried that Julia hadn't written, but understood that she would be busy.

The last email she opened was from an old college roommate, a woman named Markie Parks. Julia was surprised to hear from her: she and Markie hadn't communicated since Markie's wedding two years earlier. Markie had an enviable job at a top Boston advertising agency, a gorgeous husband, and little time for friends. The email was written in Markie's usual clipped and businesslike style:

*Julia,*

*Hope this finds you well. I heard about your sister – please accept my profound sympathies. I've heard that you are job hunting. My firm is currently in need of an assistant research project director and I remembered that you have had training in this field. It would be a starter salary, but with the possibility of advancement. If you are interested, here is the website. Be sure to let me know if you do decide to apply so I can speak with the HR department.*

*Hope to see you at one of our dinner parties real soon.*

*Yours,*

*MP*

Excitement caught in Julia's throat. Assistant Research Project Director? This could be a huge break for her. She was surprised that Markie had remembered her after all these years. Although they had shared quarters and a few classes, they hadn't exactly been close. From the start, Markie had been driven on the fast track to success, and Julia was on whatever the other track was. It felt good to know she hadn't been forgotten.

Julia followed the link and filled out the application, then she wrote to Markie, thanking her and letting her know that she had applied.

She felt much better after that. She closed down her email box and opened up a job search site, standing to stretch before scrolling.

While she worked, she saw the kids hurrying though the shelves towards her. Behind them, the window framed a rapidly darkening afternoon sky. Gathering clouds looked ready to open up at any moment.

Julia checked her watch. An hour had passed since they entered the store and the kids were probably getting bored.

She glanced at her screen in indecision. She wanted to apply for a few more positions, but the kids had been patient for a long time. By waiting, she worried that she was stretching them beyond their limits.

She had yet to make up her mind when Dana plunked herself down in the chair in front of her.

"I'm tired," she said.

Jack and Ron were fast on her heels.

"Aunt Julia!" Jack said, running over to her and burying his face in her shirt. He acted as though she'd been missing for months. "Aunt Julia!"

She stroked his head, whispering "Shhh." She looked up at Ron. He looked tired as he sank into the other chair.

Outside, thunder rumbled above the soothing new age music and quiet chatter. Rain would come soon. Had they shut the windows before they left the house? Julia tried to remember.

"Did you have a good time wandering around?" she asked, affectionately rubbing Jack's head.

He nodded into her shirt, and Julia adjusted his grip a little to make sure he wasn't causing any immodesty on her part. It was definitely time to go.

"Why don't you three go to the bathroom before we leave? I'll pack up my laptop and meet you at the front door, all right?"

Ron nodded wearily and reached for Jack. "Come on, string bean."

Jack's head popped up. "I'm not a string bean!" he protested. "I'm a *boy*!"

"Sorry," Ron grinned as they walked off. "I forgot because you *look* like a string bean."

"No I don't! I look like a boy."

Julia shut down her laptop and drained the last of her now tepid peppermint tea. She slid the computer back into its case, grabbed her purse, and headed for the front doors, searching for her car keys as she went. They had fallen among the things in her purse and she had to dig around a bit.

By the time she pulled them from the mess, she was standing in front of the author's table. Business had not been brisk. Stacks of hardcover books were piled up on the table and on the floor the front of it. A large poster with the cover of the book, and a picture of the author in a Hawaiian shirt on it, declared that the novel was "Fascinating", "Gripping", and a "Page-Turner" by the critics from newspapers and websites that Julia had never heard of.

A book stood on its spine in front of her. The cover was a graphic painting of an old, sinister looking house, silhouetted in black against a purplish-blue background. A big bay window in the middle was lit up, showing the figure of a screaming woman, leaning back with one arm up to ward off a knife held by an obscure figure. The title was, *Picturesque in Death: A Novel, by A. Glen Bernard.*

The author watched her hopefully out of the corner of his eye. He looked exactly the same as he did on the poster, right down to wearing the same Hawaiian shirt.

Julia didn't really want to speak with him. She was sorry that he was so alone at his signing, but she didn't want to buy the book and she didn't want to lead him on. But tacky as the cover was, she couldn't take her eyes off of it. There was something eerily familiar about it, something that she couldn't quite put her finger on...

"Hello!"

*Darn!*

Mr. A. Glen Bernard flashed what he doubtlessly thought was a winning smile. Now she had to talk to him.

"Oh, uh, hello," she said. She adjusted her purse strap and made sure that her car keys were in full view.

"How are you?" he asked.

"Good, thank you. You?"

"I'm doing great." He extended a huge hand and enveloped hers in it. "A. Glen Bernard, at your service. And you are...?"

"Julia. It's nice to meet you."

"Well, it's nice to meet you. You live around here?"

"Just in for the summer."

"Nice, nice. I see you've been checking out the book. They did a good job on the cover, didn't they?" He rubbed his hands together. "It was my suggestion, but it came out much better than I thought it would. Sometimes I think it's better than the actual book."

He laughed too heartily. Julia forced back a wince – if the cover was better than the book and the cover was tacky...

"I'm sure your writing justifies the cover," she said.

Mr. Bernard brightened. "You've read it?"

"Uh, no..."

"It's based on a true story," he said, picking up a book and leaning against the table. He looked like a salesman on a home shopping channel. "Set in the fictional town of Cheltham, New Hampshire. It's my first published effort."

"You must be very proud," Julia said. There was no sign of the kids. She didn't look at her watch, but it felt like a lot of time had passed.

"Oh, I am. I did a lot of research to write this book. It's based on a story a colleague of mine covered when I was just starting out in the newspaper business. A wealthy young actress, found murdered in her Victorian house, surrounded by the blood spattered posters of her movies. And who did it? Her jealous husband, who was losing his business and money hand over fist? Her co-star and lover? Or his jealous ex-wife?"

A clap of thunder from outside the building accentuated his statement. Rain began to pound against the windows and a chill ran down Julia's spine. She stared at the book cover and suddenly knew what was so familiar about it.

He was chatting away. "Honestly, I didn't really have to make up much – all the elements were there, just with different names and occupations. I may or may not have changed the ending just to punch it up a bit. Of course, one doesn't want to embarrass the family or the innocents. As I said earlier, it's set in the fictional town of Cheltham, but if you live around here, I'm sure you'd recognize it as Franklin right away. You did say you live around here, right?"

Now, he finally had her interest. "Are you saying that you based this book on the murder of that Franklin artist twenty years ago?"

Bernard's face lit up. Pleased, he straightened up and his hand went to his collar to adjust a tie that wasn't there. "You've heard of it?"

"Yes. The husband did it, right?"

"Ah, but did he?"

"Sorry?"

He grinned and tapped the book cover with a heavy hand. "Just because twelve bored men and women find a man guilty does not make him guilty, ma'am. When I was doing the research on this book, I went over all the court records and the articles written at the time. I talked with some of the witnesses and viewed some of the evidence, a luxury any author can afford when their brother-in-law is in the police force. I have to tell you, I've found plenty of room for doubt. Hence," he lifted the novel, "this book."

"You mean, you don't think the husband did it?"

"Killed Stephanie Lang? Oh, yes, *he* did it. No doubt in my mind."

Now she was confused. "Well, then…"

"What I also found, however, was wiggle room, stuff that the defense attorney tried to bring up at the trial. You see, all the evidence did mostly fit to cast Brad Lang as the perpetrator, but there were things that were never accounted for and questions that, if they were asked, the answers were not made public. I asked some of them and none of the answers contradicted my theory that Brad Lang killed his wife for the insurance. But there are still some unanswered questions, some stray pieces of evidence that refuse to be placed into the pattern."

He leaned in suddenly, before Julia could react. She smelled pastrami on his breath, and it was all she could do to keep from making a face.

"I have taken this evidence and forged an entirely new scenario," he said, in a husky voice better suited for a movie trailer.

She gazed at him for a minute, then asked, "So you're saying that there's reason to doubt that the husband, Brad, actually did the crime, but you still think that he did it. Why?"

He looked at her, puzzled. "Why?"

"Yes. I'm curious. You said there was doubt and you seem to have done your homework. So why do you still think Brad did it?"

"The jury found him guilty."

"But you just told me that their finding is not really evidence." she reminded him gently.

He flushed. "Well, yeah, obviously. I did follow up on all those loose ends, but when one is an investigator, you learn very quickly that in real life, not everything adds up. If you wait for all the bits and pieces to come together, you'll drive yourself mental. The best detectives learn what loose ends to pursue and which ones to let go."

"So, you agreed with the prosecution, that these 'loose ends' were unimportant?"

"Oh, yes. They were just the minutia of real life. Life doesn't usually wrap up as neatly as it does in books. Brad Lang is the killer, make no mistake about that. But..." He picked up a copy of the book and held it, wiggling, up next to his head, in an attempt to entice her. "Did Chase Harcourt kill his wife, the lovely actress, Daphne Maxwell-Harcourt? That is the real question."

*Which I think you've already answered,* Julia thought. It was hard to believe that this man had been an investigative reporter. His sales pitch showed a drive and polish that would have been the envy of any used car salesman.

"So, Julia," he said, flashing his 'winning' smile again. "Would you like me to sign you a copy?"

"Well, I..." Julia looked around and spotted the kids coming her way. She put out a hand to stop Bernard, but saw that he was already writing furiously on the inside of a hardcover book: "*To my curious friend, Julia...*"

"We're ready to go," Ron said, tugging Jack along behind him.

"Great," Julia said, relieved to see them.

"What are you doing?" Dana asked, staring at the poster.

"Talking with Mr. Bernard. He's signing a book for me."

Ron glanced at the author. "You're buying a book?"

Julia repressed a sigh. "It certainly looks that way."

"Ron, doesn't that look like the haunted house?" Dana said. "Look at it."

Ron frowned. "It does. Weird."

Bernard turned pink with pleasure. Without looking up from his lengthy dedication, he proclaimed, "It isn't weird at all. If you live anywhere near Franklin, you're sure to have heard about the murder in the old Victorian. Here you are, Julia, all signed and dedicated." He handed it over to her with due ceremony, cautioning, "Hang on to that volume. It may be worth a lot one day."

"Thank you, Mr. Bernard." She thought, *it won't be worth even trying to sell it on eBay, thanks to that dedication.*

"You wrote a book about that murder?" Ron asked.

Julia looked at him sharply. This murder, distasteful as she found it, was gripping enough to shake the boy out of his usual lethargic state and she was surprised. Of course, it must seem exciting to be living near a murder house when you are a youngster. She didn't particularly like the idea that he was intrigued by such a bloody and violent event, but it was better than his tortured silences and withdrawn grieving. Perhaps it was a sign of healing.

Bernard was giving them a shorter history of how he started writing the book, and Julia broke in to remind the children that they had to go.

"Thank you for the book, Mr. Bernard," she said.

"Be sure to leave your comments on my website!" he replied happily.

Julia paid for the book. It was pouring buckets when they left, and they had to run for the car, Julia with Jack in her arms. They were soaked by the time they got in. Julia started the van and looked over to make sure they were all set. Ron was studying the cover of Julia's unwilling purchase with great curiosity.

As Julia backed out of the parking space, he said, "Can I read this?"

Julia was tempted to say yes, just to encourage him, but then she had a moment of misgiving. Normally, books like these had scenes that were inappropriate for kids. She wondered what Amanda and Tim's policies were on the subject, then decided that she had to make her own decisions based on what she was comfortable living with.

Which, unfortunately, meant a commitment on her part.

"If it's any good, you can have it after I read it," she said.

He seemed content with that answer and put the book back into the bag at his feet.

Dana piped up, "It's looks creepy. *I* wouldn't read it."

"You probably shouldn't be reading books like that for a few years anyway," Julia answered.

They drove in silence for a while. Then Dana said, "Can we plant in the rain?"

Julia looked at the sheets that were coming down. The garden had to be turned over and thoroughly weeded before planting. The mud would be terrific. Julia had furniture to assemble and a few remaining touch-ups on the room upstairs. She really didn't want to spend the better part of the day cleaning muddy floors and boots.

"If it's like this, no, we probably shouldn't." She didn't need to look in the mirror to know that Dana's face fell in disappointment. "You can plant some of them in the pots, though, if you'd like."

"Really?"

"That will be fine. You and Jack can work on that while Ron and I work upstairs. Sound good to you?"

"Yes!" Dana chirped. "You'll help me, won't you, Jack?"

"Sure!"

Dana settled back into her seat with a happy sigh. "This is going to be great," she said.

Julia, driving home through the darkening streets, felt a sudden and rather exhilarating rush of triumph.

# 18

It was pouring rain when Thursday dawned. Dana spent the morning cleaning the pots that Amelia had given her, dashing in and out of the house as she filled them with rain-drenched soil.

Julia and Ron worked, attaching chair-rail to Dana's room, assembling a new bed they'd purchased that morning for Jack, and bringing the beds they'd found in the storage room upstairs for Ron and Dana.

"Well," Julia sighed, brushing her hair out of her face and breathing heavily. "It'll be nice for you to sleep in a real bed again."

"Yes," Ron said eagerly. "It will."

Julia and Dana worked in the kitchen after lunch, planting seeds in the pots while Ron and Jack set up their new room. Dana was talking about school and boys and fashion when the cell phone rang. Julia's hands were thick with dirt, so Dana answered the call.

"Oh, hi, Gran!" Dana spoke loudly to be heard over the sound of the rain pounding against the windows and the music coming from upstairs.

Julia realized that she had forgotten again to have the kids call Miriam Budd.

Dana chatted for a few minutes, talking about the rooms and the seeds that they were planting. She explained that the boys were upstairs and apparently was told not to disturb them.

She giggled a few times, saying, "How big was it? Oh my *gosh!*" and giggled again. She looked over at Julia and said, "Okay. Okay. Yep, she's right here. We're planting seeds in pots. Do you want to talk to her? Yes, we had sandwiches for lunch. Tuna. What did you have?"

It was all Julia could do to keep from making a face. She busied herself with the packets of seeds. After a few more minutes, Dana said goodbye and placed the phone on the counter with a little sigh.

"Who was that?" Julia asked, careful to keep her tone neutral.

"It was Gran," Dana said, getting back on her chair. She took a pot in her hand and looked at the seeds. "She and Gramp are on the ship again. She said that it's really hot there."

"I'll bet it is."

"She said to say hi to you, but she didn't want to bother you."

"I see. Well, it was nice of her to call. Did she have any other message?"

"Uhhh... Just to call her tomorrow, to see how we're doing."

"She's calling us?"

"No. She wants us to call her."

"Naturally." Julia reminded herself not to draw Dana into the silent feud. Best to leave the childish exchange of half-insults and half-hearted snubbing for the mature adults. "Well, let's get to planting, shall we? What shall we start with?"

"String beans?"

"I was more thinking flowers in the pots. The string beans need more space and we'll be tying them to stakes when they're big enough. Actually, we'll probably just plant them near the fence in the back garden and tie them to it."

Dana was looking at her in astonishment. "They need to be tied up?"

"Yep. Otherwise, they'll lie in the dirt and rot."

She looked over the array of seeds with a furrowed brow. "Do they all have to be tied up?"

"Oh, no. Only the string beans, the peas, the sweet peas, and the tomatoes. Everything else either is strong enough to stand on its own, or it's a vine that prefers to be on the ground." She put the packet of string beans to one side. "We'll save those for when it stops raining. How about we start with the pansies?"

Dana nodded and they ripped open the packet.

Dana insisted that they plant at least two of everything, so that Amelia could have one of each. Julia showed her how to dig the proper sized hole, where to place the seeds, and how to add the plant food to the water. Using some old Popsicle sticks that they had found in a dusty box in the storage room, they made two little signs for 'Pansies' in colorful marker and put the date on it. Then they placed the two pots on the wide window sills in the living room where they would catch the first rays of morning sunlight.

"When will they start to grow?" Dana asked as they headed back into the kitchen.

"It'll take about a week before you see something. We'll have to make sure that they get just enough sunlight and water so that they grow good and strong."

"And plant food!"

"That we only have to do once a week. If you do more, they'll be poisoned." Julia poked through the remaining packets. "It's kind of like taking care of a baby – you can't give them too much milk or they'll be sick."

"I remember when Jack was a baby."

"Do you? That was a long time ago and you were very little."

Dana nodded. "I remember he was sick and Mom said that it was because the girl hadn't warmed up his formula right. She was really mad because he was throwing up over everything. She told Dad that she would never let the girl come and watch us again. Can we do the Prince Williams next?"

"Sure."

Julia slid the packet over and watched as Dana's little fingers worked to open it. The children didn't talk about their parents much, and every time that they did, Dana ended up in tears. Now, she was so busy trying to open the slick packaging without spilling the contents that she didn't have time for tears.

After a few fruitless attempts, she looked at Julia in frustration. "Can I use the scissors, please?"

"Very good idea," Julia said.

Julia was enjoying herself immensely. It wasn't often that she and Dana had time alone together. The rain pounded outside, the boys were happily working together, and Dana was calm and peaceful. It was so nice that Julia decided that she must take steps to make sure that this happened again. Surely there were other projects that they could start doing. Maybe cooking or baking. They could bake cookies for Christmas presents this year, maybe, and then there was Easter…

Dana cut into her thoughts. "Aunt Julia?"

"Yes?"

"Are all spices seeds?"

Julia handed her the little watering can. "Some are. Others are leaves or bark, like basil and oregano."

They carefully carried the prepared pots into the living room. These were too big to put on the sills, so Julia cleared a place on the floor, where the sun was sure to find them.

"Aunt Julia, did you ever work on a farm?"

"What? I mean, no, why?"

"You know *everything* about plants, don't you?"

The admiration was genuine. Dana was looking up at her with something like awe, her big brown eyes with their delicate lashes so much like Amanda's.

Julia ruffled Dana's hair with a relatively clean hand. "No, I didn't work on a farm, but I used to have a garden of my own when I was a little girl and my mom worked with me all the time on it.

She's the one who knows everything about gardens. She used to grow prize-winning roses."

"Really? That's cool."

"Yes, it was."

Afterward, Dana fell silent and serious. Julia noticed but decided not to say anything about it. The sunflowers were planted, watered, and placed in the living room, and then they cleaned the kitchen table and put away the supplies. Some dirt had fallen on the floor, so Dana got the broom out of the dining room.

While she was sweeping, she broke the silence.

"Aunt Julia?"

"Hmmm?"

"Um... Never mind."

She continued to sweep the rest of the room, her brow puckered in concentration. Julia washed the scissors and placed them back in the proper drawer, then wiped down the counter. After that, there was nothing left to do; but as Dana obviously had something to ask, she couldn't leave. She put on the kettle, found two mugs, and put tea bags in them. She located the little plastic bear of honey and poured about a teaspoon of it into each cup.

Finally, Dana stopped sweeping and spoke.

"Did my mom work in the garden?"

It seemed a lot of effort for such a simple question. Julia answered it simply: "No, she wasn't much of an outdoors girl. She liked the flowers, though, and Mom and I would always give her a vase full for her room."

"Which were her favorites?"

The kettle whistled, and Julia took an oven mitt and filled the two mugs. "Oh, the pink roses, definitely. But she also liked the hyacinth and the tulips, especially the pink ones. She tried to get Mom – Grandmother Rachael, I mean – to plant magnolias one year. But magnolias grow on trees and we didn't have room in the yard." She put the mugs on the table and sat down. "Have some tea."

Dana left her neat little pile of dirt and wrapped her hand around the steamy brew. In Julia's opinion, a cup of tea was always welcome, even in the middle of summer's worst humidity. She took a sip, but Dana contented herself with dunking the bag in the water over and over again.

"So, you never had magnolias?" she asked.

"No, I'm afraid not. Your mother was very disappointed, of course, but then she discovered boys and she forgot all about it."

Julia took a sip, remembering her sister. Amanda had been only about fifteen when she started dating, against their parents' wishes, but you couldn't change Amanda's mind once she had made it up. Once she started, she was never without a boyfriend or a group of admirers.

"I remember," Julia said, "the first prom your mother was invited to. It was at another school and the boy who had asked her only knew her from the pizza place where they both worked. Mom and Dad weren't happy about it, but he was a nice boy and they knew his parents, so they couldn't say no. She let me sit in her room and watch her get ready. She wore this gorgeous green dress, the prettiest dress I had ever seen. I asked her if I could wear it when I got older, but she said that it would be out of style by then. I was so disappointed." She laughed at the memory.

Dana leaned closer. "Mom was beautiful," she whispered.

"Yes, she was."

Julia thought about Amanda's golden hair and how she had envied the natural color when she was a child. Amanda never understood that – she always said that brown was just the right color for Julia's eyes. She remembered dress shopping and watching movies together, arguing over shoes, giggling in the back seat, daydreaming about their futures, and all the things that sisters did, and a stab of pain struck Julia so hard that she winced.

"Grandmother Rachael told me that she was the prettiest girl in high school," Dana said. She stared at her mug, her huge, dewy eyes ready to overflow.

Julia nodded slowly. "She was very pretty, but better than that, she was very loving and kind. She was smart, too, just like you."

Dana shook her head. "I'm not very smart," she said.

"Who says?"

"People in my class. Even Tonia is smarter than me."

Julia frowned. "Nonsense."

"It's true. She gets all A's."

"That doesn't matter. I know that you're smart. I've seen how your mind works and it's very quick."

Dana sighed. "Aunt Julia, will I ever be pretty like Mom?"

Julia was taken aback. Of all the things for Dana to be worried about, this wasn't what she had expected. "What are you talking about, Dana?"

"Mom was so beautiful but I'm just – well, I'm just… me. And I don't have blonde hair like she does. Mine's like…"

She stopped, embarrassed. She was going to say, "Like yours, Aunt Julia," and realized that it was insulting. Julia had to give her points for recognizing that, in the middle of her obvious distress.

Julia didn't care about the implied insult. She took Dana's hand and the little girl gulped and looked down.

"Dana," she said, gently, "Your mother thought that you and the boys were the best thing that had ever happened to her. Do you know what she told me the day she had you in the hospital, the first time I ever saw you?"

The chin was trembling. "No."

"You and she were alone when I came in, and the first thing she did was to hold you up so that I could see. She said, 'Isn't she the most beautiful little girl you've ever seen in your life?' Do you know what I said?"

"No."

"I said that she was right. Your mother was beautiful, but she couldn't believe that anyone could be as beautiful as you. She was awed by you. She never, ever thought that you were not good enough. She didn't think she was good enough for *you*."

Dana's eyes were overflowing now and the little hand squeezed tightly.

Julia handed her a tissue. "Your mother was right, you know," she said. "And you look so much like her – it's like seeing her young again."

"Do you – do you think she misses us?"

Suddenly tearful herself, Julia said, "Oh, Dana!"

She pulled the little girl into her lap and held her while she sobbed quietly. She rocked back and forth, stroking her niece's hair and whispering things that neither one of them remembered later. Dana curled up in a tight little ball, one arm wrapped tightly around Julia's neck.

This was a different crying than Julia was used to from her niece. Before, the sobbing spurts were spontaneous, harsh, and overwhelming, almost furious in their intensity. This was soft, more heartrending. There was something about it that made Julia think that this was a healing. There was a long road ahead, still, but this was definitely a huge step.

# 19

Eventually, Dana went to the bathroom to wash her face. Julia was in the kitchen, cleaning the mugs and thinking, when the boys came in. Ron was carrying empty drawers that Julia recognized as being from the bureaus that were to go in the boys' room.

"What are you guys doing with those?" she asked.

"We're getting ready for when Robert brings them upstairs!" Jack said happily.

Ron had to keep shifting his stance to keep the drawers balanced. "We thought we'd get a head start. We're going to bring up some for Dana, too."

"That's a very good idea, guys. Thank you."

Jack beamed and they went upstairs. She could hear Jack asking Ron whether socks *had* to be folded together or if they couldn't just be tossed in.

She was just about to leave the kitchen to go into the living room when there was a pounding at the door, so loud that Julia would have been startled by half the intensity. She heard voices and hurried to answer it.

Looking up from under an enormous rain hat, Mrs. Jurta brushed past Julia, saying something so fast and so high pitched that Julia didn't understand a word. She was followed by what

SUMMER SHADOWS

appeared to be a midget in rain gear holding two leashes with puppies attached. Mystified, Julia followed them into the kitchen.

Amelia Wilde sat in a growing puddle of water on one of the
kitchen chairs, watching Mrs. Jurta fuss over the puppies with one
of Julia's few remaining clean dish towels.

"Mrs. Jurta!" Julia said. "What's going on?"

"Look, I hate to ask you, but it's an emergency and I'm out of
options."

One of the puppies escaped her and went running down the
hallway. A second later, they heard Dana's delighted voice: "Oh,
*Horatio*! What are you doing here?"

The other puppy dashed off after him and Mrs. Jurta wearily let
him go. Julia hoped that the dog was house trained.

Amelia slipped out of her seat and ran into the hall. The barking alerted the boys upstairs, and they came crashing down the
steps. They raced through the kitchen and into the hallway.

Mrs. Jurta raised her voice above the chaos.

"It's Dexter – he's taken a funny turn and I have to rush him
to the vet's right away. I've got Amelia and normally I'd take her
with me, but the vet is all the way in Concord. I've explained it
all to Robert, of course, and he was fine with me leaving her
here and said he'd be around at the normal hour to pick her up
and…"

Jack ran screeching around the corner and jumped into Julia's
arms. The tiger-striped puppy raced into the room after him and
slipped on the slick floor, colliding with the table leg.

Amelia ran in and gathered the puppy in her arms while Ron
stood in the doorway, watching them.

Julia hushed Jack and turned to Mrs. Jurta. "You need to leave
Amelia with us?"

"Yes, please."

"What about the puppies?"

"They need to have their medications, but Amelia knows what to
do."

183

Amelia reached into her pocket, pulled out a little reddish bottle, and waved it about. Dana, with the other dog close at her feet, appeared in the doorway.

Julia frowned. "You're leaving the puppies here with me?"

"Yes."

"Mrs. Jurta, I don't have any experience with dogs and I don't have any food for them. Amelia can stay with us, if her father is all right with it, but the puppies..."

But Mrs. Jurta brushed off Julia's concerns with a wave of her hand.

"They'll be no trouble. I've brought their chow and they'll go with Amelia tonight when Robert picks them up. They need their pill at six sharp and a walk before bed. Thank you, Julia. This is why I love living in a neighborhood – we're always here to help one another. I'll keep you all informed on Dexter's progress. Good night – keep dry!"

She darted back out into the rainy afternoon before Julia could regain herself enough to say anything.

There was brief silence, then Amelia yelped as Tigger slipped out of her arms. Ron jumped back as the little fellow scrambled across the floor towards Horatio.

The children waited for Julia's reaction. Ron looked annoyed, Dana was apprehensive, and Amelia's face was white.

Jack relaxed his grip on Julia's neck a little, but he tightened up the moment she shifted.

"I don't like dogs," he whispered.

Julia thought that he was in for a very long afternoon. She shifted him on her hip and brushed a stray hair out of her eyes. The sound of the dogs at play grew more intense in the background, but no one moved. They were all waiting for her.

"Well," she said with a sigh, "Mrs. Jurta certainly knows how to make a grand entrance, doesn't she?"

They didn't respond, and Julia tried again. "I hope you like macaroni and cheese, Amelia. That's what we're having tonight."

"Yes, ma'am," Amelia said solemnly.

*For heaven's sake,* Julia thought. *This isn't a Charles Dickens moment!*

"Awesome," she said. "Now, you're sure your father knows where you are?"

Amelia pulled a cell phone out of her pocket. "Oh, yes, ma'am. He texted me to tell you thank you. You can see it right here, want to see?"

She nodded. "Dana, Ron, just go make sure those dogs aren't ruining anything, will you?"

"Yes, Aunt Julia," Ron said obediently.

Dana sprang for the living room, calling for Horatio.

Amelia was still holding up the phone as Julia placed the trembling Jack on the table and reached for it.

"May I see the message?" she asked.

Suddenly hesitant, Amelia withdrew the phone; then she reluctantly gave it to Julia.

There were several messages on the screen:

Amelia: *Hey dad mrs jurta has to go to the vets dana's mom says I can stay with them until you pick me up ok?*

Dad: *everything ok with m. jurta?*

Amelia: *yes her dogs sick ok to stay with mrs Lamontaigne?*

Dad: *Yes. I'll be home at 7. Thank mrs Lamontaigne for me, give her my number and ask her to send me hers. Be a good girl.*

Amelia: *thanks I will see you home.*

It was a suspicious amount of typing for the short amount of time that Amelia had been in the house. Julia checked the time on the messages and her hunch was right: the first one was sent ten minutes before Amelia and Mrs. Jurta arrived at the house.

She looked up at the wide-eyed Amelia.

"Well," she said, handing it back. "You'd better give me your Dad's phone number."

Amelia rattled it off. Julia typed it into her phone and sent a text:

*This is Julia L. Just wanted you to have my phone number and to let you know that Amelia is with us.*

After a moment, the reply arrived: *I owe you big time. I'll cut out early tonight, if I can manage it.*

Julia grinned: *No problem. You can pay me back in furniture lugging. See you tonight.*

As she sent it, she wondered about how free and easy talking with Robert felt. It was almost as if they'd known each other for ages.

Amelia was watching her warily, concerned that Julia had noticed her lie.

She pocketed her phone and smiled at Amelia. "I hope you'll excuse the mess, Amelia. We're right in the middle of moving upstairs into the new bedrooms."

A relieved smile came over her little face. "I don't mind at all!" she said. "I can help and do whatever you want. I'll keep the dogs real quiet, so that they don't disturb you."

"Amelia?"

"Yes, Ms. Lamontaigne?"

The brown eyes were huge and fearful and Julia felt pity for her. She put a hand on her shoulder and smiled down at her.

"I'm glad you're here," she said.

A flicker of emotion crossed the pretty, tanned face.

"You are?"

"Yes, I am. You came at exactly the right moment."

"I *did?*"

"Yes, you did. Dana was just about to begin to set up her new room and she needs help. Girl help, you know. Only I couldn't do it because I need to make supper. I was going to tell her to wait until tomorrow, but, with you here, she can do it right away. That is, if you don't mind."

The face brightened and beamed. "I don't mind! I don't mind at all!"

"Great. Why don't you go get Dana and start right away?"

"Yes, ma'am!" She darted for the door.

Julia stopped her. "Amelia?"

"Yes, ma'am?"

"It's a good thing you knew about my invitation even before you got here. It saved a lot of time. But next time, wait and check with me first, all right?"

Amelia froze, horrified.

"Go on now," Julia said. "What's done is done. We don't need to talk about it anymore, right?"

She gulped. "No, ma'am."

"And it's Julia. Now run and find Dana."

She raced away, shouting for Dana.

Julia sighed and turned to Jack, who was sitting very still.

He looked at her solemnly. "What do we do now?"

"We make supper, my brave boy."

"What about the dogs?"

"We'll just have to get used to them. They're only puppies. Now, to the floor with you…"

He grabbed at her, terrified. "No! No, the dogs! They'll bite me!"

He was practically shrieking into her ear. She jerked her head away instinctively and straightened up. She was about to tell him not to be silly, that the dogs wouldn't bite him, but she remembered that they were puppies - they were probably teething.

"Aunt Julia!"

Dana appeared in the doorway, her face lit with excitement. Horatio was leaning against her leg, and he looked up at Julia with doleful eyes, his tail wagging as though he were making up for his earlier rudeness.

Something about his appearance put Julia at ease – despite all the chaos, this dog was calm and happy. Horatio would be just fine around the children, she decided. He was a handsome dog, but big, even though he wasn't yet fully grown. She had no idea what kind of dog he was and made a mental note to ask Mrs. Jurta or Amelia about it later.

Dana announced, "Amelia says she wants to help me set up my room. She says that she's staying for supper *and* that she loves *Beauty and the Beast*. Can we watch it tonight?"

"We'll have to see," Julia said. "After all, we only have the one TV and the boys to consider. We don't want to leave them out."

"Well, then, maybe we could watch *Aladdin*. She's never seen that."

"Dana!" Amelia shouted. "Ron says we have to start!"

Dana ran out of the room.

Julia shook her head and turned to Jack. "Want to help me make supper?" she asked.

He nodded reluctantly. But when she went to put him down, he clung even tighter.

"Jack, I can't make supper while holding you. You're too big and you're going to have to let go sometime."

They were interrupted by the other children trooping in with armloads of clothes and bags, Ron leading the way. The two dogs ran about their feet, threatening to trip everyone as they disappeared up the stairs.

Jack looked at Julia with raised eyebrows. "What about the dogs?" he asked.

Julia was silent for a minute. Then she said, "Well, what do you think they made chairs for?"

# 20

Officer Wilde didn't come until late. They had eaten and cleaned up, and cared for the dogs, and now Ron had his room to himself. He wasn't able to concentrate, though. He was too busy listening for the door.

It wasn't that he was one of those kids who idolized adults – far from it. He knew that he was man enough to take care of the family. But he wanted to show off the work they'd done in the bedrooms. He wanted another man's approval. It didn't necessarily have to be Officer Wilde's, but since he'd already seen the earlier work and had given them some good advice about it, his opinion held weight.

After about twenty minutes, he couldn't stand lying down any more. He hopped off his brand new bed and began to rearrange things.

He smoothed out his bedspread and re-fluffed the pillows. That action struck him as girlish, so he punched them down again.

He rearranged the drawers that he and Jack had so carefully and neatly filled, wishing, again, that he could bring up the dressers by himself. Half-filled drawers on the floor by themselves seemed so lame. He tried stacking them up on top of one another, with his drawers on one side, and Jack's on the other; but they were rickety, so he took them down again. He finally settled on two rows of two drawers on top of each other.

Jack's ball was sitting in the basket of toys near his bed. Ron began to dribble with it, faking passes and running between the beds in his stocking feet. He moved carefully, trying not to make too much noise, and threw the ball through an imaginary hoop. He raised both fists in victory and jumped lightly up and down as the ball disappeared under the bed.

After a while, Julia called him from the bottom of the stairs. He went out and saw that she was holding Tigger, the striped puppy, in her arms. For once, the little dog was quiet and still.

"I was going to put on a movie for the kids," she said. "Want to pick one out?"

He nodded and started downstairs. "Is Amelia staying the night?"

"I don't know. I haven't heard from her father yet."

Ron hoped that she wasn't. He didn't mind Amelia, really, but she always brought a lot of noise with her and made Dana act all girly and giggly. If she stayed the night, Wilde wouldn't see the rooms until tomorrow at best, and maybe not even then. That would be disappointing.

As he approached, Tigger lifted a sleepy head and sniffed in Ron's direction. Ron rubbed his head and the puppy closed his eyes contentedly.

Julia was giving him that funny, amused expression. He hadn't yet been able to decipher what it meant.

She said, "Pick out something quiet for tonight, okay? I think we need a calming influence."

Tigger began to snore as they walked through the kitchen into the living room. It was much tidier since the last time Ron saw it. The baskets of clothing had disappeared, although one remained as a make-shift bed for the puppies. A few chairs and an old couch sat in a semi-circle around the TV. Nearly all the blankets and bedding had been brought upstairs to the bedrooms, leaving only a neat pile of Julia's things. Ron remembered that they hadn't set up her bed yet.

"Aunt Julia, you can sleep in my bed tonight," he said.

She was lowering the puppy into the basket and looked at him over her shoulder with a frown.

"What?"

"You can sleep in my bed tonight," Ron said, feeling noble. "I can sleep on the floor. It doesn't bother me."

She straightened up and looked at the pile of bedding, then at him. "Oh, that's all right. I don't really mind, but thank you."

"I don't want your back to hurt and besides, it's my job to take the uncomfortable things for you."

She studied him for a moment, then said, "Thank you, Ron. I appreciate that very much. But I don't mind, and I'd rather you be with the others upstairs. You keep your cell phone in your room, right?"

"Yes."

"And you get reception up there?"

"Yes. Four bars."

She nodded and rubbed her hands on her pants. "Excellent. That's better than down here. Now, you'd better pick out a movie."

She left the room and Ron pulled out the box of DVDs, selecting an action comedy. He was halfway down the hallway before he remembered that Aunt Julia wanted a calming movie. Grumbling, he exchanged it for a musical and put it in the DVD player. He threw himself back on the couch and turned on the TV to watch the special features, puzzling over the conversation and a little offended by her refusal.

He could hear laughter and thudding feet as the three youngest got ready for bed. Horatio barked sharply once, sounding like someone stepped on his tail.

Tigger woke up and began to whine in his basket. Ron went over to let him out and the puppy followed him back to the couch. He waited until Ron was settled in, then leaped into his lap and snuggled beside Ron's arm.

After a few minutes, the girls came running into the room. Both had a freshly washed glow and were giggling. Amelia stopped short when she spotted Ron and ducked behind Dana, who ignored her.

"What are we watching, Ron?" Dana asked.

"This." He pointed to the TV.

She craned her neck to look at the screen. "Oh. Is that okay with you, Amelia?"

From behind her back, Amelia said, "Anything Ron wants is fine with me."

They raced by in front of Ron and threw themselves beside him, giggling as they drew their feet up and snuggled into the cushions. Tigger sat up and stared at them, his tail moving slowly, his ears alert. Amelia spotted him and patted the cushion beside her.

"Come on, Tigger," she said. "Come sit with me."

Tigger cocked his head and wagged his tail, but he didn't move.

Julia entered a few minutes later with Jack. Close on her heels, Horatio went immediately over to Dana. He was too big to fit on the couch with all of them, so Dana slipped onto the floor to join him. Amelia went with her, so the two brothers had the couch to themselves.

Midway through the movie, just after Julia brought them popcorn and settled down on a chair to watch with them, they heard a knock at the side door.

"Someone's at the door!" Jack announced.

"Figures," Julia sighed. "Just when I get comfortable."

Everyone was making noise of some sort by the time Ron managed to pause the DVD. In the sudden silence that followed, they could hear Julia saying, "Come in, Officer."

"Dad!"

Amelia jumped up and raced into the other room, Dana fast on her heels. Ron and Jack followed soon after.

Officer Wilde held Amelia on his lap as she talked excitedly about her day. Dana stood off to one side, watching, while Jack balanced on Julia's hip as she tried to convince the two dogs to stop running around and barking for a few minutes.

She spotted Ron in the doorway and said, "Ron, would you and Dana take the dogs into the other room for a few minutes?"

Office Wilde craned his neck to look at him.

"Hey, Ron," he said, with a grin.

"Hello," Ron mumbled, pleased to have been noticed. He left the room to put Tigger in his basket. The puppy squirmed in his grip and protested when he landed in the basket, but Ron took no notice.

Dana pulled Horatio into the living room and showed him one of the chew toys that Mrs. Jurta had left behind. While Horatio tore at it, the two left the room and shut the door behind them.

They went back into the kitchen, where they found Jack happily seated on one of the chairs with a glass of water. Julia was making coffee, and Amelia was still talking with her dad as she played with his tie.

"… and we're just at the part where they have to rescue the girl," she finished. "It's, like, the best part!"

"Sounds like it," Wilde said. He affectionately ruffled her hair and looked at her pajamas. "Are those yours? They look a little big."

"Dana loaned them to me." She smiled proudly. "Aren't they pretty?"

"Very nice. Did you thank Dana and Ms. Lamontaigne for having you over?"

"Yes, Dad," she said, with a roll of her eyes. She caught Ron's frown and changed her tone. "That is, I think so. Thank you, Dana, and Ms. Lamontaigne."

"You're welcome," Dana said.

Julia turned from the counter with a cup of coffee. "No worries, Amelia, but call me Julia, please."

"I'm really sorry about the imposition," Wilde said, adjusting his grip on Amelia so he could take the cup. "I would have called, but we were up in the northwest part of town today and reception's bad up there."

"No problem," Julia said, fixing herself a cup of tea. "It was an emergency, after all."

It struck Ron that Wilde looked rather annoyed.

"Well, thank you. There is actually a written procedure that Mrs. Jurta is supposed to follow under such circumstances. She's a nice lady but... Not very good at following directions, I guess."

Julia turned back to the table and gave him a warm smile. "Well, it all worked out for the best. As it turned out, we were in need of Amelia's help. Isn't that right, Dana?"

"That's right - she helped set up my room," Dana responded. "I've got a bed now, and drawers and *everything*."

She slid into the chair nearest to Wilde. Ron, after a moment's hesitation, followed suit, taking the chair beside Jack.

"But no bureau," Amelia said.

"No bureau?" Wilde asked. He turned to Julia. "Oh, right. You mentioned that you might need help with those. Want me to do that now?"

"Now?" Julia asked.

"Sure. Ron and I can have them upstairs in a jiffy, right, Ron?"

Ron couldn't keep from beaming. "Right!"

She grinned. "Well, all right then, if you insist."

Julia showed them the storage room, where the bureaus stood empty. Ron and Wilde moved one of the bureaus to the foot of the stairs, then started to heft them up. It was surprisingly heavy. Ron's arms strained with the load and Wilde shook his head.

"I'm not surprised you decided to wait," he said.

Creases of worry appeared on Julia's forehead. "Is it too much?"

"We can do it," Ron said, and Wilde nodded in agreement.

With some difficulty, they maneuvered it into Dana's room and stood it in the proper place.

Officer Wilde placed a hand flat on the top and tried to wiggle it. It moved slightly.

"The floor boards in here are a little warped," he said.

"Should I brace it?" Julia asked.

He shook his head. "Dana would have to really work to bring it down on herself."

They brought the next two upstairs in the same way, and Ron was sweating by the time they loaded in the last of the drawers. Wilde tested the boys' bureaus, which were taller, and decided that they were in danger of tipping. They didn't have the proper bracing equipment in the Budd house, but the Wildes did.

"We'll get them. Come on, Ron," he said, turning for the stairs.

"Right!" Ron replied, jumping up to join him.

They raced through the rain to fetch the tools in Wilde's garage and then back again. While they worked upstairs, they talked about cars and fishing, and Wilde told him that some of the best fishing was to be had in New Hampshire.

"You like to fish?" he asked.

"Yes," Ron said eagerly. "Only I don't go too often."

"I suppose Julia doesn't like it much."

"I don't know. I never asked."

Securing the bureaus to the wall took less time than it did for Julia to come upstairs to tell Wilde that there was coffee left if he wanted more. Wilde seemed willing, and as it was obviously going to be an adult conversation, Ron felt compelled to rejoin the others in the living room.

When the movie was finished, Wilde came in and told Amelia to gather the leashes.

"Time to go home," he said.

"Okay, Dad," she mumbled. She slipped onto the floor and said goodbye to Dana.

Julia broke in, saying, "Oh, but the puppies are asleep. Why don't we just leave them here for the night? Mrs. Jurta's picking them up tomorrow."

"Are you sure?"

"Oh, yes. It'll be fine."

And so the matter was settled. The Wildes left, and the Budds got ready to go to bed in their new rooms.

Dana was excited about her bedroom, especially now that it had a bureau. She dragged Ron into the room and began to chatter.

"I totally love this bureau! I can turn it into a vanity, just like Mom's, if I get a little mirror to put on top."

Ron liked her excitement. "Yeah, that's be cool."

"I should talk to Aunt Julia about it."

"I wouldn't," he said, gently. "We're only going to be here a few weeks."

Her face fell. "Oh," she said. "I forgot about that."

It felt good to be in a real bed again, with real sheets, blankets, and pillows. Ron couldn't stop himself from sighing as he slid in and Julia, who was tucking Jack into his bed, laughed.

"Feeling pampered?" she asked, coming over. She sat on the edge of Ron's bed and ran a hand through his hair. It reminded Ron strongly of Mom, and he snuggled deeper into his blankets.

"Make sure you wash your hair tomorrow, Ron. It's starting to look a little tired."

"Yes'm."

She kept stroking his head, as though she had more to say. He looked at her and she smiled down at him in the dark.

"Officer Wilde offered to take you fishing sometime. Is that something you'd like to do? I know you've been missing the Boy Scouts."

Excitement hit him like a jolt of electricity. "Do you think we could?"

She smiled and squeezed his arm. "It was a nice offer, but we don't really know him all that well yet. Let me think about it."

"Let me think about it," as Ron well knew, was adult code for "the answer is already no, but I want to let you down gently." He fought his disappointment and nodded.

"Thank you for all your help today," Julia said, softly. "I don't know what I'd do without you."

A warm feeling washed over him, as she kissed his forehead. Although he couldn't admit it, the affection felt as good to receive as it was good to be in a bed again.

"Good night, kiddo. Sleep well."

He listened to her going down the stairs, thinking about Officer Wilde and his offer. Wilde seemed to like Aunt Julia and she appreciated his help. Perhaps, if he could prove to her that Officer Wilde was an okay guy, a straight-shooter, she'd relent.

The bedroom door creaking open interrupted his thoughts. He lifted his head to see Dana shutting the door carefully behind her. She made a great show of tiptoeing towards his bed, where she leaned over him and whispered, "Ron? Are you awake?"

"Yeah," he whispered. He sat up and switched on the lamp, flooding the room with light. Dana blinked and crinkled her eyes against the sudden brightness.

"What's the matter?" he asked. "Can't sleep?"

She rubbed her eyes and shook her head. "No, I forgot to tell you."

"Forgot to tell me what?"

Dana leaned forward conspiratorially. "Amelia – she's in," she whispered.

For the life of him, Ron couldn't figure out what she was talking about. "In?"

"Yes. She said she'd help."

"Help with what?"

"With the haunted house, obviously. She says the dogs won't go near it." She leaned in, her eyes glittering. "They can smell ghosts, you know."

Ron stared at her, horrified. "You told her about Dylan? That was supposed to be a secret!"

"Amelia's good at keeping secrets," she protested.

"How do you know that?"

She fingered the trim of his blanket. "Um... Well, she told me so." When he sighed and shook his head, she gave him an anxious look. "Is it all right, Ron? Is she in?"

They heard Julia then – it sounded as though she was at the bottom of the stairs, listening. They froze and waited. After a minute, she moved on, and Ron switched off the light.

"Is she in?" Dana's voice conveyed her anxiety.

Ron nodded; then, realizing she couldn't see him in the dark, said, "Yeah, she's in, but no one else."

"Okay – thanks!"

"Better get to bed, before Aunt Julia comes back."

"Yeah, sure." She scampered to the door. She turned as she stepped out and whispered, "Love you, Ron!" Then she was gone.

"Love you, too," he muttered. He settled back down and fell asleep instantly.

# 21

Ron woke up staring through a skylight into a brilliantly blue sky. Unlike the other day, he knew where he was instantly: in his new room, in his new bed, with clean sheets and newly painted walls. The air in the room felt fresh, scrubbed clean. Someone, probably Aunt Julia, had opened the window and turned on the fan.

He didn't want to move. The brightness of the day, the clean scent in the air, and the crispness of the sheets made him want to stay in his comfortable nest of blankets for a few minutes more.

He heard Horatio's sharp bark from downstairs. The angle of the sun through the skylight told Ron that it was late. He threw on some clothes, made his bed quickly, and was halfway down the stairs with his toothbrush kit when he heard a knock at the side door. Julia called out for Dana to get it, but Ron beat her to it.

Mrs. Jurta gave him a friendly, hurried smile as she brushed past him, followed by Amelia.

"Good morning, good morning, and good morning!" she called out. "Well, hello there, Tigger! How are you today?"

Tigger wriggled with excitement. When Dana put him on the floor, he ran to Amelia and the little girl was delighted. At the table,

Julia gave up trying to hold Horatio back and let him go, causing Jack to shriek in terror.

The whole kitchen was a confusing mess of noise and calamity. Ron pushed through the kitchen and sought refuge in the bathroom, and he didn't come out until he heard Mrs. Jurta and the dogs leave.

He went into the messy, empty kitchen, too hungry to worry about anything more than breakfast. He was munching on a bowl of cereal when Julia and his siblings came back in.

"Whew!" Julia's hair was mussed and her shirt wasn't tucked in properly, but she looked wide awake despite the circles under her eyes. "Whoever said taking care of dogs was easy lied. It's only 8:30 and I'm exhausted. Good morning, Ron."

"Morning," he mumbled.

Dana sat next to him. "It was a lot of fun having Horatio and Tigger and Amelia here," she said, longingly. "I'm sorry they had to go home."

"I'm not!" Jack said. "Aunt Julia, can I go outside?"

"Finish you milk first, Jack."

"Aww…."

"Do you think we could have them over again?" Dana asked eagerly. "For a sleep over, like we did last night?"

"I don't know, honey. That would be up to Mrs. Jurta and Officer Wilde." Julia poured herself a cup of coffee.

"Maybe we could keep one?" she wheedled.

Julia sat and took a sip, looking over her mug at Dana. "A dog is a long term responsibility, not to mention an expensive one."

"But these dogs are from the pound so Amelia says they're free," Dana pointed out. "They're healthy and they're good dogs, the best there is."

"There's more to it than just the expense, Dana. Dogs need a lot of attention and time, and during the school year, you're very busy. Anyway, I don't want to take on anything new until I get my new job."

Dana exchanged glances with Ron. Both had forgotten about Julia's new job, the one she still hadn't found. Both of them knew lots of kids with parents out of work, sometimes for years at a time.

Ron decided that it was best that they did not take on a dog just yet. Before he could convey his decision to Dana, however, she was saying, "It's just that they could get adopted at any time, Aunt Julia. Then we'll never see them again."

Before anyone could respond to that, a roar from a large lawn mower erupted right outside the window, followed immediately by a sharp knock at the door. J. C. and his crew had arrived.

Julia answered the door and led Derval into the kitchen.

Derval was asking, "Do you want me to work today, Mrs. Lamontaigne?"

"Just Julia, please. And yes, that would be great. I have a lot of work to do and it's such a nice day, it would be good to have the kids play outside."

"But you said I might be able to work on my garden today," Dana protested.

"Oh, that's right, I did," Julia said, looking at her watch in indecision.

Derval said, "I can help you with that. My mom has a big garden at home and I work in there all the time with her."

Dana grinned. "Awesome. That would be *great*, Derval."

"Yes, but, um," she looked ruefully at her smoothly polished nails. "Do you have any garden gloves?"

"Yes, we do!" Dana jumped up and ran into the dining room, shouting over her shoulder, "We got them the other day for Aunt Julia and they're brand new. It's all right, isn't it, Aunt Julia?"

"Yes, its fine, Dana," she said, and then gave Derval a searching look. "Are you sure you want to go mucking about in a garden today?"

"It's fine," Derval said. "It's a good way to get a tan. Unless, of course, you need help in here?"

"No, I'll be fine, thank you. Ron and I have everything under control, don't we, Ron?"

Ron nodded and dumped the rest of his cereal into the trash. He wasn't hungry anymore and, anyway, there wasn't time.

Derval took the two younger kids outside, while Ron and Julia installed air conditioners in Dana's and Ron's rooms. The window in the boys' room was so small that they thought that it might not fit, but they managed it. Ron was glad that they had a skylight, because the air conditioner took up almost the entire window.

"The new owners should install central air," Julia commented as they went downstairs. "Of course, there's no way to tell them that without making the house look bad."

"If we lived here full time, would you install central air?" Ron asked.

"Oh, like a shot. I'm such a baby when it comes to heat. All right, time to start on the living room."

Ron thought that they should do Aunt Julia's bedroom next, but she told him she wanted to be able to invite people in without being embarrassed.

They worked until 11:30, stripping what they could of the wallpaper, which wasn't much. The wallpaper was as stubborn as Robert had warned.

Ron was hungry, and covered in sweat and dust. The lawnmowers had long since ceased to roar. Occasionally they'd see one of J. C.'s crew walking by a window with his head down, as though studying the ground.

"Would you go outside and see how Derval and the kids are doing?" Julia asked.

Ron was happy to. It looked like a great day to be outside and he wanted to get away from the dust and mold.

He found the little garden crawling with activity. Most of the dirt had been turned over and neat rows created with seed packets on Popsicle sticks (freshly cleaned off, judging by the pink stains) marking what was buried there. Jack was happily making mud castles in the corner. Derval and Dana, each with dirty knees and filthy gloves, stood off to the side, watching as J. C., Mitch, and Connor wrestled with a thin, young stump in the garden.

They were refilling the hole with dirt when Julia came out to call them in for lunch. She thanked J. C. and his crew and offered them lunch, but J. C. turned her down, telling her that they were obliged to two other lawns that day and they were already late.

"I've never in my life met boys like that," Julia told Ron as they were going into the house. "They are really remarkable."

"That's my boyfriend," Derval said, with thinly disguised pride.

Around 6:00 p.m., Ron, Dana, and Jack were outside, riding their bikes up and down the sidewalk. The road was almost completely still that Friday afternoon - only the occasional jogger or car disturbed their quiet. Derval had left a few hours earlier, and Julia was writing on her laptop in the shade of the porch.

She and Ron had worked hard all day; yet despite that, there was still so much left to do that Ron wondered how they were going to get it all done without hiring someone to help. He was silent as he rode alongside Dana, with Jack huffing and puffing on his trike behind them.

Their path fell far short of the haunted house. It seemed to watch them as they rode back and forth. Ron, for all his curiosity about the place, was content to stay in the sunlight.

Their silent riding came to an abrupt end when Amelia shot out of her driveway and challenged them to race.

The race degenerated into a chase, the two girls trying to catch Ron, and the pursuit had them crisscrossing the quiet street, going up the sidewalks and off again, into the driveways and out. They didn't notice the lengthening shadows of the trees or the steadily darkening sky. They didn't notice that Julia had long since laid aside her laptop, contentedly watching them from the sidelines.

They shouted and laughed until their lungs hurt, their sides ached, the sweat poured down their backs, and Dana complained that she was getting a headache from the heat.

Then Julia called them in for supper. She plucked Jack off of his trike while the three others circled her with their bikes.

"Oh," Amelia sounded disappointed. "Do we have to stop? I'm not hungry yet."

"I am," Dana said. "I'm starving. Aunt Julia, can Amelia eat with us?"

"When is your father coming home, Amelia?" Julia asked

"Any time now," Amelia said cheerfully. "He won't mind if you invite me over to dinner. I'll even help with the dishes."

Just then, the familiar police car pulled into the Wilde's driveway and Amelia ran to greet her father. Ron saw Julia's smile broaden when she saw the officer. Wilde gave them a friendly wave before going into the house, which Julia returned, and the Budds were left alone.

"Well," Julia said, shaking her head as though to clear her thoughts. "That's that, then. Dana and Ron, please tidy up the yard while Jack and I make supper."

"I don't want to make supper," Jack declared. "I want to play with my chalk."

"We'll play again tomorrow, pal," Julia said soothingly. "Come on. I'll make you noodle soup."

Dana and Ron started cleaning up and were still at it when Dylan rode up on his bicycle. He wore a towel tied about his bare chest like an ancient Roman stole and rolled over the new front lawn, jerking to a halt inches from Ron.

"Hey, Budd," he said, grinning.

Ron grinned back. "Hey, what's up?"

"Just finished swimming," he said, twisting to look back at Katy. "It was a good time – you should have been there. We ate a ton, too."

"Cool," Ron said.

Dana raced over. "Hi, Dylan, guess what? We have a new member on the team!"

Dylan frowned. "We do? Who?"

"Amelia, from next door. She's a real good watcher, and she has her own camera, too."

"Oh, man, Ron!" Dylan whined. "We don't need to be dragging little kids into this! They're going to slow us down, you know?"

The older boy's tone hurt Dana – her face began to crumble.

"The more eyes we have, the better," Ron said firmly. "My sister is a good observer and so is Amelia. Besides, we could use another camera, don't you think?"

"But, dude, what if they scream or something? I mean, I don't want to be babysitting the whole time we're out."

"You won't be," Ron said. "Dana's solid. She won't run or scream, will you, Dana?"

She shook her head.

"Besides," Ron continued, "Amelia also has use of Mrs. Jurta's dogs. They'd be helpful, sniffing around the place and warning us of danger."

"Ghosts don't smell," Dylan pointed out.

Ron had no answer for that, but fortunately, Katy did. "Dylan, you dope, animals sense ghosts. They won't go near the place if they detect one."

"Oh, fine, all right then. You're in, Dana," Dylan declared. "Amelia, too, I guess." He went on to the next point of business. "Okay, so, like, are you available tomorrow for a bit of reconnoitering?"

"Dylan." Katy shook her head, annoyed. "We're going to Dad's tomorrow, remember? For the Fourth of July thing he's doing?"

"Oh, bummer!" Dylan said. "When are we getting back?"

"Monday afternoon." She swatted a mosquito on her arm.

"Okay, how about Monday afternoon, Ron?"

"We can make it," Dana said confidently. "We work with Aunt Julia in the mornings, not the afternoons."

"Awesome," Dylan said. "We'll see you then."

"Let's *go*, Dylan," Katy whined. The insects were gathering and she was getting tired of fending them off.

"Oh, all right," he said. "Later, guys. Monday, remember."

They raced away, and Ron turned to Dana.

"We don't know that we're available on Monday," he said. "Remember what I told you about Aunt Julia needing extra help? We have to get everything done by the first week of August. We won't have time to play."

"This is important, Ron. Besides, we promised Dylan that we'd help and a promise is a promise." She turned her back on him and started to collect the scattered pieces of chalk from Jack's set. "Aunt Julia told me that one of the most important things we can do in life is to keep our promises."

He sighed. She was right. And, anyway, he really did want to find out.

"Okay, you're right, Dana. But we'll have to keep an eye on Dylan. I don't really trust him."

Dana stopped, staring at him wide-eyed. "You don't?" she whispered.

He reached out and patted her shoulder. "Don't worry, Dana. I can handle it."

She looked up at him and smiled bravely.

# 22

"I hope Amelia will be at Mass today," Dana said. It was Sunday, and she was standing in front of the mirror while Julia arranged her hair before church. "She said she and her dad always have to go to the early Mass because of his work."

Julia struggled with a braid as she said, "She doesn't get to see her dad a lot, does she?"

Dana shrugged. "He's a cop. She said that being a cop is a tough job and requires a lot of sacrifices. She says when she grows up she's going to be either a cop or a doctor. I like Amelia. She's smart and funny and she really, really likes hanging out with us. It's too bad that we can't babysit her during the day instead of Mrs. Jurta. Then I'd have her to play with all the time."

Julia smiled and ruffled her hair affectionately. "It is, but perhaps it's best that she goes with Mrs. Jurta. After all, all Mrs. Jurta has is her dogs. She's probably lonely, too."

"There are lots of lonely people in the world, aren't there?" Dana sighed.

"Yes, I'm afraid there is. That's why it's important to take care of the people you have in your life."

"I guess. I think Amelia's really lonely."

"Oh, she must have lots of friends in school," Julia said, as she stood and put Dana's hairbrush on the bureau. She thought, *this bureau would make a good vanity if we just put a mirror and some fabric here...*

"No she doesn't. She said that I'm the first real friend that she's made in Franklin. Except for Tigger, of course."

Julia looked at her, concerned, but said simply, "Of course."

"She said that I'm the first one who'll listen to her talk. She said that she really likes you, too. She says that you are a really good cook."

"Well, I must say, no one can whip up peanut butter and jelly quite like me. Come on, my girl. We're late."

"All right."

After Mass, they went downstairs for coffee and donuts in the hall.

The church hall was large, with a low hung ceiling, rows of folding chairs, a small stage at one end and a kitchen at the other. Julia spotted Mrs. Jurta among the mostly middle-aged crowd, talking animatedly with a tall, distinguished-looking man in a suit. There weren't many children. Apparently, there were no religious education programs until public school started again in the fall.

It was much cooler in the hall than it had been in the church, and Julia was grateful. She maneuvered the kids into line, and jumped when Amelia suddenly appeared.

"Dana!"

Although it had only been twenty-four hours since they'd seen each other, Dana greeted her like a long-lost cousin. They hugged and immediately began to giggle together.

Julia caught Ron's eye and he rolled his eyes as if to say, *Girls. What can you do with them?*

"Oh, man, I was so hoping you'd come today!" Amelia squealed. "Hello, Julia. Hi Jack. Hi... Ron."

"Hello, Amelia." Julia looked around for Wilde, but he was nowhere to be seen.

"Hey," Ron said.

"Are you guys coming to the Fourth of July party tonight?" Amelia asked eagerly. "It's going to be awesome. Last year, I went to Boston and saw the Boston Pops play, which was kind of boring, but the fireworks were cool and Kevin let me go anywhere I wanted all by myself."

"Kevin?" Julia asked.

"My mom's boyfriend. Well, he was, anyway. Now she's seeing someone else. I'm glad, because Kevin's boring and he's ugly, too. My mom is, like, gorgeous, and she should be with someone who is handsome, like Dad's handsome, you know?" She turned to Dana. "My Dad is handsome, isn't he? Mrs. Jurta said that he's the most handsome cop on the force and I think she's right, don't you, Julia?"

"Oh, yes, absolutely," Julia said with more enthusiasm than she intended.

"I do, too," Amelia said proudly.

"Who's taking you to the lake?" Dana asked.

"Mrs. Jurta, of course. Who else?"

"I don't know. You spend a lot of time with her."

"Yeah, but I won't for long. She's going to Florida with her dog to get his surgery done. She told Dad last night – he doesn't know what he's going to do yet."

Julia noticed when Wilde appeared in the door. He was dressed in his blues and was in the middle of a conversation with a heavy-set older man who appeared to be lecturing him. The other man carried himself with some authority, and Julia's instinct marked him as a town official. Wilde's calm seemed to irritate the man.

Ron caught Julia's gaze and raised his eyebrows.

Julia shrugged. They were probably dickering over a city matter – none of their business. She turned to Jack and handed him a donut.

He rejected it. "I want a powdered one!" he pouted.

"There's Dad," Amelia said. "Maybe he'll have a donut with us. Dana, you're coming to the lake tonight, right?"

"Oh, yeah, absolutely!" Dana said. "We wouldn't miss it."

Julia handed Jack to Ron, motioning him to an empty table. "We'll all be there, Amelia. I'm glad you're coming, too."

Amelia's smile widened. "I'm pretty excited, too!"

She sat herself next to Julia, chatting incessantly, while Julia was occupied with Jack's adventures with the powdered donut. After tearing into it, Jack wanted to join several other small children in the far corner of the room, but Julia felt that he ought to look less like walking powdered sugar and more like a boy before he went. They argued over it for a while, then Ron broke in.

"Come on, Jack," Ron said. "I'll take you to the bathroom, and then you can go play."

Jack grabbed his hand and the brothers took off.

Wilde was talking amicably now with the man behind the coffee machine, and he gave Ron and Jack a friendly wave as they passed.

Mrs. Jurta wandered over. "That Jack is such handsome little boy. You must be proud." She watched the boys with the keen eyes of a grandmother.

"He's great." Julia smiled at the older woman. "How are you, Mrs. Jurta?"

Mrs. Jurta snagged a chair and seated herself with a plop. Her thin face looked tired and her demeanor was one of a person who has fought great battles and sees only more on the horizon. "You're coming to the Fourth tonight?"

"Yes we are and, to be honest, I'm looking forward to a night off."

"I guess you would be," Mrs. Jurta said. "I hear that you've been tearing your little house apart."

"It sure feels that way. I'm sorry to hear that your dog is no better."

Mrs. Jurta nodded and looked into her cup. "I know. He's more than just a dog to me, you know. He's a friend, my buddy. I have a surgeon friend in Florida who's the best in the business, and he's promised to work on my boy as soon as I get him down there. I'm trying to get the other dogs settled so I can leave by the fourteenth, but it is so hard finding any foster parents on such short notice. I mean, you can't give them to just anyone."

Julia smelled a setup, but there was no way she was falling for it. They couldn't possibly take care of two untrained puppies and finish the house in time.

"It must be difficult," she commented.

"You have no idea. You see, I care about animals." Her tone made it sound as if this part of her personality made her very unique. "I want the best for them, which makes it even more difficult." She leaned forward in her chair. "I don't suppose that you and the kids would be able to..."

"Why, hello, Officer Wilde," Julia said, a little too loudly.

Officer Wilde was as delighted to see everyone as they were to see him. They chatted for a while, then it was time for the Wildes to be going. Julia, hoping to avoid the direct question, decided that they would go, too. Mrs. Jurta was noticeably disappointed.

They said their goodbyes and went home. At the house, her cell phone started ringing. Julia sent the kids upstairs to change while she took the call.

"Hello?"

"Julia?" Miriam Budd's voice sound surprised and distant. She spoke loudly over something that sounded like a mariachi band. "Julia, is that you?"

Julia felt like a noose was tightening around her neck. "Yes, hello, Miriam, how's the cruise?"

"Where are the children?"

"They're upstairs changing. Where are you?"

"Puerta Vallarta. It's in Mexico, on the Pacific. How are the children?"

"They're great. How's Walter?"

"He's fine. Actually, he's had a touch of food poisoning and he's sleeping in the cabin right now. We ate off the boat. I warned him, but you know how men are. How is Dana?"

Julia sighed. "She's fine."

"Is she eating enough?"

"Oh, yes."

"And Ron?"

"He's eating like a horse."

Miriam was not pleased. "That's unusual. He has a delicate stomach, you know."

Julia got up and began to pace back and forth, trying to work out the knot of tension in her back.

"He likes only plain things. Amanda used to have to give him just bread and milk for the longest time."

Julia sighed. "I know, I was there."

"What was that?"

"I said he's fine. He's growing tall. So is Jack, actually."

"So they need new clothes?"

"Not yet, but soon."

"I'll make a note to take Ron shopping. Kid shops will still suit Jack – the styles are so cute. But I'll let my shopper handle that for me."

"Don't worry about it, Miriam. We've got it covered."

Suspicious now, Miriam asked, "We? What is this 'we'? Have you a man in your life?" She didn't have to add "at last" – it came through loud and clear anyway.

"No, I was referring to the children and me. We've got it all set. We're going shopping this week, so I can get what they need then."

"I'll wire you some money so you can take them somewhere decent."

"No, Miriam," Julia said firmly. "That will not be necessary."

"Nonsense, Julia. Of course it's necessary. You have three children in your care. I don't think you realize just how expensive it is to raise children these days."

"I'm starting to get an idea."

"You don't have to put on the brave front with me, Julia. I know what financial difficulties you've had in the past. Some people simply aren't good with money, but there's no reason why the children should suffer. I'll send it this afternoon."

Julia took a deep breath. "I'll refuse it, Miriam. I don't need your money and I won't take it."

"Julia, I never – You are the most stubborn…"

She would have gone on, so Julia did the only thing she could do without being brazenly rude. There was a corner of the living room with no reception; she walked slowly toward it. Miriam's voice grew crackly until the connection broke off entirely.

She hung up the phone and took another deep breath. The newly installed air conditioning unit made a soothing hum and the cool air was refreshing. She looked around the empty room and, seeing so much work still to do, she felt like sinking into the floor.

Perhaps Miriam was right. Perhaps she wasn't suited for the job. Maybe she had bitten off more than she could chew. Her simple house-restoration was growing with every piece of wallpaper they tore off.

"If this house had a name," she said out loud. "It would be Julia's Folly."

"Aunt Julia?"

Dana peeked through the doorway. She looked nervous, having picked up on Julia's mood.

"Yes, Dana?"

"Can we go outside and play? Amelia's on her bike and she keeps beeping her horn."

"All right, but stay on the sidewalk in front of the house."

"Thanks!"

A moment later, Julia heard the three of them running, a door slam, and the house was quiet.

Julia grinned in satisfaction. She'd promised them no work on Sundays, and if she so much as lifted a rug, Ron would instantly appear at her side and drag Dana along with him. Now that they were outside, they wouldn't notice if she did a little work.

*What's the point? You'll never finish. Like Miriam implies, you've bitten off more than you can chew.*

She heard laughter outside and went to the window, smiling as she watched Dana and Amelia push Jack on his trike, giggling as he made race car noises. Ron, lazily pedaling his bike back and forth, looked on in amusement as the trike spilled and the three younger children went rolling on the new lawn, laughing hysterically.

Julia hadn't seen Ron smile since before the accident. Haunted by the memory of his parents and his own overwhelming sense of responsibility, he hadn't seemed to have the space or time to smile. Today, though, he looked on the verge of a smile, a huge step forward.

*I can do one thing right,* Julia thought.

It was enough to motivate her.

She changed her clothes, tied up her hair, and had just grabbed her first armload of things from the dining room when she heard a knock at the door.

"Come in, it's open!" she shouted, thinking it was one of the kids.

When she came back into the kitchen, she was surprised to see Robert Wilde there, looking around, uncomfortable. He relaxed when he saw her and gave her a shy smile.

It flashed through Julia's mind that he never, ever came upon her when she was ready for company. She always looked a mess.

Pushing the thought aside, she said, "Oh, hello. I thought you were out on patrol."

"I'm on my way," he said. "Derval Raye is coming by to look after Amelia while I'm gone, now that Mrs. Jurta is so busy with her dog's problem."

"Would you like some coffee?"

He shook his head. "Thank you, but no. I actually came because I have a little business proposal for you."

"Really? Okay, I'm listening."

"Mrs. Jurta is going away on the fourteenth, and she doesn't know when she's coming back. I go back to work on the fourteenth, and have no one else to look after Amelia while I'm gone. I've used up all my vacation time until October, and we'll be short staffed that week because several of the other officers are going to be out on leave."

*Oh, no,* Julia thought. *He's going to ask me to babysit. How can I possibly do that and still get these rooms done! I haven't even finished the kitchen yet. What is it about me that make people see 'Reliable Sitter'?*

"Next week I have off and I was wondering: would you be willing to watch Amelia for about a week or so in exchange for a week of help on your house?"

Startled, she stared at him.

He hurried on. "I know we don't really know each other well yet, but Amelia's really taken with your kids. I haven't seen her have this much fun or look this happy with anyone since we've moved here. And I'm a fair hand around the place. I renovated our house before we moved into it. Between the two of us, we could manage to get everything done in a matter of days, I think."

"There's so much work to do, though. And it's your week off..."

He chuckled. "I sit in a car all day long, on my backside, waiting for something to happen. When I'm not doing that, I'm filing reports. I'm dying for a chance to work on something real. Redoing your house, working with tools and paint, would be a great way to spend my vacation, trust me."

"What about Amelia? She's been talking all this week about spending your vacation time with you, and I don't want to take you away from her."

"Actually, it was her idea. I figure that I'll take one or two days just for her and me and we'll have the evenings together. Anyway, she'll be hanging around here with us, too, which would be better for her. You see, Amelia is..." Wilde carefully phrased his thought. "She's, how do I put it? She requires a lot of attention and a lot of stimulation." He smiled broadly. "I'm afraid that if she's with me for nine days straight without a break, she'll get tired, throw me out, and find a new dad."

Julia found herself laughing. "Okay," she said. "I could see that."

His smile deepened and he extended his hand. "Is it a deal, then?"

She looked at his hand and hesitated. She'd be a fool to turn away an honest expression of aid. It wasn't charity, like Miriam's check. This would be a fair exchange and both would benefit. And hanging out with Amelia was good for Dana: seeing Amelia as a friend in need was helping Dana to see beyond herself. Julia wanted to encourage that.

And it would be nice for Julia to get to know Amelia's dad.

She felt her face turning red, and covered by extending her hand. "A deal, partner."

Wilde grinned and took her hand in a firm grip.

"Okay, partner," was all he said.

# 23

The last person Julia expected to see at the Franklin City Fourth of July celebration wound up in line just ahead of the kids and her.

A. Glen Bernard, dressed in an appalling outfit of red shorts, blue shirt, and white socks, happily piled onions and pickles onto his hamburger, while chatting with an older couple who seemed very much enamored with the idea of talking to a semi-famous published author.

It was nearly seven o'clock and the mosquitoes were starting to show up. So far, the party had gone on very nicely. The children played on the beach with Amelia, Derval, and several other neighborhood kids. They'd worn themselves out with shouting and giggling and swimming. Julia, after taking a short dip, spent her time relaxing in the sun, swatting at insects, reading a page or two of her novel, and chatting with the few people she knew.

It seemed that the whole town was there and the line for food was long and slow. Julia's stomach was growling, and poor Jack looked white and pinched with hunger. As soon as she had a plate for him, she sent him with Ron to their picnic spot with the promise that she, Dana, and Amelia would bring the chips and sodas as soon as they could.

Caroline Ojacor was just behind Julia, dressed in a flower print dress and looking as if she'd just stepped out of a photo shoot. She leaned over and whispered, "That is the writer, is it not?"

"Yes," Julia said, keeping her voice very low. "Mr. Bernard."

"I thought so. He has been around a lot lately, asking questions and making a nuisance of himself. They say he is writing another book, but they don't know what it's about. The city council is worried about it – they think it might bring negative publicity for the town."

"Why? Are there any more unsolved murders lying around?"

"Joseph, my husband, said that there are some quite embarrassing stories about the town's people. He even mentioned the trouble that Irwin boy got into."

"John?"

"No, Michael. When he was young, he was sent to prison for a few years – drugs or some other such thing. But when he came out, he straightened up and got a good job in Canada. Of course, that doesn't make such a good story, does it?"

Bernard finished with the onions and moved on toward the plates of salad. He stood there for a few minutes, still chatting with the elderly couple.

Julia handed Caroline a ketchup bottle, saying, "Sometimes, even negative publicity can work in the town's favor."

Caroline shook her head and grinned. "It is all nothing. People will write what they want and other people will get upset, but it will pass. We needn't think anything of it at all. Are you using the mustard?"

Julia handed it to her. "I agree. It looks as though Mr. Bernard is getting along famously with that lady and her husband."

Caroline didn't look up. "They are the Mones. They like Bernard because he used a lot of their testimony in his book. They think they are celebrities now."

Julia studied the pair. The woman was of medium height, with dark tinted hair and a tidy outfit. She did most of the talking and often touched Bernard's arm when she was making a particular point. Her husband seemed to let his wife carry the conversation, agreeing with every point that was made. None of the three noticed that they were holding up the line.

Caroline spoke again. "Bernard is a persistent man. He pestered Helen Jurta for months about the first book. He went through all the court records and looked up each witness and talked with all of them. He even went to the city council and met with them about going into the house, but they wouldn't let him. He had to make do with the blueprints."

"Have you met him?"

"Not I. Joseph and I, we did not come here until five years ago. We knew nothing about the murders, except what we have read in the book. Have you read it?"

"No, not yet."

"It is very good," she said. Her 'd's, Julia noticed, were pronounced quickly, so that they sounded almost like a 't'. "A very good mystery. I will loan you mine, if you'd like."

"Actually, I already have a copy. I ran into Mr. Bernard at the bookstore a few days ago and he signed a copy for me."

"Ah, you are a fan?"

"Not hardly. I'd never heard of him before."

The lady serving the salad made an impatient gesture, and finally, Mr. Bernard understood and moved his little party down to the next station. Julia and Caroline filled up their plates, then went to find the others.

All around, people were talking, laughing, and eating. The brass band was taking a break and sat at a table near the pavilion, swigging bottles of water and downing hamburgers. The pavilion, in their absence, was being re-fitted for the annual play that the grade-schoolers were about to put on.

Ron and Jack were sitting with Caroline's husband, Joseph, who was talking with John Irwin Jr. Julia settled the kids down and then began to eat while the conversation swirled around her.

"How is your house coming along?" Caroline asked Julia. "I understand from Helen that you are completely making it over."

Julia nodded. "Oh, it's coming along. We've finished the kids' rooms, now we're working on the ground floor."

"Which house is this, now?" Joseph asked.

"It's on Whipple Lane."

"The old Purcell place," John Irwin said. "It's in good shape. I wouldn't think that there's too much to do."

Julia shook her head. "I didn't think so either, until I started working on it. Every time you pull down a cabinet or strip a piece of wallpaper, you find two more projects that need to be done. I think we're going to be seeing a lot more of each other, John."

He laughed and said, "Good heavens, what are you doing, busting down walls?"

"Just repairing some damaged ones. The living room is in rough shape."

"Whipple Lane," Joseph said thoughtfully. "Isn't that the same street that the murder house is on? The one in the book?"

"It's at the end of the street," Julia said quietly.

"It's an eyesore," Caroline exclaimed.

"The Lang house has been empty long a long time. I wonder why they haven't sold it?" Julia said.

"The family's holding on to it." Joseph was carefully tucking chips into the remaining half of his hamburger. "Brad's family is still trying to clear him. At least, that's what Mr. Bernard says. He probably knows more about the case than anyone else in town."

"Has anyone here read the book?" Julia asked.

John Irwin said, "I did. It was all right. He got Denis Gagnon to a 't', though."

"Which character was he in the book?" Caroline asked, brushing an ant off of her leg. "I don't remember a Denis."

"The Chief of Police," John replied. "He's a good guy, but he wasn't really up to the challenge of a controversial murder investigation. I was just a kid at the time, but I remember that the papers accused him of botching things up. I thought it was very unfair. He wasn't as big a fool as they said."

"What happened to him?" Julia asked, reaching over to wipe Jack's ketchup-covered mouth.

"Oh, he retired and moved to Florida. Still comes back to town every once in a while to visit."

Just then, some of the other men who were setting up a baseball game called for Joseph to come join them. It didn't take much persuading to get him to abandon his plate and go. Ron and Jack, eager to watch, followed right after.

They invited John Irwin, too, but he put them off until Joseph was out of earshot. Then he turned to Caroline and asked, "Have you invited the Lamontaignes to Joseph's birthday bash yet?"

"Why, no, I haven't!" Caroline seemed shocked by her oversight. "Would you please come? It is next Sunday at my house and it's a surprise for him. He is forty this year."

"We're trying to really pack the place," John explained. "What time did you say to arrive, Caroline? Six o'clock?"

"Yes. Rich is taking Joseph golfing and they should be home at 6:30. I want everyone to be hiding when he gets there."

"That sounds fun," Julia said, without committing.

"We still have to figure out what to do with the cars," John said. He slapped at a mosquito on his bare shoulder and Julia winced. His skin was so pink, it looked sun-burnt. "It would be pretty funny if we had everyone hiding in the house and he's walking past every car in town just to get to the front door."

"That would give the game away," Julia laughed.

"I know. Anyway, you should come. There'll be tons of food, and kids for your little ones to play with. They have a fire pit in the back yard and my wife is bringing S'mores and hot dogs to roast."

"What should I bring?"

Caroline smiled. "It's potluck, so whatever you want."

John said, "It'll be a blast. You really should come. We could use a pretty face at the party."

"I beg your pardon?" Caroline feigned offense.

"I meant to say, *another* pretty face at the party."

"I thought so," Caroline said. "Please say you will come, Julia."

"Oh, well…" Julia hesistated. She hardly knew the Ojacors and felt awkward having John Irwin ask for their invitation. But it did sound like fun. "I think we can make it… I'll have to check our schedule and it's at home. Do you mind if I give you a call later this week to RSVP?"

"Not at all. I'll give you my number."

"Terrific," John said with satisfaction. He went to join the baseball game and left the two women to finish their dinner.

# 24

Julia cleared up the picnic things by herself. It was growing dark, so she brought their belongings to the car to prevent their being lost. While there, she slipped into a pair of sneakers and grabbed her sweater. It was surprisingly cool for a summer night.

On her way back, she was so busy checking her phone that she didn't notice the approach of A. Glen Bernard and his two fans until it was too late. She nearly ran into Mrs. Mone.

"Watch it!" Mrs. Mone snapped.

"Oh, I am sorry," Julia said, sidestepping her gingerly. "I wasn't paying attention."

"I guess not," Mrs. Mone said, eying the phone with suspicion. "I know they have laws against texting and driving, but I really think they ought to extend that to texting and walking. It's usually a problem with the youth, though."

Julia's cheeks flushed.

Bernard snapped his fingers. "You're the young lady in the bookstore!" he trumpeted. "I thought I knew you! I'm sure you remember me."

"I do, Mr. Bernard."

"Please, please, call me Glen. And your name is…"

"Julia," she said, resigned. "Julia Lamontaigne."

"Of course! This is a small world. Who'd have thought we'd run into each other so soon. Are you enjoying the book? What part are you at?"

"Wait a minute," Mrs. Mone said, snapping her brittle-looking fingers, too. "I've heard that name before, too. You're the young woman who bought that rat trap on Whipple Lane, right? Just two houses down from our place. I'm Doris Mone and this is my husband, George. I've seen you out jogging in the morning. Your children ride their bikes on my walk and I'm always afraid they're going to tear up our grass."

"I'm sure that they won't," Julia said. "They've been warned against going off the pavement."

"You live on Whipple Street?" Bernard asked.

"Lane," George offered.

"Another coincidence," Bernard said, delighted. "You're living up the street from the Lang house right as you're reading about the murder. Are you enjoying my book, by the way?"

Before Julia could respond, Mrs. Mone said, "George and I actually knew the Langs, you know. We had our portraits done by Stephanie herself."

"They're hanging in the living room," George volunteered.

"Lovely bit of work, that," Bernard said. "So lifelike, and such a good use of tonal colors. Really, she would have been right up there with Rosa Bonheur, if she had only lived long enough. To be cut down in the prime of life like that was, truly, a tragic loss for the art world."

"The Boston Museum actually contacted us about the portraits," Mrs. Mone continued archly. "They wanted to build up their collection, to bring Stephanie's genius to the masses. Naturally, one wishes to do what one can for the masses, but they're too precious to part with."

"They wanted to borrow the portraits for a traveling expedition," George said. "I was hoping that they'd offer to buy them outright."

"Not that we would have accepted," his wife interjected quickly. "You can't place a price on beauty."

George looked very much as though he thought they could.

Julia decided that since they were so willing to talk, she should oblige. "You know," she said. "I've heard so much about this murder, but some of the details contradict each other. For instance, I've heard that the Chief of Police was both an idiot and fully competent."

"He was a nice enough fellow," George mused.

"Way out of his depth," Bernard said. "Did the best he could do under the circumstances, but I think he only really lost it when the thing turned into a media circus."

Mrs. Mone said, "Chief Gagnon was an ape, a great big lug of a man without a brain in his head. He should have been fired years before this ever occurred. I still don't know why we didn't run him out on a rail when we had the chance."

"Now, Dorry," George said affectionately.

"Stephanie Milano Lang was an artist, Ms... " She didn't let the fact that she had forgotten Julia's last name throw her off track. "Some people, some plebeians, didn't understand and didn't appreciate her unique genius."

Julia frowned. "You think she was misunderstood?"

"Not just her work," Mrs. Mone sniffed. "She had needs. I'm sure I don't need to explain more than that."

"She... had a bit of a reputation," Bernard said delicately.

George Mone was grinning. His wife either didn't notice, or was the most secure married woman that Julia knew. Perhaps, she simply didn't care. Some people would willingly sacrifice their all at the altar of the arts.

Mrs. Mone continued. "She was a woman," she insisted. "She had an artist's needs, a woman's needs, needs which her husband was too often away on business to fulfill."

"I was given to understand that she was the soul of decorum," Julia said. "No one mentioned anything about her running around on her husband."

"It was suppressed out of respect for her family," Bernard explained. "Her father was a well-respected politician and her mother was a diplomat. She was very well off, you understand, and quite the wild child at college, although she was careful to cover her tracks before the press got hold of them. Frankly, all her friends were surprised when she married – they never thought that she would settle down."

"She wasn't happy in the marriage," Mrs. Mone said. "She told me that commitment stifles creativity." She sniffed. "I thought Brad was a brute."

Julia was beginning to think that that everyone in Franklin was an eccentric. She understood that the publication of the book would stir up old memories, and she knew that small, dying cities were notorious for their civic spirit; but even so, this kind of passion seemed a little much.

Bernard slapped at a mosquito and asked, "So, are you enjoying the book?"

Julia hadn't started the book and apologized for it, making the excuse that she was too busy renovating the house. Mr. Bernard didn't seem to mind. It gave him a chance to use his speech about how good a book it really was.

"I'm sure it is," Julia said. "You've kept the memory of Stephanie fresh in everyone's mind."

He beamed. "That I owe to Mrs. Mone, my chief source."

Mrs. Mone smiled demurely. "I knew her well. There was a meeting of minds there. I have none of her talent or genius, but we understood one another. We would talk for hours, Stephanie and I. I consider it my duty to keep her memory alive and to vindicate her in death."

"That's right," Bernard said. "Mrs. Mone has been trying to buy the mansion and make it into a museum in Stephanie's name. A really great idea, if you ask me."

Julia agreed and then they parted company, leaving Julia wondering how a twenty-year-old murder could still stir up such deep feeling.

Despite herself, she was becoming curious. What really did happen? Why did Brad kill his wife? Why, if the true murderer was caught and punished, did everyone treat the case as though it were still unresolved?

There were no answers, and the question bothered her the rest of the night.

# 25

Despite his exhaustion from the late night, Ron was so excited about working with Office Wilde that he woke up Monday morning well before anyone else, even before his alarm clock rang. He dressed quickly and had the kids up and eating by the time Julia jogged and showered.

"You're all up early," she said.

"I wanted to make sure that we're ready to start as soon as Officer Wilde arrives," Ron explained. "What time is he coming?"

"Eight, I think."

She was right. At eight o'clock sharp, Wilde appeared, bringing his tools, his daughter, and wearing jeans, a black t-shirt, work-worn boots, and a broad grin.

"Hey, guys," Wilde said. "Ready to be put to work?"

"Oh, man!" Dana said, slumping down. She hated work. Ron shot her a reproving look that made her sit up again.

"We're ready," Ron answered eagerly. "What are we doing first?"

"We leave that up to the boss," he said.

He smiled cheekily at Julia and set off a fire alarm inside of her. Covering, she offered him coffee, then handed him the list. "I'd like to finish the two front rooms first. Ron and I have made out a list of what we think needs to be done and in what order. The second page is the list of supplies we need to get for each project - I think we've covered most everything."

Wilde scanned the list, nodding as he read. "Wow. You are ambitious. This is a lot of work for two people in one summer."

Julia smiled at Dana and Jack.

"Four people," she reminded him.

After that, it was time to get to work. They moved everything out of the dining room, then brought cloth tarps from the Wilde's house to spread over the floors. Wilde showed Ron how to prepare the wallpaper by carefully scoring it in a crisscross pattern with a retractable razor. Being entrusted with the razor made Ron feel ten feet tall. He worked slowly and carefully, so that he could prove his abilities to everyone.

After lunch, the two girls and Jack looked tired, so Julia sent them upstairs to rest for an hour and then asked Ron to watch them outside for the afternoon, to keep them out of the fumes.

Ron was keenly disappointed, but duty won over manly pride.

"Okay," he said, shoving his hands into his pockets.

Julia put a sympathetic hand on his shoulder. "I promise, you'll be right in the thick of things for the rest of the week."

He shrugged and, when their hour nap was up, led the kids outside.

It was late in the afternoon. Immovable heat and humidity seemed to oppress the entire street. Ron, more exhausted then he cared to admit, read his book in the shade of the porch. The windows of the Budds' little house were open to let the fumes dissipate, and occasionally he could hear something of the conversation between Aunt Julia and Office Wilde. They laughed a lot.

He was sitting lost in thought when Dana's shout of recognition brought him around.

Two familiar bicycles rounded the corner, and Dylan pulled up to a halt in front of them.

"Hey!" he grinned. "You guys ready to go haunted house hunting?"

His round face was pink with exertion and his brown curls were plastered down with sweat. On his back was a large, heavy looking backpack. His iPod sat precariously in his pocket with the ear bud cords dangling down his legs.

Katy pulled up, wearing a tank top and cut off jean shorts and her hair pulled up into a pony tail. She wasn't carrying a backpack, and Ron thought she looked as fresh as if she had just stepped out of the house.

Dana ran up to Dylan. "Are we going to do it now?" she asked eagerly.

"You bet," Dylan said. "Got my cameras and equipment and everything. Are you ready to go, Ron, or are you just going to sit there with your book?"

"Oh, boy!" Amelia squealed, clapping her hands. "Ghost hunting! This is going to be awesome!"

Ron tossed his book on to the chair and came down off the porch, saying, "How are we going to do this? It's private property, and people will get suspicious if they see us there."

"There's a covered side entrance that can't be seen from the streets," Dylan explained patiently. "We're not going to do anything illegal. We're just going to snoop around and take pictures and see if there's any dip in the temperature. If anyone asks, we'll just tell them it's a school project."

Katy laughed. "Science?"

"What about Aunt Julia?" Dana asked.

Dylan snorted. "She doesn't need to know as long as you're back in time for supper, right?"

Ron felt a flash of annoyance. "We're not supposed to go further than the Wildes' house without permission."

"It's not that far. You can still see the house from here."

"Want me to ask?" Dana asked Ron.

"If she finds out what we're doing, it'll blow the secrecy of the project!" Dylan protested. "She'll freak out and say no. Come on, Ron. I really want to find this thing."

"Just tell her that we're going for a walk," Amelia said. "She'll be fine if we're just going for a walk."

Ron shook his head. "I'm not going to lie to Aunt Julia."

Dana interrupted, "I'll talk to her, Ron. Just hang on a second."

She ran into the house. They could hear her excited chatter through the open windows, then she came running back out, her eyes shining.

"Aunt Julia said we can go all the way to the end, but we have to stay together and be in sight of the house the whole time."

"Sweet," Dylan said. "Let's go."

The ghost hunt was on.

# 26

U p close, the haunted house was much more intimidating. It towered two and a half stories high, and the dark sockets of the windows seemed to beckon, daring them to get lost looking into their endless darkness. The oversized front door, dark and scuffed by time, looked like the entry to a dungeon. The front porch wrapped around the front of the building, slumping with age and decay. Even the steps were crooked. The front path was overgrown with the same weeds that camouflaged the old iron gateway which surrounded the property.

Today was the first day that Ron noticed the iron fence. It was maybe five feet high, less in some places where the ground had settled, and the black paint had peeled off where rust had taken over. Each bar in the fence ended in a sharp spike, and Ron winced at the idea of falling on one of them. He hoped that the hidden entrance that Dylan had spoken of didn't include climbing over the fence.

He saw only two entrances, the front door and a side door, buried under the jungle that engulfed the driveway. Both were visible from the street.

They assembled in front of the house and parked their bikes against the fence, silently studying the house. Overhead, the sun's rays fell as warmly as before, but it felt dark and there was a cold chill where they stood. It was as though the house produced its own climate.

It occurred to Ron that if he stayed near the house for too long, the house would enter his soul and bind him to it - holding him there until he was as old, cold, and rundown as it was.

It was a foolish thought. Houses were bricks and wood, not soul-snatching demons; but once in his head, the idea took root. He shivered and tore his gaze away.

He looked down the line at the others. Except for Katy, who was looking at her phone as usual, he could tell from their pale faces and wide eyes that they felt like he did. Dana was ready to bolt, Jack was clutching the chalk he'd brought so tight his knuckles were white, and even Dylan looked nervous.

Ron drew up his shoulders, and there was a visible sense of relief when he spoke in a normal tone.

"So," he said, "what do we do first?"

Dylan dropped to his knees on the sidewalk and opened his backpack. Working quickly to get the cameras up and running, he said, "The first thing we do is get our cameras ready, then we take a scout around the house. You can use the digital – I want the cam-corder to start with, and Katy can use the Kodak."

"Oh, joy," Katy grumbled.

"We're going to go all the way around the house?" Amelia asked nervously.

"Ron, I don't want to," Jack whimpered. "It's spooky."

"We can't do that anyway," Dana said. "We'll lose sight of our house, and Aunt Julia said we weren't supposed to."

"You guys stay out in front on the sidewalk with the chalk and pre-tend like you're just decorating the place," Dylan said. "Stay in sight of your house and we'll stay in sight of you and we'll be totally safe."

"Except that you're trespassing," Katy said.

"If it isn't posted, it isn't a crime," Dylan said. "That's what Dad says. It's legal."

It didn't sound legal to Ron. It sounded downright fishy, but Katy was nodding and both of them knew more about this whole house and murder thing than he did. Surely, just walking around the house would be all right. It wasn't like they were going to break in or anything.

Dylan started off and Ron trotted after him, fiddling with the little blue digital camera. He was toying with the settings when he ran into Dylan's broad back.

Dylan stumbled. "Watch it! My camera!" He recovered without dropping anything and turned to scowl at him. "Dude, seriously?"

"Sorry."

"That's my dad's camera. You can't drop it. I don't want to have to explain it to him."

"Sure. Sorry."

They came to the edge of the property, where the old mansion gave way to a spot of thin woods. The fence ran down into the woods, amid jumbled knee-high weeds. It was dark and moist under the trees. They swatted at mosquitoes and horseflies and kept moving until Ron, keeping a constant eye out, stopped Dylan.

"We can't see the kids," he said.

"It's just a little further. Come on."

"No."

"Are you scared?"

"I don't break promises," Ron snapped.

Dylan rolled his eyes. "You didn't make one."

"I did through Dana."

Dylan sighed and pulled out his phone. He sent a text and a few seconds later, Katy appeared at the corner of the fencing. She waved languidly and turned back to her phone. Now they were in sight of her, she was in sight of Dana, and Dana was in sight of the house. It was a stretch, but Ron's conscience was eased.

He followed Dylan further into the woods until they came to a spot where the fence sank to waist height. Dylan hoisted himself over and Ron followed.

Now they were inside the yard, and the ground was a little drier under their feet. A small breeze moved the trees around, making it difficult to hear either the distant road or the footsteps of anyone who might be approaching them. It felt cut off from the outside world, and Ron's heart pounded at the idea.

"Take pictures," Dylan ordered. He was still adjusting his camcorder.

Ron began to take pictures at random, and his tension eased. Things were not so overwhelming when viewed through a lens.

They were right beside a rickety old shed, which looked ready to fall at the slightest touch. A rusted wheelbarrow was propped up next to the wall and, near it, a rake had fallen and was almost buried beneath years of neglected leaves. All that was visible were the prongs, looking like the teeth of some ancient monster.

The leaves covered most of the spacious backyard. A section had once been devoted to a garden, indicated by overgrown bushes, dying roses, and tangled weeds. All that remained were abundant lilies and one white rose that grew toward the weak sunlight. It looked, amid all that death and destruction, like the solitary ghost of former roses.

Across the way there was a pool and a patio with one old table and a pole without an umbrella. Ron stepped over to look inside the pool. It had turned into a disgusting mess of a pond, with blackened water, rotting vegetation, croaking toads, and a dancing group of insects that rose with every breath of wind. Green slime crawled up the walls, and the old ladder in the deep end was encrusted with growth. Taking it all in, Ron was glad that the kids had stayed behind.

He was avoiding the house. It loomed over everything, enhancing the eeriness. He was glad that they weren't going inside - just being in the backyard was enough to make him jumpy.

Still, he knew he couldn't ignore it forever. He was supposed to be gathering evidence, so he took a few shots of the house, zooming in on some of the windows. There was little to see. It was so dark inside that only the occasional curtain was visible.

He stepped around to the patio to take a closer look at the table. There was nothing, except for a crumbled McDonald's bag tumbling about on the ground. He wondered how old it was, and then it occurred to him that it was dry and fresh. It had been left there after the rain last week.

His blood ran cold. He stared at the bag, knowing he was being silly. It had probably been tossed out of a car and rolled by the wind until it rested here. There was no other indication that anyone else had been here recently.

Nevertheless, he went to stand by Dylan.

Dylan was struggling with his camera and starting to swear. A horsefly and several mosquitoes danced about his head and he swiped at them angrily.

"What's wrong?" Ron asked.

"Stupid battery! It's run down and I forgot to bring the other one. Shoot!"

"Just leave it. We can take stills."

"I didn't want to take stills – I wanted to film it. Oh, for crying out loud! Give me your camera."

Dylan snatched it out of Ron's palm and examined it carefully. "Okay, this has some film time left on it. It's not good resolution, though – in fact, it's pretty awful, but we can at least get some exterior and placement shots with it."

They spent some time doing that, trading off the camera to get different shots and angles. Dylan went back over the fence, and then hopped back into the yard so that Ron could get it on camera. He couldn't resist dropping to the ground in a Hollywood-special-ops pose. They got shots of Dylan contemplating the nearly-empty pool, looking up at the shed, walking around the garage, and examining some of the decomposing leaves with an inquisitive expression.

Ron decided that Dylan was more interested in becoming the star of his own video than he was in finding an actual ghost. They'd been in the yard for a long time now, and not once had the older boy looked around for signs of ghostly activity.

Finally, Dylan said, "Okay, now for the house."

"Dylan!" Katy shouted. The acoustics of the yard made her sound further away than she was. "Hurry up!"

"Hang on!" he yelled. "We're just getting started."

"Well, make it snappy," she responded. "Grandma's calling and she wants us home."

"Come on, Ron. We still need to examine the house."

Up close, the house looked worse. Dirt encrusted shutters, mud spattered siding, cracked windows, and filthy gutters were the least of it: thorny weeds scratched at their legs as they crept along the side of the house. The first floor windows were too high for them to look into, and the basement windows were pitch black. Nothing could be seen there.

"Let's go up on the back porch," Dylan said.

Up on the porch, they looked in each window. The sun started to sink behind the trees and was casting long shadows over the yard. The air was starting to cool. Strange creaking and occasional bangs came from inside as the house settled in for the night, and Ron asked Dylan about the noises as they took pictures.

"That's nothing," he said. He added, "We'll see lots more if we go inside, like proper ghost hunters do."

"That's breaking and entering."

"If we don't get caught, who cares?"

"Dylan, I'm not helping you to break in a house." Ron insisted.

"Yeesh! You know, if you don't want to help, all you have to do is say so. Oh, forget it. Let's snoop around the other side."

They made out better there. The ground was firmer, and there was an old stone path running along the house, suppressing the weeds and making it much more pleasant to walk on. The basement windows were still black and yielded little in the way of the supernatural; but they were out of sight of the awful pool, and Ron was able to breathe a little easier.

"This would be a good place to start the narration," Dylan said with satisfaction. "Come on, Ron, cameraman time."

Ron took the camera and the backpack. Dylan ran his hands through his hair and fussed over his clothes a bit. He didn't mind the patches of mud on his shorts, but he did mind those on his legs and Ron could hear him muttering and complaining as he brushed at them.

"Oh, man!" he moaned. He held up the culprit between thumb and forefinger, more annoyed than concerned. "I had a tick on my leg! Jeez." Before Ron could react, the older boy had flicked the tick into the bushes and went back to examining his limbs. "I hope there aren't anymore."

Ron, who hadn't much experience with ticks, was impressed with the blasé attitude that his friend adopted.

"All right," Dylan said, having checked everything that he could check without stripping off clothing. "Let's get to it, then. Ready with the camera?"

Ron was and started filming on Dylan's mark.

"We're here at the site of the infamous Lang murder, in the heart of beautiful Franklin, New Hampshire," said Dylan. He spoke in a hushed and awed tone and began to walk along the side of the house just like the hosts in reality TV shows. "In this spot – house, in this house about ten – no, twenty years - oh, man, stop the camera."

Ron did. "You were doing really well."

"I'll have to edit that bit out," Dylan grumbled, ignoring him. "Hand me my backpack, will you? I need to check my notes."

"Wouldn't it be better for the first shot to be in front of the house?" asked Ron. "That's what most people do, I think."

"I just don't want to be seen. People might call the cops if they saw us on the porch."

"Good point."

Dylan flipped through a well-thumbed stack of printed website pages. Ron was starting to get impatient. After all, he hadn't come on this expedition just to be a camera lackey and bag holder. He wanted to look at the house himself. Although Dylan had a point about the police, the porch was pretty well shaded and sheltered from the road by the bushes and trees. Judging from where the sun was in the sky, there was a good chance that the interior would be lit well enough to make something out.

He started for the front porch, camera in hand. Dylan, still fumbling with the pages, grabbed his stuff and followed after him.

"Wait," he said. "We'll be seen."

"The trees are blocking us. Come on."

There was a second set of porch stairs on the side of the house, made of rotting wood ready to give at any second. Ron tested the first step gingerly. It creaked and felt slippery, but did not break.

He was about to step up on it when Dylan, finally catching up with him, said, "Wait! Wait, let's film it!"

They walked up the steps. Ron followed Dylan, keeping the shot close to the older boy's flip flops, as instructed.

"The porch of the old murder mansion," Dylan said, in that same hushed whisper, "is old and decrepit. You have to watch your step carefully or you'll break through the old rotting wood. Cut. Did you get that?"

"I think so," Ron said. "I just ran out of memory. Your feet are really dirty."

"Shows that I'm rugged," he said cheerfully. "Let's take a look through the windows."

It was then that Ron heard it. A clattering sound came first, followed by a long, low moan. It vibrated through the air and sent a chill shivering up his spine. He was frozen for a moment, unable to make a sound. As the moan faded, he locked eyes with Dylan and knew he hadn't been the only one who heard it.

Dylan had jumped off the porch to the grass, bouncing on his toes, one leg bloody with the scratch he'd received leaping over the railing. He was pale, and Ron thought he looked like he was going to have a heart attack.

"What was *that?*" he asked.

Ron looked back to the house. He thought it odd that he was more curious than frightened. He tried the door handle, but it was

KILLARNEY TRAYNOR

firmly locked, and the sign on the door warned against entering these "dangerous premises".

"What are you doing?" Dylan squeaked.

Ron looked over his shoulder. "Don't you want to see where it came from?"

Dylan swallowed hard. "Well, sure," he said shakily. "Why not? I mean, that's why we're here, right?"

"Right."

"You know, it's too bad the camera wasn't on. I could have used it in the video."

He seemed to be recovering his courage, and he stepped gingerly over the fallen brambles and up the shaky stairs. Ron tried some of the windows, but they were stuck shut. He brushed some of the dirt away from the living room window and peered in.

At first he saw nothing but darkness, then, as Dylan leaned in next to him, his eyes began picking out spots of light reflecting off of what appeared to be small mirrors. He could just barely make out a bureau of some kind and maybe a chair, but nothing more.

Dylan grunted.

"Dark in there," he said. He lifted his flashlight and turned it on, but the light bounced off the dirt on the panes and they saw even less than before.

Neither said anything for minute. They didn't have to tell each other what they were listening for, but all they could hear were the kids on the sidewalk and an awful crowing sound from the trees.

"What do you think it was?" Ron asked.

"What do *you* think it was?"

"It could just be pipes or something."

"Yeah. Yeah, it could be."

They tried the rest of the windows, but their enthusiasm was waning. The project was no longer just a fun, scary way to fill their summer afternoon; now, they were waiting for something to step out of the shadows – every nook, every darkened doorway was now a hiding spot for a lurking figure.

They were glad when Katy called for Dylan to come home. They'd had their fill of the old house for the afternoon. In fact, in his eagerness to get away from the place, Dylan jumped the front fence, wounded leg and all. Ron supposed that their being caught was no longer a prime concern.

The other kids clustered around them eagerly.

"Did you see anything?" Amelia asked.

"Nothing definite, but it is a spooky place," Dylan said, regaining his normal swagger.

"Is there a ghost?" Dana whispered.

"We didn't see it."

"But is there one? Did you feel it?"

Dylan hesitated, and Ron gave him a warning look. Regardless of what either one of them might think about the reality of ghosts, he did not want his younger siblings being frightened out of a good night's sleep.

Fortunately, Dylan didn't seem inclined to commit himself. With a lingering look at the old house, he said, "Oh, there's a mystery there, all right."

The three younger children exchanged confused looks. Amelia ran over to where Ron perched precariously on top of the fence.

"Ron, you'll tell the truth," she said, looking up at him. "Did you see a ghost in there?"

She was wearing the same adoring expression that made Ron uncomfortable. He wished he could tell her to knock it off, but that would be rude.

Fortunately, he could truthfully answer her question without giving Dana and Jack nightmares.

"No," he said. "We didn't see anything."

"Good, excellent," Katy said impatiently. "Let's go, Dylan."

"Oh!" Dana was disappointed. "Then the project is done? There's nothing else to investigate?"

Dylan stopped, twisted in his bicycle seat, and gave her an arrogant look.

"Nothing to investigate?" he said. "I wouldn't say that, Dana. I wouldn't say that at all. Later, kiddos!"

He and Katy peddled off without a backwards glance, leaving the two girls confused.

"But if there's no ghost," Amelia said, "what is there to investigate?"

"Maybe the murder," Dana suggested.

"But didn't they catch the bad guy?"

"Yep."

"Then what does Dylan want to investigate, Ron?"

Ron shrugged and brushed at his clothes. He felt much safer on this side of the fence.

He rubbed the rust from his hands and checked his watch. At 7:30, it was later than he thought. His stomach was starting to rumble, and he hoped that Aunt Julia had given some thought to supper.

"Come on," he said. "I'm hungry."

They went back to the house, where they found Julia and Wilde on the front porch, dirty, tired, and waiting for the pizza delivery man to arrive.

# 27

J ulia went to bed early that night. After the kids were settled in, she took a shower, put on her nightgown, and wearily brushed her teeth. She was exhausted, and her arms were weak from hours of scrubbing walls and scraping glue. She flexed a muscle in the mirror and grinned ruefully at her image.

"Oh yeah. You're a tough girl," she said softly.

It took them all afternoon just to do those two rooms, much longer than any of them anticipated. Even Wilde was surprised.

"What did they use on this wallpaper?" he had muttered, chipping away.

"Superglue?" Julia suggested. He laughed, and she loved the sound.

Now, watching her reflection in the mirror, she wondered - if it took this long for two rooms, how much of a nightmare would the office, bedroom, storage room, and hallway be? The idea made her heart sink.

"If it isn't done before school starts," she told the mirror, "you hire someone to do the last bits and you sell it anyway. That's all."

She nodded at her reflection, then crossed herself and whispered, "Thank you, God, for Robert."

She padded out of the bathroom, almost tripping over her sleeping bag in the hallway. She set up her sleeping quarters there after the Wildes left that evening; now, she realized that she was in the way of Dana's nightly journey to the bathroom and she would probably spend half the night being tripped over.

Still, she was too tired to move it. She poured herself a cup of tea and added a spoonful of sugar, and leaned against the kitchen counter to sip it.

Julia was exhausted, but too alert for sleep. She kept going over the list of things that needed to be done to the house. She decided that she needed something to take her mind off of the projects all together.

She wandered into the office, where they had set up the temporary living room with the TV set, but it wasn't hooked up to cable and the only movies on hand were children's entertainment. All of her DVDs were buried somewhere among their things, and she simply wasn't up to digging through it all.

She was about to leave the office again when her eyes fell on a stack of books. She hadn't had time to read since their arrival. A good novel might do the trick.

The first book that she came across was *Picturesque in Death*. Standing in the silent, darkened room with peeling wallpaper and the musty smell of old rugs tickling her nose, the B-movie cover seemed ominous and creepy.

Almost against her will, she opened it. A. Glen Bernard's enormous strokes nearly covered the title page. She flipped past the prologue to about fifty pages into the novel. It was a habit of hers to check the writing style midway, to determine whether or not she wanted to read it.

*Daphne Maxwell-Harcourt lay coiled in the middle of the enormous bed, her robe a blood-red stain against the luxurious creamy down coverlet. Her hair was pulled back into a simple pony tail. Some tendrils had escaped the elastic and hung in tantalizing ringlets by her long, smooth neck. Her eyes were huge, her features delicate. Her hair was like spun gold, the red highlighted by her apparel. She was looking at the camera with a laughing smile. Somehow, she managed to look both provocative and innocent at the same time.*

*There were other photos: Daphne at work, Daphne on the beach, Daphne on her bike, Daphne in Boston, Daphne under an oak tree in the fall, Daphne coyly covering her face with her rain coat. They were all well shot, well arranged, and made full use of the woman's exquisite beauty. Her delicate features and slender figure made her a fascinating subject.*

*Hollister grunted. "You've a good eye," he said.*

*Harcourt looked up and blinked, not understanding. He looked haggard, Hollister thought. As though he hadn't slept in weeks.*

*"You've got a gift with the camera." The captain tapped the picture.*

*The bereaved husband blinked and shook his head. "They aren't mine," he said. He lowered his eyes to the scotch glass he rolled between his palms. "One of her art school friends, I think. I don't know."*

*Hollister nodded and turned his back to the wall.*

It wasn't particularly riveting stuff. Julia skipped ahead another fifty pages and tried again.

*"I don't know what to make of it," he said, as he eased his way through traffic. "Everyone loved her – no one has a reason to kill her, except maybe the husband and he's too honestly broken up about it. Perhaps Fenton is right. Maybe it was a suicide."*

*"Sure," Barbara scoffed. "Young, rich, beautiful young model, a promising acting career, her first marriage still in the honeymoon stages, if all the witnesses are to be believed, and she commits suicide by hanging. Why? No reason. She wasn't doing drugs. She didn't drink. No one had died or left her. Her husband was faithful, her career just starting, and Mom and Pop were taking her to some South-Sea island for her birthday. More importantly, she left no note. No artistic temperament could resist leaving something for the fans, a poetic end that would make her legendary. She'd have left a note."*

*The mist gave way to downpour, and Hollister turned up the wipers. They drove in silence, with only the rumble of the engine, the popcorn sound of the rain against the roof, and the rhythmic squeak of rubber against the windshield for music.*

*Barbara spoke again. "What I don't get..." She trailed off, then shook her head and continued. "What I don't get, being the nasty, small-minded kind of woman that I am, is the fact that she was so universally loved. No one has had a thing to say against her and that – that doesn't make sense."*

Barbara's point touched on something that had been bothering Julia about Stephanie Lang: everyone seemed to like her, including Doris Mone, who - even on such short acquaintance - struck Julia as the possessive type. It didn't make sense. Had Bernard come up with an explanation?

She shut the book and studied the cover. Worth the read? Probably not. Bernard was entirely too much in love with "Daphne Maxwell-Harcourt" to deliver a good procedural. But as a study of the case, it might offer a perspective that could put some of her questions to rest.

At any rate, she was certain that it would put her to sleep.

Tonight, the floor seemed harder and her sleeping bag thinner than usual. She piled up her two pillows with the blanket underneath them and settled in with her mug and book. She managed 25 pages or so before waking up to find the book had fallen from her hand. She put out the light, curled up again, and fell into a deep sleep.

The next morning, Robert and Amelia arrived just as Jack and Dana were finishing breakfast. Ron was already in the living room, studying wall-repair instructions. Wilde brought his own coffee in a Harley-Davidson travel mug and chatted with Julia while they set up. They had a full day ahead of them.

Occasionally, Julia would stop and watch. Everyone was hard at work, talking, joking, and laughing together. Ron looked happy, even if he didn't exactly smile. They were comfortable together in that room, these two families who had known each other only a week.

Julia felt a sense of peace, security, and calm that she had not known since the accident. For the first time, she felt at home. The worries about the future were far away today.

They finished the walls by noon and ate lunch out on the porch. Mrs. Jurta, looking distracted and harried, walked by with several dogs, stopping to say hello. The kids were delighted to play with the puppies for a few minutes, and Mrs. Jurta brought this to Julia's attention, slyly commenting on how well Horatio and Dana got on.

Julia escaped to the kitchen. Robert came through the living room, carrying an armload of dishes and Jack on his back. He dropped the dishes on the counter and Jack into a chair.

"Everything all right?" Julia asked.

Jack shook his head miserably as Robert explained, "We just got a little unnerved by some dogs trying to lick us, didn't we, Jack?"

"He was trying to eat me," Jack said solemnly. "I saw his teeth."

"Well, he can't get his tongue out without showing some teeth," Robert said. He turned to Julia. "Mrs. Jurta wanted to know if the kids would walk the dogs for a little bit while she made a phone call. I told them to go ahead – is that okay with you?"

Julia looked out the window and saw the three of them waiting by the side of the road, each with a leash in one hand and a plastic bag in the other. Naturally, Dana had Horatio, and Tigger was with Amelia while Ron held two others.

Julia turned to find Robert grinning at her.

"I know," he said. "It is a set-up, but I thought it would be a good opportunity to give the kids a break from work."

"As long as they stay on this street, it's fine."

He went out to tell them while Julia and Jack loaded up the dishwasher. After a few minutes, Robert came back in.

"The putty is still soft in the living room," he said. "We should let it dry before we paint over it. Where's the list?"

Julia pointed to the counter and he settled at the table to study it. Jack and Julia finished up tidying the kitchen, and then she took the little boy upstairs with Yellow Teddy. Jack was exhausted and didn't protest.

"The dog did try to eat me," he said as Julia stepped towards the door.

Julia smiled. "Then you'd better stay in here where they can't get you."

He nodded. Julia left the door open a crack as she left.

She found Robert examining the home improvement magazines that she had left on the counter. They were well worn, and some of the pages were dog eared and marked with notes. She almost wished that he hadn't found them. Some of her original ideas sounded good back in Springfield while she was sitting in Amanda's magazine-spread-worthy kitchen. Now they just seemed pretentious.

He looked up as she sat down.

"I was thinking about working on the kitchen next," he said. "But I wasn't sure, from your notes, exactly what you wanted to do."

To her dismay, the magazine lay open to one of the more elaborate and expensive kitchens that she had taken a shine to. The only way that particular plan would work was if they knocked down a few walls and enlarged the kitchen to three times the original size.

She looked around. They had been so busy the past week that she had almost forgotten what a shambles the room was. "It would be great to get this done. I feel like the board of health might come in to close us down any moment."

"Cosmetically it needs work but, otherwise, it doesn't look too bad to me. Did you have a design in mind?"

*Nothing like that magazine,* she wanted to say.

"I'd like some shelves put up," she said. "The cabinets need to be cleaned and repainted. Ideally, I'd like the walls repainted, the tiles either fixed or replaced, but that would take a lot more than I can give to just one room."

Robert folded his arms as he looked around. "So, you don't want those cabinets replaced?" he asked, nodding towards the blank space on the wall.

"No. I think an open shelving unit would brighten up the wall and make the room look larger. Besides," she shrugged, "there's no use in putting too much time and effort into it. One of the first things people redo is the kitchen when they buy a place."

He looked at her, puzzled, then shook his head. "Oh, right, I'd forgotten."

"Forgotten?"

"That you were going back in the fall," he said quickly, looking down at the magazine. "You've all fit right into the neighborhood, almost as though you've always been here – I just forgot."

Julia's heart jumped. "This is a really nice neighborhood," she murmured. "We've felt very welcome here."

"So did I when I first arrived. They're good people."

"You all are. I almost wish circumstances were different." She broke off quickly, wondering why she had said that.

Curious, he asked, "Circumstances?"

She nodded.

All it took was a another quizzical look from him and the whole story came out – about Amanda and the accident, the kids and their grieving process, the decision to come to Franklin. She told him about the job she'd lost, and the job she hoped to get, the house in Springfield and how others wanted her to sell it. She found herself talking quickly, saying more to him than she had said to anyone in months.

She worried that she was telling him too much. But he seemed immersed in her story, and he didn't interrupt except to ask questions.

She finally managed to stop and laughed awkwardly.

"I'm sorry," she said. "That was way more than you needed to know."

He cleared his throat and looked down at his hands. "I didn't know that you'd all been through so much."

"Yes, well… It's been really hard for the kids, obviously. Their entire world turned upside down."

"So did yours. You went from a swinging single to a grieving mother of three in, what, a moment? You gave up a lot for your sister."

There was a look in his eyes that Julia couldn't name. It made her feel respected - the focus of a kind of attention that she had not received in a while. The truth came out easily: "I didn't think of it like that. You do things for family, you know?"

"Yes. Yes, I know."

She grew uncomfortable. "So, back to the kitchen," she said, with forced brightness.

He nodded and scanned the room, then flipped a few pages of the magazine and showed her a 'before' picture of an old kitchen. It was done in 1970s avocado, gray, and a dull mustard trim. "How's this?"

He laughed out loud at the expression on Julia's face.

# 28

Wednesday, they had lunch in a small diner that the Wildes recommended. Robert insisted on picking up the bill. Julia objected, and the playful debate raged on until Amelia and Ron both demanded that they knock it off and play nice.

Back at the house, the children played outside while Robert and Julia painted the living room and dining room a sunshine yellow with a white trim.

After a while, Ron came in to help. They put the living room back together, keeping the furniture well away from the wet walls, and cleared out the office. Then Robert decided that they could move the refrigerator out of the kitchen so they could clean the tiled, and he and Ron began discussing logistics.

"While you guys are at it," Julia said. "I'll order dinner. Any requests?"

"Chinese!" Amelia shouted.

"Chinese is good," Robert said.

Julia went to find her cell phone and Amelia followed her, suggesting a local delivery place. After the order was placed, they began to set up the porch for a picnic dinner.

Outside, the sky turned pink and teal as the sun made its slow decline. It was quiet, except for the noise of the crickets and Mrs. Jurta's dogs barking in the distance.

Amelia sat by the edge of the blanket, her legs folded underneath her, and her hands on her knees. She nodded towards Mrs. Jurta's house. "They always get really excited when we start to bring out the bowls."

Julia asked if Amelia missed working with the dogs.

The little girl answered quickly, "Oh, they love me. They bark so loud when I come in, and none of them ever tried to nip at me, like they do the others."

"They must like you best, then."

"Mrs. Jurta says that when they do nip, it's just because they are excited, not because they don't like you. I think they do like me best. Mrs. Jurta says it's because I'm the smallest, but Annie says that it's because I like to sing and dogs like music."

Julia finished setting up the picnic, then, because the air was so nice, sat on the stairs next to Amelia and asked, "Who is Annie?"

Amelia smiled at her. "She's the vet. She's nice. She always gives me candy, even though I'm not supposed to have it because of my teeth, but I never get cavities. Do you get cavities?"

"Sometimes. I stopped drinking soda and that helped a lot."

While Amelia thought about that, Julia leaned against the railing and relaxed. She was tired, and her stomach ached with hunger. A beautiful breeze stirred the warm air, playing with her hair and soothing her.

She closed her eyes and thought of Ryan. She was pleasantly surprised to find that the memory, though still painful, had lost its sharp sting. She wondered whether Robert had anything to do with that, and the idea brought a hot flush to her face.

"I did get a cavity once," Amelia said, her tone heavy with the confession.

Julia turned to look at her. "Oh, did you?"

She nodded, without meeting Julia's eyes. "Yes. I had forgotten."

"It's easy to forget these things."

"It was a baby tooth, so they didn't have to drill. They just waited for it to fall out." There was a pause, then, "I lied."

Julia kept her voice level. "I see."

Amelia shifted closer to Julia and mimicked her pose, and they sat like that for a few minutes. Behind them, they heard the boys laughing and, beyond them, Dana and Jack were talking loudly in the bathroom, where Dana was giving her brother a bath. In a few minutes, Julia knew, the quiet on the porch would be traded for laughter and chatter. She relished the peace.

After a bit, the little girl spoke again.

"I'm not a liar." Her voice trembled. "I just... Well..."

Julia waited quietly.

"It sounds better when I make it up," she admitted. "Sometimes it makes people mad when I tell them the truth."

"The truth can hurt," Julia agreed. She couldn't resist asking, "Who would get mad at you, anyway?"

"Mom. She's really busy, and sometimes she doesn't have time for the whole story. So I make one up."

"And what does your dad think about it?"

"He doesn't know."

"No?"

"No, he's busy, too," she explained. "Sometimes Mom wants me to tell him things that'll make him sad."

"So you tell him something else instead."

Amelia lowered her head and nodded. "And then I started telling stories about other things. So that people wouldn't worry, you know? Dad worries a lot. I worry about him, too. I'm the only one who looks after him now, now that Mom's gone. He's all alone except for me."

Julia put an arm around her and drew her in close. "It's hard to be in the middle, isn't it?" She squeezed. "You're a good girl, Amelia."

Amelia swallowed hard. "But I lied. I lied to you and to Dad and to... Well, almost everyone. That's not good."

"No, maybe it isn't. But I forgive you, and you can make up for it by telling the truth from now on."

"What about Dad?"

"The next time your mom tells you to pass on a message, just ask her politely to tell him herself. She's a big girl."

Amelia's voice would have melted the cruelest heart. "Why does Mom do that?"

"I don't know, Amelia. When people are hurt, sometimes they react by trying to hurt other people. It's not right, but sometimes it's the only way they know how to help the pain."

"Like when my cat scratches because we picked him up wrong?"

Julia nodded. "Sure, like that. Your cat knows it's the wrong thing to do, but it's the only way he can tell you that he doesn't like something. Now, you don't hate your cat because he does that sometimes, do you?"

"No. I mean, sometimes I get mad, but not for long."

"And even though he may hurt your feelings, you get over it, and still love and take care of your cat, right?"

"Right."

"Because you're a big girl and you know better."

"Yes. Sometimes, though, I have to tell him to stop when he does it to other people."

"Exactly! With people it's the same. Your mother shouldn't hurt your father and vice-versa. But your father is a big boy now, and even though his feelings get hurt, he knows that your mother is just hurting, too. Eventually both of them will be all right. But you have to let them do this themselves. It's the only way they'll get better."

"I don't like it when my dad is sad."

"I know. But he has to walk through this. He'll be stronger because of it. Besides that, he has a secret weapon that your mother doesn't have."

"What's that?"

"You, of course. He's got you."

Amelia shook her head. "I don't think I'm very much help some-times," she said sadly. "I get in the way. Dad's always having to find people to look after me, and sometimes he has to cancel things with the boys just because he needs to stay home. I heard Bill tell him once that he needs to get out more, but Dad told him no because I needed him. Dad says he likes to hang out with me, and that he'd rather be with me than anyone else in the world, but, well, I don't know... What if he was just trying to make me feel good?"

"Amelia, does your dad lie?"

"Never!" The answer was swift and shocked.

"Then why don't you believe him now?"

Amelia had no answer. When Robert came out and sat on the steps to wait for the food, she curled up against him, and the three of them watched the gathering dusk together.

# 29

Later that evening, Julia was alone in the dining room. It had turned out very nicely, and she wanted a clear idea of how she wanted things arranged before they started bringing the furniture back in. The kids were in bed, worn out from the past three days, and she sat on the dusty floor with her sketch pad, a cup of coffee, and her glasses.

There wasn't room for much: the table, chairs, and maybe the narrow sideboard on one wall. She liked the sideboard, but it was in desperate need of refinishing and she doubted she'd have time to do anything about it.

She sketched out the furniture arrangements using Dana's colored pencils. Julia wasn't an artist, but as she drew, she grew excited. Her drawing became less what should be and more what could be. She drew the wooden table, imagining it polished to a bright shine with a blue and white runner down the middle. She put a vase with daisies and yellow carnations on the table. On the sideboard was another runner with more flowers in a big old pitcher and cabinetry underneath to hold dishes, cutlery, and glasses. On the light yellow walls, she hung three decorative China plates in a pyramid. There were three long windows in the room, so she dressed them in bamboo shades under light translucent green curtains that ended just short of the floor.

Julia stopped and looked at the sketch. It was cozy and warm, just right for a growing family. She imagined holidays in that room: Halloween, with a huge punch bowl and paper bats hanging from the ceiling fan; and Thanksgiving, with the two doors into the living room open, and the table extended to fit everyone. On Christmas morning, the sideboard would be loaded with pastries, garlands, and decorations, and the living room doors would be open again so that people could eat and open presents at the same time...

She berated herself. What was she thinking? They would be long gone by then, decorating the Springfield house as Amanda would have, so that the kids would have continuity. Someone else would have this house – they would probably repaint the room and maybe even knock down a wall.

Julia got up, put away the pencils, and left the sketch pad on the kitchen table. She made herself a cup of tea and pulled out *Picturesque in Death*. She read to the point where Daphne, supposedly alone in the mansion, began to be unnerved by noises that heralded the approach of the murderer.

Julia heard a knock at the door.

Her nerves nearly got the better of her. It was all she could do not to answer it with a kitchen knife in her hand.

She got to the side entry and hesitated. There was no window and no peep hole. She made a mental note to get one installed.

While she was thinking, there was another knock. Ron called to her from the top of the stairs.

"Do you want me to get it for you?" he asked.

She was about to reassure him when they both heard the voice calling through the door: "Julia? Are you there?"

It was Robert. Julia opened it and was relieved when the shaft of light fell across his friendly face. He stepped in quickly, shutting the screen door behind him.

"Don't want to let the bugs in," he said. He jerked his head towards the door. "You might want to consider getting a peep hole for that door. I didn't realize until now how vulnerable that is."

Julia was pleased that he'd thought of that, and then remembered that he was a policeman. It was probably just instinct, she decided.

Suddenly, the entryway seemed small and Robert seemed a little too close. Julia took a step back and stumbled over the bottom step of the stairway. She grabbed the banister, but not before Robert caught her arm and pulled her up.

"Easy does it," he said. "It's dark in here."

His hands remained on her elbows.

Embarrassed, she brushed a lock of hair out of her eyes, partially to cover her face with her hand for a moment, and partially to shrug his hands off. "Honest, Officer, I haven't been drinking."

"I see," he said playfully, and she could see that he was trying to ease the awkwardness of the moment. "You wouldn't want to walk a straight line for me, would you, miss?"

"I would, if you would just stop moving it for a moment."

He laughed and she felt relieved. She led him into the kitchen, where the light was. "Coffee?"

"No, thanks," he said. "I left Amelia asleep on the couch and I don't want to leave her for too long."

"Well, then, what can I do for you? Did you forget something?"

"My phone - have you seen it anywhere?"

She hadn't, and a check of the counters revealed nothing. He looked worried, and Julia suspected that their cell phones were the only ones in the house. He couldn't risk missing a call, not when it could be an emergency.

Ron came in, tying his robe across his pajamas although it was another warm night. He volunteered to look around in the living room and Robert checked the stack of things in the dining room. But it wasn't there either.

"I probably dropped it outside somewhere," Robert said, running his hand through his hair.

"Is it on ringer?" Julia asked.

He couldn't remember, so Julia called it. All three stood still, listening.

"I think I hear something," Ron said. He was in the hallway, looking back and forth. "Call it again."

She did, and she and Robert went to stand next to him. This time, they heard it as well, a distant humming sound.

Ron found it in the bathroom, under a towel on the sink. Robert looked relieved, and Julia found herself volunteering to walk him out.

"Want to make sure I get there safe?" he asked, grinning.

Julia said, "You never know who might be lurking around these parts."

Robert held the door open for her and they stepped out into the warm darkness.

Ron waited at the top of the stairs. It took several minutes for Julia to return. When she did, she slipped in quietly, and leaned against the closed door, silent and thoughtful.

After a moment, she sighed dreamily and moved towards the kitchen, catching sight of Ron.

"Did Officer Wilde get home all right?" he asked, almost too innocently.

"Yes, he did," Julia said. "Thank you for waiting up for me, but you'd better get to bed now. Tomorrow will be a long day."

She gave him a distracted kiss, and he went to bed reluctantly, curious what - if anything - was going on between Wilde and his aunt.

# 30

R on, Robert, and Julia made good progress that week, and the renovations came along speedily. But by Thursday night, Julia grew weary of paint, wallpaper, back-breaking cleaning, and tripping over surplus furniture. She wanted a rest.

"I've decided to have a yard sale on Saturday," she told Robert.

They were taking a break in the kitchen while the kids worked out in the garden with Derval. Robert, tired from their long day, mopped his sweat-beaded brow.

"This Saturday?" he asked.

"This Saturday."

"Why this sudden decision?"

"Pure laziness. I want an excuse to sit out on the lawn, tan, and read my book. I figure minding a yard sale would be the best way to do it."

"Good thinking," he said and leaned against the counter. "But who are you going to get to haul all of that stuff out? I'm bushed."

"Me, too," she admitted. "I'm not lugging it all out there in this heat."

Not long after, J. C. came in to pick up his girlfriend and Julia jumped on the opportunity. He was happy to trade in an hour or two of work for pizza and the stack of records that Ron had found in the storage room.

"I love these things," he said, examining a CCR record. "The sound is awesome when the surface isn't scratched."

While Amelia and Dana made yard sale posters, the others emptied the storage room out on to the front yard and covered it with plastic. How anyone managed to cram as much as they did into one relatively small room was beyond Julia's comprehension.

"That's the last of it," Robert said, coming back into the kitchen where Julia was preparing for the pizza delivery. Ron, pink-faced and worn out, slumped in a kitchen chair, thumbing through his texts. J. C. was there, too, pouring over his new records.

Robert leaned up against the counter. "So, boss, what am I doing while you're sunning yourself on the lawn on Saturday?"

"Joining me?" she teased.

Before he could reply, J. C. said, "Wait, you're still coming to the fishing derby, aren't you?"

Robert winced. "I almost forgot about that."

"Fishing derby?" Ron asked. He sounded uncharacteristically enthusiastic, and J. C. turned to answer him in kind.

"It's the annual Father-Son, Father-Daughter fishing derby on Webster Lake. It's a big deal in these parts. Every year, the police duke it out with the fire department to see who has the bigger catch. Last year, the firemen won, so now it's Robert's turn. Mitch and I have a bet on it and everything."

"Thanks for your enthusiastic support," Robert laughed.

"Oh, man, sounds like fun," Ron said longingly.

"You are coming, right?" J. C. asked again.

Robert shook his head regretfully. "Not this year, I'm afraid. Sorry, J. C."

"What? Why not?"

He shrugged. "Amelia won't hear of it," he explained. "She's not really the outdoors type. Last year, she nearly had a meltdown when I had her put a worm on a hook. A rubber worm on a hook, no less. No daughter, no father, I'm afraid."

"Oh, if that's the only reason," J. C. said dismissively, "just take Ron. He can substitute for Dana, can't you, Ron? You said you were a scout, right?"

"You bet!" Ron beamed. "I love fishing!"

He looked so excited that Julia couldn't say no when Robert asked her for permission. Seeing Ron look happy about anything was worth getting up at four in the morning to get him up, fed, and out the door.

That was how Julia came to be sitting alone on the lawn, barefoot and slathered in suntan oil Saturday morning. It was nearly noon, and Dana, Jack, and Amelia were playing quietly in the shady driveway while Julia read her book, napped, and sunned, with only occasional interruptions from bargain hunters.

She was engrossed in her book when she was interrupted.

"Excuse me?"

The tone betrayed impatience.

Julia wrenched herself from *Picturesque in Death* and focused on the person standing by a particularly gruesome old floor lamp. She blinked a few times and lifted her sunglasses.

The woman came into focus. She was a short lady, round, in her middle sixties, with gray hair, and a determinedly disgruntled expression. Julia was used to that look: it was the expression of choice for every experienced Yard Saler that came to inspect her offerings that morning.

"You're selling this?" the woman asked. She had one hand on the wooden lamp and the other on her hip.

Julia pulled herself up into a sitting position and removed her sunglasses to give the woman her best friendly smile.

"I am."

"There aren't any stickers." She frowned at the item, which was a combination lampstand-table with a drawer. "What are you asking for it?"

"Best offer. We're trying to clear out the house."

"It's stained, you know."

"Stained?"

"Right here." She pointed. "And here. It's paint spatter."

Julia sighed and nodded. "Well, it is rather old."

"Still, it's not in mint condition, is it?"

She fussed about the lamp for a moment and tugged the drawer open. She looked inside and frowned.

"Does the drawer work all right?" Julia asked.

"It sticks," the woman explained. She pulled out a piece of paper. "This is yours, I think."

Julia took it and found it was a glamour photo of a startlingly beautiful young woman. With sparkling blue eyes, mounds of curly golden hair, and a stunning smile, the woman was looking off into the distance, dressed in clothing that was at least twenty years out of date. In the corner, scrawled in pen, were the words, *Yours, S.*

Julia looked up, confused, and the woman said, "I'll give you ten for it."

"For the picture?"

"For the lamp."

"Oh! Oh, fine. Do you know who this is?"

The woman was making a great show of looking through her purse for the money. "Yeah," she said. "Stephanie Lang, the murdered woman. I used to clean house for her, the silly creature. You'll load the lamp into my car?"

Julia followed her and put the lamp into her car while the woman stood off to one side, studying the children. When Julia slammed the trunk shut, the woman jumped and turned, startled.

"I was just wondering," Julia said casually. "Everyone thinks that Brad Lang killed his wife. Do you?"

"No." The woman frowned. "What difference does it make?" She went around to the driver's door.

Julia followed her, answering, "I'm just curious, is all. Do you know something the others don't?"

The woman stopped with her hand on the door, staring at Julia. "I worked for the Langs," she said. "Brad Lang was a jellyfish, a silly, spoiled brat who thought his wife walked on water. Whatever Stephanie wanted, Stephanie got." She paused. "He was the type of man who would hide behind lawyers and take the easy way out. The truth was never as important as expediency. And yet, no matter how many deals the DA offered him, no matter how many times his lawyers tried to convince him to make a deal or plea extenuating circumstances, Brad Lang stuck to his guns and pleaded 'not guilty' all the way through. He sacrificed expediency for his version of the truth. That wasn't like him. That's why I think he didn't do it."

With that, she got into the car and slammed the door shut. Julia stepped back to give her room, frowning and deep in thought. The woman leaned out the open window and jerked her head at the kids. "Are they yours?" she asked.

"Two of them are," Julia said.

"Oh, yes. The other is Robby Wilde's, isn't she?"

"Yes. Amelia."

"He lives right next door."

"Yes…"

"Well," the woman sniffed. "Isn't *that* convenient?"

She drove off and Julia stared after her, gaping.

"Mrs. Donaldson."

Julia jumped.

Mrs. Jurta was behind her, watching the car speed away. She shook her head regretfully. "Mrs. Donaldson always has an opinion, and never a problem sharing it with anyone who'll listen. And she's always surprised when she finds herself alone in a crowd."

Mrs. Jurta had none of her four legged friends with her today, and Julia wondered if places had been found for them yet. She hoped so, even though she knew it would upset Dana to learn that she probably wouldn't see Horatio again.

"Oh, hello," she said. "How are you?"

"Fine. I've come to check out your sale. Mind if I nose about?"

"No, please do. It is best offer, so if you see anything you like, let me know."

Mrs. Jurta nodded and wandered off. Julia could tell that she was not really interested in furniture - she was probably here to push her dog agenda. Julia didn't want to listen, but she couldn't think of a polite way of getting around it.

She went back to her chair and looked at the photo again. So this was the infamous Stephanie Lang. No wonder the town had been so star-struck. She certainly was very beautiful, in a fresh, young way. But what was the picture doing inside that lamp?

For the second time, Mrs. Jurta made her jump.

"I'm still looking for dog sitters," Mrs. Jurta announced, rubbing the scarred surface of a tiny wooden desk. "It's tough, you know. I got a list from the SPCA, but they've just gotten a shipment of abused dogs, and every volunteer has their hands full."

"Oh, I am sorry to hear that," Julia grabbed her book and shoved the picture into it before Mrs. Jurta could see it. For some reason, she didn't feel like sharing the find. "Do you see anything you like?" she asked brightly.

Mrs. Jurta blinked at her, and then shook her head. "I was just looking at the scratches on this table." She indicated them with her hand. "Whoever owned this must not have de-clawed their cat."

"It does look awful."

"It needs refinishing. My brother does that kind of work all the time. I'm just surprised by how many scratches there are. The cat must have gone to town on it."

Julia sighed. She was getting tired of questions without answers, especially those revolving around her house. She wished fervently that someone would take the table away so that she would have one less thing to think about.

"I won't be surprised if no one takes this," she said. "No one likes buying a repair job."

"I'll take it," Mrs. Jurta said.

"No, that's okay, really."

"I'll give it to my brother," she insisted. "He's retired and has nothing else to do. How much?"

"Best offer. Make a bid."

"Oh, um, hmmm… Twenty bucks?"

"Make it ten and you've got a deal."

"You're not much of a bargainer," Mrs. Jurta commented. She fished around in her jean's pocket and pulled out a wad of crumpled cash.

"No," Julia said. "I'm afraid not. But I feel like I'm cheating you by asking for any money at all. Thanks. Are you all set for your trip down to Florida?"

"If I could find a sitter for just four more of the dogs, I'd be all set. You wouldn't…"

Julia sighed again and decided to face the matter head on.

"Mrs. Jurta, I'd help you out if I could, but I've never had a dog before and I'm just too overwhelmed with children and house repairs to add one more task to the list. I'm sorry. I really am."

The other woman nodded. "I understand."

"I'm really sorry."

"No, no, it's my problem. It's just that… Well, your little girl took to Horatio so fast and Amelia, of course, likes the little one. I just thought that – well, no matter."

She rubbed the top of the bedside table. Julia felt horribly guilty, and it was only through the strongest of self-control that she kept herself from giving in. "I'm sure something will come up," she offered.

Mrs. Jurta said, "I do have some calls out, but, well, everyone's busy, you know? And they are such well-behaved dogs. For puppies, I mean."

"I'm sure."

"They don't eat very much. And it'd only be a week, probably, before I or one of the other vets could take them back. That's not long at all."

"No, it isn't."

"If not, I guess it'll be the kennel for them."

"The kennel?"

"There's one in Concord. It's not a bad place, not at all. But it's so impersonal."

Julia had to stop herself from rolling her eyes. "I'm sure they'll be fine."

"If they were ordinary dogs, I would say so. But these little guys have been through so much in their lives already. They've been abused, abandoned, and they are finally at a point where they can start to relax and recover. Now this."

Julia felt a lump growing in her throat.

"I just feel terrible," Mrs. Jurta said. "I'm torn between my duty to the puppies and my duty towards Dexter."

Julia relented. "Mrs. Jurta, look, I can't take them in, but I will give you this much. If you can't find a place for Horatio and – and Amelia's dog, then let me know, okay?"

A smile split the gloom on Mrs. Jurta's face. "You mean that?" she chirped.

Julia nodded.

"Oh!" Mrs. Jurta reached out and grabbed both of her hands. For a moment, Julia thought the woman was going to kiss them. But the older woman merely squeezed them as she bounced on the balls of her feet.

"Oh, Julia, thank you! The boys will be so happy and your little girl will be delighted."

"Don't say anything just yet," Julia said, alarmed. "We'll wait until tomorrow night, in case you find something else."

"Absolutely! Oh, thank you! It is such a weight off of my mind, you have no idea."

"Don't worry about it," Julia said. She suspected that she might as well resign herself to the idea that two puppies were coming to stay until Mrs. Jurta's return. "That's what neighbors are for."

Mrs. Jurta showed her own neighborly spirit by taking a boxful of nick-knacks and a table lamp to go with the bedside table.

# 31

Saturday morning was one of the best mornings Ron had in a long time. He got up in the early twilight, then he and Robert joined the other guys signing in for the derby. There was lots of joking and laughing, and Ron soon felt like one of the guys.

After signing in, he helped Robert unload his boat into the lake and relished the gentle rocking as they cast off. Robert knew the best places to fish and they reeled in several catches before they found any that were worth keeping. When they finally called it a day and headed back, Ron was glowing from the fresh air, sunshine, and good feeling.

*This,* he thought, *is how summer ought to be spent.*

John Irwin Sr. had taken a break from the hardware store to volunteer at the derby. He was in charge of measuring the fish and took great delight in telling Ron that his catch was definitely one of the biggest.

"Is this your first time?" he asked, handing it back.

"No, sir," Ron said, pleased with his success. "But it's been a while."

"Well done!"

John couldn't say that Ron was the winner, of course, until all the contestants reported back in, but that didn't matter to Ron - all that did matter was that he had caught a fish, and it was way bigger than Robert's.

"Mine will taste better, though," Robert teased as they walked towards the barbeque area.

"Probably," Ron said, "but only because you already know how to cook it."

It was nearly noon and the barbeque section was hopping. They stowed their catches in coolers in the car, then went to get some food. Robert knew everyone and introduced them to Ron, bragging about Ron's catch as much as if he'd caught it himself. Ron got a hamburger, chips, and a soda, and found an empty table to sit at.

He was picturing himself as a cop when Dylan slid next to him.

"Hey, Budd," he grinned. "Catch anything?"

"Oh, yeah," Ron said and gave him the weight and dimensions. The older boy's face fell.

"Aw, man," he grumbled. "That takes mine out."

Ron grinned triumphantly, but Dylan didn't notice - he was too busy blaming the three other fishermen who'd crowded his own fishing spot on the lake.

Then he pulled his digital camera out of his pocket and turned it on. "Okay, so I set up some hunting cameras on the house the other day and, before you ask, no, I don't know if that's legal or not. It shouldn't be that big a deal because they only take photos when there's movement. Anyway, I checked them yesterday and got some images already. I think you're going to freak out when you see them."

Ron was intrigued. "Really? Did you catch a glimpse of someone?"

"It's even creepier than that. Dude, I'm thinking that we're on to something here, a real ghost."

"Isn't that what you always thought?"

"Well – not exactly. I mean, I thought there was supernatural activity and stuff, but a real ghost? Do you know how rare those are?"

"No."

"Pretty rare," Dylan admitted. He thrust the camera into Ron's face. "Look at this."

Ron studied it. It was the side of the house where he and Dylan had been earlier. There was nothing other than a cat sitting on the porch, its eyes glittering.

"What?" he asked.

"Just watch."

The picture flipped but the scene was basically the same, except the cat was jumping off the fence, fleeing the scene. Although there was nothing particularly frightening about that, it made a shiver run down Ron's spine.

Dylan hit the button and the scene shifted. It was blank.

Ron blinked, but the picture stayed the same. It was completely black.

"What?" he asked.

Dylan was grinning. "Look at it!"

"There's nothing but a black screen!" Ron protested, then did a double take and looked again. "There's nothing but a black screen? Wait – what caused the black screen?"

The older boy leaned back, looking smug. "What indeed?"

"Did it lose battery?"

"No, it didn't. See the edge, there? You can see some light."

Ron looked and saw that he was right. There was crumbly-looking light on the edge of the picture.

"What is that?" he asked.

"I found a plastic bag covering the camera. There aren't any pictures after this."

"A plastic bag? Well, that could have been anything, then. The wind could have carried it over."

"There wasn't any wind last night," Dylan said.

Ron leaned forward and clasped his hands together, imitating his dad whenever he was trying to make a point.

"Dylan, this isn't any proof that there's a ghost. It looked like it for a minute there, but the bag is pretty – um – not conclusive. I mean, an animal or something could have…"

"What? Pulled it up a tree and draped it over the camera? Katy was with me when I found it. No animal or wind put that bag there."

"Dylan, it's probably nothing."

He wasn't listening. "Someone doesn't appreciate our looking around at all. We need to step up our surveillance."

"How?"

"Stake out."

"Stake out? Overnight?"

"What's the matter? Are you scared of the dark?"

Ron glared at him. "No one's afraid of the dark, just of what's *in* the dark."

Dylan sighed, exasperated. "All right, all right. Look..." He pulled out a notebook and began to flip through the pages, doing his best to look like one of the ghost show hosts. "I've been doing a lot of studying and I think the only way we can get to the bottom of this is if we are on the scene when something happens. That means going in at night when everyone else is asleep. We'll just slip in and out without touching anything. What do you think?"

Ron shook his head. "I don't know," he said regretfully. "Aunt Julia..."

"She doesn't have to know. We'll be back before she wakes up."

Ron considered it. Dylan was right – the only way to catch a real ghost was to go at night, but Ron had never snuck out of the house before and the idea made him nervous. Nevertheless, here was chance for adventure, to see a ghost for real, to do something risky and brave. His heart pounded at the thought, and he nodded.

"Yeah, I guess."

"*Sweet.* How about tonight?"

"Tonight? Um..."

Ron looked over at the grills. Robert was a few steps away, laughing with the other guys, paper plate in hand, hamburger untouched. At any moment, he'd be joining Ron and Dylan to eat. They had only a little time to finish this conversation.

Ron turned to Dylan. "Look, I can't do it tonight, but probably tomorrow night. I'll text you."

"Why not tonight?" Dylan asked.

"Officer Wilde's going back on the beat tomorrow," Ron said. "He and Aunt Julia are probably going to be up half the night talking. They can talk a blue streak when they want to, you know."

Dylan nodded knowingly. "Oh, yeah," he said. "I know what you mean. I heard that they've been hanging out together. Grandma thinks that they're an item."

Ron blinked. "A what?"

Dylan shrugged. "You know, a couple. Boyfriend and girlfriend like. Grandma and her buddies have bets on when it's official."

"They're not a couple," Ron scoffed.

"Really?"

"Really. I'd know, wouldn't I?"

"Would you?"

"Oh course I would," Ron snapped, frustrated.

Dylan shrugged. He glanced at something over Ron's shoulder and stood up. "Whatever," he said. "Just let me know when you're available for the project, right?"

Ron nodded, relieved. "Okay."

As Robert joined him, Dylan mumbled an excuse and left. Ron thought it was a good thing that he stopped the rumors at the source - Aunt Julia would be embarrassed if she knew. Not that it would be such a bad thing, really, but they were going back to Springfield and a relationship would make everything awkward.

Ron felt much better about himself and was even hungry again.

He turned to find Robert staring after Dylan with a thoughtful expression. When he caught Ron's eye, Ron shrugged innocently.

"We beat his good fishing spot," Ron said.

Officer Wilde laughed.

# 32

After Mrs. Jurta left, Julia brought the kids in for lunch, then settled them upstairs for some quiet time while she finished *Picturesque in Death*. The detective delivered his speech, the culprit was caught, the innocent were vindicated, and the main guy and the main girl came to an understanding.

Julia closed the book with dissatisfaction.

Although the ending of the book coincided with reality and the husband went to jail, swearing vengeance, she couldn't help but feel that there was more to the case than that. She also decided that had she been on the police force at the time, she would be highly insulted at the way they were portrayed in the book.

Putting the book and the mystery aside, she checked her phone and found a voicemail from Sherri:

> *Hi Julia, it's Sherri, just calling to give you a report. The Springfield house is getting a lot of interest. I've gotten calls for walkthroughs and prices. If you're even slightly interested, call me. I want to capitalize on this. Let me know. Love to the kids.*

Julia sighed in frustration. "Of course I haven't given you a selling price, Sherri," she said softly. "I told you I'm not ready to sell."

She heard a thump upstairs and froze. It was not repeated, nor was there any wail of discomfort from the bedrooms, so she decided to let it go and turned back to the issue at hand.

To be fair, she told herself, she couldn't really be mad at Sherri. She should have stuck to her guns and refused to show the house. Julia decided to end this now.

But even as she began to dial, she hesitated. The price Sherri quoted in an earlier conversation was very tempting, especially since they had a place to live in until she found a new job. Even if she didn't get that job, running the house in Springfield was pricey: it was designed for two incomes, not one.

Julia called and got Sherri's voicemail. She left a message:

"Hi Sherri, it's Julia. This is very tempting, but I am concerned that we are misleading these clients. I have been pretty clear that I am not selling the house unless circumstances force me to and they haven't yet. Is it ethical, then, to give these people a price, allow them to do the research and financing, only to pull the rug out from under them at the last moment? I'm worried about this and would like your opinion."

"Aunt Julia?"

Jack's face was lined from sleep, and his clothes were tousled, his hair standing on end. He rubbed his eyes and looked around, and Julia couldn't stop the grin spreading across her face. He was always adorable, but he was downright irresistible now.

"Did you have a good sleep?" she asked, wondering if he'd gotten any at all with the giggling girls next door to his room.

He nodded, and came in, dragging Yellow Teddy along limply behind him. "Is it tomorrow?"

Julia patted her lap invitingly. He climbed up and curled into a ball, snuggling up against her chest with his head just under her chin. She wrapped an arm around him and started rocking without thinking about it.

"It's still today," Julia said soothingly. "You've only been asleep an hour or so. Are the girls up?"

"No." His voice was soft and sleepy. "I peeked into Dana's room and they were both asleep on the floor."

"On the floor?"

"Uh huh…"

They rocked for a few minutes in peaceful silence while Julia scrolled through her text messages.

Jack's head dropped suddenly and she realized that he had fallen asleep again. She debated whether she should wake him by getting up, but the chair was soft, the warmth inviting, and it was so quiet in the living room that she was inclined just to sit. Not a sound issued from upstairs as she settled back in the chair. Exhaustion rolled in, and the past three weeks of frantic activity caught up with her.

Dreamlessly, the afternoon slipped by.

"Hey, sunshine."

The voice was familiar, but out of place. Julia stirred. She was warm, too warm, but she couldn't move to shed the blanket. Something was weighing her down. It moved and she remembered Jack. Then she realized that she was in a chair, that the chair was in the living room, then that the living room was in Franklin. It dawned on her that she'd heard a man's voice right by her ear – while she was sleeping.

She sat up with a start, and Jack almost slid to the floor. Both she and Robert caught him in time, and Jack moaned in protest.

"Good afternoon, little man," Robert said.

He lifted Jack off her lap and set him on his feet next the otto-man where he was sitting. The little boy rubbed his eyes and tot-tered off to the kitchen, Yellow Teddy in tow.

Relieved of Jack's weight, Julia sat up and looked around. The sun was pouring through the west windows, heating the room.

Robert grinned at her. "Sleep well?" he asked.

"Yeah." She rubbed her eyes. "Are the girls okay?"

"They're still playing upstairs," he assured her. "It's a good thing the side door was unlocked, otherwise we might have busted something trying to get in."

She sank back into the chair, hands over her face.

*Great. You're sweaty, messy, and you left the door unlocked. Anyone could have just walked in here. Oh, Lord, am I ever going to be used to being a full-time parent?*

She muttered miserably through her hands, "I'm usually not - I don't know what you must think."

Brushing her hands away, he lifted her chin, studying her face. She wanted to pull away but couldn't.

"I'm thinking that you must have been really exhausted. No wonder you wanted to take the day off," he said softly.

Something in his tone was deeper than Julia felt prepared for. He had those intense brown eyes and an odd expression on his face, one that she couldn't describe but really, really liked...

"Aunt Julia!" Dana came bouncing into the living room. "Come look at the gross *fish* that Ron caught." She stopped when she saw them, confused and a little self-conscious.

Taking advantage of the broken moment, Julia pulled herself out of the chair and groaned, "Oh, ouch, that is a bad place to take a nap."

"Not exactly a great bed," Robert agreed. To Julia's relief, his tone was normal and his expression guileless.

"What time is it?"

"It's four o'clock," Dana said. She shifted uncomfortably, still looking unsure.

"Oh, good grief, it's so *late!*" Julia lamented. "You must think that we are the world's worst couch potatoes, Robert. Imagine sleeping in 'til four."

"It's not as bad as all of that," he said. "Come on. Take a look at Ron's fish. It won third place today and, if he's not bursting with pride, he really ought to be."

Straightening her clothes, she followed Robert towards the kitchen, wondering what she was going to do with a dead fish. How badly would she ruin Ron's childhood if she asked him to allow her to give the fish a decent Christian burial and substitute it with fish sticks at dinner?

"It's, like, *so* gross," Dana said. "Ron said that it nearly tore his *arm* out when he was reeling him in."

"Our Ron is quite the mariner," Robert said cheerfully. "He caught so many fish that the guys decided to nickname him 'Gorton.'"

In the kitchen, Ron stood at the table, beaming.

"Hi, Aunt Julia," he said proudly. "I've got supper." He gestured to the plate, and then something monumental happened.

The corners of his mouth tugged upwards and then he was smiling.

It left his face too quickly, but its affects remained. His face was more relaxed, his expression happier than it had been in months. Julia looked around quickly and caught Robert's knowing nod. She hadn't imagined it.

*All of this from a dead fish?*

Looking in the pan, she saw - to her relief - a nicely cleaned and cut fish nestled in tin-foil, ready for grilling. Ron handed her Robert's phone and she saw a picture of the pair of them holding their catches. Ron's was much larger than Robert's.

She gasped. "Holy cow, Ron! That's huge! What did you use for bait, a mackerel?"

"Just one of Robert's flies," he said, with more than a faint trace of pride. He handed the phone back to Robert. "We got lucky."

"Lucky, nothing," Robert said. "It was skill, Julia, pure and unadulterated skill and don't let Modest Maurice here tell you anything else."

"Send me the picture?" she asked.

"You bet. Well, I hate to catch and run, but tomorrow's my first day back on the job and I promised myself dinner and a movie with a certain young lady that I know."

Amelia gasped in excitement. She raced upstairs to get her hat and sunglasses, then back down again to say goodbye. "See you tomorrow, Aunt Julia!" she shouted as she darted out the side door ahead of her father.

Robert paused to look back apologetically. "Sorry, she must have picked it up from the others."

Julia followed him outside. "I can think of many worse things to be called."

Ahead of them, Amelia ran across the Wilde's front lawn, almost dancing in excitement. The air was humid, and warm and the shadows were beginning to get long. Julia lifted her hair up from the back of her neck and sighed.

"I'll see you tomorrow at church then?" Robert asked.

Julia felt a sudden pang. The week was over - she and Ron would continue working at the house alone.

*Oh, well. That was the deal and you knew it would come to an end.*

"Thank you again for all that you've done for my family this week, especially for today. You can't possibly know what it meant to Ron to have all this time with you and the other boys. It's – tremendous."

Robert looked embarrassed and tried to brush it off. "It was a good excuse to go fishing. And he's nice to hang around with."

"Well, it meant a lot to all of us for you to give us this time like you did. I really appreciate it. We've had so much fun this week that it's a shame that you have to get back to work."

*Did I just say that out loud?*

"It was a lot of fun." He paused. "We should do this again sometime."

"We should," she laughed, again grateful for his tact. "I owe you."

"Looking after Amelia for me is thanks enough," he said.

"Dad!" Amelia's plaintive call echoed across the lawn. "Dad!"

"Coming!" He turned to Julia. "I probably should go."

"I still feel guilty that you gave up your vacation for us."

"Don't. It was Amelia's and my idea, remember?"

"But I don't get why either of you would come up with it. I really don't."

He shrugged. "It's what neighbors are supposed to do, right? Help each other out in times of difficulty. We just lucked out that your difficulty, in this case, was an easy one. Nothing simpler than fixing up a house."

"Well, I guess. I'm glad I can return the favor, neighbor to neighbor."

He held her eyes with his steady gaze, and Julia felt her heart speed up.

"Neighbor to neighbor," he said softly.

The moment caught and held.

"Da-ad! I'm getting eaten alive out here!"

"Coming, sweetheart!" he called. Then, unexpectedly, he reached out and traced her cheek with his hand. "See you tomorrow," he whispered.

Julia watched him disappear, rubbing her cheek and wondering if there was any reason to go back to Springfield at all.

# 33

"Ron! *Ron!*"

Dylan burst through the side door, shouting. His voice reverberated off the walls of the kitchen, making everyone in the dining room jump. "Ron, where are you?"

"Call me a psychic," Julia said. "But I'm getting the feeling that someone is looking for you, Ron."

"Doesn't he knock?" Dana asked, rolling her eyes.

"I guess not," Julia chuckled. "In here, Dylan!"

Ron pushed back from the table as Dylan burst in.

"Ron!" he said, then slid to a halt when he saw that the room was full. "Oh. Sorry, Julia. I was just looking for Ron." He glanced at him, fingering his backpack.

Ron felt a shiver of excitement. Dylan must have something really important.

"You look like you're in a hurry," Julia said.

"Just wanted to show Ron my, uh, school project. Top secret, you know." He looked at Ron. "Got a minute?"

Julia got up. "It's all right, Ron. Why don't you take Dylan upstairs, show him your room, and take a look at his project. But, remember – we're having an early night tonight."

Dylan was bouncing on his toes with excitement. Ron led the way upstairs into his bedroom where Dylan slung his backpack on the bed and scanned the room approvingly.

"Nice," he said. "Wait until you check this out, Ron, just wait."

Ron's stomach squeezed with excitement. "New evidence?"

"Just wait. I've got it right here."

The older boy's hands shook as he opened the laptop. Soon Ron's neatly made bed was covered in Dylan's battered and somewhat grimy equipment.

"Dude, this place is seriously haunted. I'm not kidding. We're on to something *huge*. We're going to have to step up the investigation, big time. We seriously have to go in and we can't do it alone anymore. I've already texted a few of the guys, and they're all going be at the birthday party tomorrow. We'll talk, figure out what to do, when to go in, what to take with us – have to play it safe for now... oh, sweet, the program's up. Now watch this."

He worked the keyboard for a few minutes and pulled up a picture of the side of the house, showing a couple of the windows on both floors. He manipulated the image so that it shuddered, grew, and diminished. After a few failed attempts, Dylan got as close as he wanted, but Ron still didn't see what was unusual about the side of the house. He was beginning to think that this was just Dylan's wishful thinking.

"Now, look" Dylan demanded.

Ron leaned in and his stomach dropped. In the window, partially covered by a tattered, gray curtain, was a human hand. A translucent human hand.

Dylan was regarding him with grim anticipation.

"What – *what?*" Ron gasped.

"Meet Mrs. Stephanie Lang," Dylan said in a hoarse whisper. "The *late* Mrs. Stephanie Lang."

"But..." Ron said, trying to come up with some reasonable explanation. "It's a person... right?"

"Look," Dylan pointed. "You can see right through the hand there to the folds of the curtain. Transparent."

He was right. Ron felt dizzy. "But ghosts don't exist!"

"Oh yes, they do." He tapped the screen triumphantly. "They're in Franklin and tomorrow night you, me, and the guys are going to slip out of the Ojacors' party and go down to that old house and get the final proof that we need. Isn't this awesome?"

Ron couldn't think of anything to say.

They stared silently at the photo; then, just when Ron thought he couldn't stand it anymore, Dylan abruptly shut down the program and turned off the computer.

"Enough of that," he said, hastily. "I gotta get home before dark."

Ron finally found his voice. "But why?"

"Why what?" Dylan asked, shoving everything into his backpack.

"Why would someone haunt the Lang house?

"I dunno." He paused. "Unfinished business, maybe?"

# 34

Later that night, with the kids ready for bed and watching a movie, Julia found that she couldn't settle down. Not for the movie, not with the cup of coffee that she made for herself, not for the budget she was trying to balance, or the help-wanted ads she was searching through. She blamed her restlessness on her mid-afternoon nap and avoided thinking about what happened outside with Robert. She needed activity, and she hunted through the house for something to do, but found nothing.

She paced and wandered, and wound up in the back bedroom. It was in a dismal state. The wallpaper was sagging and torn, the carpet was stained and threadbare, and the windows were dirty. It bothered her – it was unfinished, and she longed for it to be done, for the house to be done so that they could get on with more important things.

Julia reached out and tugged on a torn bit of wallpaper. It came off easily in her hand.

She could start on the wallpaper: it would be the ideal way to work off her excess energy. There was a lot to do, but anything that she could get done tonight was one less thing for her to do on Monday.

She went into the office for the supplies. Working quietly, so as not to alert Ron, she spread the tarp over the rug, then decided that this was a silly precaution: she was going to throw the rug away anyway.

Julia went to work, humming to the music she brought in with her. Tugging carefully, she found a second layer of wallpaper under the first. When she came to a tear in the paper close to the floor, she seized it, and tore an enormous strip of if off in one quick motion.

That's when she saw it – a wide, spattered, reddish-brown stain.

At first she thought it was coffee, and she wondered why someone would cover it rather than just cleaning it. But there was something about it that didn't fit with a coffee spill. She got on her knees and took a closer look. Stunned, she yanked her fingers back from the stain.

It was blood.

She gasped out loud. Dana was passing by and stuck her head in the doorway.

"Are you okay?" she asked.

Julia stood, blocking the stain. "Yes, fine. Is the movie over?"

"No, but I had to go to the bathroom. What are you doing in here?"

"Just taking down the wallpaper."

"Oh. Do you need help?"

"No, I'm fine."

"Okay!"

Dana slipped back out and ran down the hallway.

Julia listened until the sound of her bare feet slapping the floor faded away and the dull hum of the movie resumed. Then she turned and examined the stain again, this time determined to look at it logically. There was nothing to fear, after all. The stain was as old as the wallpaper.

The spatter pattern indicated that it hit the wall with force. It was about knee height, and some smudging indicated that something had been rubbed on the wall, but not enough to clean it off. She wondered if someone, sitting on a chair, got cut somehow and fell backwards, spattering and smudging the blood as they fell. But what sort of cut would have caused that much blood?

Which, naturally, lead to the next question: under what circumstances had the wound been received?

She shivered, then reminded herself that the stain was at least a decade old, if not older. There was no danger here and now. Ancient evils were only dangerous in the movies. In real life, there was safety in the passage of time.

*It was probably an accident, covered up by a lazy person. A lazy person who'd rather paper his walls than clean them.*

Julia recalled the hidden picture of Stephanie Lang. Perhaps that was what put the dark thoughts into her head in the first place. After all, there was no reason to think that there was anything suspicious about this stain – aside from the size of it, of course.

She shuddered and rubbed her temples.

Julia decided that there was nothing more she could learn from the stain tonight, and she was much too unnerved to work any longer. She would cover it up again and not mention it to the kids. It would only frighten them.

*I should show this to Robert. He'll know what to say to put my mind at ease.*

After covering the spot as best she could, Julia shut the door to the bedroom and went into the kitchen to make another cup of coffee. She opened a drawer to find a spoon, and her gaze rested on the picture of Stephanie Lang. The sight of that lovely face was enough to send shivers down her spine. She picked it up and studied it.

What was it about this woman? What made her so fascinating and so repulsive at the same time? Julia was beginning to wish she'd never heard of the Lang house or the murder mystery it contained.

*What was this picture doing here?*

The kettle's whistle brought her back to the moment. She pulled it off the stovetop, then went into the dining room to find her purse. She shoved the picture in her wallet.

*I'll show it to Robert tomorrow.*

Still nervous, she went around the house, checking the windows and relocking all the doors. Only when she was certain that everything was secure did she pour herself a cup of coffee. She held the warm mug in her hands until they stopped trembling.

# 35

The night was filled with uncomfortable and frightening dreams, all variations on the same theme. Julia was trapped in the small bedroom where fresh blood dripped off the walls. She would try to clean it, but the blood would get all over her. She would start to panic, and the dream would start all over again.

The last dream was the worst: Amanda was helping her wipe the walls, chatting in the way she always used to.

Julia was ecstatic. "Oh, Amanda, I've missed you so much! The kids have been crying. Where have you been?"

"Right here, goose!"

"But I thought you were dead."

Amanda laughed. "Oh, no. I'm not dead. It was all a silly mistake, Julia. I never left you at all."

Julia threw her arms around her, only to have her hands pass through the image. Amanda wasn't there. She was crumbled on the floor, dead, and it was her blood on the walls. Julia heard Ron and the kids approaching the room. The last thing she remembered was running for the door to stop them, and realizing that she was covered in Amanda's blood.

Julia woke up sobbing, clutching the blankets to her hot face and rocking back and forth. The pain of the loss roared back to life, as sharp and fresh as ever. She didn't think she would ever stop crying. She tried to keep it quiet – she didn't want to wake the kids.

As her sobs subsided, all that was left was one thought: *Oh, Amanda, how could you leave them? Why did you leave me?*

Sleep took a while to come again, but when it did, there were no more dreams. There was only darkness, and silence… And a wish for peace.

After Mass, Julia, the kids, and Amelia were downstairs in the basement, in line for donuts. Once again, Robert had been grabbed by someone needing to talk with him, so Julia had taken Amelia with them.

Julia dropped a few dollars into the donation basket and poured herself a cup of coffee as the boys followed the girls at a more sedate pace. She was distracted, and didn't notice when Mrs. Jurta stepped in next to her.

"Good morning, Julia!"

Julia's coffee sloshed out over her hand and she winced as the hot liquid bit her skin.

Mrs. Jurta snatched a napkin out of the basket and handed it to her. "There you are, girlfriend. Look, I'm afraid I've got some bad news."

"You can't give me the puppies?"

Her voice, Julia realized, sounded just a bit too excited. Mrs. Jurta didn't seem to notice.

"I *might* have a home for them," she said, cautiously. "An elderly couple who already have a pair of pugs might be interested in taking them. I dropped them off at their house yesterday and if all went well last night, you're off the hook. Can I still rely on you as my plan B?"

Julia nodded. "Sure, no problem."

Mrs. Jurta reached out and squeezed Julia's hand, then pulled her in and kissed her on the cheek. "You are a love!" she exclaimed. "How come someone like you hasn't been married yet, huh? What's wrong with the men today? How about it, Officer Wilde? Can you make sense of it?"

Robert was striding over, grinning. "You've got me, Mrs. Jurta. It's a mystery that even our crack team of experts couldn't solve."

His tone was light and humorous, but Julia couldn't bear to look at them, so she stared at the floor, wishing it would swallow her up. What was it with these elderly women and their matchmaking?

Mrs. Jurta's voice carried though-out the parish hall.

"...and all I can say is, that a smart young man wouldn't let this one get away, am I right?"

"Yes, ma'am," Robert said, and Julia could hear the smile in his voice. "I think... Mrs. Jurta... Isn't that Donald Mack trying to get your attention?"

They turned and Julia saw the man waving to them from one of the far tables.

"Oh, brother," Mrs. Jurta sighed. She folded her arms and frowned. "What does he want now?"

"Perhaps he's thinking," Robert said lightly, "that a smart man wouldn't let the right one get away."

Julia held back a laugh as Mrs. Jurta fixed Robert with a withering look.

Donald Mack was approaching. Mrs. Jurta sighed again and began to make her way to him.

Julia looked back to Robert. Now that Mrs. Jurta was gone, he seemed preoccupied.

"Everything all right?" she asked.

He looked weary as he nodded. "Yes. Just getting back into the swing of things."

"The first day back to work usually has me in a tailspin, too. Is there a lot for you to catch up on?"

"Catch up…?" He took a sip of his coffee, then shook his head. "Oh, no, nothing more than usual. I just… Well, I just got reassigned a new route today, which isn't a big deal, I guess."

She waited a moment before suggesting, "But it troubles you."

"The reasoning bothers me."

"Oh?"

"We've been having a problem with vandalism lately, and we think there may be a drug connection. We've been working on it for weeks, but haven't been able to get any real leads. There's the usual group of suspects, of course, and some of the guys have wanted to put them under closer surveillance." He paused. "I've had my own ideas, but in the week that I've been gone, the chief has decided to go the other way." He rubbed his chin and admitted, "Yeah, it bothers me."

"Do you think that they're targeting the wrong suspects?" she asked.

Robert shrugged. "Not necessarily. I think there's a good chance that they are involved. But if we squeeze them too tightly, they'll get nervous and go underground - and then we'll lose them."

"What do you think you ought to do?"

"We've established an M. O. and from that, we've been able to determine possible targeted areas. I think we ought to keep watching them and see what happens."

"Well, that seems reasonable."

He grinned wryly. "To you, maybe. But not to the guy in charge."

"Frustrating, huh?"

"Yeah, but I'll get over it. He's the boss, not me, and the crimes haven't been violent or anything. So I suppose we have a margin for error."

She looked at her hands. "Does Franklin… have a problem with drug abuse? Trafficking, I mean?"

"We've got some users, but compared to Manchester, Franklin's pretty clean. Chief Putnam likes to stomp on that sort of thing really hard. He's got a son and a daughter in the school system, and he doesn't like the idea that anyone might try to pass stuff on to them."

She turned her gaze over to the police chief. He may have upset Wilde, but it seemed he had his priorities straight about one thing, at least.

"The local parents must love that," she said.

"Yeah. He's pretty popular." He stretched his back and then checked his watch. "He's a good guy. Tough, and usually fair. He's clean, too, and that can be rarer than you think."

"That doesn't always mean that he's easy to work with," she suggested.

He flashed her a grateful smile. "No. That, it doesn't."

Their gaze held for a minute, until Julia remembered Mrs. Jurta's earlier comments. She dropped her eyes to her cup.

Robert looked at his watch again and stood up.

"I've got to get going," he said, moving his chair back into place. He was relaxed and moved easily, looking much more like the Robert that had been such a fixture at her house for the past week. "Is there anything you need before I go? Are you all set?"

"We're fine," she assured him. "We've got to go shopping for the party tonight, and then we'll be home for the rest of the afternoon."

"What time is the party?"

"Um, six, I think."

"Oh, good. I'll be back in plenty of time to pick Amelia up before then. You have my cell phone number?"

"Yes. And you have mine, I think."

"Yours and Amelia's. Thanks again."

"It's really no problem at all. The girls have such a good time together. Good luck on your first day back."

He laughed and pulled out his keys. "Thanks. I may need it."

Julia watched him go over to hug Amelia goodbye for the day, then stride out of the room.

*He looks ready for anything,* she thought, as she settled back into her chair. She caught Ron watching Robert's departure with an admiring look on his face.

*Hero worship,* Julia thought. *It's good to know that he has at least one good male role model in his life. I wonder what Miriam would say if Ron decided to become a cop like Robert.*

She grinned at the thought, and then realized that she'd forgotten to tell Robert about the wall. She thought about running after him, but decided against it. He already had enough on his mind. The wall had kept a long while, and it would last another day or two. She'd just have to make sure no one went in there before he'd had a look.

# 36

Sunday passed quickly for Ron. Aunt Julia had forgotten to buy a present for the birthday party that night, so they all went shopping and bought a basket that they filled with barbeque stuff. At home, Aunt Julia and the girls wrapped the gift while Ron and Jack watered the garden and played a game of catch.

Around five o'clock, they started to get ready for the party. Ron was looking forward to it now that he was going to meet Dylan's other friends to plan their next move on the house. He was glad that more people were involved. There was safety in numbers, even up against ghosts.

As they were getting ready, Julia got a call from Robert.

"They got an emergency call and it's going to take a while," she told them, when she finished the call. She saw the look on Ron's face and added, "It's not dangerous, just a lot of paperwork. Don't worry – I asked."

"Does that mean I get to go to the party, too?" Amelia asked, beaming.

"Yep. Go get ready."

It was a cool evening, so when six o'clock came, they decided to walk to the party. Julia fussed with making sure everything was locked, that they had everything that they needed, and then realized that she had forgotten her pasta salad. They had to wait for her to go back into the house to find it and a bag to carry it in. It was about six-fifteen before they finally set out.

They were halfway there when Ron heard his name being called. He turned to see Dylan and Katy riding up on their bikes with their grandmother, Sheila, trailing behind on hers.

Dylan rode up to him and jumped down. "Hey, Budd!" he said. He was wearing his helmet – a concession to his grandmother, no doubt. He fell in step with Ron while Katy rode in lazy circles around them. Sheila caught up with Julia and dismounted from her bike gratefully. Her face was pink from effort and she was winded. In her basket were a gift bag and a bundle wrapped in a plastic grocery bag.

"We decided to ride over, since it was so nice out," Dylan said conversationally. "And Grandma needs the exercise for her heart."

He said nothing about the haunted house, and Ron figured that he was being cautious in front of the others. Ron was glad of it; he'd decided that he didn't want Dana and Amelia involved anymore. It was getting too dangerous.

Caroline Ojacor met them at the door in an African caftan. The house was already humming with activity, and the spacious living room was crowded and warm.

John Irwin arrived with a cooler full of soda and beer and was delighted when he found them in the crowd.

"Hey, you guys made it, great! Now I just hope Joseph arrives before we all melt in here."

When Joseph Ojacor's car was finally spotted, there was a lot of noise and confusion as people doused lights, told each other to be quiet, and made futile attempts to hide themselves. Ron glanced at Dylan, and the older boy rolled his eyes. Ron agreed – adults could be as silly as children.

Joseph came in to their shouts of "Surprise!" The honoree pretended to be shocked, and the party spilled out into the backyard, where Caroline had set up games and grills.

Two other boys came up to Dylan, and a natural order was established: Dylan was the head of the pack, while the other two, as Dylan's older friends, outranked Ron, the newcomer.

Jamison 'Mac' McCullough was gangly, wore glasses, and talked a lot about comic books and literature. He had brought his eBook with him and showed Ron his library. Ron spotted *War and Peace*, a slew of Shakespeare plays, *Dracula*, and the *Harry Potter* series, among others. He wondered if Mac really read all of those or if he was just borrowing his parent's reader.

George Simpson was a jock. He had the shoulders of a football player and seemed more interested in playing the yard games and eating than in the business at hand. But he had a good sense of humor and immediately took to Ron, for some reason. No sooner had Dylan introduced them than George insisted that Ron join his side for volleyball. Dylan decided to play, and all the boys ended up playing on the same team.

They played for an hour, until dinner was announced. They ate at the same table with Dana, Amelia, and Katy. The girls mostly talked among themselves and left the boys alone, but their presence was enough to keep the boys from talking shop.

After a bit, Julia and her new friends, Sheila and Mrs. Jurta, came to sit at the table. At a wordless signal from Dylan, the boys swallowed their food and excused themselves.

Dylan found a spot behind an old oak tree with the remnants of a tire swing still hanging from its branches. It offered cover from the curious eyes at the table.

George sprawled out on his back, one arm over his eyes, and Mac sat cross-legged and facing the picnickers while cleaning his glasses. His face wasn't nearly as red as it had been when they were playing, but his hair was still plastered tight against his skull.

Dylan rummaged through his backpack until he found his cell phone.

"You all know why we're here," he said formally. "Ron and I are in the middle of a scientific investigation of the Lang mansion."

"The haunted place," George said. "Yeah, we know it."

"We haven't proven that it's haunted yet," Ron cautioned.

"I think we have," Dylan said. His voice was growing excited, despite his attempt at scientific detachment. "We've pick up some movement on film that can only be explained by supernatural activity."

Dylan showed them the picture of the hand behind the curtain and they were both impressed. George said that he always had a feeling about that place. Mac, however, pointed out that it might just have easily have been a squatter's hand moving that curtain.

"But you can see right through it!" Dylan protested.

"I don't know about that," Mac said. "That screen is awfully small. It may just be a trick of the light or the fact that it's low-grade film shot in the dark. Ron's right – it doesn't mean that there's a ghost. It could just be a bum."

"Bummer," George said, and laughed at his own play on words.

"Well, if you don't believe that…" Dylan was scrolling through the phone again, his fingers trembling with excitement. "Check this out, guys."

It was a shot with the same footage, showing the side of the house, only Dylan had gone in closer to one of the second story windows and fixed some of the pixilation. The window was dark, with no hand showing.

"Awesome, dude," George said. "A dark window."

"Look closer," Dylan insisted.

They did. Then Ron saw it, a small circle of light nearly obscured by the ancient curtains. It was too small and too concentrated to be a shaft of moonlight. Ron's hands felt icy as he pressed them against his knees. He felt frightened, then annoyed at his cowardice. Dylan wasn't afraid and Ron wasn't going to be, either.

"That is a ghost orb," Dylan said in a low voice, resonating with awe. "That room is the studio of the dead woman – the place where they found her body."

George said, "Holy cow," but his voice was so solemn that the words weren't quite as funny as they might have been.

Mac was impressed, but not convinced. "It's probably a lamp or something. There are no such things as ghosts."

"How can you see this and say that?" George demanded.

Mac shook his head. "Ghosts aren't real. They're archaic explanations for known scientific phenomenon."

Dylan grew impatient. "Look, Mac, I am one hundred percent sure that there is something supernatural going on in that house, and so is Ron and he's as smart as you think you are. If it's not a ghost, then it's a poltergeist."

"Cool!" George said.

"Ridiculous," Mac countered. "Come on, Dylan, we're too old to believe in bedtime stories."

"This isn't a story – its reality. And we can prove it."

"How?" Mac asked, folding his arms.

"By going into that room and seeing if there are any footprints or wrappers and stuff. Ghosts wouldn't leave that behind, but bums would."

"Uh uh. No. Bad idea, Dyl, bad idea."

"Oh, come on!" Dylan sputtered.

"Dude, think about it," George said. "If it's a ghost, we're running the risk of upsetting it and getting dragged into hell. If it's a bum, he's probably high and has a knife or something to kill us with. Neither is a good option."

Mac rolled his eyes. "Ghosts don't drag you to hell, George. Demons do."

"And how do you know this isn't a demon?"

"Dude, seriously?"

"What difference does that make? Besides, if you don't believe in ghosts, how do you *know* that they don't drag you to hell?"

Ron was annoyed. He wondered why Dylan thought that he needed George and Mac when they were such obvious doubters;

but since he was the outsider, he kept quiet and tried to maintain that air of intelligence that Dylan had assigned him earlier.

Mac sighed loudly. "George, ghosts do not drag people to hell, all right? Demons do."

"But you don't believe in those either." George protested. "And how do we know that ghosts aren't also demons?"

"Because they aren't," Dylan said dismissively. "They are a completely different thing. Ghosts are the spirits of dead people and they hang around because they either don't realize that they are dead or because they have some final business to take care of. Demons are devil-spawn or fallen angels. The two are entirely different things. What we have here is a ghost, plain and simple."

"I still say it's a bum," said Mac.

"Look, Mac - if you're going to be a jerk, you can just leave now, you know. We're going to the house after dark to find out and I say we go tonight, after the party."

Mac shook his head. "Isn't breaking and entering illegal?"

"It's been empty for nearly twenty years. That makes it public property. Besides, I'll bet half of the doors and windows are unlocked."

"So we'd only be entering," Mac said. "Is there an alarm?"

Dylan paused. "I don't think so."

"Well, don't you think we should find out?"

"We will," George said. "When we open the door, we'll find out."

"Come on, Mac," Dylan said. "Knock off the scared talk and tell me if you're in or not? You sounded stoked on the phone."

Mac considered for a long moment. As he did, the crowd around the tables began to get up and come out into the yard. In a few minutes, they'd be surrounded and would be unable to talk.

Finally, Mac nodded.

"All right," he said. "But if we find anything, *anything*, we tell the police, right?"

The plans were quickly made. There was an old riding path that ran behind the houses which they could use to avoid being seen on the road. The other two boys were sure that they'd get permission to stay out late, but Ron wasn't. To his relief, the older boys seemed understanding.

"Just tell her that we're doing video games or something," Dylan said.

"We'll actually play some afterwards, so it won't be a total lie," George said.

"Just a partial truth," Mac added.

"I'll think of something," Ron said. He didn't want to lie to Aunt Julia. He worried about it until Dana ran up to invite them to volleyball match that some of the fathers were organizing.

"They said if you weren't too tired, to come up and play," she said.

"Too tired!" George jumped to his feet. "We'll show them old guys: come on, team."

# 37

When Jeanne Simpson found out that Julia lived on the same street as the Lang mansion, she could hardly contain herself.

"Goodness," she exclaimed. "I would be so unnerved living by that spooky old place, and I wasn't even here when the murder happened. How do you manage it?"

Julia was sitting between Jeanne and Mrs. Jurta at a long table filled with neighborhood mothers. Mrs. Ojacor was flitting from table to table, seeing to her guests.

"It was twenty years ago," Julia said. "And they did catch the guy. Or so they say."

"What do you mean?"

"She means," Mrs. Jurta said, spearing a slice of cucumber with her plastic fork, "the justice system in this country leaves much to be desired. They're always getting it wrong."

"Besides," Julia said, "according to people who knew him, Lang seemed too prissy to be a murderer. It's hard to imagine him getting blood on his hands, let alone his suit."

"But I thought Stephanie had been strangled," Jeanne asked.

"Oh, no," Mrs. Jurta said. "She was beaten to death, blood everywhere. It was a crime of passion, no doubt."

Jeanne shivered. "It's so creepy. All that murder and scandal right here in this little town. It's like one of those Agatha Christie novels. Even her name sounds like the name of the tragic heroine in an epic novel, doesn't it?"

"Maybe in a 1980's miniseries," Mrs. Jurta scoffed. "People aren't named Stephanie anymore."

Julia leaned closer. "Mrs. Jurta, is it possible that Brad Lang didn't kill his wife?"

Mrs. Jurta considered the question. "It's possible, I suppose – he didn't really seem the type. He was gone a lot, on buying tours for the gallery, and she had loads of free time here, alone. She did what she pleased, but for all that, she did seem to love him. She was always doing portraits of him, and whenever they were together, she was all over him."

"He was a looker," Sheila O'Reilly said. "In the upper-class, Harvard-man way, you know. Very WASPish, the two of them. We used to say that they were the only two real Yuppies in town."

"So," Julia said, wishing that she had brought a notebook, "you think that she loved her husband but that she was also having an affair?"

They nodded emphatically.

"Very discrete, though," Mrs. Jurta said. "No one wanted to know. This was Stephanie *Milano* Lang, the heiress and rising star in the art world. She and her husband donated lots of money to the civic projects and local charities, and they even went to church every once in a while. Who would speak out against them? It was like having a Kennedy move into town or something."

"I always said, though," Sheila said, "that she was asking for trouble. No one can play with that many lives and hope to keep their own."

The power that this dead woman still wielded over the town was fascinating, Julia thought. Every detail that would defame her character was given as though it were a mere personality quirk, or it was hastily covered up.

"So what *did* happen that day?" Jeanne asked. "I've never heard the full story."

Mrs. Jurta looked past Julia to answer. "I didn't have much to do with Mrs. Lang except for the fact that she offered to give my daughter some lessons. As it happens, I was supposed to meet her on the day she was murdered to discuss those lessons, only I ran into her jogging on the street in the morning. She was a health nut, kind of like you, Julia."

Julia shivered, but said nothing.

"She looked very distracted by something when I stopped," she continued. "I thought that she'd forgotten who I was, but that wasn't it. She knew exactly who I was and even thought to ask about a dog that was ill. She told me that she couldn't keep her appointment with me in the afternoon, but that if I could come over at around seven, she would probably be in then."

"Did you find the body?" Jeanne interrupted.

Mrs. Jurta shot her a scornful look. "Of course not!" she said. "Brad did. Anyway, she runs off, and I go home. At six-forty-five or so, I was out walking the dog again when I notice that she was riding her bike down the street, away from her house."

"On which street?" Julia asked.

"Why, ours, of course. I was at the end of the road and turning, so I didn't see which way she went after that."

"Did you go on the witness stand at the trial?" Jeanne asked eagerly. "Were you for the defense or the prosecutor? You must have been an important eyewitness."

Mrs. Jurta snorted. "That was a hassle. I had five kids and six dogs. Being a star witness was not exactly something I had the time or energy for. Anyway, I knew then that she'd forgotten our appointment, but Liz made such a fuss that I called anyway and no one answered. We thought nothing of it – she was an artist and got caught up in things and whatever. Besides, I thought it was good for Liz to know that sometimes things didn't work out. Later that night, I was watering the garden and..."

"At night?" Jeanne asked.

"It was hot that day," Mrs. Jurta explained, exasperated by the interruption. "Anyway, I was in the front yard watering, when I saw Brad's car pull up. He went inside and I stayed outside to finish up. The light was off in Stephanie's studio, but some of the other lights were on, so I remember thinking that she'd probably returned, too. Then, while I was packing up the hose, I thought I heard something, like a shout or a cry, but it was very distant. When I looked at the house again, the studio light was on and I saw shadows moving in front of it."

"He was probably doing it right as you watched!" Jeanne said, rapt with attention.

Mrs. Jurta shrugged. "Maybe. I don't know. I went back inside and a few minutes later, we heard the sirens. Len and I went outside to see what was happening and we were told to stay away, that there had been a robbery and murder. Mrs. Lang was dead, some sketches and knick-knacks were missing, and Mr. Lang had collapsed. The whole neighborhood was terrified. We thought some gang was ransacking the area. I didn't sleep well that night, I'm telling you."

Sheila said, "I remember that. We thought it may have been the Rooney boys. It was only later that we realized that the monster was Brad Lang."

"Who were the Rooney boys?" Julia asked.

"The local drug lords."

"It's less exciting than it sounds," Mrs. Jurta assured her. "They were lazy bums who pushed dope, is all. They were never really violent."

"Except when they were drunk," Sheila countered.

"True. Even then, they broke a few bottles and called it a night. Hardly worth worrying about."

"So Brad Lang stole his own stuff to make it look like a robbery," Jeanne said, quietly awed.

"That's what the police thought," Mrs. Jurta added. "He must have stashed the knife with the other things."

"So they found it, then?" Julia asked.

"The knife? No, they never found the knife."

Julia frowned. "That's really odd. I mean, he didn't have all that much time to hide it before the police showed up. It must still be nearby."

"What about the sketches that were stolen?" Jeanne asked. "Were they ever recovered?"

"No, they weren't," Sheila said. "They'd be worth some money now: original Stephanie Langs, evidence in a murder investigation."

"It would have been good if they had been found," Mrs. Jurta said. "They would have proven Brad Lang's guilt one way or the other, and Doris Mone would be the happiest woman in the world. She was insufferable when the verdict came down."

"Yes, she was..." Sheila said. "I remember her saying that a life sentence was not enough. She kept saying that this was New Hampshire and we had to use the death penalty, otherwise, he'd be out to do it again."

"They must have been great friends," Julia said. "Mrs. Lang and Mrs. Mone, I mean. She speaks so highly of Stephanie."

"They weren't," Sheila said firmly. "Mrs. Mone is a follower. She was always trying to get in good with the Langs just because they were the closest thing this town had to aristocracy. I heard Stephanie charged double her normal rate on their portraits just because Doris was such a pain in the neck."

"Wouldn't surprise me," Mrs. Jurta said archly. "Doris has terrier-like tendencies and always had. She's gotten worse over the years, too."

"Noel Hickey was another one I couldn't understand," Sheila said. "He was in good with the Langs and I never understood why."

"Noel Hickey, the postman?" Jeanne asked.

"Stephanie took a fancy to him and drew him a few times," Sheila said. "She even did a portrait of her handyman for free – I can't remember who he was at the time, but that wasn't uncommon. She'd do that if the subject interested her enough."

"*She* took a fancy to *Noel?*" Jeanne asked, her tone heavy with disbelief.

"An artistic fancy," Mrs. Jurta explained. "Stephanie Lang may have been many things, but she had standards."

"I would hope so!"

"Noel never got to see his portrait. It disappeared the night of her murder. It was one of the things missing. He went on about that for years." Sheila glanced beyond them, then brightened and sat up straight. "Cake time!" she said, with a grin.

They twisted in their seats to see. John Irwin and J. C. carried an enormous sheet cake, ablaze with candles, to the table where Mr. Ojacor sat. Caroline followed, her face bright with anticipation and carrying a giant bowl that seemed to be filled with whipped cream. All other activity and conversation stopped as John Irwin boisterously led the crowd in an off-key birthday song. Mr. Ojacor stood and blew out all the candles with the help of some of the children.

They cut the cake as the younger kids crowded around the serving table, anxious to get a piece of cake with a candied letter on it and a scoop of the whipped cream.

Julia used the opportunity to excuse herself from the table and away from all of the talk. Looking around, she realized that Jack was no longer with the other little boys, playing with chalk on the patio.

Fear gripped her stomach. She made her way through the crowd towards the house and the serving station. It was growing dark. Julia checked her watch and saw that it was 8:30.

She located the girls soon enough. They were in a corner of the porch with several other girls, giggling and talking movies. Amelia hopped up when Julia beckoned, and Dana did so more reluctantly.

"Have either of you seen Jack?" Julia asked, trying to keep her voice even.

"He was with Tim last time I saw him," Amelia said.

"They were playing on the concrete," Dana added.

"He's not there now," Julia said, biting her lip. "I can't find him." She saw Dana's face grow pale with anxiety. "Have you seen Tim around?"

"He's there by the counter." Amelia pointed.

The little boy was there, but Jack was nowhere to be seen. Dana put her plate down on a nearby seat and said, "Maybe he's in the bathroom. I'll go look. Come on, Amelia."

"Thank you, Dana," Julia said. "You two look in the house. I'll look outside and meet you on the porch."

Julia began to search, trying not to look as anxious as she felt. She called out his name softly, responded politely but quickly to anyone who tried to engage her in conversation and kept walking.

Ron was sitting on the grass next to Sheila's grandson and several boys that Julia did not recognize. When he saw her, he jumped up and ran over.

"Something wrong?" he asked.

"Have you seen Jack?"

"He's missing? Where did you see him last?"

Julia didn't have a chance to answer. There was an uproar from the house and she knew instinctively that Jack was involved, even before she saw Amelia running toward her. She met her halfway.

"Jack hurt his head!" Amelia gasped. "It's all bloody – come quick!"

Ron beat them to the bathroom, but by only a few steps. They had to thread their way through the crowd and squeeze into the small room. Jack was crying in short, painful gasps. His shirt and forehead were covered with blood and for one short, terrifying moment, Julia thought that something had happened to his eye. But then he turned, and she saw that it was fine.

Jeanne Simpson and Sheila were tending to him while Dana kept them supplied with wash cloths. Caroline fluttered about, assuring everyone that it wasn't as bad as it looked, while her husband sorted through medicines and ointments.

Jack reached for Ron as soon as he saw him.

"Hey, buddy!" Ron swept him up and out of the women's grasp. Jack buried his head into Ron's shoulder, and then spotted Julia. He held out his arms to her and Julia was glad to scoop him up.

"Oh, honey, what happened?" she crooned, trying to calm her own palpitating heart.

"Tim pushed me!" Jack sputtered into her neck.

"Tim?"

A horrified looking little boy was clinging to Jeanne Simpson's jeans. He looked ready to be sick. Jeanne put a protective hand on his shoulder.

"They were playing on some chairs and Jack fell," she said.

"He pushed me!" Jack asserted.

"I didn't mean to!" Tim protested. "We were playing pirates and he was chasing me!" He burst into tears.

"I'm sure it was an accident," Julia said. "Let me see your head, Jack."

She propped him up on the sink and lifted the hair out of the way. It was a shallow gash, just deep enough to bleed profusely. She felt a rush of relief.

A fresh trickle of blood traced the outline of Jack's forehead. Julia took the wet wipe that Caroline offered her and carefully cleaned around the cut. The boy sniffled and looked up at her pitifully.

"My head hurts," he whimpered.

"I know," she said gently. "We'll get you cleaned up, and we'll go home so you can rest."

"Go home?" he wailed. "I don't want to go home. I'm feeling much better, see?"

He smiled up at her, but Julia stayed firm. "I think it'd be best, honey."

"Here is the ointment." Joseph handed her disinfectant and a cotton swab at the same time. "We have bandages. Do you want me to call the hospital?"

"Hospital?" Jack cried, turning white.

"I don't think so," Julia said. "I think he'll be fine with a bandage if we can get him home to rest."

Jack protested that he was well enough to stay, even though he yelped every time Julia touched near the cut.

Dylan arrived then. Julia wasn't too busy to notice his disappointment when he learned that the Budds were going home. She noticed that he drew Ron aside to speak with him.

"Dana," she said, "why don't you go and find our things so we can leave."

Dana was as reluctant as Jack. "But we were supposed to meet Robert here, Aunt Julia. Shouldn't we wait for him?"

"Oh, I'd forgotten," Julia sighed. "You'd better give your dad a call, Amelia, and see where he is."

Amelia darted out, followed closely by Dana.

"Mrs. Lamontaigne," Dylan said, brightly. "Would it be all right if Ron stayed longer? We just started a game, and J. C.'s dad went to his truck for the S'mores supplies. We'll walk him home after."

Julia was about to say no, then hesitated when she looked at Ron. He was looking at her apprehensively.

"Would you like to stay a little later, Ron?"

"Sure." He added, "I mean, unless you need me."

"I think we'll be all right," Julia said. "I'll just speak with Sheila about it and make sure that she's up to making the detour."

"I'll get her." Dylan bolted from the bathroom, but Ron stayed where he was and silently began cleaning up the discarded first aid supplies.

Dana and Amelia returned with news that Robert wasn't picking up his phone, so Julia called him herself while Jeanne offered to hold Jack. She listened in carefully as Julia left a message, informing him that they were all headed back to the house and he could pick Amelia up there.

Sheila came in and promised to keep an eye on Ron and bring him home safely.

"Not that he needs an eye kept on him," she said, as she watched Julia gathering up their belongings to head home. "That one was born thirty-five years old, I think."

"I think you're right," Julia laughed.

Ron was pulled outside with the boys and, with a final thank you to their hosts, the rest of his family stepped out into the night.

As soon they were outside, Dylan had turned on Ron with an elated smile.

"Ready for a little haunted house-snooping?" he asked.

Ron's heart started to pound. This was it. They were actually going into the house to find a ghost. It was possibly the most thrilling, dangerous thing Ron had ever done.

Dylan turned to go find the other boys, and Ron followed him, trying to keep his face clear of excitement. No need to tip anyone off.

"What about Aunt Julia?" he asked, keeping his voice low. "We'll pass her on the road, won't we? What'll we say?"

"Nothing," Dylan said. "We're not going to run into her. If we use the bike trail, we'll avoid the road and get there without anyone seeing us. We'll be in and out and no one will ever know we were there."

Ron hoped he was right.

# 38

Mrs. Jurta decided to walk Julia and the children home. She'd eaten her fill of cake and didn't want to leave Dexter alone for too long.

It was a nice night for a walk. The two little girls were ahead of them, talking confidentially. Jack was limp with sleep in Julia's arms. All around them, tree frogs sang harmony to the tune carried by the crickets, and bats darted industriously overhead.

Julia took a deep breath. The air was fresher than it had been lately, and she was glad to be outside. It was peaceful, a perfect summer night.

Mrs. Jurta did most of the talking, still angling for a commitment from Julia. Julia let her go on as she indulged in her own thoughts. She thought about Jack's injury, and how quickly her neighbors had sprung up to help him, as they had so many times already these past few weeks. After months of feeling isolated, it was comforting to know that there were others around who cared enough to help.

*Too bad this situation is only temporary...*

They rounded the corner to Whipple Lane and the two girls began to run towards the house. Julia was too tired to try to catch up or to stop them. She felt her phone vibrating in her back pocket and shifted Jack to reach it.

It was a text message from Robert. Julia was surprised by the rush of relief she felt. She hadn't realized how much she'd worried that his delay was being caused by some problem or disaster at work.

*If I'm this worried about a cop I'm not even in a relationship with, how much worse is it to be his wife or daughter?*

It was a fleeting thought, but it was enough to give her a different perspective on the former Mrs. Wilde and her reasons for leaving her husband.

The message was short: *On my way. Sorry I'm late.*

It was almost too short. No mention of why he was so late, but he was probably on the road and couldn't say any more. And Julia wasn't about to start nagging.

She replied: *No prob. We're at my house now.*

"I've never seen that there before," Mrs. Jurta said suddenly, drawing Julia out of her thoughts.

Julia blinked and looked around. "I'm sorry? Haven't seen what before?" She slipped the phone back into her pocket and hiked Jack up on her shoulder.

"That truck. I don't recognize it. Odd."

She gestured towards a big pickup truck parked in front of her house. It was sitting there, dark and ominous. It probably belonged to a friend of a neighbor, having a beer and watching a game. Even so, Julia felt a chill go down her spine.

"I don't like it," Mrs. Jurta looked frightened. "What if they're robbing my place? What if they're waiting for me in there?"

That seemed to Julia to be a huge jump in logic. "Your dog would be barking, wouldn't he?"

"Not if he's been drugged. Or worse. Oh, Lord, I wish I had my gun! I'd go over there right now and confront them. No one's cleaning *me* out and getting away with it!"

There was a touch of hysteria in her tone, and Julia was very glad that the gun wasn't there.

"Why don't you come in with us and wait," she suggested. "We can watch the house from my place until Officer Wilde gets here.

It's probably nothing – just a friend staying over who parked at the wrong house, maybe. These places can look alike in the dark."

Mrs. Jurta didn't answer right away. She couldn't take her eyes off the truck, and Julia wondered if she was going to flip out. She didn't know what to do if she did.

"We won't do any good waiting out here," Julia said. "Come on inside with me. I could use a cup of coffee and a chat while I wait for Amelia's dad."

"But what about my dog?"

"He'll be fine. Come with me and let's get the kids in the house."

Julia propelled the older woman along until they reached the side door. As they passed the two girls, Julia told Dana to follow her. Then she stopped to find her house key while Mrs. Jurta, hiding in the shadow of the van, tried to catch a glimpse of the imaginary thieves.

It was impossible to search her purse with Jack in her arms, no matter how she shifted him back and forth. She finally gave up and tapped Mrs. Jurta on the shoulder.

The woman jumped and turned around.

"Would you hold Jack for me, please?"

Mrs. Jurta took him reluctantly. Jack woke up during the transfer and rubbed his eyes solemnly, and she bounced him up and down in her arms while glaring across the street.

"I'm probably being cleaned out even as we speak," she said. Her hushed and dire tone was in keeping with the drama she was creating. "I should call 911."

"Let's wait for Robert before we do that."

"Where are the police, I ask you? Never where you need them, yet always around when you're going a teensy bit over the speed limit."

"There's nothing in the back of the truck yet and there's no light coming from your house," Julia said. "They'd hardly be working in total darkness. They would at least have flashlights."

"That's true, I suppose. Dexter's been so sensitive to light lately that I haven't left even my bedroom lights on, like you."

"Like me?" Julia was pawing through her purse, trying to remember which compartment she'd placed the keys in.

"Like you, leaving the back room light on. Always a good idea. People will notice the shadows on the shades."

Julia's head snapped up and she looked around the doorway to the back of the house. Sure enough, there was a dim light emitting from the back bedroom, the one with the blood-stained walls. She could see the faint glow through the windows of the other bedroom. A chill washed over her for the second time that night.

She had turned off all the lights before they left for the party that afternoon.

"Come on, Budd, keep up!"

Ron hurried through the underbrush after Dylan. Bushy branches scratched his legs. Twisting roots tried to trap his feet, and insects swarmed them every time they stopped for a breather.

"How much further?" Mac wheezed. He sounded awful. Ron was winded, but at least he didn't sound as bad as the leggy nerd did. It wasn't much comfort, but he'd take it.

"Almost there," Dylan said now. He was leading, doing his best to keep ahead of George.

"Good night for a hike," George said.

Mac wheezed, "Sure, if you don't mind ticks going up your back and – other places."

"Quit moaning. You didn't have to come."

"Shut up," Dylan muttered. "We're here."

The house loomed before them, looking even more like a set for a horror movie than Ron had remembered. He looked around at the other boys for their reactions.

Theirs weren't obvious. Mac adjusted his glasses and studied the wall, while George brushed twigs from his shirt and checked his phone. Dylan crouched next to his backpack, rummaging through it.

After George fiddled with his phone for a few moments, he thrust it in front of Mac's face and took a picture. Mac jumped back and tripped over an exposed root, falling flat on his back.

George laughed and showed Dylan the photo.

"Nice," Dylan laughed. "All right, Ron, you're cameraman again and Mac, here's my night vision binoculars. Be careful with those – they're my granddad's."

"What's the game plan, Dyl?" George asked.

"We're going to split up," Dylan began, but he was immediately interrupted.

"Uh, no, bad idea," George said. "People always get killed when they split up."

"That's just in the movies."

"I have to go along with George on that one," Mac nodded. "We're already breaking and entering – I don't want to add criminal stupidity to the charges."

"I meant, we *pair* up," Dylan said, patiently. "Me and Ron, you and George. We take the opposite ends out of the house and see if we can't flush out this ghost. We each have a cameraman and a leader, and Mac and I will stay in touch by cell phone. Sound good?"

The two older boys nodded, but Ron raised his hand.

"I don't think we should break in," he said.

"We'll try not to. Start looking for unlocked windows. That way it won't be breaking in."

"Just entering," Mac agreed.

"Let's move!" George said.

They stepped over the low wall of bushes. The other two hurried around the back, and Ron and Dylan were alone.

"Okay, Ron," Dylan whispered. "Just keep the camera rolling and follow me. Watch your step and don't trip."

Ron fumbled with the buttons, embarrassed by his shaking hands, and then brought the camera to bear on Dylan. "Ready."

Dylan turned with a theatrical flourish and began to creep around the house. Ron sighed, exasperated, and then followed him.

They went around the corner and stopped while Dylan peeked through windows and tapped on the glass. Nothing stirred, but that didn't deter him. He didn't miss one window without stopping to rap on it or shine his flashlight into the darkened space. It was so ridiculous that Ron forgot about being scared and started wondering what the professionals Dylan was trying emulate would think of his "footage".

Dylan stopped, gazing soberly into the camera.

"It's still relatively early at night. Most ghosts don't come out until after midnight, but if we're lucky, we might catch an early one. My friends are on the other side of the house, trying to stir something up right now. But I'll tell you," and here he leaned forward in an attempt to look cool, but he looked even sillier than before. "Tonight, I feel lucky."

Ron shook his head and looked up to a big window on the second floor.

Someone was staring back at him.

Julia tried to calm herself, tried to think. Mrs. Jurta's talk of burglars had her on edge: she expected to be hit over the head with a mallet by a malevolent criminal at any moment.

Had she forgotten to turn the light off? It was possible, but she couldn't go in there with the kids until she was sure.

"Mrs. Jurta, would you stay out here with the kids while I take a look inside?" she asked, trying to keep her voice steady.

Mrs. Jurta was alarmed. "What? Why? What's wrong?"

"Nothing," she assured her. "I just want to look around a bit before I let the kids in, that's all. Normally I would have them wait with Ron, but he's not here now. Would you mind?"

"Well, I guess not..."

"Why aren't we going in?" Amelia asked.

"You will in a second," Julia said, keeping her voice low. "You two wait here with Mrs. Jurta, okay?"

"Now, you know, Julia," Mrs. Jurta said. "If you had a dog, you wouldn't have to worry about this."

"Thank you for that, Mrs. Jurta."

Julia's fears seemed silly to her now, and she wished she hadn't made such a big deal out of the whole thing. She probably wouldn't have, if Mrs. Jurta hadn't gotten her all nervous with talk about burglars and murderers.

She found her key and inserted it in the lock, keenly aware of the sound as she turned it. The door swung open quietly, as it always did, and she stepped inside.

The face was motionless, white and distorted, watching them with a terrible intensity. Its eyes were two empty holes, boring into Ron's, holding his horrified gaze.

His heart stopped as the camera fell from his hand and hit the ground. After two failed attempts to speak, Ron managed to gasp, *"Dylan!"*

Dylan half turned, then lost his footing and fell to the ground with a wail. He swore, and Ron glanced at him before looking at the window again.

The face was gone, but a white circle played about the panes in its place, a fog left from someone breathing on the glass. Through a haze of fear, Ron recognized this, and a different sort of fear took root.

He ran to Dylan's side and grabbed the boy's arm.

"Come on, come *on!*"

"Wait, ow, my ankle! Dude, stop pulling! What's the matter?" Dylan yanked his arm out of Ron's grasp, but Ron grabbed it again.

"We've got to get out of here. Call the others, call them right now! Move!"

"We're not leaving until I catch that ghost on film!" he snapped. "Fine time to lose your nerve."

"There isn't any ghost!"

"Shut up, Ron…"

"It's a guy, Dylan, a man, a person! Let's get out of here before he comes at us…"

Then they heard the shot.

♉

As soon as Julia was out of sight of the kids, her fears came swarming back. The entry was dark, the air oppressive - even the dampness seemed ominous. She slowly put the key back into her purse and stepped into the kitchen without flipping on the light. In the gloom, it was difficult to see; but the room was as she left it, right down to the van keys on the counter.

But something was wrong. She could feel it. As she stood there, trying to calm her racing pulse, she heard something.

It was faint - a murmur, almost. If it was daytime and the room was flooded with light, it probably would sound normal. Tonight, it was enough to stop her heart in her throat and make her break out in a cold sweat.

Moving quietly, she went over to the counter and felt along the edge until she found the knife drawer. She opened it carefully and felt around until her fingers wrapped around the handle of a steak knife. It had a short, dull blade, but it was better than nothing.

Leaving the drawer open, she tiptoed into the hallway. Light spilled from the back bedroom and she realized that the light was wrong – it was too little to be the ceiling light and she had no lamps in there. It had to be coming from a flashlight. One that was resting on its side, perhaps, and there was no way she would have left one of those on without remembering it.

A shadowy figure crossed briefly in front of the light. She almost dropped the knife.

*Oh my God! If I move, he'll hear me…*

Looking around frantically, she noticed that someone had stacked her laptop along with their CDs and DVDs in a pile near the office doorway, preparing for a quick getaway, perhaps. But what were they doing in the back bedroom? There was nothing in there but painting supplies and tarp.

She heard a creaking sound, like nails being pried up out of wood. It was a bone-chilling sound under the circumstances, but she realized that, if he was prying up floorboards, he didn't think anything was wrong. She could slip out undetected. She took a step back.

There was another creak and then the sound of wood splintering. She heard a mumbled curse, and then an irritated, "Come on…"

The voice… She almost recognized it.

What could be under the floorboards? Without realizing it, she found herself moving quietly back toward the bedroom to take a look. If he was tearing things up, he would not be paying attention to possible intruders.

Ignoring the screaming warnings in her head, Julia crept forward, step by step, until she was at the doorway and could peer around the corner. Clenching the knife, she could see a bulky shadow crouched on the floor. The intruder was grunting as he struggled with something.

The rug was pulled back. A few of the floorboards were pried up, and the pry bar laid next to them. A flashlight lay on its side on the ladder, shining on the work in progress. The rest of the room was in darkness.

The intruder shifted suddenly, in response to the sudden hum of a cell phone. Quietly cursing, he stood and pulled the cell phone out of his pocket. He sounded exasperated as he hissed, "*What?*" into the speaker.

Julia pulled back, her heart pounding. She'd heard that voice before. If she could just catch a glimpse of his face... She waited a moment, then slowly leaned in again until she could see him. He was standing, looking at something in his hands. He was of medium height and build, but his face was in shadow and there was nothing else distinguishable.

He swore again and shoved the phone back into his pocket. He grabbed the flashlight and the pry bar next to it and whipped the light around. It caught Julia's half exposed face.

Julia didn't stop to think or to negotiate. She turned and ran.

*Get out! Get out!*

She heard him following her and panicked, thinking that his hands were inches away from her.

Something caught her foot and yanked. She fell blindly, dropping the knife as she hit the ground hard, losing her breath.

He stepped on her hand, and then something fell on her head, hard. She was lost in a swirling sea of stars, struggling to stay afloat in a liquid darkness.

She heard someone scream. It might have been her.

Far away, a door slammed. Dana screamed, a shot rang out, and panic gripped Julia. She fought desperately but she couldn't hold off the dark tide. She saw nothing more.

# 39

At first, Ron thought it was a car backfiring. It happened all the time back in Springfield, where the neighbors were always working on old junkers that they like to call "classic cars". But this wasn't Springfield, and this wasn't a car.

The sound ricocheted around them, making it impossible to tell which direction it came from or even from how far.

Ron's attention was quickly captured by another sound: from the other side of the house, he could hear scuffling, grunts, and what sounded like someone prying wood.

"What was that?" Dylan said, in a small voice.

Ron, with his head cocked to one side, said, "George and Mac..." He jumped up. "They don't know about the guy!"

"Wait!" Dylan shouted, but Ron was already rounding the back corner of the house.

A second shot sounded.

This time, there was no mistaking it. It was close by, maybe even from inside the house. Ron skidded to a halt and listened.

His legs were rubbery. He found his feet, and he started to run, to get to the others before anyone was hurt.

Behind him came an explosion, and the backdoor burst open.

He whirled around and froze. The tall figure on the porch had an enormous sack slung over one shoulder and held something in his free hand, something small and metallic.

*A gun!*

Ron made a small sound, and the figure turned to him for a second, then jumped off the porch and raced through the backyard, coming to a stop at the fence. He threw the heavy sack over the fence into the trees, then made a move to climb over.

Without thinking, Ron took off after him. The figure was halfway up when he got there. Ron grabbed hold of a leg and yanked. The figure shouted in surprise and nearly fell, but grasped the top of the fence. He tried to kick the boy off, but Ron held on tight. He was thrown against the fencing again and again, losing his breath and bruising his side.

"Guys! Help!"

The boys spotted him and came running, Dylan lingering behind.

The man spotted the boys. He thrust downward with a vicious kick that caught Ron on the cheek and mouth.

He saw stars. He tasted metal and he fell, blindly, into the moist tangle of weeds on the ground below. His side landed on a rock, knocking what little remained of his breath out of him. Through the tears, he saw the man pull himself nimbly over the fence. Then the figure was gone, and George crashed into the wooden wall above where Ron lay.

Dylan was there, too, grabbing George's arm.

*"Are you insane?"* he screamed. "Let him go!"

Mac took the flashlight out of Dylan's hands and shone it through the gaps to the woods beyond.

"Let's get back," Dylan said suddenly. "He might come back."

"Geez," George whispered. "Good thing he took off. We could have been in real trouble."

"Yeah, no kidding," Mac said, tossing away the stick. "Nice ghost you got here, Dylan. I didn't know they were able to kick people around like that."

"Let's get out of here." Dylan was already moving toward the house. "He's probably a criminal hiding from the law."

"We almost caught him, too," George said, disappointed.

"We almost got killed," Dylan whispered. "Let's get out of here." He was acting far differently from the way he had when he thought that there was only a ghost.

Mac crouched down beside Ron.

"Are you okay, Ron?"

Ron nodded, but the movement hurt. "My mouth," he muttered thickly. His head throbbed, and he wouldn't unclench his teeth for fear that they would fall out. He tried to lift himself up, but it was painful, and he fell back again with a groan.

George leaned over him, his expression difficult to make out in the gloom. "Dude, can you move?"

"Yeah, yeah," Ron muttered, forcing his mouth to move. It hurt, but not nearly as much as he had anticipated. He carefully propped himself up, and this time there were extra hands to help him.

Dylan bounced on his toes a few yards away. "Hurry," he said, panic raising his tone again. "Come on, he might be coming back."

"Dude, chill," George snapped. "Ron's hurt. Come give us a hand, will you?"

Dylan took an unwilling step closer. The two other boys hefted Ron onto his feet and propelled him along through the yard towards the back porch.

As they reached the back door, George said, "Let's take him inside."

"What?" Mac squeaked. "Are you crazy?"

"Dude, Ron can't go too far as he is and, if we're inside, we'll be able to hear the guy if he breaks in. Besides, I really want to see."

They stared at him incredulously.

Ron shrugged off their hold on him and leaned himself against the wall. His mouth was starting to throb and he wished that they would stop arguing.

"Aren't we going to call the police?" Mac insisted. "That guy beat up Ron."

"We can't. We were trespassing," Dylan said. He was shaking like a leaf, and Ron wondered if there was something actually wrong with him. "Look, if they find us like this, they aren't going to believe another guy was here. They're gonna think we beat up Ron ourselves."

"Unless we find the bullet holes," Ron croaked.

"What bullet holes?" Mac asked.

"Wasn't he shooting at you?"

"Shooting? No! Those came from down the street somewhere." Ron winced. "He was holding a gun."

"That was a phone," George said. "We saw him making a call just before he ran to the window in the other room."

"That's when George had the brilliant idea to try to break in while he was out of sight," Mac sighed. "Great idea, George. Never listen to a jock. Anyway, the upshot of it is, we found a squatter who beat up on Ron then took off. I think we should call the police and let them handle it."

"No," Dylan insisted. "Not without proof."

"Fine," George said. "Then let's go get some proof."

He wrenched open the back door and stepped into the inky blackness. Mac groaned and followed with the flashlight.

Dylan hesitated, looking to Ron for guidance.

Ron found the phone number he was looking for and called it, but the call went directly to voice mail: "This is Robert Wilde. Please leave your name and number, and I'll get right back to you."

Ron said, "Hi, um, Officer Wilde, this is Ron. Not an emergency, just wanted to talk to you. All right, um, talk to you later."

He hung up and faced Dylan's disapproving stare.

"You call the cop?" he demanded.

Ron drew himself up and off of the wall to stand toe to toe with the taller boy. For once, he didn't feel intimidated. Dylan had cowered in the shadows, refusing to help a wounded friend, and now didn't want to do the right thing by reporting this to the authorities. Ron couldn't believe that he had been so foolish as to follow him.

His voice dripped with contempt as he replied, "Well, doing it your way hasn't really worked, has it?"

Before Dylan could overcome his surprise enough to respond, they heard George shout, "Guys! You've got to see this!"

With a look of disgust, Ron went inside.

He found himself in a shadowy room that he thought was a kitchen. The floor was hard beneath his sneakers, and it smelled of mildew. The only light came from Mac's flashlight in the other room. Walking carefully, his hands out in front of him, he followed it until he joined the boys in what appeared to be a living room.

Mac was in the middle of the room, shining his flashlight on George, who looked out another door into what Ron assumed was the entryway.

When Ron appeared in the doorway, Mac dropped the flashlight beam to the floor. "Look," he said, grimly. "Proof."

There were fast food wrappers, a pile of blankets, unopened cans of beans, a knife, and some musty old pillows. A messy pile of newspapers spread out near the kitchen doorway where Ron stood, and some clippings were tacked to the wall.

Ron shivered, then jumped when another beam of light appeared from behind him, and joined Mac's playing out on the floor. Apparently, Dylan had recovered somewhat.

Moving the light around quickly, his voice trembled as he asked, "What is this?"

"It's an incident room," Ron said grimly.

George snapped his fingers and stepped into the circle of light. "*That's* the word," he said. "That's what I was trying to think of. Incident room."

"Incident room?" Dylan asked.

"Someone was researching something," Mac said. "See the clippings on the wall?"

Dylan flashed his light over the clippings as he and Ron leaned in. One of them was an article about the Mones and their museum, another was of a painting of Stephanie Lang's. The third was not really a clipping, but a copy of one that had been carefully cut out. There were a few other pins pulled halfway out with jagged bits of paper clinging to them, as though someone had been in a hurry when he tore them off.

"All of these have something to do with the murder here," Ron said, glancing at Dylan. "I wonder if he was investigating it."

The older boy nodded.

Mac snorted. "I don't think this was an ordinary private eye, Ron. This is the room of an obsessed man."

"Let's get out," Dylan begged, but George shook his head.

"That guy was terrified," he said. "He ran like a scared rabbit and left half his stuff. Besides, no one would be dumb enough to take on the four of us. I want to look around. Maybe he left more clues."

Ron moved toward the other doorway where George lingered, staring out into the dark. Nothing moved, there was no sound except the creak of the floorboards under their feet.

George said, "Come on, Mac, let's go upstairs. This is a murder house, you know. Maybe we'll find a body or something."

"Great," Mac grumbled. He adjusted his glasses and leaned into the clippings so far that his nose was nearly touching the wall.

Ron looked out into the darkness of the entry way. "The studio is upstairs."

George was intrigued. "Studio?"

"The dead woman's. Someone told me it was on the second floor."

"Let's go check it out."

He took the flashlight from Dylan's limp hand, and then disappeared into the gloom of the entryway. Dylan didn't even protest, and Mac was too absorbed in the clippings to notice.

Only Ron limped after George, calling out, "Wait up."

The entry was big with a sweeping staircase that looked as though it had been torn out of an old movie set. The railing was covered in cobwebs, and the stairs were slick with years of dust. When George shone his flashlight on them, there were footprints.

"He's been up here," he whispered.

They hurried up the stairs. Ron slowed when his foot slipped and nearly cost him his balance. He didn't need any more injuries to explain away to Aunt Julia.

On the landing, they had their choice of doors. George halted, unsure; then Ron said, "Look at the floor."

The footprints in the dust went into only one room.

Ron didn't let George touch the doorknob, reminding him that they would disturb fingerprints. Fortunately, the door opened with a light push, and they found themselves in an enormous, shrouded room.

Big windows were covered by dingy shades. Drop cloths lay haphazardly over tired piles. In the middle of the room, the intruder had uncovered a paisley-clothed chaise lounge and propped up an empty easel next to it. Against one of the walls, empty frames, bolts of canvas, and canvasses stretched on wooden frames of all sizes and shapes lay waiting for the artist that would never return. Another wall was loaded with shelves and, under these, old sketch books lay scattered and open. They weren't dusty. Someone had been using them recently.

"Geez," George mumbled. "Dude, right down the street from you and everything."

The old drop cloths gave the room a ghostly feel and the old, dried drops of paint on the floor were still shiny. From underneath one of the piles of clothes, tape snaked out. It was coated in dust, but Ron was willing to bet that it was the police's crime scene tape.

He shuddered. The whole room felt like a crypt – all that was missing were the coffins.

Mac and Dylan came in then, and Mac said, "This is weird."

"Tell me about it," George said softly. He crossed to the lounge and sat on it, looking around thoughtfully. "She was killed in here, right?"

Ron, his voice clipped, answered, "Yes."

"What do you think the guy was looking for?"

Mac shrugged. "I dunno. Souvenirs?"

Ron limped slowly around the edges of the room. "I don't think he picked this house just because it was empty. I think he wanted something that was here, something valuable - evidence, maybe."

"Something in this room," George said. "Remember, the footprints only went into this room."

"I wonder if he found it," Mac said quietly.

"Probably not. I mean, he was still here, wasn't he?"

"But he was carrying that bag awfully tightly," Ron countered. "He had something in there. More clippings maybe. Where would he get those? They were pretty old."

"Newspaper office, I guess," George mused. "They keep back copies and stuff, right?"

"I don't know," Dylan muttered. He stood by the door, his hands jammed in his pockets, his manner sullen. "It's creepy either way."

"However he got them," Ron said, "you're right, Mac. He is obsessed." He thought back to all the people they had met in the past two weeks. "You don't think it's that writer guy, do you?"

"Who?"

"The one who wrote that mystery. He told Aunt Julia that he spent months researching it, and it's based on this murder. Do you think he's the one who is..." He stopped, shaking his head. "No, that's silly. He can get in here with permission and stuff. He doesn't need to hide."

"Check it out," George said suddenly. He was bent over the floor next to the lounge, shining his light on the floorboards.

They gathered around him and looked at the dark spot on the floor.

George traced it with his finger, then withdrew it quickly before looking up. "She was stabbed or something in this room twenty years ago and this thing is still here. It's like - time froze or something." He looked at Ron. "Man. Imagine that night, living right next door to a murder, hearing the sirens and everything and realizing that there was a killer only a few yards away? Got to be scary. Sirens always give me the creeps."

As he said this, they heard sirens. Then they heard the deeper sound of an approaching fire engine. It stopped at a distance, but it was close enough to cause pulsing lights to play around the edges of the heavy curtains.

Dylan visibly relaxed.

"It's not coming here," he said, relieved. "It's down the street."

*Down the street…*

Ron was sure that it had nothing to do with his house. After all, Aunt Julia and the kids were walking home, and probably hadn't even gotten there yet.

He hobbled over to the window, stepping carefully around the debris, and pushed back the heavy curtains.

An ambulance was pulling around the corner onto his street, lights on, but the siren was silent. He followed it up to the fire truck, parked on the road just in front of Mrs. Jurta's house. Swarms of firemen, cops, and medics wove through the parked vehicles.

Then he realized that the focus wasn't on Mrs. Jurta's house at all: it was on his own.

His heart caught in his throat. He rushed across the room, his injured ankle forgotten. He was out the door before the others even noticed, and on the stairs before they could react. He hopped onto the railing and slid down as the others rushed out.

"What is it, Ron? What's wrong?" they shouted, but he was in too much of a hurry to answer them.

He slid off the bannister and managed to land on both feet. The front door was locked. Fumbling, he managed to draw back the bolt and unlock the handle. He threw the door open and charged outside just as Dylan reached the door.

Together, they raced up the street. It seemed to take forever. Up ahead, the house was ablaze with lights, and groups of firemen talked together while a couple of cops blocked off the street. A medic near the ambulance was on his phone.

"Oh, man," Dylan panted.

Ron grunted and pushed himself harder. In another minute, he had reached the Wilde's driveway, where the cops had set up cones.

One of them tried to stop the boys.

"Move along," he said, stepping out right in front of Ron. "Nothing to see here."

"That's my house!" Ron snapped.

The cop looked doubtful.

Ron glared at him. "If you don't believe me, ask Officer Wilde."

"Officer Wilde, huh? Sorry, kid, I need to see ID."

"I don't have any," Ron said, growing desperate. "Look, is anyone hurt?"

"I can't say," the cop said, but his voice softened a little. "I don't know."

"Dude, that's his family's place," Dylan said, trying to help. "They've just come up for the summer, and they're friends with Wilde, all right? Let him go in, seriously."

"Wait here," the officer said, but Ron didn't wait. He slipped past the cones and darted around him.

"Hey!" the cop yelled.

Ron raced as fast as his legs would let him, dodged another policeman, and took the porch steps two at a time.

The front door was open. Inside he could see Jack held by a female cop. He was crying.

He burst into the room, into the middle of what appeared to be an interrogation. All the doors were open. In the hallway, medics were bent over a prone figure; beyond them, people were in the back bedrooms, and someone was taking pictures. A policeman stood guard next to the dining room door, through which Ron could see Mrs. Jurta seated at the table. A gun, a small automatic, lay on the table in front of her.

He saw all in a second, before anyone had time to react to his appearance. And then:

"*Ron!*"

Dana threw herself into his arms, almost knocking him over, and he shouted in pain. Amelia wasn't far behind, wrapping her arms around the both of them. They sobbed into his shoulder, and all he could hear was "Aunt Julia" and "shooting".

Jack squealed, wriggling to get out of the policewoman's arms.

One of the medics stood up and snapped, "Get them out of here. We need quiet."

"Outside, all of you," the female officer said brusquely, and another cop yanked Ron by the arm back on to the porch and down the steps. The others followed, protesting.

Ron tried to break the policeman's grip, but to no avail. "Where's Aunt Julia?" he demanded. "What's going on?"

"Kid, you're in a lot of trouble," the officer said.

Across the yard, Dylan was standing against a cruiser. Another cop was with him.

The officer holding Ron barked, "Harry!"

"What's this?" Harry turned. Recognizing Ron, he said, "Told them to wait, but they rushed me."

"Nice. Contaminating the crime scene. You're in a lot of trouble," he said again.

Ron stopped short and yanked his arm out of the man's grip. He raised his chin and glared at him.

"Listen," he said. "My name is Ronald Timothy Budd, and those are my siblings, and this is my house. If you touch me again, I'll file charges against you."

The cop stopped short and stared. Ron readied himself for whatever came next, but at that moment, a familiar voice called from the porch:

"Have you located the brother yet, Warren?"

Warren looked up as Ron whipped around to see Robert Wilde. Wilde looked stern, but he was surprised to see Ron running up to him.

"What happened?" Ron demanded. "What's going on?"

Robert was calm. "There's been a break-in. Your aunt's hurt."

It struck him like a thunderclap. Ron staggered, and Warren steadied him from behind. Visions of February, when his parents died, flashed in his memory and he was aware of the same sinking, nightmarish feeling rolling over him now that had come then.

*Steady. You can't go to pieces. You need to look after the kids.*

It was a huge effort, but he regained control. His voice sounded level and calm as he said, "Is she all right?"

The lump in his throat was huge. It was difficult just to get that much out.

"The medics are taking care of her right now. She needs to go to the hospital, but they think she'll be all right."

Ron relaxed a little. She wasn't dead.

Robert examined his face. "What happened, Ron? Were you in a fight?"

He didn't explain. Robert was obviously just giving him the watered-down version, and Ron was determined to get the whole story.

"But – but there was shooting?" he asked.

"We think Mrs. Jurta was trying to scare off the burglar. She's inside, and everyone else is okay." His face turned rigid. "We're just waiting on your aunt."

"Wilde." Another cop near Dylan was listening to his collar radio. "We got another break-in, just down the street. The Lang place. Silent alarm was tripped."

"Silent alarm!" Ron said, astonished. "But…"

Robert was barking out orders, and after a few unsuccessful attempts, Ron finally got his attention.

"It's not burglars," he said. "They're – my friends."

That got their attention. Robert turned to Ron and the others clustered around to listen.

Ron's mouth went dry, but he explained. "We were ghost hunting, that's all. We weren't going to go inside, but then the guy left the back door open and we just thought that…"

"Wait. Guy?" Wilde demanded. "What guy?"

"The homeless guy who was living there. That's where I got this fat lip. But he's gone now, and we went in to see if he had disturbed anything and he, um, had."

Robert was angry now. He turned to Warren.

"Take Harry and get down there to secure the area. If it looks okay, leave him, and bring the boys back here."

Warren nodded and signaled to Harry, leaving Dylan free. He looked hesitatingly at Ron, and when Robert spotted him, he waved the boy over.

"I suppose you're in on this ghost hunting bit as well, Dylan?" he asked.

Dylan nodded miserably, giving Ron a wounded look. Ron ignored it.

Robert glared at the both of them. "Breaking and entering is bad enough," he growled through gritted teeth. "But you were stupid enough to challenge a squatter? What were you thinking? You might have been hurt!"

"He was," Dylan muttered. He gestured to Ron. "The guy kicked him."

Robert glared at Ron's bruise. "He did?"

Ron nodded slowly. On the inside, he felt as though the foundation was slipping out from under his feet. Worse still, tears hovered just behind his eyelids. He never cried, and he certainly wouldn't do so with Dylan and the police - and Wilde - staring at him.

"Are you all right?" Wilde asked.

"Fine." It was an effort just to make the sound.

Robert put a hand on his shoulder and turned to the ambulance. "Charlie?"

A medic poked his head around the ambulance door. "Yeah?"

"Got another one for you."

"Send him over."

The yard was getting busier. Robert was being called from a hundred different directions, but he remembered to ask, "Dylan, where is your grandmother?"

"At the party," he mumbled.

"Call her, and tell her that we're going to have to question you and your friends about what happened tonight." He turned to Ron. "As soon as Charlie's done with you, come and find me."

"Yes, sir."

Dylan gave him one last, pained look before he marched up the porch steps and into the house.

# 40

Julia drifted in and out of the blackness. She heard voices, but they were distant, and she couldn't make out what they were saying. She kept trying to call out to them. There was something urgent she needed to do, something she needed to say, but she couldn't remember was it was.

She was aware, though, and trying to force her eyes open. Unfamiliar voices were talking about someone, telling each other to be careful, and watch her respiration. She became aware that her head was aching and she thought, for a moment, that it had been broken open. Other areas were hurting, too, but they weren't as bad.

"...possible concussion... stabilized..."

They were talking very fast and their voices were growing stronger. She tried to ask them what was going on but she couldn't. Nothing in her body seemed to exist anymore except for the pain and the headache. She was detached from everything but those anchors. If she wanted to, she could just let those go and sail away back into the dark nothingness...

Then she heard someone say, "The house is clear. No other victims."

*Robert.*

Partial memory returned, enough to grip her with terror, and it forced her eyes open a little.

The world spun. Robert's back was towards her. She tried to lift her hand but it didn't respond. She opened her mouth, but all that came out was a small squawking noise.

It was enough. Robert turned, and suddenly he was much closer. He was holding her hand.

"Julia."

His voice sounded far away. The dizzy spell was making her nauseous, and she longed to close her eyes to block it out. But she couldn't. There was still the question, the one that she couldn't remember.

The tide was turning – she was being pulled out to into the dark sea. Desperate to speak before she was swept out again, she tried to talk, but nothing came out. She tried again, harder this time, but the effort made her weak and the current was gaining ground.

"They're all right," Robert said. "Amelia, Jack, Ron, Dana, they're all right, they're fine."

*Dana is okay.*

*The boys are fine.*

Julia felt deep peace overtake her anxiety. That was the answer. The kids were all right. The kids were safe. They were with Robert. Robert would take care of them. The sea beckoned, and this time she didn't fight it.

"Julia, you're going to be all right. Just hang in there, Jules..."

His voice faded, but the peace remained.

Julia awakened alone, staring at a white ceiling from a soft bed. There was no noise, except for the gentle beeping of the monitor. Her head hurt, but her mind was clear - empty of all thought except for how comfortable she was. She had no idea what time it was or how she had gotten to bed, but it didn't seem to matter.

*I must have been really tired...*

She could tell from the shadows on the wall that it was still dark outside. She closed her eyes and tried to roll over, but something tugging at her arm prevented her. Annoyed, she glanced wearily at it.

It was an I. V.

She tried to raise herself, but her head throbbed and a wave of nausea threatened her. She leaned back against the pillow and looked around. She was in a small, but comfortable hospital room. The beeping sound came from the machine she was hooked up to. She was wearing a shapeless gown, and her clothes, the ones that she had so carefully picked for the party, were piled up on one of the bureaus. In the mirror, she could dimly see her bandaged head and sunken eyes. Her knee hurt now, too.

*The kids.*

Panic gripped her, then subsided. Robert had them. He had told her they were all right. She couldn't remember when he had said that, but she knew that he had.

Maybe it was a dream. Nothing here felt real. She fumbled around the bedding and found the call button.

The nurse was delighted to see that she was awake and bustled off to find a doctor. He came back with two, both of whom assured her that the kids were fine and staying with Caroline Ojacor. She could see the kids tomorrow, when she was more rested and the doctors had completed the tests to their satisfaction.

They examined her, asked questions, some about her condition, others about the incident, then planned the tests, and increased her medication.

"That's it for now," said one doctor, whose name Julia had already forgotten. "We'd better let you get some sleep. You've got a lot of healing to do."

"I want to see the children," Julia murmured as the drugs took effect.

"Sorry, but you need rest and quiet. You can see them tomorrow afternoon, perhaps. Right now, just rest."

Julia could barely see him as he spoke. She was out before they left the room.

♈

When morning came, Julia felt much better. The nausea had subsided, her aches were responding to the medication, and her doctor jokingly informed her that she had a very hard head.

"My mother could have told you that without an MRI," she laughed.

"We'd like to keep you for a few hours more for observation and tests," he said. "They're just routine and probably aren't necessary, but I want to be sure we're not missing something. You've got a lot of people waiting for you to come home."

Julia wondered if she would be able to go back, knowing that her house had been violated.

After the doctor was done with her, she had a light breakfast of dry toast and weak tea, then called Caroline's house. Joseph answered on the third ring.

"Oh, hello, Julia," he said, cautiously cheerful. "How are you feeling this morning?"

"Better, thanks. And thank you for looking after my kids. You've no idea what a weight it is off my mind."

"Oh, it's a pleasure. We haven't had children stay with us in a long time. Are you looking for Caroline?"

"Yes, or Ron."

"He's still talking to the police, but I'll get Caroline for you."

Ron was talking to the police? Julia wondered about that until Caroline picked up the phone.

Caroline assured her that the children were fine, causing no trouble, and that she and Joseph were delighted to have them as guests. Julia asked about Ron's chat with the police.

"I suppose it's about the break-in, right?" she said.

Caroline's answer was too vague to be very reassuring. "I'm sure that's so. The police allowed me to go into your house to get some clothes for the children and I took a look around. Only that back room was damaged."

"Yes – that's where I saw him." She winced at the memory.

"It must have been terrible for you!"

"It's just so odd. I mean, why *our* house? It's pretty obvious that we just moved in, and we don't have anything fancy. Do the police have any clues as to who did it?"

"I don't know, but Officer Robert said that he's coming over to see you as soon as he's done with Ron. He probably has all the information – he worked straight through last night, I think. I'll be taking the children up to see you later. I know Ron said that they called your parents, but they still haven't answered their calls. Should we be concerned?"

Julia was tired again. "No, it's not unusual. They like to take weekend trips with the cell phone turned off. Dad says people have entirely too much access to them."

"When they do get the message, it just says to call Ron. We didn't want to panic them. When do you think you'll be released?"

They discussed the particulars of Julia's medical condition, then Caroline had the kids, except for Ron, talk to her on the phone. Dana was enjoying her new adventure in the Ojacor household, and Amelia said that Joseph and Caroline were taking them to the park for lunch. Jack told Julia that Yellow Teddy had survived, but that he had sustained a tear in his arm for her to fix. All of them wanted to know when she was coming home.

Julia promised to fix the teddy bear, left a message for Ron, thanked Caroline, and then hung up the phone. She thought about calling her parents, but she was still drowsy from the medication, and she sank into a light sleep.

A few hours and a couple of tests later, Robert came for his promised visit.

When he arrived, one of the nurses was fussing over Julia's charts and hookups and adjusting her I. V., all the while making comments and observations that had Julia convinced that she was this particular nurse's worst patient in a long career.

They were starting to wean her off some of the more potent medications, so her mind was clearer and her limbs felt lighter and stronger. A snack restored some of her energy, and the notepad that someone had thoughtfully left on her nightstand already had some pages filled with ideas and questions that she hoped to have answered by Robert when he arrived.

The nurse interrupted her own tirade to note that there was someone waiting out in the hallway to see her.

Julia's heart skipped a beat. "Who is it?"

"He's a cop. Probably wants to ask you about last night. That's all anyone's been talking about."

Julia wished that the nurse would quit adjusting her tubes and let Robert come in. There were so many questions that needed answering.

After what seemed liked forever, the nurse left, and Robert was there.

Julia felt like she'd been waiting all day to see him, but all she could think about when he walked in was how awful she must look, with her silly hospital nightgown and the bandages.

He came in his uniform, pulling out his notepad and looking very official. Julia felt somewhat letdown.

*Official business,* she thought, as she settled back against the pillows. *Oh, well. What did you expect? Flowers?*

He smiled then, and that lightened the moment.

"How are you feeling, Julia? You got quite a nasty bump on the head."

"I'm feeling much, much better. Robert, I am so sorry about everything."

"Everything?" He pulled up a chair.

Julia was so busy talking that she didn't notice how the smile didn't quite reach his eyes like it usually did.

"About Amelia and all. One day in my care and she's in the middle of a shootout – oh my gosh, I'd forgotten - someone was *shooting.* Was anyone hurt? That man had a gun? Someone could have been killed! One of the kids, or Mrs. Jurta or..."

"Or you?" he asked pointedly.

His tone made her break off. Now he looked angry. Julia was astonished: she'd never seen him angry before.

He was saying, "You didn't think of that before you went charging in? That maybe he might have a weapon and that you might have been killed? What possessed you, Julia?"

"Well, I..."

"Why didn't you call *me*? Why didn't you wait for me? What if something happened to you? Lord, Julia, didn't you have better sense than to stick your neck out for some stupid burglar ripping off cheap stuff to front his habit?"

He was up now, pacing, his voice growing in intensity. He slapped the pad of paper into his palm, his other hand curling into a fist that crumbled the sheets. Julia hadn't felt so cowed since she had been a teenager, getting lectured by her father over some minor violation of family rules.

"I'm sorry," she found herself saying. "I guess I just didn't think anyone was really in there. I thought I'd check before I called and bothered you."

"It would have been too late. If he had wanted to kill you, no one would have gotten there in time to save you. It was a stupid, *stupid* move. You should have waited. You should have gone to Mrs. Jurta's house, called 911 - called *me* - and waited. We can handle things like this. We're *supposed* to take the risk, not you. Geez, Julia!" His voice broke. He stopped in front of the window, his back towards her.

After a moment, she said again, "I'm sorry, Robert."

Robert looked out over the crowded parking lot and took a few deep breaths.

"No, I'm sorry," he said after a moment. "I'm acting like an idiot. It's just that you were hurt. You could have been killed." He paused. "And I wasn't there to stop him."

"You couldn't have known. I didn't call."

He faced her then. "That should help, but it doesn't."

There was a moment of silence while Julia mentally regrouped. Then gently, she asked, "Was anyone else hurt?"

He shook his head. "No. Everyone's fine, just a little shaken up."

"Then he didn't hit anyone when he was shooting?"

"He didn't shoot. Mrs. Jurta remembered that she was carrying and tried to stop him with a nine millimeter. Fortunately for him, she's a lousy shot. The only thing that got hit was the neighbor's car. I think Mrs. Jurta will be hearing from their lawyers any day now."

She sighed in relief and fell back against the pillows. Everyone was safe. She was the only one wounded, and that had been her own fault, the result of poor decision making. Hadn't Miriam been accusing her of that ever since she'd been made guardian?

A few minutes of uncomfortable silence went by, with Julia wondering how to break it and Robert obviously unwilling to. Then he sighed, and ran a hand through his hair, smiling faintly.

"Look, Jules," he said. "I know I shouldn't have come in here yelling at you like that. I apologize. My reaction was way out of line."

She shook her head. "No, it wasn't. I put your daughter in harm's way and I'm sorry."

"It's not just her…" He stopped, seeming ambivalent. "Look, promise me that if something happens, you'll call me first, okay? I can't be everywhere, but let me do my job, all right? Please?"

Once again, she felt like she was losing herself in his dark eyes.

"All right," she whispered.

He took her hand. "Thanks," he said.

Somehow, Julia broke away from his gaze and sat up straighter in her bed. "Can you tell me what's been happening since I've been out of commission?"

He looked grim again. "All right. I need to get some facts from you and tell you a few before you give an official statement. Why don't you tell me exactly what happened from the time you left the party until you can't remember any more."

There wasn't much to tell. She told him everything, answered the few questions he had, and waited as he finished jotting down his notes. She had time to think about his reaction earlier. It was kind of flattering, really.

"Do you have any suspects?" she asked.

Robert shook his head. "We think he was wearing gloves because we didn't find any fingerprints on the tools he left behind."

She frowned. "But why was he prying up the floorboards? Was there anything under there?"

He put his notepad back into his shirt pocket. "Okay," he said. "This is where I report to you."

He had arrived just ahead of the other squad car and in time to see Mrs. Jurta still toting her automatic. Mrs. Jurta said that a man came running out of the house, too fast for her to identify him. The intruder had shoved her aside and jumped into a pick-up truck, and Mrs. Jurta recovered herself enough to pull out her gun and fired several shots at him - but only hit the neighbor's car.

When they investigated the back room, several of the floorboards had been pried up, and they found something wrapped in old painting rags. And when they unwrapped these, they found...

"The missing Stephanie Langs?" Julia guessed.

"The sketches, yes," he said. "How did you know?"

"It was just a guess. The Lang murder seems to be coming up an awful lot lately. In fact, I found a signed picture of her in an old lamp-table, and I was going to ask you to take a look at it." She stared wide-eyed at him. "This is getting creepy. How did those get into my house?"

"That's what we've been wondering, too," he said. "You're right, the sketches were all there, including several that had not been listed as missing. They're unfinished, our resident expert tells us, and it's possible that the cataloguers weren't aware of their existence when they made the list."

"But that doesn't make sense," Julia insisted. "Brad Lang made the list with the museum expert, according to Bernard's research. Why would he steal them only to omit them from the list, when the robbery was his cover story? And how did he have access to my house? I don't remember seeing his name on the list of previous owners."

Robert shook his head. "I don't know. Maybe he had an understanding with the owner at the time, a girlfriend, maybe."

"There's no mention of that in any of the stories."

"That only means he was more discreet than his wife. We have no reason to suppose that she was the only one cheating."

"No. Only I got the impression that he was far too busy with his career to spend time with his wife, let alone a girlfriend. Will the discovery of these sketches reopen the case?"

"They have to be authenticated first," he replied. "After that, who knows? To be honest, if I wasn't so concerned with catching the man who broke into your place, I'd be cracking into the old case files myself. Don't throw away that picture you found, whatever you do. It may be important."

She leaned back against the headboard. "We've felt drawn to that old house ever since we moved in, the kids and I. It's so weird to think that there might actually be a connection."

Robert cleared his throat. He was rubbing his hands together, seeming uncomfortable.

"That's not the only connection to that old house," he said, and Julia gave him a sharp look. She suspected this had to do with Ron.

"Last night, at about the same time as you were getting hit over the head, a couple of the neighborhood boys discovered a squatter in the old Lang house. After they chased him out, they – broke in themselves. Dylan O'Reilly was one of the boys… And I'm afraid Ron was with him."

She gaped at him. "That can't be. I left them at the Ojacors' house."

"Apparently, they left early and were hoping to catch a ghost on film. Dylan has been staking the house out and thought he saw paranormal activity. What he actually saw was a squatter. We've impounded the tapes and cameras and are going over them now for clues as to who the person was who was living there."

Julia stared in disbelief.

"From what the boys told me, they were outside looking in when they startled a man. He ran outside, Ron tried to stop him, and the suspect kicked him." Catching her expression, he quickly added, "He's all right. The paramedics looked him over and gave him a clean bill of health. He has a fat lip but other than that, he's fine."

Her hands were shaking. She pressed them against her eyes, trying to steady herself.

Robert said, "We found out about it when the boys accidentally tripped the alarm system by opening the front door. What's confusing is whoever was living in the house knew enough to dismantle the alarm on the back door while leaving the rest of the system intact. The other strange thing is what the boys found in the living room, where the squatter was camping out – clippings referring to the Lang murder. An incident room, if you will. He grabbed some of the evidence when he ran. Mostly, it was copies from library film, but some of it was from newspapers at the time of the murder. Stuff that even the Mones had a hard time locating."

Julia moved her hands from her eyes to her mouth, then spoke through them. "But – why would he have that?"

"We don't know. Maybe he's obsessed with the case. He probably selected that particular house because it was the scene of the murder."

"If he's obsessed, he's dangerous."

Robert nodded. "The lawyers in charge of the house are install-ing a new alarm system as soon as our boys are done there. They're going to get in contact with Brian Lang, who, I hear, is out on pa-role right now, somewhere down south. In the meantime, the chief is putting extra patrols in the neighborhood until this squatter is caught. We're hoping that he left some identifiable fingerprints, but the going is slow because the boys messed up some of the evi-dence. It's been a busy night."

"Do you think that the squatter and the burglar are the same person?"

"They can't be. At the time Mrs. Jurta was shooting at your burglar, their intruder was escaping out the back door. In fact, the boys remembered hearing the shots and actually thought that he had fired them. It's a miracle that none of them were hurt."

"Oh my God," she said and meant it as a prayer. "Oh my God. I can't even..." She began to tremble, and he leaned forward to put a hand over hers.

She squeezed it gratefully.

"I don't know what I would have done," she confessed, and drew a shuddering sigh. "We rely on him so heavily. I don't think I could have handled it. Those poor kids..."

"No need to go there. Nothing happened to him."

"What now? A breaking and entering charge? What will that mean?"

"The chief is sorting that out. The fact that Ron left me a mes-sage on my phone to report the illegal activity will play in his favor. I don't think he'll get much more than a slap on the wrist, maybe some community time if the judge is in a bad mood. The media have already gotten a hold of the story, by the way. They're calling it 'a modern twist on the Hardy Boys.'"

"Oh, poor Ron," she whispered. "He's going to be so humiliated."

"It'll be good for him," he grinned. "A good way to remember not to go along with everything your friends tell you to do. I'll be around, whatever the outcome, to make sure that things go smoothly." He looked at his watch. "I've got to get going. I've got a bunch of reports to fill out. I'll keep you informed. When are you getting out?"

"Maybe this afternoon, if the tests come back all right."

"Just send me a text and I'll come and pick you up."

She flushed a little. "Oh, no, really - that's okay."

"Do it. Besides, I'll probably have more to tell you by then." He stood over her and his smile faded. "Are you all right?"

She nodded and looked at her hands. "I'm fine," she said.

"Really?"

"I… I don't think I've really had time to process everything. It'll probably hit me a week from now, and one of the kids will find me in a puddle on the kitchen floor, stuffing myself with ice cream. But really, everyone's been so kind – I don't know how I'll be able to pay them all back."

He gave her hand a squeeze. "Everyone is just pleased to be able to help."

Julia let her head, which was growing increasingly heavy, fall back against the pillows. A wave of exhaustion washed over her.

"Thank you so much for coming, Robert. Thank you for everything."

"Get better, Jules." There was an odd, low tone to his voice as he spoke.

Then he was gone, and the nurse took his place.

"Ready for the next round of tests?" he asked.

# 41

R on trailed slowly after Mrs. Ojacor, rubbing his sore jaw. The hospital was not very busy, and few nurses and staff were visible in the hallways. It was very quiet and smelled of antiseptic and plastic - familiar, but not comforting.

The last time he'd been in a hospital was back when he was seven or eight. They'd gone to visit his dad's aunt, who was dying of cancer. She was a wizened little old lady in flowered pajamas, an oxygen tube up her nose, and great dark patches on her skin. She couldn't sit up or move very much, but she had been excited to see them and wanted to touch Ron's face. Ron tried to avoid her, but his grandmother kept pushing him back within reach, oblivious to his discomfort.

"Your aunt is going to be tired," Mrs. Ojacor reminded them gently. "So we'll have to be very quiet and calm."

She was holding Dana's hand and Amelia was on the other side of her. Both girls were wearing the same dress, but in different colors, with their hair pulled up in the same high, tight ponytail. Amelia had explained to Ron that they were twins today. Each held a sad bunch of flowers that they had cut from the Ojacor's little garden.

Jack's warm, moist hand was tight in Ron's. The little boy slept badly the night before, sharing a makeshift bed with Ron on the

Ojacor's living room floor. He kept asking Ron if they could go home. When told no, he would start crying, asking if Aunt Julia was dead. No matter how many times Ron assured him that she was fine, and that they had to stay away from the house until she was well, the boy wouldn't understand.

Jack asked, "Is this where Aunt Julia is?"

"Yes," Mrs. Ojacor answered.

"Is she dead? Like Mom?"

"No, she's just hurt," Ron said, ignoring the tight feeling in his chest.

They reached the elevator and waited for the doors to open. Jack looked thoughtfully at Mrs. Ojacor for a moment.

"Our Mom died, you know," he offered.

"I know," Mrs. Ojacor replied soothingly.

The elevator door slid open and she ushered them inside, pushing the button for the third floor.

Jack stood next to Mrs. Ojacor, his face pinched, as though he was thinking something through. It was the first time that Ron had ever heard Jack talk about their parents' death to someone outside of the family. Even inside of the family, he never verbalized it beyond asking where Mom and Dad were, and then bursting out into tears. He hadn't done that in quite some time. Ron wondered why he was talking about it now; it had to be because of Aunt Julia's injury.

Jack looked up at Mrs. Ojacor.

"My Dad died, too," he said quietly. "Aunt Julia said that they went to Heaven, but I don't know for sure, because I haven't seen it. Where is Heaven?"

"It's where God is," she said, her tone solemn.

"Aunt Julia said that God is taking care of Mom and Dad until we can see them again."

"She's right, you know. He's taking very good care of them."

"That's good," Jack said. "They were very nice. They didn't want to die, you know. But they had to because God missed them and wanted them with Him. I think He wanted Mom to make Him chicken fingers."

Mrs. Ojacor smiled. "Did she make good chicken fingers?"

"Yes. She put lots of sauce on them. Dad liked them best. Granddad says that Dad is playing golf with St. Peter now. So I guess they are both happy, except that they miss us a lot."

"You must miss them a lot."

He nodded. "When the lightning scared me, Mom hugged me. Now, Ron does that."

Ron took Jack's hand, pulling him close. He saw that Dana's eyes were shiny, like she was about to start crying.

"When we see your aunt, we have to be very careful," Mrs. Ojacor said. "Her head is still hurt and she needs peace and quiet."

They were at the door. It was open, but a curtain was drawn, dividing the room in two. Mrs. Ojacor knocked gently on the door jam.

Ron didn't want to enter the room. He didn't want to see Aunt Julia looking like Great Aunt Alice. She wasn't supposed to be ill or wounded – she was supposed to be healthy and well. He didn't want to see the tubes, the bruises, the withered expression, and tired eyes. He wanted Aunt Julia out of the hospital and back home, sanding the walls with him and laughing at the jokes that they made.

*If Aunt Julia doesn't recover, we'll be split up. How am I supposed to be the man of the house then?*

He flushed with anger and helplessness, thinking about the intruder breaking into their home. The emotions roiling inside him were powerful, but this was no time to be angry. The kids needed him to be strong, now that Aunt Julia was wounded.

As she called out for them to come in, Julia's voice sounded stronger than he expected, but perhaps the excitement of seeing them had given her a temporary lift.

The hospital room was small. Equipment and furniture lined the narrow quarters. Yet when Mrs. Ojacor pulled back the curtain that divided the room, sunlight flooded the tiny area and made it feel welcoming.

At the sound of Julia's greeting, Jack wrenched his hand from Ron's and wriggled past the others.

"Aunt Julia! You *aren't* dead!"

"Careful, Jack," Mrs. Ojacor said, but her warnings went unheeded. The two little girls broke ranks to run around the bed as Dana burst into tears.

"Aunt Julia," was all she could manage.

Julia looked bright and alert, with her hair neatly combed and her face clean and smiling. She was sitting on top of the bedding, dressed in a hospital gown. She was attached to monitors, and there was a bandage wrapped around her head, and dark circles shone under her eyes. But she was laughing and hugging the kids, trying to thank Mrs. Ojacor.

"It's all right," she murmured to Dana as she hugged her. Jack climbed into the bed and snuggled up against her. "It's all right, guys, I'm fine. How are *you* all doing?"

"Okay." Dana's voice sounded hoarse. "We thought that he killed you."

Julia sighed heavily. "I thought so, too. It was stupid for me to go into the house like that, but thank God we're all safe. I'm so glad to see you. You must have been so scared when Mrs. Jurta started shooting."

Dana nodded.

Amelia shrugged. "I wasn't, really. My dad takes me to the shooting gallery sometimes, so I'm used to guns." Then her cocky façade crumbled and she wrapped her arms around Julia's neck. "I'm just glad you're okay."

Julia stroked her head, then reached to trace Dana's face with her hand. That started another flood of tears that Mrs. Ojacor stepped in to tend to.

Ron felt separate from the scene. He was in too much trouble to be any help. He was, after all, a felon - or so Mac had told him last night when they were questioned by the police.

Julia noticed him hovering near the foot of the bed and gave him a welcoming smile. Ron smiled back, but stayed where he was. She had to be upset with him for his stunts at the Lang house, and there would be a long lecture in his future. He decided to stay back – the little kids needed time, he decided.

"Ron."

Julia gently slid Jack off to the side, then Dana, and gestured for him to come closer. As he did, he saw that her smile was pained but genuine.

"Are you all right?" she asked.

He nodded silently.

Suddenly, she pulled him into her arms and held him.

"Oh, Ron," she sighed into his hair, "I almost lost you." Her grip tightened.

Ron felt like he was melting on the inside. Aunt Julia knew what had happened earlier, she knew about the house... But she was still glad to see him. Something inside threatened to give way, but he held it in tightly as he returned her hug.

He was loved.

For a few seconds, he felt almost whole.

# 42

J ulia was released that afternoon. The doctors said she was
fine, but might have headaches and dizziness for the next
couple of days. They gave her a cane, some prescriptions, and
cautioned her to rest.

Julia was feeling well enough to joke, "Maybe next year."

Mrs. Ojacor offered to have them all stay at her house for a few
more days, but to Ron's relief, Julia refused. She wanted to go see
the house, she said, and she simply couldn't intrude on the Ojacors'
hospitality any longer. Amelia called Robert and let him know that
Julia wouldn't need a ride, and then they all squeezed into Mr.
Ojacor's extended cab pickup.

"I am very lucky to have this truck," Mrs. Ojacor commented.
"Joseph never lets me borrow it, but today I told him it was an
emergency - anyway, he was at work and couldn't really stop me."

Now that Julia was back, the whole atmosphere had changed.
The kids were able to appreciate Mrs. Ojacor's good humor, and
the funny way she liked to tell her stories about Africa and coming to America for the first time. She kept them entertained the
whole way from Concord back to her house in Franklin, and they
never thought to put on the radio or listen to their iPods.

When they got to Mrs. Ojacor's house, she insisted that they
come in and have afternoon tea.

"It is too early for supper and too late for lunch," she pointed out. "And I think you would like to have something a little better in your stomach besides hospital food before you go and face that place again."

"That would be very nice of you," Julia said. She was tiring out, so it probably was a good idea. She rested in the living room with Jack curled up on her lap while Dana helped Mrs. Ojacor in the kitchen, and Ron and Amelia packed up their things from the guest room and living room.

Over lunch, Ron asked if he could go inside the house first, but Julia shook her head.

"I want us all to go together," she explained as they sat around Caroline's table enjoying tea and sandwiches. "I think we need to face what happened as a family unit."

"It's amazing to me that you want to go back at all," Caroline volunteered.

"I'm just so mad that someone broke in and tried to ruin our hard work. It's *my* house, and no one has a right to just walk in and frighten us."

"Well, good for you, girl," Caroline said.

Despite her bold stance, Julia didn't seem to be in a hurry to get home. After they'd eaten, Caroline invited her to see the workshop where she made homemade cards and did a little pottery.

They sent the kids outside to play, but Ron didn't enjoy himself at all. He sat on the back porch steps, watching the others and wishing he could go home and check around for intruders. Robert had told him that the police would patrol the area more often and that he would keep a personal eye on the place, but this was Ron's responsibility, not his.

Dana came running up to him. "Come on and play tag with us, Ron," she begged.

"Can't."

"Why not? You're not doing anything."

"I'm thinking. Did Mrs. Jurta find a home for Horatio?"

She sighed and shrugged. "I don't know. I think so."

"Bummer."

"You know, if Horatio was with us, he would have warned us. He would have bitten that burglar and held on to him until the police came."

"Maybe," Ron muttered.

"Do you think Aunt Julia will ever let us get a dog?"

"Maybe if we could convince her that a dog would be a good guard for the house. But we can't ask her about it just yet. She's still got a headache."

"And *you're* still in trouble," she said pointedly. "Was it cool in the haunted house?"

"No," he said shortly. "And there weren't any ghosts."

"Was there…"

"I can't say, because of the police," he announced. "Go play with Amelia."

Looking hurt, she trudged off. Ron felt guilty, but was glad that she was gone and not asking him questions.

Long after Ron was ready to go, Julia called them in to leave. They took their bags and thanked Caroline, who insisted that she not only drive them back over, but walk them through the house before she left.

"The last time I let you go by yourself, it was a disaster," she said. "We won't make that mistake again."

Julia didn't protest. Ron thought that she was glad for the company, but he resented the idea that they couldn't handle an empty house on their own. Today wasn't like the other night. Today, he was there with them.

He knew he had acted foolishly with Dylan. He deserved punishment; yet wondering if he'd be trusted again shook him right down to his toes.

At the house, Ron was about to tell Julia that he was going in when they were interrupted by barking.

"Horatio!" Dana cried.

The puppy, who seemed bigger since they'd last seen him, raced across the lawn. The girl opened her arms to receive him, and he nearly knocked her down in his excitement. His whole body trembled as he barked and wagged his tail and licked Dana's face. Then he bounded toward Julia and licked her hand, jumped up to Ron, ran around Amelia three times, and then leaped back on Dana.

"Oh, Horatio, I've missed you!" she squealed, and Horatio barked his reply. She giggled and wrapped her arms around him.

"Tigger!" Amelia shouted, delighted. Tigger was crossing the street, straining at the leash that Mrs. Jurta held as Amelia ran to him. The small dog covered Amelia's face with kisses, seeming as happy as Horatio.

Mrs. Jurta surrendered the leash to Amelia and turned to Julia.

"How are you feeling today?" she asked.

Julia smiled, nodded, then winced, and touched her head. "Better," she said. "Thank you. But aren't you supposed to be on your way to Florida?"

Mrs. Jurta shook her head and lifted her hands in disbelief at what she was saying. "Stupid burglar," she said. "He almost kills you, and then - because I do the right thing and try to shoot him - I'm probably going to be sued because I accidentally hit a neighbor's car instead. Nice, huh?"

"Oh, no!"

Mrs. Ojacor interrupted: "My dear, are you being charged?"

"I could be," Mrs. Jurta said. "I've called the lawyers and every-thing, but since I had a pistol permit and because the man was ac-tually trying to rob a house and attacked you, Julia, the lawyers say that the cops probably won't push it."

"Well, that's good," Julia said.

"Except that I can't leave town until they say so," Mrs. Jurta con-tinued. "I tried to explain to them that I had a mortally ill dog, but our beloved police chief wouldn't budge on the matter. He says I can't leave the state."

As the women chattered, Ron saw an opportunity. The three kids were playing with the dogs, so no one noticed him when he slipped past the van in the driveway to put his key in the side door.

He would get through the house, survey the damage, and make sure everything was safe before Aunt Julia noticed he was gone. He'd even put the water on for coffee, that way he'd be brave, responsible, and considerate, all in one swoop. Maybe, he thought, it would make amends.

But the door was already unlocked. He froze, unsure what to do.

Then the handle moved.

Ron jumped back, fists up, and tripped over some of Jack's outdoor toys. He sprawled onto his back, scraping his elbow against the old pavement. But that wasn't the worst of it.

The figure in the doorway who was offering him a hand was Officer Wilde.

"Are you all right, Ron?" Robert said, pulling him into a sitting position.

Ron was too embarrassed and confused to answer.

"Oh goodness, are you all right, Ron?" Julia rushed over, her movements unsteady.

"I startled him," Robert said apologetically.

"You weren't trying to go in by yourself, were you?" asked Mrs. Ojacor.

"He was just trying to help," Julia said. "Honey, how's your head?"

They were clustering around him like a bunch of concerned hens. In a matter of seconds, Ron had gone from reliable, a pillar of strength, to a clumsy victim of poor judgment.

Waves of frustration washed over him, and it was only with huge effort that he was able to keep himself under control.

Julia saw the struggle and thought he was in physical pain. With a wave of her hand, she indicated that the others, except Robert, should give him some space.

Ron might have held it together had Julia not looked up at Robert.

"You were inside?" she asked.

Robert nodded sheepishly. "Amelia said that you were coming back tonight, so I wanted to look things over before you arrived. Hope it doesn't bother you."

He looked anxious, but Julia's expression turned soft. "Oh," she said. "That's really nice of you."

They gazed at each other while Ron shifted uncomfortably.

"Almost like having a man around the house, isn't it?" Mrs. Jurta suggested.

If she had slapped him across the face, Ron would not have felt more stung. He turned to glare at Mrs. Jurta, but she wasn't paying attention.

*Almost like having a man around the house?*

Bitterness rose up inside him, and suddenly, he had to get out of there. He rolled over and up onto his feet.

*I've got to get out.*

Julia pulled herself out of her reverie enough to say, "Ron? Honey, where are you going?"

He began to run. His head throbbed, his ankle hurt, but he didn't pay any attention. The pity in his aunt's voice made him want to get as far away from the house and those people as fast as he could. He heard Amelia shout, "Wait!" but he ignored her, too.

*Almost like having a man around the house...*

He ran on and on, the phrase chased itself around in his head, like a manic dog after its own tail.

*How dare he go into my house? How dare he take my place?*

He was halfway down the street, nearing the old Lang place. When he reached the stop sign at the end of the road, he stopped for a moment to wipe his eyes.

*You're the man of the house now, Ron.*

*I tried, Dad. They won't let me.*

He was having difficulty breathing. The pounding in his chest and ears made it difficult to hear. He bent over and took a few deep, steadying breaths, but it didn't help. He was shaking all over and it was growing worse by the second. He wasn't far enough away from the house; they could still see him from there, and he didn't want them to see him that way.

*Almost like having a man around the house...*

Ron ran into the street.

A horn blared, and he saw the truck. It was too close to stop and too big to turn.

A car was approaching from the other direction. If Ron moved back, the car would hit him.

He couldn't move. His mind suddenly cleared of all thoughts but one:

*I'll see Mom and Dad.*

Something smashed into him, knocking the breath from his chest and throwing him through the air to the pavement.

The ground met him with a bone-shaking impact. The truck horn sounded a long blast as it passed him and the car's tires squealed.

Something was on top of him, pinning him to the ground. Ron realized he hadn't been hit by an automobile at all. A person had hit him. Someone had saved him. He wasn't going to die, not today.

"Ron, are you all right?"

It was Robert.

Ron lashed out. His first strike landed on Robert's face, but the man caught the next one in a strong grip.

"What the...?"

Ron began to fight with his whole body, squirming and kicking, wanting to hurt Robert in the same way he was hurting. But his strikes were ineffective, and he decided that he would settle for just getting away. He didn't want to be helped. He didn't want to explain, or apologize, or listen to reason. He wanted the whole world to know that he was furious.

The most frustrating thing was, he couldn't break free of Robert's grip.

His desperation grew, but no matter how hard he fought, Robert was bigger and stronger and pinned him down. Ron was beginning to get dizzy from the effort.

"Ron, *calm down*," Robert yelled.

"No!" Ron shouted. "I *won't! Let me go!*"

"Ron, you almost killed yourself! Didn't you see that truck?"

"Leave me alone!"

"Let me help you."

"I *hate* you!" Ron tried to hold back the sobs. "Go away!"

"Ron…"

"*Shut up!*" he yelled, and Robert snapped his mouth closed, staring at Ron with alarm.

"You're all stupid," Ron shouted. "All of you! My Dad told *me* to be the head of the house, not *you!* I hate you! I *hate* you!"

Then he was sobbing, crying too hard to talk. He forgot who he was mad at and why. He forgot that he was supposed to be the quiet one. All he could think was that Mom and Dad were dead, that they were never coming back.

Dad would never tell him that he was doing a good job again. Mom would never tell him how handsome he looked. They'd never be there for anything. He would be alone forever.

He stopped fighting. Jagged sobs threatened to rip through his chest. He felt himself falling apart, and he gripped at the closest thing he could find.

Robert.

After a moment, Robert hugged him back.

When Julia finally made it to the end of the road, she found Robert cradling Ron, who couldn't see for the crying.

# 42

The next few days passed quietly. Between Julia's physical injuries and Ron's emotional collapse, everyone needed time
to recover.

Amelia insisted on coming over during the day to help and, to
Julia's surprise, she and Dana took over the running of the household. They made the meals, walked the dogs, watered the garden,
and kept Jack happy so that Julia and Ron could rest.

Julia was glad for the respite, even though it was punctuated by
calls and visits from various well-wishers. Julia's parents called, frantic; then they told the Budds, even though Julia begged them not
to. She managed to get Miriam off the phone in a record-breaking
six minutes and thirty-five seconds.

Mrs. Jurta was over almost every day, bringing pots of soup and
neighborhood stories. Mrs. Ojacor brought baskets of supplies. Mrs.
Mone came by, as did others, and Derval showed up on Wednesday
and weeded the garden with Dana. And everyone commented on
the enormous bouquets from John Irwin, one of flowers and the
other of fruit, both with kindly notes.

"I just can't believe how nice everyone is being," Julia told Mrs.
Ojacor when they were alone. "I feel overwhelmed and a little
embarrassed."

"No reason to feel that. You give when you can, and when you can't, the best you can do is accept graciously."

It was good advice, but Julia had to swallow a bit of pride with it.

Robert phoned twice a day, as much to check on Julia as to check on Amelia, and joined them each night for supper. The police department was investigating the break-ins. Robert was convinced, as Julia was, that there was a connection between the break-in and the Lang Murder, and Robert had taken it upon himself to pull out the old files and start reinvestigating the evidence. Although it wasn't normal procedure to talk shop around the dinner table, Julia and the others were too curious about his progress to allow him to keep mum.

At first Ron was shy and quiet around Robert; then, as he grew more comfortable, he began asking about the investigation. There wasn't much to tell.

Robert told them that the sketches had been positively identified as Stephanie's, and now her family was demanding that they be turned over to the Lang trust. They had even flown in their big-shot lawyer from New York to talk to the police chief, but the works were evidence in a robbery, and they could not be turned over until the D. A. said so.

"The lawyer must have been mad," Amelia commented.

"He was a cool customer," Robert said. "Great poker face, but we all got the impression that he wasn't used to taking no for an answer. By the way, we made copies of the pictures, and I thought maybe you guys would like to see them."

He handed the pictures around, and everyone thought that they were very nice, if a little boring.

"They're just staring," Dana said.

"They're called character studies," Julia said. "Artists do them to decide how to draw someone's portrait."

"Lot of detail in these for just character studies," Wilde commented.

"Hey! It's J. C.!" Ron exclaimed, holding up a picture. Then he frowned. "But, wait a minute – he wasn't born then, right?"

"No, he wasn't," Julia said. "Let me see."

He passed it to Amelia, who commented before handing it off to Julia, "Besides, J. C. doesn't have a mustache."

"Maybe Stephanie painted one on as a joke," Dana suggested.

"This isn't J. C." Julia studied it carefully. "It does look a lot like him, though. It must be his father, John."

"Let me see," Wilde said, and she handed it across the little table with the comment, "I imagine the family must have been thrilled that these were found at all."

"You more got the impression that they should have been found long ago," he said dryly. He examined the picture closely, frowning. "This does look like John. Funny – I don't remember him ever mentioning that he sat for Stephanie."

"Well, he wasn't the only one," Julia said. "I gather half the town sat for her."

"Yeah, or..." He looked up, remembered that there were children in the room, and actually blushed when Julia laughed.

The next night, with the kids playing in the living room, Robert and Julia sat on the front porch steps and talked. At first, they simply sat side-by-side, talking about commonplace things, then Julia shivered in the rapidly cooling air.

Robert slipped an arm around her shoulders and drew her close. He smelled of soap and aftershave, and she liked it.

She was starting to daydream when Robert said, "I was waiting to get you alone. I've got something to tell you, and I didn't want the kids to know yet."

Her heart quickened, but she wasn't expecting what he said next. "There's been a development in the Lang case."

She lifted her head and frowned up at him in the dark. "In the *Lang* case?"

He nodded. "We took samples of the blood you discovered on your wall and sent it in for testing."

"Why?"

"The chief and I were looking over the old photos with a blood-spatter expert today, and he confirmed what we already thought. There doesn't seem to be enough blood for the wound discovered on her head. We can't prove it yet, but there's room for doubt that the studio was the scene of the crime."

She felt a cold chill wash over her. "You think that she was killed in *my* house?" she whispered. "But why would she have been here?"

"I don't know, Jules." He reached up and brushed a lock of hair out of her face. "The stain is the right age, and there's the evidence under the floorboards. I have no explanation for why she would have been there. The town information says that the house was owned at the time by a Henrietta Purcell, but there aren't any Purcells mentioned in the original investigation. I suppose Stephanie could have known Henrietta, but there is nothing to connect the two, not even a painting or sketch in the known Lang collection of any Henrietta or Purcell."

"And there weren't any women in the sketches we found under the floorboards," Julia mused. "Just one of the little Jurta girl." She stopped and looked at him sharply. "Then do you think that the person who broke into my house was..."

He interrupted before she could finish. "He's already desperate enough to hurt you, Julia. He's dangerous, whether or not he was actually Stephanie's murderer, too." He looked away suddenly and swallowed hard.

They sat in silence for a moment or two, looking out into the street, his hand gently rubbing her back. Julia wished he would hold her again. When he didn't take the initiative, she did, leaning in close until her head was on his shoulder. His arm came around her waist, and Julia was struck by how natural it felt.

"What happens now?" she asked quietly.

She could feel his heart pounding in his chest. "Unless we can bring something more concrete to light, the D. A. isn't going to re-open the case. Officially, we're just working on the break-in as an unrelated matter."

"And unofficially?"

"The chief told me that I can study the Lang case files as much as I'd like. He's not convinced that we know everything."

"Oh, Lord," she whispered. "That's so frightening. I would have preferred a real ghost to this."

His armed tightened around her. "Me, too."

Later that night, when they were at the door saying good bye, Robert suddenly asked her, "Are you all right staying here alone?"

Julia nodded. "Oh, yes. We've got the window alarms and the dog. We'll be fine."

His grip tightened on her hands as he explained, "These past two nights, the chief has ordered an extra patrol around this area, but he's shorthanded tonight and had to cancel it. If you're nervous, though, I can stay…"

"No." Julia pulled back, her cheeks flushed. "No, that's all right. We'll be fine, Robert, really. I'm not worried."

"Well, I am. This is serious, Julia. This man is still at large and dangerous. He may come back to finish what he started."

She kept her voice steady. "We'll be fine. I'm not taking your warning lightly. Besides, you're right next door. I'm not worried."

He nodded, but he didn't leave.

"Julia…" he sighed, "there's something I didn't tell you."

"Oh?"

"Brad Lang's out of prison and hasn't reported to his parole officer in over a week. We think he might be in the area."

Julia froze. Brad Lang was out of prison. She thought it odd, that even under these circumstances, she couldn't think of him as the murderer.

"Do you think he was the one in my house?" she asked.

"We don't know," he said. "He may have been the one in the Lang house with Ron or he may be in South America somewhere.

All that we know is he's loose, and he's dangerous. Either he killed his wife or he has a grudge against this town. In any case, he might just decide to take it out on you and the kids..."

"But..."

"Julia." He took her hands again and his eyes held hers. "I'm right next door, but that can be awfully far away."

His eyes were so dark, so penetrating, and she so wanted to be able to tell him, "Yes, please stay." She thought about how she felt when he was holding her on the porch, and about the children, about how Ron's eyes shone whenever they were talking, and she thought about the long, lonely days ahead of her. Even without the threat of a break-in, the invitation was very tempting.

But it was too soon, too complicated by circumstances, for her to agree. And she was too bound by her beliefs to allow herself to give way now.

Julia shook her head regretfully. "We'll be fine, Robert. I know where you are. He probably does, too."

They were quiet for a while. He was holding her hands, gently massaging them with his thumbs. The darkness outside the door framing Robert's figure was as soft as velvet, and just as warm. If she looked over his shoulder, she could see a circle of light: porch light at Amelia's house, a reminder that he had other responsibilities, a person with a prior call on his time and attention. Just as she had.

She looked down at their entwined hands and tightened her grip just a little.

When he spoke, his voice was gentle. "You'll call if you need me? No more heroics?"

She smiled in spite of herself. "I don't think I can afford any more. I'll call."

"Be safe." He smiled, pained. "Don't open the door for anyone you don't know."

She laughed. "Now you're sounding like my dad. I've lived alone before, Robert. I know the rules."

"All right. Just... be careful."

For a long moment, they stood looking into each other's eyes. Then he leaned in and brushed her cheek with his.

"Be careful," he breathed in her ear.

When the screen door shut behind him, she stood for a second or two longer, then eased the door closed and stood quietly beside it, her heart pounding.

When she raised her head, she spotted Ron and Dana peering through the upstairs banister. They raced back to bed when they realized that she saw them. Julia shook her head, drew the bolt on the door, set the alarm, and went into the kitchen to make some tea. She curled up on the couch with it, and just when she started to feel lonely, Horatio wandered over and snuggled next to her with his head on her lap.

She smiled and stroked his head.

"Okay, but you aren't Robert."

He just whimpered and looked up at her with a hurt expression.

# 44

*Hi Julia,*

*Just a note to let you know that the position has been filled. I put in your name, but, unfortunately, the boss already had someone in mind.*

*Good luck on the job hunt. My best to you.*

*Markie*

Julia fell back against her chair, stunned. Until that moment, she hadn't realized how much hope she had put on Markie's recommendation. She had let the other job searches go, she'd charted out her new work route, and budgeted around the pay cut. In her mind, she'd approached the move with the children, bought a new house, hired moving vans, and argued Miriam down to the ground about putting Ron into a lesser, more affordable junior high. She'd built an entire life for them, based on the slender promise of a nearly forgotten school friend.

She pressed her hand to her mouth and fought the welling tears. Around her, the bookstore café hummed with muted activity, the rustle of pages, and the clink of dishes. The kids were in the children's section, listening to Story Time. They were there to just keep Jack company, or so Amelia said. For all their protests that they were too old for a story, they had been awfully worried about missing the opening.

It was Friday. After several quiet days at home, everyone needed a break from the little house, Ron especially. He'd done a lot of crying and a lot of talking with Julia, and he was doing lot a better, but he was still fragile.

Now, Julia stared at the computer screen and fought her rising panic. She'd been so certain of Markie's job, so wrapped up in the house and the murder mystery and then the robbery, and Robert, that she hadn't been paying proper attention.

She scrolled through her emails and logged on to her job search engines, finding no responses. Her resume had netted her nothing but the standard invitation to attend a conference on insurance salesmanship – which would cost her only an "affordable" amount.

She shut down the websites and opened up an email from Sherry, who wrote that she hadn't any interest in the Franklin house yet, but was expecting an offer on the Springfield house. Wouldn't Julia reconsider and sell?

Julia thought she'd soon be in a position where she couldn't afford to refuse a decent offer. Taxes were due soon, and she'd have to find health insurance by the end of the month.

She shut off the computer and leaned back into her chair again with her cup of coffee, thinking about her conversation with Robert the night before. If his suspicions were correct, Stephanie was killed in her back bedroom and then brought back to the house, where the murderer set the scene to look like a robbery gone bad. That was a new spin on the original story, but did it automatically clear Brad Lang?

From what she'd been able to gather about Brad, he was crazy enough about his wife to commit murder during a jealous mood swing, but then why move the body out of the Purcell place and into his own house? Aside from trying to preserve the fiction of his happy marriage, having Stephanie found in his house would only make things more difficult for him.

Julia pulled open her purse and pulled out the copies of the sketches found under her floor boards. There had to be a clue among them.

She shuffled through them. Even the most unfinished ones were impressive. The art world had, indeed, lost a great talent when Stephanie Lang died. She paused when she came to the one that resembled J. C. Irwin. Looking at the sketched design, she studied the lines on the face, the scruffy goatee, and the jeans with the torn pocket. He had a devil-may-care pose, his back to the artist while looking over his shoulder. There was a mark on his upper arm that was either a mistake of the artist's or a tattoo partially covered by his short sleeves. Julia tried to picture the courteous, almost servile John Irwin living a James Dean youth on the back of a motorcycle.

"Aunt Julia!"

Dana and Amelia raced to the table and dropped a heavy book onto it. A black and white photo of Stephanie Lang, paint brush in hand, smiled up at her, her large eyes looking dreamily off into the distance.

"Look what we found!" Dana announced a little too loudly for the quiet confines of the café. Julia got a few startled and annoyed grimaces. "See! It's all about the dead lady!"

"Hush, now, Dana," Julia said, staring at the book.

"Isn't it cool?" Amelia plopped down in the seat across from Julia, then moved to the side so Dana could share it. "It has tons of photos and stuff, and it even has a picture of the postman!"

"Noel Hickey?"

"Yes, him. He's funny looking in it."

"He's funny looking anyway," Dana said, and the two started giggling.

Julia knew that she should correct them, but she was too taken up with the book to pay attention. It was expensive, finely bound, and thick, with glossy pages that were light on text but rich in color photos and reproductions. She flipped through a few pages, noting the celebrities, the expensive clothes, and the familiar locations of the photographs. There was even a picture entitled, *Young Stephanie Meets Jackie Onassis*. Stephanie's family was *very* well connected, apparently. It was a wonder that the local police had been able to hold onto the artwork at all.

Another giggle from the other side of the table brought her attention back to the girls.

"Aren't you two supposed to be with Ron and Jack?"

"Yes, but we saw that, and we had to show you," Dana grinned.

"We know that you're really into the murder and everything," Amelia added.

"And, plus, there's a picture of our house!"

Julia's mouth fell open. "A picture of what?"

"Of our house! That's what was so exciting. Come on, I'll find it for you." Dana slipped around the table, under Julia's arm, and began flipping pages.

"We were hoping to see some pictures of the body," Amelia said. "But all they had was of the police at the house, which was still really cool, but not really creepy. Can I take one of those sugar cookies?"

"No."

"Bummer."

"It's around here somewhere," Dana fretted. "I know I saw it. It's in this section and there was a picture of a dog on the other side… Oh! Here it is!" She tapped the page and beamed up at Julia. "See? It's our house!"

Julia took a good look. The picture was grainy, even on the glossy pages of the brand-new book. Stephanie Lang was on her bicycle, her painting kit strapped on the back, laughing into the camera. She had been caught off guard while talking to a man in a dark, collared shirt and the white, grainy jeans that were so popular at the time. It was impossible to say who he was, as his back was turned, and he was wearing a baseball cap. The photographer must have been standing across the street, because the house was very visible.

It was, indeed, their house, the one her sister had bought: there was the same porch, windows, walk-way, drive-way, even the same bushes, although they were much smaller at the time.

*Here's proof of the connection between my house and the murder.*

But, a second later, she thought, *don't be silly. So the woman stopped in front of the house. She lived right down the street, for Pete's sake. Of course she must have passed it.*

"Isn't that weird?" Dana said. "It's kind of creepy."

"Why?" Julia asked.

The answer was simple: "Because she was at our house and now she's dead."

Julia looked back at the photo and stopped short. The man in the photo was wearing jeans with a torn back pocket – the same tear captured in the sketch of John Irwin. This wasn't a random stranger that Stephanie was talking to. It was her subject.

The two girls were chattering, distracting her, so Julia asked, "Aren't you missing the ending of the story? Jack and Ron will be wondering where you are."

"The story is really boring," Amelia said. "Is it all right if we go look at the magazines instead?"

"Sure." Julia scanned the picture again, taking in the smaller details, like the way Stephanie was brushing her hair back from her face. At first glance, she seemed as cool and confident as in every other picture, but something about this one made Julia think that she had been caught unaware – and didn't like it.

She read the caption:

*Stephanie, only a few weeks before her murder. Photo courtesy of the Lang Memorial Museum.*

Julia realized that the photo belong to the Mones. They must have known that John Irwin and Stephanie knew each other, so why hadn't they brought up the connection before now?

More importantly, why hadn't John Irwin brought it up?

If he knew Stephanie well enough to have his portrait sketched, certainly he would have mentioned it – it would be a bragging right in a town like this. After all, the murderer had been caught, so there was no reason not to claim the relationship.

Unless there were reasons that he didn't want the world to know.

Perhaps he had known her too well. Stephanie was an acknowl-edged man-eater who nevertheless stayed with her well-connected husband. Perhaps she'd pursued John, then rejected him, and he killed her in a fit of jealous rage. Hating her husband, he might very well have planted the body in the Lang house and arranged the rob-bery in order to frame Brad, the man he'd then been thrown over for. His keen interest in Julia's renovations could easily be explained by his concern that she was going to turn up the old evidence.

Julia suddenly felt very cold.

This was John Irwin she was thinking about, not some stranger in a book. This was a living, breathing man who had not only been one of the first to welcome her into town, but had sent her two bou-quets after her attack. They were sitting on her counter at home right now - over-flowing vases that had embarrassed her when they arrived. She'd been confused why a happily-married man she hard-ly knew should be so generous. It hadn't made sense.

Unless the gifts weren't prompted by generosity, but by guilt.

Julia looked at the pictures in the book again. There was Stephanie and John in conversation, her worried expression captured for poster-ity. She didn't look like a vixen in that photo. She looked like a victim.

But John Irwin Junior as the killer? That still didn't feel right.

Then, as Julia's eyes ran over the picture again, she saw some-thing that changed her mind.

Behind Stephanie, in the driveway that was now Julia's, a pickup truck sat, shiny and new in the photo. Only half of it was visible in the picture, and part of that was obscured by Stephanie's bicycle wheel. But she didn't need to see the whole truck to recognize it as the same type of truck that she'd seen on Sunday night - the one that Mrs. Jurta had taken a shot at, the truck that had driven off with Julia's attacker behind the wheel.

# 44

The more Julia thought about her new-found revelations, the more she was convinced she was right. Yet she couldn't bring herself to call Robert yet. There was still too many things unexplained, the chief among these being, why would John Irwin and Stephanie Lang be in Julia's little house at all?

If he was at the party at the Ojacor's, how could he break into her house and be there in time to surprise her? And who had called him while he was there?

Surely there were explanations, but she couldn't find them - and until she did, she was not about to drag J.C.'s family through the muck.

She was silent on the way home. When Ron asked her if she was okay, she answered that she was still tired from her head injury. He seemed to accept that, settling back in his seat to listen to his iPod. The kids in the back of the van were too caught up in their own conversations to notice her mood.

Back at the house, the girls let the dogs out, and they chased the squealing Jack all around the backyard. Ron helped Julia unload the van and was in the kitchen when Mrs. Jurta let herself in.

"Good afternoon, Julia," she said cheerily. "I hope you're feeling better."

"Like a million bucks," Julia said, and gestured towards a chair. "Make yourself at home."

"I can't stop. I have some news to tell you. First is that, since I can't take Dexter to Florida, the SPCA found a vet in New York who can do the surgery there. They've arranged transportation and everything."

"Oh, that's wonderful!"

"Mmm. Unfortunately, I'll have to pay full price, but what can you expect? Anyway, I wanted to know if I could borrow some of your kids for an hour or so to lend a hand. Now that I'm not going to Florida, the pound sent over a few new dogs for me to look after, and I need help taking them for a walk."

Julia looked at Ron, who nodded eagerly. Unlike his former self, Ron was starting to enjoy the dogs, spending all of the afternoon before trying to teach Horatio how to fetch. Even Jack was starting to warm up to them.

"I think that'll be fine," Julia said. "How many did you want?"

"Ron, Amelia, and Dana, if you'll let me. They're a rambunctious bunch."

"Ron?"

"Fine by me," he said. "We can take Horatio and Tigger at the same time."

"Why don't you go and get them leashed up and ready to go," Mrs. Jurta suggested. "I'll be out in a minute."

"Right." He dashed eagerly out the door.

Mrs. Jurta chuckled as she turned to Julia. "He's really coming out of his shell, isn't he?"

"Yes," Julia said, sitting down herself in a kitchen chair. "It's nice to see him smiling. Horatio's been a huge help in that respect."

"Dogs are wonderful creatures," she agreed, then surprised Julia by dropping into a kitchen chair and leaning forward eagerly. "Have you heard the news?"

"News?" Julia frowned. "No, what…"

"John Irwin Junior's been arrested."

Julia's mouth dropped open. "John Irwin? When? Why?"

"Two hours ago. The police came right to the hardware store and took him away in the patrol car. One of the clerk's said that his fingerprints were found on the sketches your intruder found in the back room. The whole town's in an uproar."

"John…" Julia sat back. So John Irwin had been involved. The voice she'd almost recognized was his. She felt a strong sense of disappointment wash over her. "Oh, his poor family…"

Mrs. Jurta was looking at her curiously. "I'm surprised. With you being so tight with Robert, I'd have thought he'd call you about it."

She shook her head, biting her lip. "No, he didn't tell me."

"I suppose they're trying to be discreet, although taking him away in the middle of the day wasn't the best way to do that." She gestured to the two bouquets, one of them looking a little wilted now. "It explains those. You know, some of us were thinking that he had a crush on you."

Julia looked at Mrs. Jurta, puzzled. "Why would John have been in my house?"

"Retrieving those Lang sketches, of course," was her prompt reply. Mrs. Jurta leaned forward and whispered confidentially, "You know, John Irwin was working on this place at the time of the murder. Henrietta, God rest her, was in Oregon at the time, visiting her daughter when the whole business happened. She hired John to redo the place while she was gone, and Sheila O'Reilly and I have the suspicion that more went on here than a little wallpapering."

"So he was *working* here," Julia exclaimed. "But why didn't that come out at the trial?"

"It did, but he was out of town at the time it happened, so he was in the clear. Or so he said."

"So you think he murdered Stephanie?"

Mrs. Jurta hesitated and looked doubtful. After a moment, she shook her head.

"You know, up until Sunday, I would have said no. John Irwin couldn't hurt a fly, hasn't the stomach for it. But knowing that he was here, knowing that he sent you to the hospital – if a man can do that, why couldn't he kill, too?"

At that moment, Ron appeared at the door.

"Ready to go, Mrs. Jurta," he said. "Aunt Julia, Jack doesn't want to come."

"He's probably ready for a time out," Julia said. "Why don't you bring him in before you go?"

"Right."

He left again, and Mrs. Jurta hopped up, as energetic as ever. "I've got to fly. Dexter has another appointment later today."

"I hope he's doing better."

"Well, you must be feeling much better, anyway. Knowing that the intruder is caught and behind bars must be a huge load off your mind."

"Yes," Julia murmured. "It should be."

But it wasn't. It worried her as she set to work, starting a dinner of baked chicken, and then tucking Jack up in his room with Yellow Teddy and instructions to rest.

Back downstairs, she set the table, paced, and puzzled. While green beans warmed on the stove, she took out the sketches and spread them on the table before her, with John Irwin's sketch set out on top of the rest. Tapping the table with nervous fingers, she studied it.

Something about the sketch bothered her. Something about the whole situation bothered her. Julia thought back to the Fourth of July party, to her sitting on the picnic blanket, talking with John and Caroline about the party, and John insisting that she come. He was setting her up, of course, but how did he get to her house and back without arousing suspicion at the party? Who called him in the middle of his investigations? Was it a warning? It had to be – he had bolted from the room as soon as he got the call, which meant someone else was involved. But who? His son, J. C.? Julia couldn't believe that. It was almost as hard to believe as it was to know that John Irwin was the one who'd hit her over the head and terrified her children. And knowing John was in her house didn't explain who was in the Lang House, kicking Ron at the same time.

The pot began to boil, and she automatically got up and adjusted the heat. When she turned back to the table, the sketch caught her eye again and she picked it up.

She broke the sketch down to components: subject, John Irwin. The background had only a few strokes, but seemed to indicate trees and a yard. Her backyard? No, too expansive. The Lang backyard? Julia had never seen it, so she didn't know.

She then catalogued the subject's clothing. Torn jeans, beaten boots, a printed t-shirt, scruffy facial hair, a tattoo on his shoulder, half-hidden under the short sleeves...

*A tattoo.*

Again, she pictured the picnic: John's smiling face, his insistence that they should come to Joseph's party, slapping his bare arm at a mosquito, the skin on his arm bright pink with sunburn... And nothing else.

Whipping around, she scanned the counters until she found her phone. Her fingers trembled as she pounded in the password and found Robert's numbers.

She pressed call and the phone went right to voicemail. Trying to keep her voice from shaking, she spoke quickly.

"Hi, Robert, it's me. Look, I know that you've taken John Irwin in for questioning today in connection with the break-in and the sketches, but I think I've uncovered something about that sketch." She was about to say what, but another thought struck her and she wanted time to play it out before explaining it in a short message, so she finished by saying, "I... Well, give me a call as soon as you can, okay? Thanks."

She hung up and stared at the picture. Of course, John could have had the tattoo removed, but Julia was willing to bet that he'd never had one to begin with.

"This isn't John," she said out loud. "This is his brother, Michael."

"Well, well," said a familiar voice from behind her.

Julia's heart leaped into her throat. She turned.

Someone who looked very much like John Irwin stood at the other end of her kitchen. His hair was grayer, his skin more weather-beaten, and he now wore a jacket over his t-shirt, but the cocky stance and the insolent smile were unmistakable. It was Stephanie's last subject. And he was holding a nine millimeter handgun.

"Looks like I don't even need to introduce myself," Michael Irwin said.

# 45

J ulia looked down the barrel, her focus narrowed and clari-
fied. She noticed the slight tremble in his grip and the gray-
black dirt on his hands.

Then she took in the worn leather of his boots, the glint of the
charm he wore about his neck, the delicate webbing of wrinkles that
lined his face, and the steely glint in a set of blue eyes that reminded
her of John. He had none of his brother's attitude – Michael was all
business.

Julia quelled her rising panic and drew herself up.

"What do you want?" she asked, managing to talk despite her
suddenly dry mouth.

"Only what's mine," he said. "You're Julia?"

She nodded, and he grinned.

"We met the other night, but I didn't catch your name. My
brother speaks highly of you, though."

"You're the one who hit me?"

"That wasn't my fault. John was supposed to keep you at that
party, but he's never very good under pressure. You're alone here?"

She thought about Jack, upstairs and asleep.

*Please God, don't let him wake up.*

"For now," she said slowly.

He grinned again. "Good. We can have a little one-on-one then."

Julia clenched her teeth and her hand unconsciously tightened around the sketch. He noticed and held out his hand. After a moment, she slowly gave it to him. He stepped back, glanced at it, and raised an eyebrow.

"I was good looking back then, wasn't I?"

"You were her subject, not John."

"Yeah. First time anyone ever preferred me over John. Everyone else only saw an ex-con, but Stephanie – she could make you feel like a rock-star, you know." He gazed longingly at the sketch. Something deeper than regret played briefly across his weathered face. "She sure was something, that Lang woman."

Then with a sudden fierce motion, he crumbled the paper and threw it to the side. He took a step closer to Julia, his eyes bright and hard.

"Let's go into the back bedroom, you and me," He gestured with the gun. "After you. Slowly, please."

Fear of a different sort rose inside her, but Julia turned and led the way, her mind racing. What did he want? What was he going to do? She had to get him out of the house before the kids returned with the dogs.

They were in the hallway now, and she paused in front of the storage room. Without turning to look at him, she asked, "Which way?"

"The bedroom," he answered.

Julia couldn't control the shiver that ran through her. She turned to the left and opened the door to the bedroom.

It was still and dark. Julia had hung makeshift curtains earlier that week, to discourage passersby from looking in. The police had taken all the intruder's tools and some of Julia's as well, leaving the ladder, the bucket, and a few other things. The rug was still pulled back, leaving the hole in the floor exposed.

She halted in the middle of the room, waiting for her next order, but it didn't come right away. When she risked a look over her shoulder, she saw Michael with his gun still trained on her back, staring at the bloodstain as though hypnotized. A small segment of the stain had been cut away by the police lab technicians.

She turned slowly and his head snapped back to look at her. His eyes were wild, but Julia kept her calm. She indicated the stain.

"Stephanie?" she asked.

He seemed confused, but quickly recovered.

"Stephanie," he said. "Lovely, privileged, the-world-is-my-door-mat Stephanie Lang." His gaze wandered about the room, taking in the shabby details, nodding absently. "God. This brings it all back..."

Unconsciously, his hand tightened on the pistol, and Julia stepped reflexively back. He noticed and brought the pistol back up and level.

"Easy, duchess," he said.

"Just take what you want and get out," Julia said quietly. "I won't stop you."

Michael looked her up and down and leered. "No," he said. "I guess you won't. You gave me a real scare when I saw you the other night. Lucky I didn't kill you then."

"Like Stephanie?"

"Yeah, like Stephanie. That was an accident, too, you know. I didn't mean to kill her, I didn't want to. It just happened. She found out, and she was going to tell her husband. I would have gone back to prison. I'd just gotten out. I wasn't going back in, not for her, not for anyone. I couldn't let her tell the police."

"Tell them what? About your affair?"

He glared, clearly disgusted by her naiveté. "No. I was in debt to some nasty creditors and needed something fast. John and I weren't going to get paid for this job until the end of the month, so I used the key she'd given me and took some knick-knacks from her place while they were in Boston. Only she came back earlier than I figured and went ape. I gave her the pawn tickets, but she was crazy. She slapped my face and screamed that she was going to have Brad put me away. Brad!" He snorted derisively. "As if he could. He couldn't even hold on to her. He hit her, you know. He'd drink a bit and smack her around, but she wouldn't leave him. Crazy woman. I would have helped her if I could."

"You *killed* her."

"She was going to send me *back*!" he shouted, the roar echoing throughout the tiny room.

Julia unconsciously stepped back, her heart tightening.

*Jack, oh, please don't wake up. Please don't come downstairs.*

His expression was twisted, fear and anger wrestling for dominance. "She was going to send me back to prison. Do you know what they do to a man there? She did. She knew everything that happened, and she was going to send me *back* rather than face *him*. I'd just gotten out, out of prison. I was not going back. So I hit her, and she fell, and there was blood everywhere. I didn't want to kill her, but I wasn't going back then and I'm not going back now."

He stopped then, drawing a deep, shuddering breath, still glaring at her.

"Go over and kneel in the corner with your hands on your head," he ordered. "Quick."

Julia obeyed, facing him and putting her hands on her head where he could see them. She strained to hear upstairs, but heard nothing to indicate that Jack was awake.

Michael kept his eyes trained on her as he began to move about the room. When he got to the far wall, he reached out and felt along it with his hand. After going a few inches, he grunted and stopped. Pulling a long hunting knife out of his belt, he pried at the panel until it was large enough to fit his hand through. He returned the knife to his belt and reached in, pulling out a rolled piece of canvas.

As he glanced at Julia, she ventured, "Your portrait?"

Startled, he asked, "How did you know?"

"Someone told me that she did a portrait of her handyman, that she found his face interesting. But if you were on their payroll, how did you avoid investigation?"

He smirked. "Who said I was on the payroll? I liked to keep things under the table and so did the Langs. I sat for her, yes. She thought I was interesting. No one ever called me that before. Then, when she died, I gave this to John to get rid of. He was too sentimental and hid it instead. Fool."

"How did you get him to help you?" Julia asked, carefully looking around for some weapon, something she could use to disarm him while he was focused on his find. "He wasn't involved with her himself, was he?"

"No, John was the good boy. He had the hots for her, but he never had the guts to do anything. He doesn't know I killed her. He thinks we were having an argument and she fell and hit her head on the wall." He shook his head in disbelief. "No one but John would be simple enough to buy that story."

Julia spotted a wooden handle sticking out from under a pile of paper and she recognized the hammer. It was too far away for her to reach, but if she could keep him talking, keep him occupied with memories, perhaps he wouldn't notice when she started sidling over to it.

That she had to do something was obvious. There was no way Michael was going to let her live to tell what he'd told her today. What surprised her was that he hadn't killed her already. Perhaps he was afraid the shot would alert one of the neighbors. Either way, the more time she had to think, the better chance she had to survive.

He unrolled the canvas and studied the portrait, holding it so close to his face that Julia wondered if he was nearsighted. She hesitated, then scooted a little to the side.

His head jerked up and she hastily spoke, saying the first thing that came to her head, "Is it yours?"

He glanced at it again, and she looked at the hammer. If she flung herself forward, she could reach it, but she was too far away to use it before he could squeeze off a shot. Cold sweat trickled down her back.

"It's mine," he said gruffly. "It's the only thing that concretely connects me to Stephanie. There's no paper record that I was working with John on this house, or that Stephanie asked me around to her place to pose and to do some work. I was strictly a handshake and cash back then. There was only ever the sketch, this portrait, and that bloodstain."

"And if only John was known to have been working on this house, the bloodstain would only incriminate him."

"Nothing should have incriminated him. We had it set up perfectly so that her husband would take the fall. It would have worked... if it hadn't been for you and those damn renovations."

He dropped the portrait, pulled a tie-wrap out of his pocket, and Julia's heart started to pound.

"He called me the day you arrived." Mike's voice was low, even, and cold. "Told me that you were moving into the Purcell place, but that he thought you'd be gone before long. Then you started to change things and he panicked and begged me to clear the evidence out. He was supposed to keep you at the party, but you didn't stay. That's unfortunate, Julia. If you had stayed, you would only have been robbed. Now..." The gun trembled in his hand. "Turn around, Julia, and put your hands behind your back."

Julia froze. "You don't need to do this," she whispered.

"Oh, but I do. I'm not going back to prison, Julia, not even for my brother." His grip tightened on the gun. "Turn around."

As slowly as she dared, she did, dragging out her motions to buy time. She heard him advance, fumbling with the tie and the gun. He was going to tie her up, then kill her, and she couldn't think of a thing to stop him. Michael had her wrists, was breathing on her head, so very close...

Then they both heard something.

"Aunt Julia?"

*Jack!*

His voice cut through the air like a knife. Michael gasped and his grip loosened for a second.

Julia threw herself backwards, knocking him off balance and sending the gun skittering across the floor. Rolling on to her knees, she felt desperately about for the hammer.

Jack stood in the doorway, Yellow Teddy in one hand, opened mouthed. Michael lunged for the gun.

Julia screamed, "Jack, *get out!*" just as her hand wrapped around the handle of the hammer.

Jack hesitated. Michael brought the pistol up to bear on him, but Julia was already swinging the hammer. She smashed it into his hand, and the gun went off. Jack screamed, and the bullet went wild as Michael lost his grip on the pistol. He roared in pain.

Julia tried for another swing of the hammer, but slipped on some wallpaper and nearly lost her balance. Michael, now furious, gave her a vicious backhand that sent her spinning. She fell this time, hitting the floor hard.

He was on top of her before she could recover, raining down blows, as she fought with everything she had - twisting her body, pulling, scratching. She knew if she stopped, Michael would go for Jack.

She fought desperately, but Michael was a big man with nothing to lose. He managed to land a stunning blow across her face, and Julia saw stars. She was reeling as he got on top of her, pinning her arms under his legs, his weight crushing the breath out of her chest. His hands came down on her neck.

She couldn't breathe. Twisting her head from side to side, she couldn't shake his grip. Her sight began to fade, and the world shrunk to a pin point.

Then, just when she was about to submit to the blackness, something roared. Michael's hands jerked painfully, then he fell on top of her. She panicked, her screams coming out in hoarse breaths, fighting to get him off, when he rolled off seemingly on his own. Then other hands were there, grasping her shoulders, touching her face. From far away, Robert's voice came.

"Julia! Julia, it's all right, we're here. Julia, oh Julia."

She was in his arms then, pressed tight against his chest, his uniform rough against her cheek. Julia reached up and grabbed him tighter. For the third time that week, Robert had come to their rescue.

Another uniformed officer was checking Michael's prone body, looking for a pulse. He turned and looked grimly at Robert.

"He's still with us," he said.

"Call an ambulance," Robert said, his voice rumbling against Julia's ear.

Jack was sobbing, at her side, trying to get into her arms, and she pulled him tight against her.

"We're okay," she whispered. "It's all over, Jack. We're safe now."

Robert pulled her tight, burying his face in her hair.

# 46

Michael Irwin confessed to Stephanie's murder while recovering in the hospital, and ignited a firestorm of news coverage in Franklin. For days the downtown was crawling with news vans and crews, pestering the locals and taking photos not only of the old Victorian, but of Julia's house as well. A. Glenn Bernard was back on the interview circuit: he was more than happy to give his expert opinion on the case - along with the news of his next novel, which had just found a publisher.

Brad Lang was found and arrested for parole violation. He also admitted to breaking into and hiding in his old house in a vain attempt to prove his innocence. As it was his house, there was some question about whether he could actually be charged with anything. In either case, an army of Lang family lawyers descended on New Hampshire, demanding an investigation. The fiasco brought both the Lang and the Milano family considerable media influence, and Stephanie's paintings enjoyed a sudden boost in popularity.

The story was running on all the news channels. The fact that Brad Lang, even after years of imprisonment, was still a good-looking man made the story even sweeter.

At first, Robert and the police tried to keeps the Budds out of it. However, thanks to the coverage of Ron and Dylan's exploits on the previous Sunday, it wasn't long before a reporter put the two together. A week after the Lang/Irwin story broke, reporters began swarming the house, begging for interviews and spinning stories about intrepid investigator children, and the courageous single mom who held off a murderer until the police arrived. They spoke with Mrs. Mone and the neighbors, and even called Mrs. Jurta, who'd somehow made it to New York to be with Dexter. The press tried to corner Julia or the kids when they were out walking or shopping and called the grandparents in Florida and in the South Pacific.

*Children uncover evidence of murder in bedroom of family summer home. Boy detective solves murder case. Single Mom Brings Murderer to Justice. Family Vacation turns Deadly. New Hampshire's own Hardy Boys and Nancy Drew solve the Case!*

All sorts of ridiculous headlines plagued them, but the worst were the ones that dug into the family background and discovered the February accident: *Tragedy Drives Family to Franklin, only to uncover a murder.... Struggling single mom solves murder case. Orphans bring killers to justice. Unemployed foster-mother's conversation with a killer: Full story inside.*

Miriam was furious. Far away as she was, she got the news from concerned friends, and she called Julia one night to lambaste her for embarrassing the entire family.

"It looks as though we are cold and hard-hearted!" she fumed. "Everyone knows that we're well off, and they're wondering why we aren't helping, why we aren't supporting you. Your selfish pride is making us look like the evil grandparents. I'm wiring you money right now, Julia, and I won't hear of you not accepting it. These are *my* grandchildren and I won't have them starving."

The call threw Julia into such a panic that she called Stephen Hall and left a desperate message about the guardianship of the children and her fears that Miriam would start proceedings again. Stephen Hall didn't call back until the next day. If Robert hadn't stopped by when he did, Julia might have gone frantic with worry.

"If that lawyer's any good, he'll know how to handle this, Julia. No judge is going to want to take the children away from you – it wouldn't look right, not after all the publicity you've been getting from the neighbors about what a good mother you are."

"People have been saying that?"

"What else could they say?" After a few moments, he asked, "Is he any good?"

"Who, Stephen?"

"Yeah, that... lawyer."

"Very good. I don't know what I'd do without him."

"Oh. Really."

She laughed at his suddenly dour expression. "I mean, professionally, Robert."

He looked embarrassed. "I knew that," he protested.

They were sitting on the porch, side by side on the front steps. As he put his arm around her shoulder, Julia asked him what brought him to the house in time to save her.

"Ron. Dana and Amelia saw the truck parked near the lot behind your house and recognized it. He called me and told me that he thought that you might be in trouble. That kid sure is something. He never lost his cool."

Julia had to agree with him there.

"It's done John a lot of good, having this out in the open," Robert continued. "On the way to the station, he kept telling me what a weight it was off of his shoulders. He was worried about J. C. 'I've made such a mess of everything,' he kept saying. 'I don't know how I'll tell my poor boy...'"

She nodded, and her head hurt again. She reached up a hand to gently touch the latest wound, which was healing nicely. "He must have gotten nervous when he learned that I was renovating."

"He was. He kept apologizing for your getting hurt. Even if we hadn't found the fingerprints, I think he would have confessed sooner rather than later. He was frightened of his brother."

"He's not the only one."

He didn't answer, just pulled her closer.

Eventually things started to quiet down. One hot, sticky day in August, Robert and Julia packed a picnic lunch and took the kids to the lake. Dylan came along at the last minute. He'd become a fixture at the house, now that his others friends were away at their camps and summer schools.

At the beach, they set up a picnic and rubbed on sunscreen and copious amounts of insect repellant. Robert brought an area lamp to keep the horseflies at bay, but the horseflies were brutal out of the lamp's range. The only way to keep them off was to keep moving, which the children managed to do easily. They hit the water and didn't leave it, swimming, playing Marco Polo, or jumping off of the floats they'd brought, seeing who could make the biggest splash. Robert came in to play, too, to their delight and to Julia's amusement.

Julia thought the water was absolutely delicious. The designated lifeguard, she left her book more than once to join in the fun. It seemed that the stresses of the world melted away.

After one of her brief swims, Julia relaxed on the picnic blanket, propped up on her elbows. Next to her, the tiny portable barbeque snapped and hissed as thick hot dogs roasted and dripped over the heat.

It was all so happy and peaceful that Julia felt contentment growing inside her. With the warmth of the sun on her back, the scent of the hotdogs, and the sight of everyone that she loved having fun, she could have laid there for hours and wanted nothing more.

The jangle of her phone jolted her out of her pleasant reverie. She sat up and dove into her bag for the phone. She managed to pick up halfway through the third ring.

"Hello?"

"I've got great news for you, kiddo," Sherri crowed loudly in her ear. "When you hear it, you're going to say that I'm the best realtor you've ever dealt with in your life. I just got you the asking price on the house. The *asking* price, Julia."

Julia felt her stomach fall.

*The asking price for the Franklin House?*

After everything that had happened in that house, she ought to be relieved to sell it and never see it again. It took her a week after Michael Irwin's attack before she could look in the mirror without wincing, and she still struggled with nightmares involving blood-stains and men with tie-wraps. She had decided more than once to sell it.

But she couldn't help thinking about all the dinners they'd had in the kitchen and the now-functioning dining room, the kids' lazy morning in their pajamas around the TV, and the boys' room with the new basketball hoop. There was the nook in the kitchen that Horatio liked to sleep in, the little garden out back that Dana and Amelia had grown so fond of, and Robert and Amelia next door, so close that Robert could stop for a cup of coffee on his way to work. So much good had happened in those walls that it was hard to re-member the evil.

They'd always known that they weren't in Franklin for long, but now that the end had arrived, it was a jolt. She looked over to the kids in the water, steadied herself, and forced herself to speak calmly.

"Well, that is good news, Sherri..."

"I can't believe it myself, kid, I was so shocked. You know how bad the housing market has been lately. It's been tricky getting any house to move, let alone at full asking price. I could have gotten more, too, if I'd mentioned that the Smith family from Boston was also looking at it."

"You are amazing."

"More like you lucked out – these people have just come into some money and wanted to move up. They practically bought it from the pictures on the website, but I insisted that they have a look at the place. They walked through three rooms when the hubby – I assume it's the hubby – might just be the boyfriend… Anyway, he turned to me and said…"

Julia stopped her. "Wait a minute, wait a minute. When did you show the house?"

"Yesterday, silly. Something wrong?"

"Then – you mean the Springfield house?"

"Of *course* I mean the Springfield house! What else would I mean? I'm telling you, Julia, no one's looking at the Franklin house. Franklin is dead. There's nothing moving there."

Julia looked out over the lake, where another family with small children was being welcomed into the water by Dana and Amelia.

"I have to disagree with you there, Sherri," she said. "There's lots of life still here."

"Well, there may be life, but not a lot of real estate prospects. So, what do I tell the Jensens? They're meeting with their lawyers now and will make a formal proposal this afternoon. Should I give them the go ahead?"

It was a question that she'd been putting off all summer. Could she sell Amanda's house or did the kids still need it? And if she did sell it, where would they live then? Could she really move them up to New Hampshire without having a job in place first?

She rubbed her forehead, feeling a headache moving in. "I don't know yet, Sherri. I'll have to get back to you…"

"Oh, Julia!" She was very annoyed, and Julia couldn't blame her.

But she was firm. "I can't make a decision without talking to the kids. I'll get back to you this afternoon."

"But…"

"By then the lawyers will have had a chance to draft the proposal. I'll get back to you, Sherri, I promise. Thanks for everything."

She hung up and threw the phone back into her purse. Sizzling from the barbeque alerted her, and she turned the hotdogs to reveal the crispy, brown grill marks on the bottoms. She set out things for lunch, but all her contentment was gone, leaving behind the stress and insecurity that she'd been struggling with for weeks.

Summer was slowly creeping to a close, and she was no closer to being employed than she had been back in June. If it went on for much longer, the unemployment checks wouldn't be enough. Letting Springfield go would make so much sense. But were the kids ready? Could she do that to them?

Dana came running then, her skin glowing.

"I'm starving," she said. "When do we eat?"

"In a few minutes, honey."

"Good."

Dana plopped down on the blanket and sighed happily. In the water, Amelia squealed as Robert tossed her in the water.

Julia turned the hot dogs over and lowered the heat on the barbeque, still musing. Her phone buzzed with a text, but she ignored it and went to the cooler to get out the condiments. When she came back, Dana was holding her phone, looking at a follow-up text from Sherri.

"Are we selling the house, Aunt Julia?" she asked.

Julia nearly choked. She snatched the phone away, snapping, "Dana! That's private."

"Sorry." She was wide-eyed. "I'm sorry, Aunt Julia. But why are we selling the house?"

Julia put the phone in her pocket, regretting her outburst, but too shaken to apologize yet. "We aren't selling anything yet, Dana. Let's talk about it later, okay?"

"Okay," she whispered.

Julia busied herself setting out lunch, watching Dana out of the corner of her eye. She was clearly unhappy, plucking at the grass, and frowning. When Horatio came over, he put his head in her lap and she sighed as she stroked his fur.

Julia was pulling out the salad when Dana spoke.

"We can't do it, you know," she said.

Julia steeled herself before she turned. "We can't do what, Dana?"

Her blue eyes were steady, unafraid. She was certain. "We can't sell the house. It would be wrong."

Julia sighed heavily. She'd been right – the emotional attachment to Springfield was still too strong. Dana couldn't let go and the others probably couldn't, either. Where did that leave Julia?

She was about to respond when Dana burst out, "It's just so wrong, Aunt Julia! Ron says we need the money, but money's not as important as people. We can't just *leave*."

"Dana, Dana, please listen to me…"

She shrugged off Julia's hand and shook her head. To Julia's surprise, she continued, her voice steady, not shedding a single tear, even though her eyes seemed misty.

"There are *people* here who need us, Aunt Julia. Where would Amelia be without me? Who's going to walk Mrs. Jurta's dogs? Who is going to fish with Robert if Ron isn't here? And who's going to keep Dylan out of trouble if Ron isn't here? He needs a friend and Ron's the best friend anyone could ever have. Who's going to be your friend, Aunt Julia, if we don't have Caroline and Joseph and all those people? And Steven Hall is nice, but he doesn't like you nearly as much as Robert does."

"*What?*"

Dana looked surprised. "I thought you knew that," she said. "Aunt Julia, I know some scary things happened, but you were right to bring us here." She paused reflectively, then said, "I mean, I'll miss Mom and Dad's house, but Mom would want us to live where our friends are. She told me all the time how important people are. Well, I think these people are important. I think they helped us. Jack's not scared of dogs anymore, and I didn't know anything about gardens until we came here and now I have one. I always wanted a sister, like you and Mom were sisters. Now I do, with Amelia, and I like her, Aunt Julia. I really, really do. You don't worry here as much, because Robert is nearby."

Julia nodded, listening intently.

"And Ron *smiles* now. He laughs here. He has friends here, and he didn't at home. I want to stay here. Our home is here, not at Mom's house. That was our home when Mom and Dad were alive and with us, but it's not anymore. Please, please, *please*, Aunt Julia, please say we can stay. We can't go back. We don't belong there anymore. We belong here."

She stopped and took a deep breath, her cheeks a bright pink. She looked up at Julia, her eyes wide with anxiety and hope.

Julia sat next to her, not knowing what to say, and they were silent for a minute.

Dana put a hand on her arm. "Don't you think we belong here too, Aunt Julia?" she whispered.

Julia looked up towards the lake. The others were coming in now, enticed by the scent of the hotdogs.

Jack was riding on Robert's shoulder, squealing as Robert pretended to trip. Amelia romped around him with Tigger chasing her, while Ron dunked an unsuspecting Dylan, laughing when his friend popped back out and charged at him. His laughter echoed around the lake.

"Yes, Dana," she said, softly. "Yes, I do."

# EPILOGUE

Julia sat alone in the dining room. It was December 23$^{rd}$, close to midnight, and she was still wrapping presents. Soft, instrumental Christmas music filled the room as she worked, humming along.

Around her, garlands of green decorated the edges of the room and a tiny Christmas tree stood on the side-board that they'd brought up from Springfield. It was draped in a Christmas cloth and already set with Amanda's holiday china for Christmas morning brunch.

They'd invited Robert and Amelia, of course. Later on Christmas afternoon, J. C. and his friends, the Ojacors, Mrs. Jurta, the O'Reillys, and a lot of people from the neighborhood would be coming for a Christmas party.

The party was Ron's idea, and when Julia expressed concern that they wouldn't be able to fit everyone, he'd assured her that they could. They were going to have a very full house, because her parents were coming up to stay Christmas Eve night. Miriam and Walter Budd, still disgusted with Julia, had elected to go to Europe for the holidays, but promised to see them after the New Year. Neither Julia nor the children were very upset about that.

As she prepared the gifts, Julia felt a serenity that she'd never known. The dining room table heaped with wrapping paper, tape, boxes, and instruction manuals. Thanks to her new administrative assistant job at the school and a generous Christmas bonus, she was well able to fill the space under the tree this year.

In the open doorway, the living room was awash in the gentle glow of colored lights, dancing among the tinsel that Jack had covered the tree with. Ron had picked the tree and cut it down at the local farm himself, and they'd made a party to decorate it with Robert and Amelia. They spent nearly two hours on it. New, shiny ornaments hung alongside of old family favorites. A garish and sparkly tree skirt covered the tree stand, and a perky angel winked from her perch at the top of the tree. Jack had placed it up there, held up by Robert, and he never failed to mention this whenever visitors came by to look at the tree.

The rest of the house was decorated, too. Garland hung around every doorway, because Amelia and Dana insisted that it made the whole house look like a fairy's Christmas castle.

Amelia was even more excited about this Christmas than she usually was, according to Robert.

"Her mother's on a cruise this year," he'd told Julia the night of the tree decorating. "I was worried how Amelia would take it, but she was so excited about spending Christmas here that she didn't mind a bit."

Later, Amelia confided to Julia that her mother was on a trip with her new boyfriend, but that Amelia didn't mind because she hadn't wanted to miss her first Christmas with her new family.

"I know that you and Dad aren't married or anything," she said as Julia blushed. "But it's okay, because they're already my brothers and sister, in *spirit*, you know. And that can be even more powerful than being a real family." She sighed happily and twirled about the room. "I am sooo glad that you guys didn't move! So glad I almost don't need presents this year. Almost."

She didn't know it yet, but Robert and Julia's big present to Amelia and Dana were matching tutus to go with dance lessons that would start in January. Julia herself was not a huge fan of dance, but that was all the pair of them had asked for this year - and since Dana had been so good about the sale of the house in Springfield, she thought it was the least she could do. Besides, the girls needed their girl time.

The kids had handled the transition better than anyone had expected. After the hard work of closing the house and moving began, Julia landed her new job - and between her new work schedule and the children starting school in Franklin in September, they had to rush.

Robert helped them out whenever he could, even taking a few days off to help with the lugging and loading. Sherri, ecstatic to have a real sale and a good profit for once, loaned them her strapping nephew and the use of her moving van. They cleared the house in record time, but the basement and the office of the Franklin were still filled with unopened boxes. Julia thought she could go through everything over the Christmas holiday. That was looking less and less likely as time went on.

The sale of the house went through without a hitch, and the bank account filled up. There were some healthy tears, but having to adapt to a new school and a new schedule helped everyone move toward closure faster than they might have otherwise.

Thanks to Ron's private school, he had advanced a grade and was now in class with Dylan and his friends who, due to Ron's good influence, were no longer the troublemakers they had been. Dylan, in fact, was researching and writing a book about his experiences in the Lang house while Ron was seriously pursuing his studies, and finding out that he was actually a pretty good athlete and scientist.

Dana and Amelia were in the same class. Dana was emotionally stable now, and her friendships were much better. Both she and Amelia had a group of girls that they liked to hang out with, and they had them over for movie nights on occasion.

Jack was thriving. He liked his school, even though he was initially intimidated by his teacher and new schoolmates. For a while, Julia worried about him, but then he met Judah. Judah was a little boy who was absolutely terrified of dogs.

"He's just like me, only scareder," Jack had explained to Julia.

Jack introduced Judah to Horatio, and by the time he'd cured him of his phobia, Jack had made a fast friend.

As for Julia, the new job was a challenge, but in a good way - and she was considering taking an online degree course to further her job prospects.

Brad Lang's attorneys had demanded that the state reopen the case, and it looked as though he would be cleared. As yet, no one knew what he was going to do with the house. It was well known, however, that A. Glenn Bernard had been hired to write a history of the case from Brad's point of view. What Stephanie's family thought about it could only be imagined.

Both Michael and John Irwin were arraigned and awaiting trial. J. C.'s family had a lawyer who felt very sure that they'd be able to reduce John's charges, thanks to his emotional state at the time and his impeccable reputation in town.

The last gift was assembled and wrapped. Julia stood up, stretched, and checked her watch. It was 12:30 and she was exhausted. She stowed the wrapped boxes in bigger, cardboard ones, then carried them into her room, which the kids had been strictly forbidden from entering. She was just about to go around shutting off Christmas lights when she heard a soft rapping from the kitchen door.

She went over to the kitchen door and peered through the window. Out of the shadows, a hand held up a bottle of sparkling grape juice.

Laughing, Julia pulled the door open and let Robert in. He was wearing his heavy weather coat over his jeans and sweater, and a swirl of chilly wind followed him into the house. Julia shut the door behind him.

"What are you doing here?" she whispered, following him into the kitchen. "It's after midnight!"

"I came to celebrate," he said. He put down a plate of cheese and crackers on the kitchen table. "Break open the wine glasses, Jules, we are living large."

"With sparkling grapes, no less! And what," she asked, as she got out the glasses, "are we celebrating?"

"Santa Claus! He just finished all his wrapping tonight."

"By a strange coincidence," she handed him a glass, "so did Mrs. Claus."

"I knew that," he said, twisting open the bottle. "How's Amelia?"

"She and Dana fell asleep an hour ago. I didn't think they'd ever get tired."

"So we have the place to ourselves for a little while." He swept his arm toward the living room. "Shall we drink by candlelight? Methinks I hear good old Nat King Cole playing."

"Good ears."

"Well, I'm not as old as I look."

"Neither am I."

"Oh, geez, then, is this legal?"

"You tell me. You're the cop."

"In that case, it's legal. Here, you take the glasses and settle down on the floor right there."

She sat where he gestured and he settled next to her. He filled their glasses as she took the plastic wrap off of the plate. They reclined against the couch, toasted each other and sipped the fruity drink.

"Umm…" she said. "Nice vintage."

"Only the best for you, Julia."

"Mmmm…"

They sat in easy silence for a while, listening to Nat King Cole, Dean Martin, and Frank Sinatra serenade them.

Julia kicked off her shoes and Robert followed suit, slipping his arm around her shoulders as they leaned back against the couch. It was warm and comfortable, and she leaned into his shoulder and relaxed. He pulled her a little closer and brushed the top of her head with his lips.

"Nice," she murmured. Her eyes were heavy, and she was so relaxed that she nearly dozed off.

"I think so, too," he said. "I'm glad you're here, Jules."

"Me, too. Springfield was never my kind of town."

"And Franklin?"

She lifted her head and pulled his face down to hers. "Very promising," she whispered.

Ron woke up at the first rap. He heard Julia opening the door, and then the sound of Robert entering. After a few minutes, they left the kitchen and went into the living room. Intensely curious, he laid in bed straining to listen, yet afraid of what he might hear. He was exhausted anyway, so he decided to go back to sleep.

He was just nodding off again when Dana came to his bedside.

"Aunt Julia let someone in," she whispered.

"I know," he said. "It's Robert."

She got that curious, excited look on her face that he'd learned to mistrust. "Really? What's he doing here?"

"I don't know, Dana. Go back to bed."

"I want to see."

"Don't!" he warned, but she ran out of his room and shut the door behind her. He thought about going to get her, but he was still tired, so he laid down again and closed his eyes. It seemed as though he'd just done that when he felt someone pulling on his arm.

Dana was as excited as if Santa Claus had come a day early.

"It *is* Robert!" she whispered, jumping lightly up and down. "And he's *kissing Aunt Julia!*"

Ron rolled his eyes. "Gross," he said, but he was secretly pleased.

"Amelia and I are going to be real sisters. See, I told you!"

"You did. Now go back to bed."

She turned to leave, but a moment later she was back again, shaking his shoulder.

"What *is* it, Dana?"

"Our houses are both too small for all of us," she said. "We're going to have to move again."

"Oh, brother!" He threw himself back down on the pillow. "They aren't even engaged yet, Dana."

"But I'm right, aren't I?"

"Yes, they are too small. Why?"

"Well, because I was thinking. J. C. says that the Langs are going to sell the haunted house at the end of the street. Wouldn't it be
cool if we bought that one?"

"Creepy, more like."

"Romantic," she said dreamily. "That house brought us all
together." She yawned and smiled sleepily. "The stars are out tonight. I'm going to wish on one for the house. I want to live in it and
it'll be fun to work on it like we did this house."

Ron laughed. "You're wishing on a star? That's for babies, Dana."

She paused at the door and grinned at him. "No it's not. I wished
for a sister and I've got Amelia. Amelia wished that we would stay
and we did. Both of us wished for Aunt Julia and Robert to get married and now they are…"

"Dana!"

"Well, they're kissing aren't they? Anyway, I'm going to wish for
the house and I'll get it. You'll see. Good night! Love you!"

She slipped out and shut the door behind her.

Ron waited until he was sure that she wasn't coming back, then
he rolled over and looked up through the skylight. Stars glinted
above him, too many to count. He picked out a constellation and
smiled as he found the North Star. Robert was right. It was easy to
find, once you knew how.

He thought about Dana and her wish for the Lang house. How
could she want to move in there? Terrible things had happened in
that place – loneliness, murder cover-ups, Ron being attacked. But,
then, worse things had happened in their own house. Stephanie
Lang had been killed, Michael Irwin had broken in, tore up the
floorboards, and attacked Aunt Julia, all in the downstairs room.
They really ought to hate the house, or at least be nervous around
that room.

Only they weren't.

Aunt Julia and he had removed the bloodstained wallpaper,
repaired the wall, and painted it a pretty shade of lilac, which
Aunt Julia said was the state flower. Then, despite everyone

warning her that she'd have nightmares from the attack, she made it her bedroom.

"I'm not going to let the past dictate the future," she'd told Ron when he asked her about it. "We've cleaned it up and we're giving it a new history now. That's all that matters."

Whether she had nightmares or not, she never said, and it wasn't long before everyone sort of forgot that these things had happened in her room. It was as though the room had been healed of its tragic history. Like the wall itself, the brokenness had been fixed. From dust, dirt, and death, new life had sprung. A new history was being written in the house.

That, Ron decided, was what Aunt Julia did best: she made things come to life again. She took an ugly old house and turned it into a bright, happy home. She took care of a lost Amelia, and made her feel secure and comfortable. She brought Jack out of his shell, and gave Dana the security she needed to heal. And even though Robert was a strong, capable policeman, ready to handle anything, Ron suspected that he, too, needed a family. He needed Julia.

Ron thought about his parents and that awful night in February. His family had been shattered by his parents' death, broken until they could barely hold on to each other, frightened by a dark, empty future. He, himself, had been so hurt that he couldn't feel anything, and poor Dana and Jack bore the brunt of his unhappiness. Aunt Julia had been there the whole time, taking care of them, comforting them, giving them time and safety to heal, until now they were a new unit, whole and strong. He'd never stop missing his parents, of course, and things weren't the same as they were before, but they were good, very good. Ron, Dana, and Jack had a home again, thanks to Aunt Julia.

Ron loved her for it.

He looked up at the stars and thought about the Lang house again. It was an ugly shambles of a place, with a dark history, and would require even more work than this place had. But thanks to his experience working on this little house, Ron could see that once the work was finished, the Lang house would be a grand place to live in. He imagined it with new windows, clean siding, and a new porch, and his heart expanded with the idea.

They could do it. Between him, Julia, Robert, and the others, with a little faith and a little work, they could bring that old house back to life, just as they had done with this house. Just as they had done with themselves. Together, as a family. Life from death, whole and strong and new.

Ron gazed up at the sky and concentrated. "Wish I may, wish I might..."

It was practically in the bag.

# ABOUT THE AUTHOR

Killarney Traynor is a New England-born writer, actor, and history buff living in New Hampshire. *Summer Shadows* is her debut novel. Find Killarney on the web at killarneytraynor.com.

Made in the USA
Lexington, KY
26 November 2014